Pose For Me
Maree Rose

Maree Rose Publishing

Pose For Me

by Maree Rose

Copyright © 2025 by Maree Rose

All rights reserved

First Edition: March 2025

Published by Maree Rose

This book is a work of fiction. Names, characters, places and incidents (outside of those clearly in the public domain) are products of the author's imagination or are used fictitiously. Any resemblance to actual events, locales or persons, either living or dead, is entirely coincidental.

Foreword

Content Warnings

Apologies if I missed any, please reach out to me on social media if that is the case.

Playlist

I know how much you all love a
good playlist to set the mood...

For your listening pleasure:
https://spoti.fi/3EYTff4

PLAYLIST

I Want It All (Slowed Down) - Cameron Grey
Show Me - Alina Baraz, Galimatias
Come Follow Me Down - George Taylor
Dirtier Thoughts - Nation Haven
Cravin' - Stileto, Kendyle Paige
Play Dirty - Kevin McAllister, [SEBELL]
Good Girl - Morganne
Psycho - EMM
I'll Make You Love Me - Kat Leon, Sam Tinnesz
Savage (bitmastr remix) - Bahari, bitmastr
Between Wind and Water - Hael
Where Your Secrets Hide - Kleryg, Katie Garfield
Almost Touch Me - Maisy Kay
Dark Room - Foreign Figures, Jonny T

Welcome To Your Nightmare - UNSECRET, MAYLYN
Easy to Love - Bryce Savage
Good People Do Bad Things - David Thomas Connolly, Max Samuel Rowat
River - BRKN LOVE

To the beautiful, unapologetic rebels who dare to worship their own darkness and see the beauty in themselves, this book is for you.

Embrace every scar, every sinful twist, and let your obsession with your own raw power set your soul on fire.

Fuck the rules, love yourself fiercely, and revel in every damn flaw that makes you uniquely irresistible.

Also...
Don't hover... they don't need air that much...

Prologue
Unknown

MY ATTENTION IS DRAWN to her, an almost magnetic pull. She isn't exactly what I'd call stunning by society standards, but there's a beauty to her—a quiet, unassuming kind that doesn't command a room but leaves a lasting impression. It's the sort of allure that doesn't shout but lingers, whispering for a second look.

I know I shouldn't be staring, especially not here, in the middle of a grocery store. Yet here I am, unable to look away as she meanders down the aisle. Her hair, black as a raven's feathers, is swept up in a loose bun atop her head, with a few stray pieces escaping, framing her face in a way that seems both deliberate and carefree. It's clear she didn't spend much time on it, a testament to her confidence or perhaps her disregard for others' eyes.

She's wearing a loose, formless dress, something that hangs on her rather than clings. It suggests a lack of self-consciousness, as though she's indifferent to how others might perceive her. And yet, as she moves, I catch hints of curves beneath the fabric—gentle and elusive, drawing my gaze in a way that makes it hard to look away.

She steps out of the aisle, and a strange, unexpected urge to follow her grips me. There's something undeniably compelling about her, something in the ease of her movements and the way she seems oblivious to anyone else. I force myself to walk at a normal pace, fighting the instinct to rush after her as I reach the end of the aisle and peer subtly down the next one.

She's kneeling now, inspecting something on a lower shelf, and the graceful line of her neck is exposed as she bends forward. Strands of her hair brush against her skin, drawing my attention to the softness there. Her profile is delicate, her cheek gently rounded, her nose a soft, subtle slope. There's an understated elegance to her features that draws me in, a quiet allure that's easy to overlook but impossible to ignore. The way she tucks a loose strand behind her ear, how her lashes flutter as she blinks, completely unaware of my gaze—it's entrancing.

Amid the fluorescent lights and shelves stocked with mundane goods, she radiates a calm, quiet confidence that sets her apart. Maybe it's in the unhurried way she moves, the sense that she's unbothered by the noise around her. Or perhaps it's the focus in her eyes, a glint of determination as she continues her task, seemingly miles away from the bustling store.

When she turns down another aisle, disappearing from view, I find myself curious to the point of obsession. Skipping the aisle she left, I move to the next, hoping to continue observing her in this subtle game of hide-and-seek. But to my surprise, I don't see her right away. I frown, glancing down each row until I catch sight of her, heading toward me, focused on the shelves.

She stops just a few steps away, examining the options in front of her with a slight frown, worrying her lip as she ponders different laundry detergents. My pulse quickens, my heart thudding as I take in the details—the way her dress shifts and hugs her frame as she reaches up, accentuating the body she's hidden. The faintest stir of attraction pulls at me as I watch her stretch to reach a box just above her line of sight. My gaze lingers on the way her dress clings for a moment to her skin, emphasizing the soft swell of her chest and the contour of her waist, and an undeniable, primal desire ignites within me.

As she huffs softly in frustration, giving up on whatever she was reaching for, I step forward, closing the gap between us. I glance around to ensure the aisle is empty before reaching up to grab the item for her, I inhale a faint whiff of her scent—a blend of fresh linen and something soft, almost like lavender. When I hand it to her, she murmurs a quick thanks, her gaze fixed on the shelf as she turns to leave, completely unaware of the effect she has on me.

I don't need laundry detergent, but I reach up and take one for myself. The scent lingers in the air, a reminder of her. As I watch her disappear around the corner, I know I'll spend the rest of the evening thinking about her—this woman in the loose dress, in this ordinary setting, yet unforgettable.

And after only a moment's hesitation, I continue to follow her.

Chapter 1
Rayne

My photography studio sits in near-total darkness, every light off except for the one casting a soft glow over my computer screen. The dim, quiet atmosphere allows me to immerse myself in the images from my latest shoot. A grin tugs at my lips as I scroll through them; it was a rare session—one I'm sure will stay with me.

The couple reached out to me, wanting a shoot with a special twist: to bid farewell to her breasts. Due to the BRCA genes that ran in her family, she had chosen to undergo a double mastectomy, and the shoot was a playful way to say ta ta to her "tah tahs." She wanted a celebration, not a solemn farewell, and that playful approach made it one of the most joyful, endearing sessions I'd ever done.

As a boudoir and erotic photographer, I've become pretty desensitized to most things, but this couple's infectious laughter pulled me into their happiness. She'd told me they were this way at their wedding, too, sharing private jokes that had them laughing at completely inappropriate times during the ceremony. I felt honored to give them another cherished memory in light of what she'd be going through soon.

As I review the shots, the rich, vibrant colors in the images perfectly capture the mood of the session, from the glint in her eye to the playful flashes of purple lace in her lingerie. With the initial edits done, I begin assembling their proofing gallery, satisfied at being part of such a meaningful moment.

The late-summer heat seems to seep through the walls, and even with a fan running, the room feels thick with warmth. I hesitate to open the window, knowing it would only invite the sticky humidity inside, so I settle for twisting my long black hair into a loose bun, feeling the relief as the air cools the back of my neck.

As I start the upload, my phone rings, startling me. It's not late, but certainly past typical work hours. For a second, I consider letting it go to voicemail, but curiosity wins, especially since unknown numbers are a regular part of running my business.

"Hello?" I answer.

"Hello, is this Midnight Rose Boudoir?" The voice on the other end is deep, with a hint of roughness that sends a flutter through me, catching me off guard.

"Yes, that's correct. How can I assist you?" I reply, shaking off the unexpected reaction.

"I apologize for calling so late, but I stumbled upon your website and am interested in booking a couples photoshoot for myself and my partner."

His request is straightforward, something I've handled countless times. "Of course! Do you have a specific time frame in mind?" I ask, reaching for my calendar.

"We were hoping to schedule something within the next week."

"That sounds doable," I reply, scrolling through the schedule, though I see that it's packed. "How about Friday? I have other obligations during the day but could do an evening session around 5 p.m. I won't be able to organize any hair and makeup on such short notice, so you'd need to arrange that yourselves."

A brief pause follows before he says, "No problem. Friday at 5 p.m. sounds perfect."

"Great, I'll pencil you in," I confirm, jotting down the details. "And could I get your name for the booking?"

"Knox Bishop," he replies smoothly.

"Thank you, Knox. I have you down for Friday at 5 p.m. I assume you know where my studio is located?"

"Yes, we do."

"Looking forward to meeting you and your partner then," I say, a smile in my voice.

"So are we, Rayne," he says, his voice lingering for just a beat before the call clicks off.

When I hang up, a brief wave of confusion hits me—wondering how he knew my name—until I remember my website has it right at the top. Chuckling at my own forgetfulness, I refocus on the upload, feeling a spark of anticipation at the thought of Friday's session.

As the upload finishes, I linger on the screen a moment longer, watching the bar fill and then disappear as the files are sent off to the couple. There's a satisfying sense of closure in finalizing a project like this—knowing I've helped someone capture an intimate, joyous moment that might help them through a difficult time. With one last look at the closed email confirmation, I power down the computer, the soft light winking out and leaving the room in complete darkness.

I stand, stretching slightly to ease the day's tension from my shoulders, and move through the darkened studio to the stairwell. It's completely silent in here, save for the faint hum of the fan still whirring on my desk. The blinds are all drawn, thick and heavy, ensuring no wandering eyes can peer inside; that boundary between my professional space and the outside world has always been essential. Still, as I approach the stairs, a small sound—a slight scrape, maybe?—makes me pause.

The noise prickles at my awareness, unexpected in the stillness. I strain to hear, standing motionless, my gaze flicking toward the windows even though I know no one could possibly see in. In the quiet, a chill curls its way up my spine, making me hyper-aware of the silence around me. After a few tense seconds, the noise doesn't repeat, and I realize I've been holding my breath. Exhaling slowly, I shake off the momentary tension and step forward, dismissing the sound as likely a trick of settling wood or the echo of someone moving outside.

At the foot of the stairs, I place my hand on the rail, feeling the familiar smoothness of it beneath my palm, and begin the climb up to my apartment. The old warehouse has served me well, its converted layout providing a perfect separation between my workspace below and my living area above. Each step up feels like shedding the day's intensity, a transition from the bold, evocative images I create to the solitude and simplicity of home.

As I reach the top of the stairs, I glance back once more, half-expecting to catch a flicker of movement in the shadows below. But there's nothing. Just the comforting quiet of my studio, now tucked away for the night.

Opening the door, I step through and into my living area, breathing in the calm that washes over me. The apartment's open layout stretches before me, a bright, welcoming contrast to the moody darkness of the studio below. High ceilings and wide windows amplify the sense of space, and even now, under the warm glow of ceiling lights, the apartment feels expansive. During the day, sunlight streams in generously, casting patterns on the imitation concrete floors, but now the softer light lends a gentle ambiance that invites me to unwind.

The exposed brick walls and steel beams show the building's original industrial character, but I've softened it with touches of color and warmth. A cream-colored sectional dominates one corner, piled with an assortment of pillows in jewel tones—emerald, ruby, and sapphire. A fluffy rug sprawls across the floor, its deep, teal color adding a cozy splash against the neutral tones. Here and there, potted plants bring a touch of green to the room, their leaves lush and healthy thanks to the natural light they drink up daily.

As I walk deeper into the space, a familiar presence slips around my ankles with a gentle purr. "There you are, Luna," I say softly, crouching to greet her. She responds with a delighted arch of her back, rubbing her face against my hand, her dark fur soft under my fingers. Luna's large amber eyes blink up at me, expectant, reminding me it's her dinner time. Her petite form follows me eagerly to the kitchen, her soft paws padding silently as she weaves around me, occasionally brushing against my legs as if to make sure I haven't forgotten her.

Once I reach the kitchen, I scoop her food into a bowl, watching her dive in with enthusiasm. Her gentle, contented purring is a sound I never tire of—it's grounding, a reminder of the small comforts in life. I reach for the cookie jar as Luna eats, selecting a chocolate chip cookie and biting into it, savoring its soft, buttery sweetness as I lean against the counter. The kitchen is small but functional, with a sleek black countertop and open shelving that holds neatly organized dishes and an assortment of spices and teas. A bowl of fresh fruit sits on the counter.

I think about putting on a movie, settling onto the couch, and letting myself unwind in front of a screen. The thought is tempting, an easy way to zone out after such a charged day, but a deep exhaustion is already dragging down my limbs, a weighty reminder of the intense session I had earlier. It's the kind of tiredness that only sets in after an especially emotional or physically demanding shoot, and I know from experience that sitting down now would make it nearly impossible to get back up.

The ache in my arms reminds me of the day's work, a dull throb settling into my muscles from hours of lifting and positioning my camera equipment. Photography is physically demanding, and though I'm used to it, today's shoot has left me sorer than usual. I have an early morning tomorrow, too, and the promise of a hot shower sounds more restorative than the flickering lights of a screen.

I make my way down the hallway to the bathroom, flipping on the light to reveal the sanctuary I've created there. Warm-toned tiles and a few candles give it a spa-like feel, and I waste no time turning on the shower, letting the steam fill the room.

Under the hot spray, I let the water work its way over my tired muscles, easing the tension that's built up across my shoulders and back. I linger longer than I normally would, indulging in the sensation as the heat seeps into my skin, soothing every knot and ache. My eyes drift closed, and I let the day slip away, focusing solely on the rhythmic sound of water hitting tile.

When I finally step out, I feel a satisfying sense of relief, like I've shed the day's weight along with the steam lingering in the air. I towel off, change into my favorite worn-in pajamas—a soft cotton tee and flannel shorts—and make my way to the small drawer beside the bed where I keep my pain relievers. The soreness has lessened, but I know this will help me relax fully, allowing for a deep, restful sleep.

Pulling back the covers, I sink into bed, feeling the cool sheets against my skin. The mattress molds around me, familiar and comforting, and Luna, finished with her dinner, hops up beside me, curling into a ball near my feet. I reach down to give her one last scratch behind the ears, smiling as her purring grows faint, her contentment seeping into my own sense of calm.

As my eyelids grow heavy, my mind briefly drifts to the week's schedule but the thoughts quickly slip away. The pain reliever begins to take effect, leaving me in a gentle haze, and soon, I'm completely enveloped in the soothing quiet of sleep.

Chapter 2
Knox

I BRIEFLY TAKE IN the space, it's dark but I'm used to the dark. I thrive in the dark. There is enough light filtering through the few small high windows that I can see. It's an elegant photography studio, but that doesn't come as a surprise, already feeling familiar with her after watching her for months.

I linger by her desk, letting my gaze drift over the details scattered across her workspace. It's neat but lived-in, with a few stray papers and bills resting on top, almost like an open invitation for prying eyes. With a gloved hand, I carefully nudge a few aside, spotting a large planner lying open to the current week. It's immediately clear she keeps her schedule meticulously by hand—every entry inked in her delicate handwriting. My name is there, newly added for Friday. The sight of it stirs something in me, a quiet thrill at being woven into her plans, even if she doesn't fully realize what she's invited in.

Her scent lingers faintly in the air around her desk, something soft and calming. Lavender. The subtle fragrance wraps around me, unexpectedly warm, like the comfort of falling asleep in a well-worn blanket. I take a steady breath, drawing it in as though I could hold onto this fleeting moment. But I'm not here to linger; I know her routine well by now, and she will be in bed after the day she's had.

At the base of the staircase, I pause, listening carefully. Silence. Just as I expected. I tread lightly, each step up purposeful and soundless, one hand gliding along the railing where her fingers had traced only an hour earlier. The intimacy of the small gesture sharpens my focus, but when I reach the door to her apartment, I pause once more, listening for any sign of movement inside. Nothing. Slowly, I turn the handle, slipping inside and shutting the door soundlessly behind me.

My entrance doesn't go unnoticed, however. A small, cautious sound draws my attention to the floor. The cat is watching me, its amber eyes narrowed with curiosity but not alarm. Reaching into my pocket, I pull out a small bundle I'd prepared earlier, a little cloth pouch filled with fresh catnip. The cat's gaze is fixed on it immediately, its attention rapt as I place the pouch on the floor. That should keep it occupied, at least for the time I need tonight.

I had learnt the hard way, several times, that unless I brought some sort of offering—otherwise called a bribe—for the little feline guardian, then I wasn't getting past her razor sharp claws.

Moving with calculated steps, I make my way down the hall. I reach the entrance of her bedroom, and there, I stop, taking in the sight before me. She's fast asleep, her form wrapped in a loose sheet, her dark hair spilling over the pillow like ink against its soft fabric. The steady rise and fall of her chest is hypnotic, her breathing slow and deep, oblivious to my presence.

My eyes fall to the small bottle of pills next to her glass of water on the bedside table. I recognize them easily enough: pain meds that are effectively a mild sedative. A small smirk tugs at my lips—no wonder she's so deeply under, her breathing steady and untroubled, her face softened in the haze of sleep. I let myself savor the moment, watching her chest rise and fall, a slight shift in her limbs betraying the ease and warmth of her slumber. It's a vulnerable beauty, one that pulls at a desire I'd kept under wraps until now.

The faint light filtering in from the window barely touches her, but it's enough. I peel off one of my gloves, wanting to feel her warmth directly against my skin. Tentatively, I reach out, brushing a stray strand of hair away from her face. Her skin is smooth, warm, and as my fingertip trails down the curve of her cheek to her jaw, a quiet hum rises in my chest. Gently, I trace along her neck, savoring the softness, lingering just a moment longer to feel her pulse, strong and steady beneath my touch.

The sheet has slipped down, exposing the gentle slopes of her body, and though it covers her, it's thin enough that the silhouette of her figure is still visible. My fingers drift lower, tracing over the sheet where her collarbone meets the swell of her breast. She sighs in her sleep, her body shifting slightly, and I pause, watching for any sign that she might awaken. But she doesn't stir beyond that gentle sigh, and her chest rises again, the steady rhythm of her breathing undisturbed.

Beneath the sheet, her nipple hardens at the slightest graze of my finger, and I let my touch linger there, skimming over the peak. The response is immediate and delicate, a slight tremor in her body that brings a faint flush to her cheeks.

I let my hand drift lower, tracing the shape of her body, taking in every subtle line and hollow. The rise and fall of her chest is a steady, unguarded rhythm, her breath warm and sweet. Leaning down, I let myself get closer, close enough to breathe her in fully. Her scent is stronger here, filling my senses—lavender and something uniquely hers, delicate and calming, yet potent enough to pull me in further. I hover over her, my face so near that the faint brush of my lips against hers is almost inevitable, a whisper of a touch that she'll never know happened. Her breathing remains steady, her lips soft and slightly parted, and I allow myself the faintest pressure, feeling the warmth of her breath.

I know I shouldn't linger, that being here is already pushing too close to the edge, but I can't tear myself away. The vulnerability of it, of her, sends a thrill through me, but I know the risk. The allure of this moment is intoxicating. She has no idea of the intensity of the attention she's drawn, no knowledge of the dangerous shadows circling around her now, the killers that have been pulled into her orbit.

My control teeters at its edge, and with a ragged breath, I force myself to step back, dragging my glove back on with deliberate movements. My time is slipping away, and I know I must make use of it. I take a look around her space, absorbing the details now that I'm close enough to see them without the filter of distance.

This space is a stark contrast to her photography studio, a quiet refuge that serves as a distinct boundary between her work and her life. The elegance is understated, filled with touches that are deeply personal yet inviting. A small mirrored dresser catches the muted light, its surface adorned with trinkets that tell stories I'm not yet privy to. I wonder what secrets those little objects hold.

Against the wall, a bookcase stands, the bottom shelf crammed with books on art history and photography. Titles that I can only assume are filled with knowledge she cherishes and draws inspiration from. My eyes scan the other shelves, and I can't help the smile that tugs at my lips—most of the spines are dark, well-worn, hinting at stories that are anything but sweet romances. She seems drawn to tales with edges, narratives steeped in conflict or darkness, and I find myself intrigued. Perhaps she might be more receptive to my attention than I first imagined.

I drift closer to the bookcase, fingers trailing over the spines, absorbing the details, each title a small window into her soul. There's something about the way she curates her space that resonates with me—a quiet rebellion against the sweetness that so often pervades life. It paints a picture of a woman who embraces the complexity of emotions, who finds beauty in the darker corners of existence.

Just as I'm lost in the allure of her space, a flicker of movement catches my eye. The cat, curious and emboldened, stalks back into the bedroom, its amber gaze sharp and watchful. In that instant, I know my time is up. A rush of adrenaline surges through me; I can't afford to be caught here, not now, not when I've come this close to her.

With a last lingering look at the dark-haired beauty sprawled across her bed, I let my feet carry me silently from the room, each step calculated and light. I can't help but steal one final glance back at her, the way her dark hair frames her face, how serene and unaware she is, a world apart from the dangers that hover so very close to her.

I retrace my steps back to the entrance of her apartment, moving with the precision of a dancer who knows the stage well. The soft thud of my heart mingles with the low hum of silence around me as I keep my focus sharp, every sound amplified in the stillness. I can feel the pulse of the moment—so fragile, so electric.

I lean down, retrieving the catnip pouch I'd left for the curious feline, slipping it back into my pocket. I take a moment to ensure there is no evidence of my presence left behind. I don't want her to know just yet. Soon, though, she will. The thought sends a shiver of anticipation through me.

Soon.

Chapter 3
Rayne

I STIFLE A YAWN as I change the opacity of the editing brush I'm using to refine an image on my screen. It's one of the galleries from the previous week, where the client took their time deliberating over the images they wanted as part of their final package. I can almost feel the weight of their expectations pressing against me, the mix of excitement and anxiety that always accompanies a client's choices.

The day is dragging, and it doesn't help that I woke up unexpectedly in the middle of the night. There was something lingering in the back of my mind, an itch I couldn't quite scratch, keeping me from sinking easily back into sleep. I tossed and turned, trying to recall the thread of my dreams, but they slipped away like sand through my fingers. Eventually, the restless hours crept by until morning light finally broke through my curtains, forcing me to rise early for errands I couldn't skip. My schedule is packed tighter than ever with the newly added shoot tomorrow, and the thought of falling behind sends a small wave of panic coursing through me. Mentally I tell myself not to stress and even if I do fall behind, the schedule is lighter after next week anyway.

I contemplate getting my groceries delivered but dismiss the idea as quickly as I usually do. There's something about the personal aspect of wandering through the aisles, getting lost in the crowd of people bustling about doing their own errands, that I find oddly comforting. I enjoy the little moments of choosing fresh produce, feeling the weight of a ripe avocado in my palm, or the crispness of a head of lettuce before deciding to place it in my basket. It's not that the delivery service is hard to come by—there are plenty of apps that promise convenience and speed, a true perk of living on the outskirts of a bustling city—but I just prefer to do some things myself.

I focus on the screen, the vibrant colors of the images providing a welcome distraction. Each photograph tells a story, and I pour my energy into enhancing them, trying to capture the essence of the moments I froze in time. As I work, I can feel my eyelids growing heavy again, the day's exhaustion settling in like a thick blanket. I take a moment to stretch, rolling my shoulders back and inhaling deeply, hoping to shake off the need for sleep that still clings to me.

Getting up from my desk, I shuffle over to the little coffee station I've set up for clients, even though I use it more for myself than anyone else. The compact machine hums softly as I pop in a coffee pod, the promise of liquid gold fueling my motivation. In just a few minutes, I'll have a steaming cup to revive my senses. As the aroma wafts through the air, I toss in an extra spoonful of sugar, craving that sweet kick to help jolt me awake.

As I make my way back to my desk, my computer chimes with a notification, pulling my attention away from my editing. The alert catches my eye, and my heart races as I bring it up on the screen. The headline jumps out at me: "Gruesome Murder Shocks Local Community." The title is enough to grip anyone's attention, and it sends a shiver running down my spine.

The article loads slowly, the vague details about the brutality of the crime emerging piece by piece. There's something haunting about the lack of concrete information—no photos, no specific victim mentioned, just a collection of ominous statements about the violence and the absence of leads for the police.

I narrow my eyes and read through the article again while taking a sip of my coffee. It gives no more detail than it did the first time, leaving only unsettling hints of the horror that had unfolded nearby. Frustrated, I search for more articles, but after sifting through a few more sources, I come up just as empty. It's clear the authorities are keeping the details under tight lock and key—no images, no additional information on the crime, and not even a suggestion about whether this was an isolated event or something larger. The ambiguity hangs like a weight, leaving a question mark over the event. There aren't even any statements from the investigators on the case

I lean back in my chair, my fingers tapping against my coffee cup. It's almost worse for the community this way, not knowing if the threat is contained or still lingering in the shadows. Like an open question of should we all be looking over our shoulders? Just the thought has a dark thrill going up my spine, one I'm sure a normal person wouldn't have but this sort of thing had always fascinated me.

Pushing the thought aside, I return to my editing. I pull up the photos I was working on, focusing on the colors and shadows, losing myself in the familiar rhythms of my craft.

I manage to work for a few uninterrupted minutes before my phone starts ringing, the sharp sound jolting me from my thoughts. Glancing down, I see an unfamiliar number flashing on the screen and after a brief pause to regain my professional mask, I pick it up. But the voice on the other end catches me off guard—it's deep and slightly rough, carrying a faint edge of familiarity.

"Good afternoon, Rayne. This is Knox. We have a booking with you tomorrow evening."

For a brief moment, my stomach dips, and I can't help but think he's calling to cancel. It wouldn't be the first time a client had second thoughts about a boudoir shoot and backed out. The silence stretches as I realize I haven't responded yet, and I rush to fill it.

"Oh, hi, good afternoon! Yes. Is everything okay?" My voice comes out overly bright, betraying a bit of my nerves.

There's a hum on the other end, his tone shifting to something more serious, and I find myself frowning in response. "I hope this is okay, but I forgot to mention something when I initially booked. Our privacy means a great deal to us, and there are reasons regarding our careers that make it necessary that whatever images or footage you take as part of our photoshoot are not shown or shared with anyone but us."

Relief washes over me, my heart easing from its quickened pace. "Of course! That's no drama at all. I wouldn't be able to share anything without a signed release anyway, so that's completely fine."

"Good to hear," he says, his tone slightly softer. "Oh, and I should have also mentioned—we're actually wanting the full Rose Garden Package."

My eyes widen at his words. The Rose Garden Package is my top-level offering, worth thousands of dollars. Not only that, it's a full erotica shoot, featuring a breadth of images and video where anything goes. The realization hits me, and I struggle to keep my voice steady. "Oh, um, wow! That's a significant choice."

"Yeah," he says, a hint of a chuckle in his voice. "We're looking to go all in for this shoot, so I hope you're ready."

I take a deep breath, excitement mingling with nerves. "Absolutely! I'll make sure it's everything you hoped for."

"Oh, I'm sure you will. Then you won't mind that I've just emailed you an NDA?" he adds, and I mentally groan, suppressing the urge to roll my eyes. I click over to my emails, and sure enough, see a message from Knox Bishop. I open it, skimming through the attached document.

"No problem," I say, keeping my voice professional but warm. "I'll review it and send it back to you as soon as possible."

"Appreciate it, Rayne. And thank you." There's something in his voice, a faint warmth, like he's genuinely grateful. Before I can respond, he adds, "See you tomorrow," and then the line clicks off.

I stare at my phone for a moment, processing the conversation. Knox's request was a bit intense, but I can respect the need for privacy. With a sigh, I push aside the distraction of Knox's call and turn my attention back to finishing the gallery, carefully refining each image with the editing brush. The client had taken their time deciding, and now I'm determined to exceed their expectations. After what feels like hours, I finally complete the gallery and move to order their album and wall art, double-checking everything before sending it to print.

Once that's handled, I turn to Knox's NDA. I hit print, and the hum of the printer fills the studio as I stretch, feeling the day's tension start to settle. The document seems standard as I skim the details—clauses about confidentiality, image ownership, no sharing on social media. It's not the first time I've signed something like this, so I quickly add my signature, scan it, and email it back to Knox.

Shutting down my computer, I realize that the daylight has faded. With a sigh, I head out to the store, choosing to walk the few blocks for a breath of fresh air. I always enjoy wandering through the grocery aisles, grounding myself in the simplicity of everyday errands. It's a small break from the studio, where so much of my time is spent immersed in other people's stories.

Back home, I'm greeted by Luna's dramatic meow. She coils around my legs as if I've been gone for days instead of just a few hours, so I scoop her up, chuckling as she nuzzles my cheek. "Alright, drama queen, let's get you fed." Once she's happily munching, I fix myself a quick meal and settle down with a movie, hoping to unwind a little before tomorrow's big shoot.

As the film's storyline drifts on-screen, I can feel my eyelids growing heavy. Just as my eyes flutter closed, I hear the soft sound of Luna curling up beside me, her purring a comforting lullaby. I relax into the moment, letting the day's worries slip away as sleep finally claims me.

Once again, I startle awake in the middle of the night, at a loss for what woke me. Looking around, I can't see Luna near me, but that isn't uncommon, as she sometimes wanders out to scavenge some of her leftover food or have a drink. But after a moment, I frown, glancing around my bedroom again and down at my clothes from the day, not recalling how or when I moved from the couch to my bed or why I fell asleep so hard, so quickly.

Chapter 4
Rayne

THE MORNING HAD BEEN full of errands, and I was glad to check each item off my meticulously planned schedule. An early drop-off to deliver a gift to a special couple was first, and then another quick stop to pick up a different gift for storage. I swung by to restock some supplies, making sure everything was in place for the days ahead. Thankfully, the timeline had fit just right—this session was wedged perfectly into my schedule, leaving the next few weeks light and open.

Once everything was settled, I took a quick break in my apartment, finally slowing down enough for a late lunch. I showered, letting the hot water work the tension out of my shoulders, then dressed in my usual outfit for shoots—a soft, loose top and comfortable cotton overalls that allowed plenty of movement. I pulled my hair back into a loose bun, tucked my phone into a pocket, and gave Luna a quick snuggle. Her purrs always made me feel a bit more centered.

But as I headed back to the studio, preparing to set up, I could feel nerves buzzing under my skin. They weren't unusual—any shoot with new clients left me a little on edge. But today, the feeling was heightened.

Usually, the female partner arranges everything, with a process I'm used to—consults, questions, confirmations. But with Knox, everything is different, from the abruptness of his booking to the absence of my usual pre-shoot routine.

I try to shake off the anxiety, focusing instead on setting up the studio. I turn on the air conditioning to combat the outside heat, and knowing how hot I always get while moving around during the shoot makes it a requirement. Then I move to adjusting the lighting, arranging props, checking that my equipment is in order. But even with all the preparation, that feeling—an unsettling mix of nervous anticipation—refuses to go away.

My studio is a sanctuary of dark and moody elegance, exactly the atmosphere I've crafted over the years to bring out my work's intensity and depth. The main room is spacious, its walls painted in rich blacks and muted golds with accents in deep, jewel tones that shift slightly with each section of the room, providing a blend of color that compliments skin tones beautifully on camera. On one side, a luxurious blue velvet Chesterfield sofa stands out against the dark walls, offering a soft and inviting texture for my clients to sink into. Across the room, a canopy bed with a striking gold frame sits against the wall, its bars doubling as a perfect support for more adventurous clients who enjoy the darker tone of BDSM scenes. A Saint Andrew's Cross is secured nearby, adding an extra edge for those who want to explore the deeper, grittier side of intimacy.

I make my rounds, ensuring each light is in its place, casting the right shadows and highlights. They're all connected to a single remote, which I slip into one of my pockets for easy adjustments mid-session. For the kind of session Knox booked, I set up additional equipment. Besides my main camera—a high-end mirrorless Canon that captures every detail—I've placed four smaller video cameras around the room, angled to catch different perspectives without being intrusive. They're not as high-quality as my main equipment, but they capture a surprising level of detail. Alongside them, eight stationary cameras are arranged strategically to snap photos at intervals, capturing different angles and candid moments. Not all of the shots will be usable, given they don't move, but every so often, those unexpected images become client favorites or even behind-the-scenes glimpses I can use with permission.

The final touches are a careful inspection of each piece of equipment, checking that all batteries are fully charged and ready to go. My main Canon video camera sits firmly on its tripod, capable of capturing every frame of this carefully curated shoot. Each camera, each light, even the smallest details, represents a small fortune of investment—worth every cent given how my reputation has grown. By the time I'm done, everything is just right, and I feel the satisfaction that comes from knowing I'm fully prepared, even as the nerves simmer under the surface. I glance at the clock. It's almost time.

As if sensing that everything is ready, there's a firm, solid knock on the studio door. I take a deep breath, steadying myself as I head over, plastering on my best friendly smile. When I swing open the door, the man filling the entryway practically takes up the entire frame. Dressed sharply in black pants and a brown button down that strains over his well-built body, he exudes a quiet, powerful intensity. His dark brown hair is cropped short on the sides with a hint of curl on top, and a rugged stubble highlights his sharp jawline. He pulls his sunglasses off, revealing piercing hazel eyes that sweep over me in a quick, appraising glance. The gravelly voice I'd grown familiar with over the phone rolls out smoothly.

"Nice to finally meet you. I'm Knox," he says, and the words seem to resonate from somewhere deep. I find my smile widening instinctively as I extend my hand.

"Nice to meet you too," I reply, feeling the roughness of his larger hand as he shakes mine. Hints of tattoos peek from the edges of his cuffs, giving him an added edge. I motion him to come in, and as he steps inside, another figure enters the doorway behind him.

The other person catches me off guard. I could say I wasn't prepared for a same sex couple but I'm always prepared for pretty much anything with what I do. His striking blue eyes—like staring deep into the Caribbean sea, with darker, ocean-blue rings around the edges—meet mine, stopping me in my tracks. His dirty blond hair is styled just so, slightly tousled, longer than Knox's with strands that shimmer like spun gold in the dim light. There's a shadow of golden stubble on his jaw, highlighting an easy smile that feels as if it could disarm even the most guarded person. A scar that intersects his left eyebrow is the only thing that mars his perfect features.

"I'm River," he says, extending his hand toward me. The voice is smoother than Knox's, with a husky edge and an undercurrent of amusement, and I find myself a little breathless as I return the handshake. He is dressed similarly to Knox, but in black on black, and vaguely, I wonder if either of them are feeling as hot under their collars as I am.

"Nice to meet you," I manage to say, hoping my voice sounds steadier than I feel.

As River steps further inside, I close and lock the door, taking a moment to collect myself. Turning back, I find the two of them surveying the studio, taking in the dark atmosphere and the equipment I've prepared. The aura they bring with them—powerful, confident, and utterly captivating—threatens to unravel my carefully constructed professionalism.

I focus on running through my checklist once more to mentally ground myself. The buffet of hotness in front of me is really going to test my ability not to call a ten minute toy break and disappear upstairs. It will push my focus to the limits, but if I can hold it together, the results are bound to be unforgettable.

I take another steadying breath as Knox and River make themselves comfortable. Knox's sharp gaze lingers on the various pieces of equipment—his mind likely ticking off each detail with military precision. River, on the other hand, seems more relaxed, casually surveying the room with a quiet confidence that matches his presence.

I can feel their eyes on me, the weight of their attention a constant pull on my focus. I push back the sensation, forcing myself to concentrate on the task at hand. "Feel free to make yourselves at home," I say with a smile, my voice sounding far more composed than I feel. "I'll just do a quick final check before we start."

I motion toward the velvet sofa, trying to give them a moment to settle in, but I can't help but notice how they stand close to each other—close enough to blur the line between a shared space and the subtle tension that radiates from them. They seem at ease together, and it's hard not to imagine how that ease will translate in front of my cameras.

As I walk back to my equipment, I can't stop myself from sneaking glances at them—Knox, with his chiseled features and intimidating presence, and River, who exudes an effortless charm that makes me want to pull him into the frame immediately. His smile is so disarming, I almost wonder if he's aware of the effect it has. Knox seems more reserved, but there's something about his silence that speaks volumes. It's clear they complement each other in a way that's almost magnetic.

I start adjusting the lighting again, despite already ensuring everything was perfect earlier, needing the distraction to push past the growing heat in my chest. The setup needs to be flawless; this shoot demands it, especially with the tension I can already feel simmering between them. It's the kind of dynamic I live for—the kind that creates electricity in every frame.

I feel my pulse quicken as I slide my camera into position, making sure everything is in place for when I'm ready to begin. They're close now, Knox giving me an almost imperceptible nod as River drops onto the velvet couch, his posture relaxed but with an air of anticipation. The air between us crackles with expectation, and I wonder just how far this shoot will push me.

I swallow hard, forcing myself to stay professional, and dive into the usual pre-shoot spiel I give to all my clients. My voice sounds surprisingly steady, despite my pulse racing at a dangerously fast tempo. "Alright, before we get started, there are just a few things I like to go over. I want you both to feel at ease, so if there are any injuries or sensitivities I should be aware of, let me know. And as best you can, try to forget I'm even here—just go with the moment."

River's soft murmur, smooth and almost amused, throws me off and has my words stumbling to a stop. "I think that'll be... impossible," he says, his tone filled with unspoken implications.

Knox, meanwhile, has drifted through the room, his sharp eyes taking in the setup with a focus that borders on inspection. Every glance he throws around the studio seems to catalog each detail as though evaluating the space, the lights, the positioning of the furniture, until he finally circles back to the couch. As he passes me, I catch a subtle whiff of his cologne, something woodsy and dark, almost grounding. I barely suppress a shiver as the brush of his presence feels close enough to make the fine hairs on my arm stand up.

"So," I continue after a moment, doing my best to keep the tremor out of my voice. "Is there anything I should be aware of that you absolutely won't do?" I hold my breath, knowing this question often draws out boundaries that help me navigate the tone of the session.

Knox's gaze meets mine with unblinking focus. "We have safe words if it comes to that," he replies, his voice low and edged with assurance. I nod, storing the information as he takes a step closer, stopping just shy of where I'm standing. He looks down at me, the weight of his stare cutting through the air between us. "But do you have one?" he asks, voice dropping almost to a murmur, eyes gleaming as he adds, "We can both be... intense, sometimes."

The suggestion makes my mind stutter as I blink up at him. "I don't—" I begin, then shake my head, trying to regain my professionalism. "I mean, it doesn't really matter since I'll just be behind the camera."

Knox's sharp gaze remains steady, his lips curving just slightly as though I've missed something crucial. "But it does," he murmurs. "We wouldn't want to push you past your own comfort, would we?" There's a dark amusement dancing in his eyes, and the hint of a smirk on his lips sends my heart racing faster than I care to admit.

The words hang in the air between us, heavy and full of unspoken meaning. I barely manage a nod, my brain spinning as he finally moves to sit down, settling into the corner of the couch. River leans into him, casual yet intimate, like it's the most natural thing in the world. But there's something about the way they're both looking at me—steady, unwavering—that has my pulse racing, and a warmth building against my will.

I'm suddenly very thankful for the air conditioning I turned on earlier.

Chapter 5
River

I WONDER IF SHE knows that all her careful planning and schedules are about to be thrown out the fucking window.

Chapter 6

Rayne

"As you know, the package you selected for today means that there are no limits to what you want to do so long as it isn't illegal."

My words seem to amuse them both, subtle smirks playing on their faces. Knox stands again, fishing something out of his pants pocket as he makes his way toward me with a casual confidence that somehow feels anything but. He stops directly in front of me, his presence dominating the space between us as he extends his hand.

It takes more effort than I'd care to admit to pull my gaze from his face to the item he's offering. In his hand is a stack of cash, folded neatly and secured by a gleaming gold pin. My hand reaches out, instinctively, and he places it into my palm, but he doesn't let go immediately. His hand lingers, large and warm against mine, holding it in place with a deliberate slowness that sends a surge of awareness through me.

I drag my eyes back up to his, meeting his sharp, unreadable gaze. His eyebrow raises just a fraction, and the intensity behind his look has my stomach dropping as if I'm teetering over the edge of a cliff.

"Thank you," I manage, my voice barely a whisper, fighting the inexplicable urge to add a "sir" to the end of it. The word dances on my tongue, caught somewhere between instinct and compulsion.

River, still lounging on the couch, watches us with a gaze that is almost lazy in its curiosity, but there's something sharp in the way he studies me. Knox's lips curl in the slightest of smiles, one that borders on dangerous amusement. He finally releases my hand, and I take a moment to steady myself, clutching the cash as if it were an anchor. Clearing my throat, I remind myself of my role, slipping back into professionalism even as I feel the weight of their presence.

Knox takes a step back as I tuck the money into another of my pockets, his eyes never leaving mine. He gestures to River with a slight tilt of his head.

"Ready?" he asks, his voice deep, and there's an unmistakable excitement in his tone as he looks over at his partner.

River pushes himself up, his movements graceful as he joins Knox's side, his easy smile now carrying a hint of mischief.

"Always," he replies, his gaze flicking between me and Knox.

The weight of their attention, their raw, magnetic energy, makes my nerves spark again, but I manage to keep my professional demeanor as I pick up my camera and adjust the lens. Walking over to the sound system I have set up I ask, "Do you have any preference on music?"

River's grin widens, a playful edge to his smile as he glances over at me. "Put on something that makes *you* feel sexy," he says with a tease in his voice, his eyes sparking with amusement as he watches me for my reaction.

It's a request that throws me off guard for a second, but I recover quickly, my mind already working through what would fit the mood. It's not uncommon for clients to not have a preference on the music—they're usually caught up in the moment. With a subtle nod, I go to the sound system, my fingers lightly grazing over the smooth surface of the controls.

I don't waste any time; I know exactly what to play. I press a button, and soon the air is filled with the deep beats of a playlist I've carefully curated over the years—songs that speak to my body, that resonate in my skin, that heighten the sensual pulse of the room. They've become a backdrop to so many shoots, but tonight, it feels a little different. The music, heavy with bass and haunting melodies, sinks into the space between us. It's a rhythm that seems to match the rising tension, the heat in the room, as I glance over at Knox and River.

"Alright," I say, turning back to face them, my voice steady even if my heartbeat is anything but. "Whenever you're ready, just start, however it feels natural to you, and I'll be here to capture... everything."

I turn on the switches for all the cameras around the studio before I lift the one in my hands, hiding a faint smile behind it as the two of them move to stand by the bed, their focus fully on each other now.

I expected them to start slowly, maybe take a moment to grow comfortable, to ease into the space like many of my clients do. But the studio must feel as much like home to them as it does to me; they are entirely at ease, moving with a confidence that feels strikingly intimate. Knox reaches for River, threading one of his large hands through River's hair, his fingers tangling and pulling with a firm, unspoken command. River responds immediately, leaning closer, his eyes heavy-lidded as Knox pulls him in.

Both men are tall, but Knox's additional height and broader build dominate the space between them. He lowers his head, brushing his lips lightly, almost teasingly, against River's mouth. The slight tilt of his head, the way his grip tightens possessively, speaks of a well-practiced connection—a dynamic woven of familiarity and an almost palpable tension. Through my lens, I capture their every movement, adjusting the focus as the subtle shift in their body language evolves, sharpening from a quiet closeness to something charged.

Knox murmurs something, low and just loud enough for River alone. River's response is a soft husky laugh, filled with anticipation, as he slides a hand to the back of Knox's neck. Their shared ease reveals layers of history between them, a trust that's both bold and mesmerizing. I can feel the heat of their connection radiating through the room, bringing an edge of tension to the air.

I circle them, capturing every angle, every shift in their expressions. They aren't putting on a show for me; rather, I'm simply there, allowed to witness something private and profound.

Knox's gaze occasionally flicks toward the camera, his eyes meeting mine through the lens with a knowing focus, as though he's fully aware of the effect he and River have—not just on each other, but on everyone in their presence. There's an unspoken invitation in that look, a challenge that makes my heart beat a little faster.

The camera clicks, capturing the rawness in each frame, the looks of unfiltered desire, the press of lips against skin, the hard press of fingers. I adjust the lens again, my fingers slightly unsteady. There's no denying the electric pull I feel as I watch them.

Knox's hand shifts, trailing from River's hair down his cheek, his thumb brushing over River's lower lip with the faintest touch. The way they look at each other feels both intimate and passionate.

I find myself captivated, drawn in as I capture frame after frame. Knox murmurs something else, and River's laugh, low and breathless, fills the air as Knox starts to unbutton his shirt. They move together fluidly, with a comfort and ease that makes it clear this is as natural for them as breathing.

Just as I'm adjusting the camera for a new closer angle, Knox's eyes flick to me, sharp and assessing. It feels as if he's testing me, seeing if I'll flinch or pull back. I don't.

River's fingers make quick work of Knox's shirt, slipping buttons through loops with practiced efficiency, and in a few moments, both men shed their shirts, revealing expanses of tattooed skin that take my breath away. It's not just a few scattered tattoos here and there; both men are covered in intricate, mostly grayscale designs that tell stories across every inch of their bodies. The hints I'd seen on Knox's hands were just the beginning, faint shadows of what lies beneath.

As an artist, the sight is mesmerizing. As a woman, I wish I could trace every dark line on their bodies and see where they lead.

Through my lens, I capture the striking contrast of ink against their skin, the interplay of light and shadow emphasizing the strength in their frames and the fine details of their tattoos. Despite myself, my body responds with a thrill I'd typically be embarrassed by, an instinctual reaction to the raw, powerful beauty they project.

As River's hands move to Knox's waistband, fingers working deftly to undo the button and slide down the zipper, Knox kicks off his shoes, his eyes dark and unwavering on River's face. In one smooth motion, River pushes Knox's pants down, his fingers grazing along Knox's legs as he peels the fabric away, leaving him in only a pair of black boxer briefs that do little to hide the large solid length pressing against the fabric. Knox sits back on the edge of the bed, his powerful form relaxed, a silent expectation that River will continue.

With a faint smirk and an answering fire in his eyes, River moves to straddle Knox's lap, their frames fitting together perfectly. My camera captures the moment Knox's lips descend, trailing slowly along the lines of River's tattooed chest, his mouth brushing along inked skin with a reverence and heat that speaks volumes. The press of Knox's lips and the scrape of his teeth as River arches into him, his head tilting back, exposing more of himself in an unspoken offer.

I continue pressing the shutter as I draw closer, focusing in on the subtle shifts of their expressions, the way Knox's hand moves to cradle the back of River's neck while his mouth continues its exploration. My pulse races as their eyes suddenly flick to me, their attention hitting me like a physical force, as though they can feel my reaction even from behind the lens. The heat in their gazes takes me by surprise, and I swallow hard, suppressing the soft sound that escapes me.

Knox catches it, his eyes narrowing slightly, and I can sense the challenge in his low, steady tone. "Did you want to say something?"

I bite back a smile, shaking my head, trying to maintain my composure. But his gaze pins me, unwavering. "Say it," he commands, his voice firm, expectant. The edge in his voice sends a shiver through me, and my breath hitches as I find myself responding.

"I... I just thought..." My voice is soft, my words slipping out before I can reconsider. "I thought you seemed like the more dominant one, so... I assumed things would be the other way around."

This time, Knox chuckles softly, the sound low, dark, and somehow both amused and dangerous. "I can still top from the bottom," he replies, his words laced with a quiet intensity that leaves no room for doubt. He punctuates his point by fisting a hand in River's hair, pulling his head back sharply, exposing the long line of his throat to his waiting mouth. Knox's tongue traces a slow, teasing line along River's neck, savoring the exposed skin, and River's reaction is immediate—a moan that's half gasp, half plea, his hips instinctively rocking forward in answer.

But both of their eyes remain locked on me, heavy-lidded with desire, pulling me into the current of their connection with a look that's almost possessive, as if they're inviting me to be part of it, to feel the heat that's quickly consuming the room. And as I capture frame after frame, my own pulse races, the professional distance I usually maintain slipping as the desire and tension between them seem to seep through the camera, leaving me feeling raw, exposed, and undeniably affected.

As River's eyes continue to stare into mine, a mischievous grin tugs at his lips. "Have you ever done an erotic shoot yourself?" he asks, his tone light but edged with something mischievous.

I clear my throat, the unexpected question making my heart skip a beat as I lower the camera briefly. "No, I haven't," I admit, a touch of self-consciousness creeping in.

Knox releases his grip on River's hair, both of them still watching me. "Ever done self-portrait, then?" River asks.

I raise an eyebrow, caught slightly off guard by his question. "You know much about photography?" I ask, my tone gently challenging. River's expression softens slightly, almost nostalgic, as he nods.

"In a previous life, yes," he says, his voice carrying a weight I don't understand.

I nod, and before I can catch myself, I respond. "I have done self-portrait before, but... I'm not sure they're any good."

River's grin returns, laced with an undeniable playfulness. "My experience tells me that artists are their own worst critics," he states with a knowing smile, his gaze holding mine for a beat longer. The insight makes me pause, his words catching me off-guard. "Would you let me take your photo?"

The unexpected request catches me off guard, and for a moment, I'm lost for words. I lower the camera further, blinking in confusion as I try to process what River just asked. The weight of his gaze on me feels heavy, and I can't help but notice how much more intense the room has become, like it's on the edge of a knife, despite how relaxed and playful his tone is.

I glance at Knox, but he's simply watching us, his expression unreadable, though there's something about the way he looks at me that holds a faint dark amusement. I find myself wondering how much of what's happening here is part of some unspoken game between the two of them.

I clear my throat again nervously, trying to regain my composure, but the air feels thick with anticipation. "You want to take my photo?" I ask, my voice sounding a little breathier than I intended, betraying just how affected I am by the request.

River chuckles, the sound rich and full of intent as Knox leans back on the bed and allows River to stand. The way River approaches me is like a stalking lion, the sway of his hips is pure sex and makes my mind quickly wander to how he will look when he does have sex.

I'm so distracted that he easily manages to take the camera from my hands before I can even protest.

Chapter 7
Rayne

MY MIND IS STILL spinning, caught on the brief, featherlite brush of River's fingers grazing mine. That single touch lingers, subtle yet electrifying, as he uses his free hand to press against my lower back, guiding me forward. His touch is gentle, yet firm, his fingers press against my spine, and I feel myself sway, my steps faltering as he propels me toward Knox. I feel the low beat of the music in each step, in each beat of my heart and each shallow breath.

Knox rises from the bed, filling my vision. The room seems to shrink, every detail blurring at the edges, except for him. Hard, tattooed flesh covers his body in mesmerizing patterns, and my gaze is drawn to the ink tracing his arms, his collarbone, his abs, slipping just beneath the fabric of his briefs. He is towering, steady and unyielding, a wall of power before me, and for a moment, I lose myself in the intricate details of his tattoos.

I almost stumble forward, but strong hands catch me. Fingers press into my hips, firm and steadying. Knox's hands are scorching, their heat seeping through the thin cotton of my overalls, and I'm acutely aware of every point of contact, every inch of space that separates us. His hands seem to burn through the fabric, branding me with the strength of his hold, and the simple act of him steadying me feels intimate, possessive.

I look up, drawn to his face, only to find his gaze already locked on me, molten and intense. There's a hunger in his eyes that makes my stomach flutter, and I feel a shiver race down my spine, pooling into a slow, simmering ache at my core. His presence is overwhelming, consuming, and the air between us grows heavier with each passing second.

A slow smile tugs at the corner of his mouth, a knowing curl that promises both danger and thrill. His gaze drifts over me, taking in every inch with an appreciation that leaves me feeling bare, vulnerable. "Is this okay, little Rayne?" His voice is low, rough, the gravel in his tone sending a pulse of heat through my body.

For the first time, I realize how much power he holds over me with just a few simple words. It's a question, but there's no real uncertainty in it. He's not asking for permission, not really—he's commanding, yet giving me the choice. The intensity of his gaze makes my heart race, and the ache deep inside me intensifies in response, urging me to surrender.

I'm not small. I know I'm not. I'm tall, with curves that most people notice the moment I step into a room, but standing here with them—standing between Knox and River—I feel smaller than I ever have. Their height, their confidence, their strength—all of it dwarfs me in a way that makes my mind spin, but at the same time, it pulls something from deep within me, a desire to submit, to give in to what they're offering, even without fully understanding why.

The heat in my body is overwhelming, so I close my eyes for a moment, trying to steady myself, to regain control. I can't make sense of what's happening, why this is affecting me so much, but the tension in the air is all consuming. And when Knox rumbles again, his voice low and almost dangerous, my body betrays me, responding to him even before I have a chance to process the words.

"I can stop this if it's too much," he murmurs, his voice dark and tempting, "Simply say the word, and he will obey me."

I could stop this. I could end it all, draw a line, regain control. But the truth is, I don't want to. I want to feel everything, to let go of the control I've clung to so tightly in my life and embrace the wild uncertainty they're offering.

I open my eyes, and the world narrows to just Knox's gaze, dark and unyielding, as it locks onto mine. The magnetic pull between us is undeniable, and for a moment, I wonder if I'll crumble under the weight of it. But then, something inside me shifts, and I find my voice, though it's barely a whisper.

"No, don't stop."

It's all I say, but it's enough. The moment those words leave my lips, Knox is already moving, and before I can even register what's happening, he's unhooking the buttons of my overalls with an ease that makes my breath catch in my throat. I feel the fabric slip down my body, pooling around my hips, and my stomach dips. But I'm not afraid. Not yet.

His lips hover just above mine, his breath warm, almost teasing. I can feel the steady beat of my pulse as he leans in, his lips brushing against mine as he pushes the overalls past my hips and the fabric falls away. It's slow, deliberate, and then his lips press more firmly against mine, his kiss deep and demanding, pulling me in as if we've been here before—like we're both aware of the game we're playing.

I can hear the beat of the music and under that the faint click of the camera shutter, but everything else blurs away. I'm acutely aware of Knox's hands, of the way his fingers press into my waist—drawing my body closer to him.

I let myself melt into the moment, surrendering to their presence, to what they're offering. There's no hesitation, no second-guessing.

It's as if I was made for this—made to exist in the space between them, caught in the current of their dominance, their hunger, their gaze.

As Knox pulls away from the kiss, I'm left breathless, my body reacting to every touch, every movement, every click of the camera. I feel exposed, vulnerable, yet more alive than I have in a long time. Their attention is all-consuming, and I can no longer bring myself to care how much it's affecting me.

Knox's gaze never leaves my face, watching every flicker of emotion as his fingers drag slowly up my waist, each inch setting my skin alight. He moves with a deliberate, almost teasing precision, the thin material of my top sliding along with his touch until his thumbs brush against the sensitive skin just beneath my breasts. I can barely breathe, anticipation building as he leans closer, his breath a warm caress against my cheek, his eyes dark and intense.

"What is your safe word, baby girl?" The question is soft, but the words vibrate in my chest, setting every nerve on edge.

I gasp as his thumbs brush higher, grazing over my bra, the lace catching against my skin, sending a sharp wave of sensation through me. "Aperture," I manage to whisper, my voice barely audible, caught somewhere between disbelief and desire.

A low, knowing chuckle rumbles from him "Of course it is." The warmth in his voice somehow makes it feel like a shared secret, as if he'd known I'd choose something tied to my passion, something familiar to ground me. Then he is pulling my top up and over my head, his hands brushing along my arms as he does. The room feels cool, goosebumps erupting across my skin, but the exposure only amplifies the heat simmering underneath my skin.

I'm acutely aware of River's presence just a few steps away, the quiet shutter of the camera marking moments I barely comprehend.

Standing there in nothing but my bra and underwear, Knox steps back just enough to take in the sight of me, his gaze intense and hungry. Every inch of my skin tingles with awareness of the man towering in front of me.

Knox reaches up and gently unclips my hair, letting the long, dark strands tumble down my back. His fingers sift through the waves, lingering for a moment as he watches my reaction. It's a strangely tender gesture, a contrast to the dominance simmering in his gaze, and my heart pounds in response.

On instinct, my hands press against his chest, fingers meeting the hard heat of his skin. I push slightly, a half-hearted attempt to create space, but he doesn't move an inch. Instead, his hand twists in my hair, tightening sharply and tugging on the strands. The brief flare of pain makes my breath hitch, and he leans closer, his lips just brushing my ear as he growls, "You're not in charge here anymore, sweetheart. If you want this to stop, you know the word. That's the only thing that will stop this now."

A shiver runs through me at the low command in his voice, the raw authority that thrums in his words. I shouldn't find this attractive, but I do—more than I can admit, even to myself. His grip on my hair is firm, unrelenting, and every ounce of control I'm so used to holding onto slips away in his hands.

He drags my mouth to his, and there's nothing gentle in the way he claims me this time. His kiss is searing, deep, his tongue parting my lips and tangling with mine, leaving no room for thought, only sensation. Heat blooms inside me, a fierce wave of need that overrides everything else, erasing any last scrap of professionalism I'd been clinging to. I moan into his mouth, my body responding before my mind can catch up.

My senses explode with the taste of him—smoky and fierce, tinged with something dark that makes my pulse race faster. Knox seems to pull every lick of fire from within me, igniting a hunger I didn't know existed. He groans low when I arch into him, wanting more than just his mouth, yearning for the vise-like grip of his body around mine. He brings his free hand between us and deftly unhooks my bra, the lace parting as his hand cups and squeezes my flesh.

"Good girl," he whispers against my lips, the praise sending shockwaves through me. It blooms like a wildflower, vibrant and untamed, threading tendrils of pleasure through my veins.

I don't even realize he has moved us, my whole focus is on his hands and mouth, the heat of his touch branding me, until the backs of my legs hit the bed. His push is firm and suddenly I'm on my back on the cool sheets, a contrast to the warmth radiating from my flushed skin. Knox stands over me, a dark silhouette against the studio lighting. His gaze is heavy and heated as it trails over the contours of my body—every part of me laid bare before him.

An instinctual vulnerability prickles at my skin, and I reach to shield myself, to hide what doesn't fit the mold of small and delicate. But his growl slices through the air, a single command that roots my hands to my sides. "Don't."

Narrowed hazel eyes pierce into me as Knox tilts his head, drinking in my body. "Never hide this perfection from anyone, Rayne." His voice is a gravel-laced growl. "A body like yours deserves to be worshiped, like Aphrodite herself."

I gasp as he suddenly drops to his knees in front of me. His large tattooed hands gripping my thighs, jerking me toward the edge of the bed with a forceful tug. Heat pools low in my belly at the dominance in his movements.

"And that's exactly what I'm going to do," he rumbles, hooking his fingers into the waistband of my underwear and pulling them down my legs in one swift motion.

I swallow hard as he leans forward, the rasp of his stubbled jaw brushing my inner thighs. Then his tongue traces a molten path along my slit.

The world around me slips away, fading into an overwhelming ocean of sensation. I arch my back involuntarily, gasping as Knox's tongue glides over me with a tantalizing slowness one moment and then a savage passion that ignites every nerve ending in my body. My hands curl into the sheets, gripping the fabric like a lifeline as he brings me to the brink and whisks me only inches from it—teasing, tantalizing.

"Please," I manage to breathe, though whether I'm begging for more or for release, I can't tell. Knox looks up at me through dark lashes, his eyes shimmering with something primal—a hunger that mirrors my own.

"You taste as good as I imagined you would," he rasps, the words curling around me like smoke, seductive and intoxicating.

Before I can respond, he delves deeper, his mouth devouring me with an urgency that sends shockwaves of pleasure rippling through my entire being. Each flick of his tongue sends me spiraling, drawing out sounds I never thought I could make. It's been so long since I've been with anyone sexually and even those were quick, meaningless and unsatisfactory.

His hands hold me firmly in place as I try to shift my body closer to him, seeking more, craving the release he undoubtedly knows how to provide. He seems to find delight in my helplessness, his eyes glinting with mischief and a darkness I can't identify as his tongue circles my clit teasingly. I can already feel this is going to be over quickly, my body barreling toward a cliff as his mouth closes over my sensitive bundle of nerves and sucks. A desperate whine escapes my lips as I feel that tight coil deep within me begin to unravel.

I throw my head back on a cry as a ripple of pleasure pulses through me, radiating from my core until my body tingles. Some small part of my mind is faintly aware of River leaning over me, the camera capturing the look on my face as I come apart.

My eyes flutter open, meeting his striking blue gaze. There's an potency there that sends a shiver down my spine, a mix of adoration and something darker, more predatory.

"God, you're fucking gorgeous when you come," he says, his easy smile doing little to mask the hunger in his eyes. "Isn't she, Knox?"

I can feel Knox's breath hot against my inner thigh as he chuckles. "Absolutely breathtaking."

As I attempt to regain my composure, Knox rises from between my legs, his eyes locked on mine. He reaches out, his tattooed fingers gently brushing a strand of hair from my face.

"You have no idea how long we've waited for this moment," Knox murmurs, his gravelly voice sending shivers down my spine. Does he mean they planned this from the moment they saw my website?

My mind races, trying to process the situation. How did I end up here, caught between these two men? Part of me wants to run, to escape the growing sense of danger. But another part, a part I'm not proud of, craves more.

Chapter 8
Rayne

Knox stands at the foot of the bed, eyes blazing with desire as they rake over my flushed body. His tattooed hands slowly push his boxer briefs down, freeing his impressive length.

"Fuck..." I swallow hard at the sight, my rational thoughts overridden by pure want. How had I gone from professional photographer to this? The fact that I'm about to be fucked in my own studio, by a client, is beyond unprofessional of me. But with pleasure still humming through my body, I can't bring myself to stop.

River shifts, a feral grin on his handsome face as he watches his boyfriend. All sense of propriety has fled–I'm utterly transfixed by Knox stroking his rigid cock.

"You want this, don't you, Rayne?" His gruff voice makes me shudder. When had I thrown all professionalism out the front door of the studio?

I give the tiniest nod, mouth dry. Knox steps closer to the edge of the bed, that dark and commanding energy rolling off him in waves. My pulse thunders, skin tingling with forbidden thrill as he pushes my parted thighs wider before gripping one of my hips. Then the thick head of his cock rubs torturously against my entrance, slicking up with my arousal, before slowly pressing forward.

"So goddamn tight," he growls, slowly burying himself into my welcoming heat inch by delicious inch.

A guttural moan tears from my lips at the full, stretching burn. My eyes squeeze shut as I arch backward, my lips parting on a gasping breath. It has been far too long since I've had a man inside me like this. He stills for a moment, a bruising grip on my hips.

He thrusts the rest of the way. "That's it, take every fucking inch of me."

When I hear the sound of the camera shutter close, my eyes part wide and all I can see is the reflection of my own flushed face in the lens as River captures the look on my face as his boyfriend buries his cock deep inside me.

Knox's muscular body hovers over me, his hands bracketing my shoulders, his intense eyes locked on mine. With agonizing slowness, he pulls back until just the tip of his thick cock remains inside me. I whimper in anticipation, my nails raking down his tattooed arms.

A small, dark grin pulls at his lips before he slams back into me, the force stealing my breath. He doesn't stop then, setting a deliciously hard pace that has me clawing at the sheets.

I cry out at his relentless thrusts, losing myself in the exquisite fullness and the liquid heat pooling between my thighs. River's presence in the room fades from my awareness as I become lost in Knox's powerful body working above me, his cock stretching me so perfectly with each punishing stroke.

The seductive beat of the music blends with the lewd sounds we're making—skin slapping, gasps, and groans. It's the most erotic experience I've ever had, and a part of me vaguely registers River circling us, camera in hand, capturing every moment.

"Look at you," Knox murmurs, bending closer until his chest brushes mine, our heated breaths mingling. One of his tattooed hands moves, wrapping around my throat with calculated pressure. "So fucking gorgeous. Will you take River so well too?"

My reply is a choked whine as my hands encircle his wrist, nails digging into his flesh when his hips snap forward with force. Knox licks his lips, gaze flickering between my eyes and parted mouth mere inches away. "That's it, you want that too, don't you? I can feel you squeezing my cock. Go on, sweetheart. Let me hear that pretty voice when you come again for me like a good girl..."

Incoherent cries fall from my lips as waves of ecstasy crash over me and I come undone, legs squeezing Knox's hips. His intense gaze drinks in every flicker of pleasure across my face from just inches away. As the pulses slow, my orgasm subsiding, he rolls us until I'm seated astride him, his cock still buried deep.

Still gripping my throat, he pushes me up until I'm sitting, straddling him. I let out a gasp at the new, deliciously deeper angle. So close to the bed's edge, his legs dangle off, feet planted. Hands braced on his chest, I steady myself as he rasps, "Move for me. Let me see those beautiful tits bounce."

My brain short-circuits as my hips start rocking of their own accord. I swivel and grind against him, drawing delicious groans. Nails scoring his chest, I ride him harder when he thrusts up in response.

Just as I'm getting into the rhythm, his hand leaves my throat to grip my hip. For a second, I think he's going to control the pace. But then a warm, solid chest presses against my back and another large hand encircles my neck from behind.

River's scent surrounds me as he moves my hair aside and licks up the skin of my neck, sandalwood and sin. Panic spikes through me for a moment and I try to turn, to find my camera that he was using earlier. "Tripod," he pants hotly against my ear. "Timer's set to capture everything." He sucks on the lobe, making me shudder.

His teeth graze that sensitive spot below my ear, biting down and I'm instantly melting again, pussy fluttering. "Ready for me too, beautiful?"

His meaning doesn't register until I feel thick fingers pushing into me alongside Knox's thick length. "No, please..." I whimper, my eyes flying wide when I realize their intent. "I can't..."

Knox levels me with a stare that doesn't allow an argument. "You can, and you will."

I keen softly as River's fingers stretch me further, prepping me for what they plan to do. The burning sensation dulls momentarily and I squeeze my eyes shut, bracing for what is to come. When he pulls his fingers out and replaces them with the thick head of his cock, searing pain lances through me as he slowly pushes in alongside Knox's cock.

"Fuck, you're so tight," River growls, squeezing my throat.

I whimper, tears leaking from the corners of my eyes as they stretch me beyond my limits. The overwhelming fullness steals my breath.

Knox brushes a calloused thumb over my cheek, catching a tear. His lips pull into a slow, wicked grin as something dark flickers in those piercing eyes. Like he's savoring my pain and whimpers, getting off on my distress.

"You love feeling us split you open, don't you, sweetheart?" His gravelly voice caresses the words, both soothing and menacing.

I can only cry out softly as they begin moving in tandem, the drag of their cocks rubbing deliciously against my inner walls even as it feels like they are cleaving me in two.

"Such a good girl, taking us both so well." River practically purrs, his fingers fisting in my hair as his hips snap forward.

Their words heat my blood even as I sob from the exquisite pain of them stretching me wider than I ever imagined. But underneath it, I feel the pleasure building. I feel so full, I can feel every ridge of their thick cocks moving inside me. This is bliss and torture intertwined so perfectly, I never want it to end.

The viselike stretch and burn slowly morphs from agony into exquisite pleasure as my body adjusts to accommodate them. I cry out with each thrust, nails raking down Knox's chest as they set a brutal pace, their cocks driving relentlessly in and out of my pussy.

"Fuck, you feel so goddamn tight wrapped around our cocks," Knox growls.

A whimper tears from my lips at his filthy words, my inner walls fluttering around their thick lengths. The skin of River's chest rubs deliciously against my back with each powerful snap of his hips, his harsh pants fanning across my neck.

Sweat beads on Knox's brow as he hammers into me, his abdominal muscles clenching and flexing with the effort. I drink in every sculpted line of his body, taking in the sight of where my nails have cut into his skin, drawing blood.

Wave after wave of pleasure crests, building higher with each stroke of their cocks inside me. I'm utterly lost to anything but the euphoric fullness and the sound of our skin slapping together obscenely and the filth dripping from their lips.

"You're going to be a mess when we're done with you," River promises darkly in my ear, his fingers tightening around my throat. "A beautiful, wrecked mess leaking our cum."

I should be concerned that I hadn't even thought about protection, but those words, combined with another perfectly angled thrust, shatters what little control I have left. I come apart at the seams, inner muscles fluttering and clenching as I cry out hoarsely. Knox's grip on my hips turns bruising as he loses his rhythm, hips snapping erratically. With a low growl, he buries himself to the hilt and I can feel the thick pulses of his climax as he spills himself inside me.

River isn't far behind, his fingers biting into my throat and cutting off my air as he ruts shamelessly into my fluttering pussy. A harsh groan punches from his lungs when he erupts, his hot cum joining Knox's inside me.

Weak and utterly spent, I slump forward bonelessly against Knox's broad chest. When River slowly pulls from inside me and slumps on the bed beside us, I can't stop the whimper escaping and they chuckle. Knox rolls me gently until I'm on the bed between them before he pulls out of me also.

I feel the cum trickling obscenely from my abused folds. "Such a gorgeous fucking mess," Knox murmurs with dark satisfaction, sweeping his thumb over the swollen lips of my pussy.

His fingers slide from between my thighs, drenched and glistening. A grin curves his lips as he brings them to his mouth, his eyes darkening as he sucks them clean with an obscene groan.

My body flushes hot, breath catching as River leans over me. Knox captures River's mouth in a hungry, possessive kiss, fisting his fingers through River's golden hair. When their lips part, Knox rasps, "Clean up the mess."

Oh god.

River slides down my body, heated blue eyes flicking between us. His tongue licks the entire length of my pussy, and for a second all I can think about is the fact that he's cleaning up not just mine and Knox's cum, but his own too. Then I thrash my head side-to-side as his tongue laps at my swollen, sensitized clit. A broken cry escapes me, hips bucking involuntarily as jolts of sensation lance through me.

"Knox...no, I can't—too sensitive..." I plead desperately, even as arousal tightens low in my belly.

His large hand clamps over my hip, pinning me firmly to the bed. "You'll come for us again," he growls, voice dark and low. "Keep going, River."

River groans in pleasure, the vibration making me whimper. His tongue swirls firmly over my aching clit, sucking it between his lips to lave and tease relentlessly. Objections die on my lips, harsh pants escaping instead as heat coils tighter...tighter...

My back bows, thighs trembling uncontrollably as that first searing rush of release crashes over me. Knox leans in, lips brushing my ear, breath ghosted across it, sending shivers down my spine. "You're perfect for us, Rayne," he whispered, his voice dark and full of promise. "We have so many plans for you."

My breath catches in my throat at his words. Plans? What kind of plans? A mixture of fear and excitement courses through me.

River's tongue continues its relentless assault, drawing out my climax with merciless skill. My body convulses, waves of pleasure crashing over me again and again. I gasp for air, feeling lightheaded as the intensity builds to an almost unbearable peak.

My vision begins to blur, spots dancing at the edges as the sensations overwhelm me. I gasp for air, feeling lightheaded and dizzy.

"River," Knox commands, his voice sounding distant. "Make her see stars."

With renewed vigor, River redoubles his efforts. His fingers join his mouth, thrusting and curling inside me, hitting that spot that makes me see white. I cry out, my body arching off the bed.

"Oh god, oh god," I chant, my mind reeling. "I can't—it's too much—"

Knox's hand cups my face, forcing me to look at him. I can't focus, I can vaguely see his eyes are dark, filled with a possessive hunger that both terrifies and thrills me.

"You can and you will," he growls. "You're going to give us everything, Rayne."

The potency in his gaze, coupled with River's relentless assault on my senses, pushes me over the edge again. My eyes roll back as the most intense climax of my life rips through me. I distantly hear myself screaming as my body convulses.

The last thing I register before darkness claims me is River's gleeful laughter and Knox's satisfied growl.

Chapter 9
River

I GENTLY LOWER RAYNE onto her bed, her limp form pliant in my arms. Her skin is flushed and glistening with a sheen of sweat, dark hair fanned out across the pillow like spilled ink. My eyes trace the contour of her body, drinking in every detail–the gentle rise and fall of her chest, the marks our hands and mouths have left on her skin, the slight parting of her lips as she breathes deeply in unconsciousness.

"I'll clean her up," I murmur to Knox, who nods and settles into a chair nearby, his piercing gaze never leaving Rayne's body.

I move through her apartment with practiced ease, having memorized the layout during my previous visits. The familiarity of the space sends a thrill through me–how many nights had I spent here, watching her from the shadows, imagining this very scenario? And now here we are, the fantasy made gloriously real.

In the bathroom, I fill a bowl with warm water, adding a splash of the lavender-scented soap I know she favors. The gentle floral scent fills the air, reminding me of all the times I've breathed it in while standing unseen in her bedroom, watching her sleep. I grab a soft washcloth and towel before returning to where Rayne lies sprawled across the bed.

Knox's eyes meet mine as I enter, a silent conversation passing between us. The satisfaction and dark promise I see there mirrors my own feelings. We've waited so long for this, planned so carefully. And now that we have her, we're never letting go.

I set the bowl on the nightstand and dip the cloth into the warm, fragrant water. Wringing it out, I start at Rayne's face, gently wiping away the traces of tears and sweat. Her skin is soft beneath the cloth, and I can't resist trailing my fingers along her cheekbone, marveling at finally being able to touch her freely.

Working my way down, I clean her neck, paying special attention to the almost imperceptible marks we've left. A possessive thrill runs through me at the sight knowing we put them there—visible proof that she belongs to us now.

I take my time washing her breasts, admiring how much larger than my hands they are. Even unconscious, her body responds to my touch, nipples hardening as I pass the warm cloth over them. It takes all my self-control not to lean down and take one in my mouth, to wake her with the sensation of my tongue and teeth on her sensitive flesh.

But no, not yet. We have time now. No need to rush.

I continue down her body, wiping away the mingled sweat and fluids from her stomach and thighs. When I reach her pussy, I'm extra gentle, carefully cleaning any of our combined release I missed with my mouth and tongue from her swollen folds. The sight of her like this–used and marked by us—sends a fresh wave of arousal through me. Already, I'm craving more of her, aching to bury myself inside her again.

I almost can't believe this day finally arrived. Only yesterday I was in this very apartment, watching her from the shadows and restraining myself from reaching out to touch her. It took every ounce of willpower not to climb in beside her, to pull her warm body against mine and breathe in the intoxicating scent of her skin.

I let my fingers stroke against the fur of the grey cat, scratching just the way I have learned she likes it. It took more visits than I care to admit—and certainly wont admit to Knox—to win the little feline over without resorting to bribery. I watch Rayne settle back onto her bed and fall back to sleep from where I'm standing in the shadows of the apartment hallway. The soft vibration of the cat's purr against my palm is oddly soothing, a stark contrast to the electric anticipation coursing through my veins. I knew I didn't just have to learn every little detail about the woman in that room, but also the little feline she called hers. After all, she was my first obstacle, the gatekeeper to Rayne's most private moments.

My eyes never leave Rayne's form as she shifts in bed, her dark hair splayed across the pillow. The sheet clings to her curves, rising and falling with each breath, and I find myself matching my breathing to hers, syncing with her unconscious rhythm. It's intimate in a way that makes my skin prickle.

The cat's ears perk up suddenly, and I feel the change in her posture before I hear anything. The air shifts toward the apartment entry, and I know without looking that Knox has arrived. I give her fur one final scratch before setting her down gently.

Moving silently through the shadows, I retrace my steps back to the living area where Knox stands. His presence fills the room, a familiar comfort that settles over me like a second skin, and our eyes meet in the dim light.

I almost snort out loud as Knox leans down, placing a small pouch on the floor like an offering to a god. The cat eyes it warily for a moment before pouncing, attacking the offering with gusto. It's amusing to see him try to win over the feline guardian, especially when I've already gained its trust.

Stepping closer to Knox, I can feel the tension radiating off him in waves. His jaw is set, eyes dark. I know that look well—it's the same hunger that burns in my own veins, a craving for the woman sleeping just down the hall.

"How long have you been here?" Knox asks, his voice a low rumble that sends a pleasant shiver down my spine.

"Long enough," I reply with a smirk, my gaze drifting back to where Rayne sleeps. "She's beautiful when she's unaware, isn't she?"

Knox nods, his eyes following mine. "Did you...?"

"No," I shake my head. "Just watched. Touched her hair. It's as soft as it looks. And her scent..."

He inhales sharply, and I can see his control wavering. It's intoxicating, this dance we do—pushing each other's limits, seeing how far we can go before one of us snaps.

The cat rolls onto its back, still fixated on the pouch. Its purrs fill the silence between us, a soothing counterpoint to the tension in the air. I crouch down, running my fingers through her soft fur. She blinks up at me lazily, completely at ease.

"You've charmed her little guardian," Knox observes, a hint of admiration in his voice.

I shrug, a smile playing at my lips. "What can I say? I can calm even the most savage beast."

Knox chuckles, the sound low and warm. "That you can."

Standing, I move closer to him, close enough to feel the heat radiating off his body.

"She stirred not long ago," I whisper, my voice barely audible even in the stillness of the apartment. "But she's sleeping deeply again now."

Knox nods, his gaze drifting toward the hallway that leads to Rayne's bedroom. "Good," he murmurs, and I can hear the restrained desire in that single word. "Did you disturb anything? Leave anything behind?"

I shake my head. "Of course not. You trained me better than that."

His answering smile is sharp, predatory, and it sends a thrill down my spine. This is the Knox I fell in love with—the meticulous planner, the careful hunter. He reaches out, his fingers ghosting along my jaw, and I lean into his touch.

"Let's go," he says softly. "We have work to do before tomorrow's shoot."

As we make our way to the door, I can't help but cast one last glance down the hallway. The darkness seems to pulse with potential, with the promise of what's to come. Rayne has no idea how her world is about to change, how we're going to consume every aspect of her life until there's nothing left that we don't touch, don't own.

Shaking off the memories, I finish cleaning between her thighs and down her legs. Once I'm satisfied that I've washed away all traces of our activities, I use the towel to gently dry her skin. My touch lingers perhaps longer than necessary, savoring the softness beneath my fingers.

I take the bowl back to the bathroom, rinsing it out and watching the cloudy water swirl down the drain. As I set it aside, my eyes catch on Rayne's hairbrush sitting on the counter. Without hesitation, I grab it, running my thumb over the soft bristles as I make my way back to the bedroom.

Knox is still seated in the chair, his piercing gaze fixed on Rayne's sleeping form. As I enter, his eyes flick to the brush in my hand, and a small, knowing smile pulls at his lips. He doesn't say anything, but I can see the approval in his eyes, the understanding of what this simple act means.

I settle on the edge of the bed, careful not to disturb Rayne. Her hair is a glorious mess, tangled and wild from our earlier activities. Gently, I begin to run the brush through the dark strands, starting at the ends and working my way up.

I lose myself in the task, marveling at the silky texture of her hair between my fingers. It's something I've dreamed of doing for so long—touching her like this, caring for her in these intimate ways. The reality is even better than I imagined.

As I work, I tilt her head gently from side to side, careful not to wake her. Her skin is warm beneath my touch, and I can't resist trailing my fingers along the line of her jaw, down the graceful line of her neck. Even unconscious, she's captivating, and I find myself drinking in every detail of her face—the fullness of her lips, the delicate arch of her eyebrows, the tiny beauty spot at her temple that I want to kiss.

The room is quiet save for the soft sound of the brush moving through her hair and Rayne's deep, even breaths. It's a moment of peace, a chance to simply be with her, to care for her in this small way.

I catch Knox's eye as I work, and the look we share is heavy with meaning. This is more than just cleaning her up or brushing her hair. It's a statement of intent, a promise. We're going to take care of her in every way possible, tend to her every need, whether she knows she has them or not.

As I finish brushing out the last tangle, I run my fingers through her hair one last time, savoring the silky feel. Rayne shifts slightly in her sleep, turning her face into my touch, and my breath catches in my throat. Even unconscious, she's responding to us, seeking our touch.

I move to join Knox and he reaches out as he stands, pulling me close, his hand warm on the small of my back. "Beautiful," he murmurs, his eyes never leaving Rayne's sleeping form. "Both of you."

I lean into him, drinking in the warmth of his body, the familiar scent of his skin. We stand together, watching Rayne's chest rise and fall with each peaceful breath.

"We should go," Knox murmurs, his breath warm against my ear. "We have work to do."

I nod reluctantly, not wanting to leave her but knowing we need to clean up the studio. With one last lingering look at Rayne, I move back to the bathroom, replacing her hairbrush exactly where I found it. My fingers trail over the bristles, still holding strands of her silky dark hair.

Back in the bedroom, Knox is adjusting the sheets around Rayne's body, tucking her in with surprising gentleness. His large hands look almost incongruous as they smooth the fabric over her silhouette. When he's satisfied, he steps back, and I can see the possessive gleam in his eyes as he drinks in the sight of her.

"Sweet dreams, little Rayne," he whispers, voice low and dark with promise. "You're going to need your rest."

We make our way silently through her apartment, pausing only for Knox to retrieve the now-empty catnip pouch from where the cat has abandoned it.

As we descend the stairs to the studio, anticipation thrums through me. The space is thick with the lingering scent of sex and sweat, visual evidence of our activities scattered everywhere. Clothing strewn across the floor, sheets rumpled and stained, cameras still set up on their tripods.

"I'll start with the bedding," I offer, moving to strip the sheets. Knox nods, already gathering up discarded clothing. We pile them all into the small washing machine in the tiny bathroom in the corner and start it. We move efficiently, falling into the familiar rhythm we've developed over years of cleaning up after our... other activities.

Knox wipes down all of the furniture while I straighten Rayne's equipment. As I place Rayne's cameras carefully on her desk, my eyes linger on the thick bundle of cash Knox had given her earlier. I can still vividly recall the way her eyes had widened slightly when he pressed it into her palm–that flicker of surprise mixed with a hint of awe. It was clear she wasn't used to clients valuing her work quite so highly and I wonder how often she gets clients who pay that much for a single session.

My fingers brush over the crisp bills, a small smile playing at my lips as I remember her reaction. The way her breath had caught, just for a moment, before she composed herself. How her fingers had curled around the money, almost reverently. But beneath that professional mask, I had seen the spark of desire in her eyes–not just for the cash, but for Knox, for me, for what was about to unfold.

If only she knew that we would have gladly paid a hundred times that amount to make tonight happen. The cash was just a formality, a way to maintain the illusion of a standard transaction. But what transpired between us was priceless.

And only step one on the path to changing her whole world forever.

Chapter 10
Rayne

I JOLT AWAKE, HEART pounding, disoriented. Sunlight filters through the curtains, casting a soft glow across my bedroom. It takes a moment for my foggy brain to catch up. I'm in my apartment, not the studio. Luna's warm weight presses against my legs, her furry body curled atop the sheet covering my naked form.

Frowning, I mutter to myself, "I could've sworn I locked that door..."

My eyes narrow as I study Luna. How did they get past her? She's a terror with strangers.

Reaching for my phone, I notice it's plugged in. A considerate touch that sends a chill down my spine. The time makes me groan, 6:17 AM.

"Shit," I hiss, sitting up abruptly. "I'm so behind."

Luna gives an indignant meow as she's jostled from her perch.

"Oh, stop being dramatic," I tell her, throwing off the sheets. "That's my job today."

As I stumble towards the shower, my mind races through my packed schedule. Edit the farewell breast shoot. Client pickup. Drinks with Kahlee. And somehow, I need to clean the studio after... everything.

The hot water does little to ease the tension in my shoulders. I can't shake the way my heart races at the memory of what happened. But I push it down, lock it away. I have a business to run.

"No days off for the self-employed," I remind my reflection as I get dressed, carefully choosing clothes that don't accentuate my curves.

In the kitchen, I grab a quick bite before dealing with Luna's dramatic pleas for breakfast.

"You'd think I never feed you," I mutter, pouring kibble into her bowl.

As she eats, I pause, my hand resting on the doorknob leading downstairs. My studio awaits, likely still bearing evidence of last night's unexpected events. I take a deep breath, steeling myself.

I descend the stairs, each step echoing in the silence. At the bottom, I pause, listening intently. The studio is eerily quiet, the music that was playing last night now silent. My heart rate quickens as I approach the larger bedroom set.

Stepping inside, I freeze, my eyes widening in disbelief. "What the..."

The room is immaculate. The bed is stripped bare, no trace of last night's activities visible. My clothes, which I distinctly remember being scattered on the floor, have vanished. The lights are all off, and the tripods are neatly packed away.

A wave of panic washes over me as I realize the cameras are missing. "No, no, no," I mutter, frantically searching the studio. After several frantic minutes, I spot them in my office lined up perfectly on my desk, exactly as I would have arranged them after a normal shoot.

My mind reels. How did they know? It can't be a coincidence, can it? The precision, the attention to detail – it's unsettling.

Sitting next to the cameras, the bundle of cash, complete with its shiny gold pin. It gleams as though mocking me, like *'here is an extra something for letting us ruin you for other men'*.

I shake my head, trying to clear the fog of confusion and unease. *Focus, Rayne, you have work to do.*

Grabbing my other keys from a drawer, I head towards the basement and connected parking garage. As I descend the second flight of stairs, the feeling of being watched fades away. This is the one area I know prying eyes can't see or get into.

It doesn't take long to run my errand and I'm back in my studio again by 8 am. I work through moving the data from last night's shoot from the storage cards and into the large server I have for storing client images. I don't look at them, the memory of the night before is far too fresh to bring myself to look at them.

Instead, while the computer is processing the data, I start on editing a different set of images. The photoshoot from the other day, the one where they were saying farewell to her breasts. I take a moment to admire the set again and the beautiful purple lingerie. It's a guilty pleasure of mine that I love lingerie even though I don't wear it often. When I do, I feel sexy, but they don't make sexy lingerie that is ideal for the way I have to constantly move around when I'm photographing someone.

The shoot for this couple wasn't an erotic shoot and was a little more posed than candid, but the images still looked amazing. I spend several hours working through most of the selected images, until my eyes are strained from looking so closely at my computer screen. There are also so many tiny edits in a photoshoot–little stray strands of hair in the wrong place, random pieces of string from lingerie, a tag that's suddenly showing on the best images, temporary blemishes from nerves. I have lost count of the number of times I've had to edit out a hair band around a wrist that was forgotten.

I lean back in my chair, rubbing my temples. The tedious work is necessary, but it takes a toll. My mind starts to wander, drifting back to the events of last night. The thrill, the rush, the mind blowing pleasure. A small smile tugs at my lips.

A notification chimes on my computer and I click on it, noticing I missed one from the previous morning as well. Both have my heart racing as I bring up the news articles about the new murder victims. There is still a frustrating lack of detail in both articles, but somehow the police have been able to contain the details of two more murders without anything being leaked to the press. The only new details I garner from the articles is that they are being investigated by two detectives who specialize in serial killers. It's the first time the words "serial killer" have been used and a shiver goes through me, my body tingling slightly. I'm beyond fascinated.

In the article from today, it simply says that when approached for comment, one of the detectives, a Detective Maddox, said they are completely focused on finding the person responsible.

Closing down the articles, I return to the editing, but my mind keeps drifting back to the murders. I take a break and head upstairs for lunch and Luna snuggles, though she seems highly offended that it's only me, causing me to frown at her again. Her behavior has been odd lately, and I can't shake the feeling that something is off.

After lunch I return to editing and get the gallery finished and the art and album ordered. I've just hit submit when there is a knock at the studio door, checking the time I see that I've timed it perfectly for my appointment.

I make my way to the door, smoothing down my dress and plastering on a warm, professional smile. As I open it, I'm greeted by Lacy Matthews' beaming face.

"Lacy! Come on in," I say, gesturing her inside.

She practically bounces through the doorway, her eyes sparkling with excitement. "Oh, Rayne! I can't tell you how excited I've been for this day!"

As I close the door behind her, Lacy turns and grasps my hands in hers. "The photoshoot was just... magical," she gushes, her eyes never leaving mine. "You made me feel so beautiful, so empowered. I've never experienced anything like it."

I smile, used to such effusive praise. "I'm so glad you enjoyed it, Lacy. That's exactly what I aim for with every client."

As we walk towards my client's sitting area where her album and wall art are waiting, I can't help but notice how Lacy's gaze seems to drink in every detail of the studio. It's almost as if she's replaying the photoshoot in her mind.

"You know," I say, trying to fill the silence, "most of my clients come in nervous, but leave feeling much more confident. It's really rewarding to see that transformation."

Lacy nods enthusiastically. "Oh, I can imagine! You have such a gift, Rayne. Such a special way of... capturing people."

There's something in her tone that makes me pause, but I push the feeling aside as we reach the seating. I pick up the boudoir album from the coffee table, its leather cover cool against my fingers.

"Ready to see the final product?" I ask, opening the album.

Lacy's eyes widen, and she leans in close as we begin to flip through the pages. "Oh my god," she breathes, her finger tracing one of the images. "You've made me look... perfect."

As we continue through the album, Lacy talks animatedly about each photo, pointing out details I hadn't even noticed.

"This one," she says, lingering on a particular shot, "it's like you saw right into my soul, Rayne. Like you really know me."

I laugh softly, ducking my head. "Well, that's part of my job – to capture the essence of my clients."

Lacy looks up at me, her eyes shining. "You certainly captured mine," she whispers.

I smile, feeling a mix of pride and unease at her intense gaze. Clearing my throat, I stand and move to the large, framed wall art I'd prepared.

"And for the pièce de résistance," I say, unveiling the piece with a flourish.

Lacy gasps, her hands flying to her mouth. Tears well up in her eyes as she stares at the enlarged image of herself, artfully posed and bathed in soft light.

"Oh, Rayne," she whispers, her voice choked with emotion.

I quickly grab a tissue from a nearby box, offering it to her. "Here you go," I say gently.

She takes it, dabbing at her eyes while fanning her face with her other hand. "I just... I look so sexy and beautiful," Lacy says, her words tumbling out. "Thank you, thank you so much."

I feel a warmth spread through my chest at her reaction.

Lacy suddenly straightens, composing herself. "Oh, I should get out of your hair," she stammers. "I'm sure you have a lot to do, and you don't need me gushing at you all evening."

I laugh. "Actually, I just have drinks with a friend tonight. Nothing too pressing."

Her smile falters for a moment, becoming strained. I wonder if I've said something wrong. Does she not socialize with friends?

Or worse, does she not have any? I mentally kick myself for not considering that before mentioning my plans.

"That's nice," Lacy says, her voice tight. She moves forward suddenly, enveloping me in a hug. As one of the only women I've met who is taller than me, it's a little strange to be surrounded by her. "Thank you again, Rayne. This means more to me than you know."

As she collects her things to leave, I can't shake the feeling of sadness that presses in at the thought she might not have anyone. Although I am glad she chose to do the photoshoot for herself. My professional mask slips for just a moment as I watch her go, trying to remember back to her photoshoot and if she spoke of having anyone in her life.

Shaking my head, I tidy up the sitting area, lock the studio door behind her and head upstairs. A client's excitement and happiness is what I live for – helping people feel empowered and beautiful. Lacy felt that in a profound way, and to me that was a good thing.

It's nearly time to meet Kahlee for drinks so I grab my purse, pausing to scratch Luna behind the ears. She purrs contentedly, seemingly back to her usual friendly self after her earlier dramatics.

"Be good while I'm gone," I tell her with a wink. "No wild parties."

Chapter 11

Knox

Leaning against the cool brick wall, I let the shadows swallow me whole. From this vantage point, I've become just another piece of the city's forgotten architecture. It's a skill born from necessity—being invisible—and it comes in handy in this part of town, where the industrial gives way to the residential in a patchwork of gentrification.

I watch as Rayne steps out of her studio, locks the door with an absent flick of her wrist, and starts down the block. She doesn't see me; she never does. My gaze follows her every move, intense and unwavering. The desire to be near her pulls at me like a relentless current. It's not my first time standing here, consumed by the sight of her, and it won't be the last. There's a compulsion in my veins that sings to the dark tune of obsession.

I saw her client leave in tears. Satisfaction twisted inside me. That raw emotional response meant Rayne had done her job well, as always. But those clients don't know her like I do; they haven't felt her warmth envelop them, the taste of her skin lingering like a promise. The memory alone sends a surge of hunger through me, but I push it down. Patience is a virtue, even for men like me.

Keeping to the shadows, I start to follow, maintaining enough distance to remain unseen but close enough to keep her within my line of sight. My raven-haired beauty moves with a grace that belies her oblivion, narrowly avoiding a street sign, then a discarded box. Her black dress plays against her contours, simple and unassuming, yet it's the red lipstick that captures my attention—it screams to be smudged, to be worn by more than just her lips.

A growl builds in my throat but remains caged behind clenched teeth. I've waited too long, plotted with a meticulousness that rivals my need for her, to ruin everything with impatience.

The streets fill with people as we approach a more populated area. It affords me the chance to close in a little—until she suddenly turns, pushing through the door of a bar. My hands flex involuntarily, ready for violence if she's meeting a man. If anyone else dares touch what's ours, I'd take pleasure in peeling their skin from muscle, in gouging out their eyes so they'd never again see what they can't have.

Inside the bar, the crowd swarms, and I watch—always watch—as someone's arms wrap around Rayne. Fire licks through my veins, a visceral blaze until I see it's a woman who holds her briefly before letting go. Relief crashes into me, swift and cold. Yet, it doesn't quell the drive to follow her inside, to continue watching her. The patrons provide enough cover for me to stay hidden, to observe without being observed.

Because I can't stop watching her. Because she is, undeniably, irrevocably, ours.

Chapter 12

Rayne

THE HUM OF THE bar surrounds me, a mix of laughter and clinking glasses, the occasional burst of music from the speakers drowning out conversations. It's not deafening, but it's enough to set my teeth on edge. Bars aren't really my thing—too many people, too much noise—but for Kahlee, I make exceptions. She always picks the least chaotic spot she can find, and tonight is no different. We're tucked away at a small table in the corner, far enough from the crowd that we don't have to raise our voices over the din.

I wrap my fingers around the stem of the glass she had waiting for me. White wine, exactly as I like it. Kahlee's unspoken rule: whoever gets there first orders the first round. "Two drinks max," she'd said once, after a long night years ago. A tradition we've stuck with ever since.

"God, Rayne," she says, her voice warm, familiar, tugging me out of my thoughts. "It's been way too long since we did this."

She leans back in her chair, a small smile tugging at her lips as she takes a sip of her drink. The deep red of her cocktail matches the flush on her freckled cheeks, her brownish-red hair catching the low light of the room.

"Far too long," I agree, swirling the wine in my glass before taking a slow sip. It's smooth, crisp, just sweet enough. "How are you? And how's Ivy?"

At the mention of her daughter, Kahlee's expression softens instantly, her green eyes lighting up with that unmistakable maternal love.

"She's so good," she says, her voice dipping into that fond, dreamy tone she always gets when she talks about Ivy. "She's learning this silly little dance routine right now. Keeps running around the house, making me her 'audience.'"

"She sounds like a handful," I say with a laugh, though warmth pools in my chest at the thought of Ivy's endless energy.

"She is," Kahlee admits, but there's no mistaking the pride in her smile. "But she's worth every second of it. That girl..." She trails off for a moment, staring down at her glass. When she looks back up, the edges of her smile have tightened, just slightly. "I'm just glad she doesn't have to deal with... Well, you know."

"Her father," I finish quietly for her, watching the way her shoulders stiffen slightly before she nods.

"Yeah." She sighs and sits forward again, brushing a hand through her hair. "Thank God he's locked up where he belongs. She deserves better than—" Her words catch for a moment before she shakes her head, forcing another smile. "Better than that mess. But I'm okay. We're okay. Better than okay, actually."

"Good," I tell her, meaning it. Watching Kahlee's confidence grow these past few years has been something else entirely. "You both deserve nothing less."

Kahlee swirls the stem of her glass between her fingers, her nails catching the dim bar light as she watches me with a raised brow. The faint hum of conversation and clinking glasses fills the space around us, but here in this corner, it feels almost private. She leans forward slightly, her elbow resting on the table.

"It's been three years," I say suddenly, the thought bubbling to the surface as I watch her. "Can you believe that?"

"Three years since…?" she prompts, though the smile tugging at her lips tells me she knows exactly what I'm talking about.

"Since you walked into my studio. Ivy was, what? Not even walking yet?" I chuckle softly, taking another sip of my wine.

"She was seven months old," Kahlee says, her voice softer now, reflective. Her gaze drops for a moment before she meets mine again. "I almost didn't go through with that shoot, you know."

"Why?" I ask, though I already know the answer. Still, hearing it from her feels different—like proof of how far she's come.

"Because I was… just so broken," she admits, her fingers tightening briefly around the base of her glass. "I didn't think there was anything left worth capturing. But then you…" She pauses, exhaling softly. "You saw me differently. You made me feel like I could be someone again."

"That's because you *are* someone," I say firmly, setting my glass down. "You always have been, Kahlee. You just needed a reminder."

"Well, you gave me more than that." Her lips spread into a warm smile, genuine and filled with gratitude. "You pushed me to pick up my camera again. Do you know how hard it was to even look at it back then? Let alone start shooting again?"

"Now look at you," I say, gesturing toward her with an exaggerated flourish. "The go-to family photographer in town. Everyone wants Kahlee Pearce to take their Christmas card photos."

"Stop it," she laughs, swatting at the air between us, but there's a pink tinge rising to her cheeks. "It's not like that."

"Yes, it is," I insist, grinning. "Don't argue with me. I've seen your calendar. Booked solid through next spring, aren't you?"

"Okay, fine," she concedes, laughing again. "But seriously, Rayne... Thank you. For everything. I don't know where I'd be if—" She cuts herself off, shaking her head as if to banish the thought. "Anyway, enough about me. What about you? How have you been? Anything exciting happen since we last caught up?"

Her question catches me mid-sip, and I nearly choke on my wine. I set the glass down carefully, avoiding her gaze as I try to compose myself. My mind races, images flashing unbidden—Knox's piercing eyes, River's wicked grin, the heat of their touch. My cheeks burn, and I press my lips together tightly.

"Wait a minute," Kahlee says, narrowing her eyes at me. She points a finger in my direction, a teasing smirk spreading across her face. "That hesitation. That's new. Something happened, didn't it?"

"Uh..." I start, but the words won't come. How the hell do I even begin to explain *last night*?

"Spill it," she demands, leaning forward eagerly. "Come on, Rayne. Don't leave me hanging. You know I live for drama. Did you meet someone? Go on a date? Hook up with some ridiculously hot stranger?"

"Not... exactly," I mumble, feeling the weight of her expectation pressing down on me.

"Not *exactly*?" she repeats, her grin widening. "Oh, this is going to be good. Tell me everything. And don't you dare hold back."

"Alright, fine," I say, setting my glass down and leaning in so Kahlee can hear me over the hum of the bar. A sly grin is already tugging at her lips, anticipation glinting in her eyes. "You're not going to believe this."

"Try me," she says, her voice dripping with curiosity as she rests her chin on her palm.

"Okay." I take a breath, trying to decide where to even begin. "So, last night, I had this... photoshoot. A couples' erotic shoot."

"Wait, wait—" Kahlee sits up straighter, her hand flying out to stop me. "I knew you did boudoir stuff, but *erotic*? Since when?"

"Since forever," I reply with a shrug, though I feel the faintest blush creeping up my neck. "It's rare, but yeah, I do those sometimes. Anyway, this couple comes in—two men."

"Two men?" Her brows lift, intrigued. "Hot?"

"Beyond hot," I say, and immediately my heart kicks up a notch just thinking about them. My fingers toy with the stem of my wineglass as I lean closer, dropping my voice. "One of them was this tall, brooding type. Gruff, commanding, the kind of guy who doesn't need to raise his voice because one look does all the talking for him. And the other—" I shake my head, a small, involuntary laugh slipping past my lips. "Mischievous as hell. Wicked smile, sharp tongue. You could tell he loved stirring up trouble. Both muscular and tattooed, and did I say hot?"

"Good God," Kahlee breathes, her eyes wide. "That's not fair. That's too much sexy for one relationship. Let me guess—they seduced you during the shoot?"

"Ummm, actually yes," I admit, biting my bottom lip before continuing. "Somehow, before the photoshoot had even gotten fully started, I ended up in the bed with both of them. And let me tell you"—I pause, meeting her gaze firmly—"it was the most erotic experience of my life."

"Shut up," she whispers, her jaw dropping slightly. Then, as if catching herself, she lets out a dramatic sigh and clasps her hands together like she's praying. "Rayne, you won the goddamn lottery. Two insanely hot guys, and you got both? Please tell me you're about to give me every single dirty detail because I need to live vicariously through you."

Her enthusiasm bubbles up, pulling a laugh from me. "Alright, alright," I say, holding up a hand. "Where do I even start?"

"Anywhere!" she insists, practically bouncing in her seat.

I'm about to dive into the memory, the heat of it still fresh enough to make my skin tingle, when something catches my eye. Movement, a flicker in my peripheral vision. My words falter, and I glance toward the far side of the bar.

For a moment, it's like the rest of the world goes out of focus. My breath hitches, and I swear my heart skips a beat. There, weaving between the tables, is a tall figure with cropped dark hair that's just long enough to curl at the top. His broad shoulders and muscular frame are impossible to mistake, even under the dim lighting. Hazel eyes, piercing and intense, seem to flash in my memory, and I feel the ghost of his touch on my skin.

"Rayne?" Kahlee's voice tugs at my attention, but I barely hear her.

I blink, forcing myself to focus, but the figure is gone. My gaze darts around the room, scanning for him. Knox. It had to be Knox. But how? Why would he even be here?

"Rayne?" Kahlee asks again, this time sharper. "What is it?"

"Nothing," I say quickly, shaking my head as though to clear it. But I can't help glancing toward the hallway leading to the restrooms. For just a fleeting second, I could have sworn I saw him heading that way.

"Hold on," I murmur, pushing back my chair. "I'll be right back."

"Hey, what—" Kahlee starts, but I don't wait to hear her finish. My pulse pounds in my ears as I weave through the crowd, following an invisible pull toward the hallway.

The hallway is dimly lit, the hum of the bar fading into a muffled buzz behind me. My heels click softly against the worn floor as I step further in, my eyes darting between the men's and women's restroom doors. The faint scent of cleaning solution lingers in the air, sharp and sterile compared to the beer-soaked haze of the main room.

I hesitate, my gaze shifting to the door at the end of the hallway, its edges scuffed from years of use. It probably leads to an alleyway, but instinct keeps me rooted where I stand. For a moment, I feel ridiculous. Maybe I imagined him. Maybe the wine and our conversation about *them* had stirred something in me—something that conjured his presence out of thin air.

With a sigh, I turn on my heel, ready to head back to Kahlee and laugh this off as some weird coincidence.

Then I hear it—a soft creak of a hinge, the distinct sound of a door opening behind me. My breath catches, and I swivel back toward the noise.

Knox steps out of the men's room.

Chapter 13

Rayne

TIME SEEMS TO SLOW as he moves, his tall, broad frame commanding every inch of space in the narrow hallway. His dark hair catches the faint light overhead, the subtle curl at the top just as I remember. Tattoos snake down his forearms, the ink looks like it's bleeding down his skin from the sleeves of his casual black shirt. And then there are his eyes—piercing hazel with gold and green flecks that lock onto me like a predator sighting its prey.

A slow, deliberate smile tugs at the corner of his mouth, and it's devastating. Dangerous.

"Knox," I whisper before I can stop myself, my voice barely audible over the thundering of my pulse.

"Rayne," he drawls, his voice low and gravelly, like smoke wrapped in velvet. He doesn't stop walking until he's right in front of me, close enough that I catch the clean, woodsy scent of him.

His gaze drags down the length of me, lingering on my dress. It's modest by most standards—simple and black, with a high neckline—but the way his eyes darken as they rake over me makes me feel utterly exposed. Heat rises to my cheeks, a traitorous flush that betrays my thoughts. *He knows.* He knows exactly what's under the fabric, and I hate how much that realization sends a shiver down my spine.

"What is it that guy says in the movie? Are you lost, baby girl?" he murmurs, his lips curling around the words like a promise.

My breath hitches, my lips parting as the memory of his voice calling me that—just hours ago, in the throes of pleasure—spirals through me. My knees feel weak, but I refuse to let him see just how much power he has over me.

My lips are dry, and I wet them quickly before responding—anything to break the magnetic pull between us.

"I didn't think that movies would be your thing," I manage, cocking an eyebrow in what I hope passes as casual confidence. "But I can see why that one holds a certain appeal."

His smirk deepens, a low chuckle rumbling from his chest like it's been dragged up from some dark, hidden place inside him. "There are several things that hold... a certain appeal to me." The weight of his words is deliberate, his tone dropping just enough to make my stomach tighten involuntarily.

I swallow hard, forcing myself not to react, but the heat creeping up the back of my neck betrays me. He doesn't need to say it outright for me to know he's talking about me. Still, something cold cuts through the warmth of his attention—a reminder. Knox has a boyfriend and as good as it felt to be between them, for all I know, I was just a passing moment of fun.

"Right," I mutter, trying to deflect, my voice tight against the spiraling tension. But before I can say more, there's a faint noise behind him—the unmistakable creak of a door hinge. But I don't look, my focus on Knox, too distracted by his presence to care.

"Did you get impatient, my love?" A velvety, teasing voice reaches me before I even register the movement. A hand, masculine yet graceful, snakes around Knox's waist, its grip easy, familiar—as if it belongs there.

My gaze drifts toward the voice, and I'm suddenly staring into those impossibly blue eyes. Caribbean blue, framed by a darker ring. River's grin spreads wide, wicked and full of mischief as he steps closer, his body brushing against Knox's side.

"Well, hello, gorgeous," he says, his voice honeyed with charm yet edged with something sharper. Dangerous. "Fancy seeing you here."

The air shifts between the three of us, charged and electric. They're both dressed casually tonight—tight jeans that cling to every inch of their powerful legs, shirts snug across their broad chests, tattoos on all the visible skin. It's almost unfair how effortlessly captivating they are, how they command attention without even trying. My fingers twitch at my sides, the urge to touch them again, to trace the ink on their skin, burning through me like a fire I can barely contain.

River moves with deliberate ease, his body a sinuous line of confidence and intent as he steps around his boyfriend. A flicker of something wicked dances in his eyes, and that grin of his—a weapon disguised as charm—broadens as he closes the space between us.

I don't move. I can't. My breath hitches as his fingers lift, brushing against my collarbone, their touch featherlight yet searing. The heat from his skin radiates into mine, and though the gesture is barely invasive, it's intimate enough to make my pulse stutter. His gaze doesn't just meet mine—it pierces me, rooting me where I stand.

"Rayne," he murmurs, my name rolling off his tongue like a secret only we share. He steps closer, his frame eclipsing mine, and I feel the weight of his presence settle over me. His hand slides upward, curling loosely around my throat. Not tight—not threatening—but enough to send a shiver down my spine. His face dips, his lips brushing the shell of my ear as his warm breath fans across my skin.

"Are you sore, can you still feel us?" he whispers, his voice rich and low, each word a deliberate caress. The air between us thickens, charged and suffocating all at once. "Because I can still feel your pussy wrapped around our cocks. I can still taste you on my tongue." His teeth scrape lightly against my earlobe, making my knees threaten to buckle. "I desperately want to play with you again, beautiful Rayne."

The ache that had been simmering low in my belly ignites, spreading like wildfire through my veins. My body betrays me—my thighs clench, my lips part, and a shaky breath escapes before I can catch it. But beneath the haze of desire, a sliver of restraint claws its way forward. Kahlee's waiting for me. She's out there, sipping her wine, expecting me to return any second now.

I steel myself, forcing my voice past the lump in my throat. "I can't," I manage, the words trembling but firm. "I'm here with a friend."

River pulls back slightly, his touch falling away, though the intensity in his gaze remains. His grin softens into something almost playful, yet no less dangerous, as if he finds my resolve amusing. With a languid step, he retreats to Knox's side, his movements unhurried, unapologetic.

Knox's arm snakes effortlessly around River's waist, pulling him close until their bodies align. The other hand rises, claiming River's throat in a way that mirrors what River had done to me moments ago. There's a possessiveness in the gesture, an intimacy that feels both raw and deliberate, like a silent display meant for my eyes alone.

"Well," River says, his voice light but tinged with disappointment, "that's a shame." His gaze lingers on me as if he's savoring the sight of my flushed cheeks and the way I struggle to maintain composure.

Knox leans in toward him, his lips grazing River's ear. Whatever he whispers is too quiet for me to hear, but the effect is immediate. River's lashes flutter closed, his mouth parting slightly as a look of sheer bliss crosses his face. It's mesmerizing, maddening. I want to know what Knox said, what has that look crossing River's face—and it makes my feet itch to move toward them despite every rational thought screaming at me to stay put.

I wrench my gaze away, breaking the spell they've cast over me. My legs feel heavy, unwilling, but I force them to carry me back down the hallway. Each step feels like a betrayal of the fire still burning in my core, but I cling to the memory of Kahlee's expectant smile, her laughter over glasses of wine.

By the time I reach the table, my hands tremble as I pick up my glass. I take a long sip, desperate for the cool liquid to drown the inferno raging inside me. Kahlee looks up with curiosity, but I manage a strained smile, tucking the encounter away for later—when I'm alone and far from their intoxicating presence.

Kahlee's green eyes narrow slightly as she tilts her head, studying me like she's trying to capture the perfect frame. "Are you sure you're okay? You look a little flushed." Her voice is soft but probing, a familiar warmth undercut by curiosity. She leans in closer, resting her chin on her hand, her freckled face lit by the dim amber glow of the bar.

I nod quickly, too quickly, and raise the glass again. The chilled rim presses against my lips, and I take another long, deliberate sip, letting the sweetness coat my tongue, hoping the act will buy me a moment to pull myself together. When I set the glass down, Kahlee's gaze hasn't wavered.

"Alright," she says, drawing out the word, her tone teasing now. "Then spill it. What happened with them? And don't even think about leaving out the juicy details." She smirks, leaning forward like she's settling in for a story she knows will be good.

But instead of the knee-jerk response I usually have—the automatic urge to share everything with her, no filter—I feel an unfamiliar weight pressing down on me. A strange, protective instinct coils in my chest, wrapping tightly around the memory of *them*. It's mine. The way they moved, the way they looked at me, the way they—no.

My fingers tighten around the stem of the wine glass until the delicate glass threatens to snap. The tension surprises me, and I force myself to loosen my grip, placing the glass back on the table with a trembling hand. My pulse thrums unevenly, and I try to ignore the telltale prickle at the base of my neck. They're here. Watching. I can feel their attention like a phantom caress sliding over my skin, intimate and invasive all at once. My breath catches, and I fight the maddening urge to turn around and search for them in the shadows of the crowded bar.

Kahlee's voice cuts through the haze. "Rayne?" She frowns, concern flickering in her green eyes. "What's going on with you?"

"I'm fine," I manage, though my voice sounds thin, strained. I straighten in my seat, forcing a smile that doesn't quite reach my eyes. "It was nothing, really. Just...a simple one night stand. I'm sure they were just ticking something off a bucket list."

Her eyebrows shoot up. "Simple?" she echoes, latching onto the word. "That's all you're giving me? Come on, Rayne, you've got to give me more than that!"

I shake my head lightly, my smile growing tighter. "Honestly, Kahlee, it's not that interesting." The lie tastes bitter, but there's no way I'm unraveling this tangled thread for her. Not tonight. Not with *them* so close, their phantom presence burning into me like a brand.

Desperate to steer the conversation away from dangerous territory, I reach for my phone on the table and tap the screen. "Anyway, how did *your* shoot go yesterday? You said you had some new clients?"

She hesitates for a moment, clearly unsatisfied, but something about the shift in my tone must convince her to drop it. With a shrug, she sighs and launches into a detailed account of her latest photoshoot—something about an engagement session at sunset near the lake.

I nod along, trying to focus on her words, but every nerve in my body remains taut, aware of the invisible strings tying me to the shadows where I know they're lurking.

Chapter 14
Knox

I'M QUIET AS I open the door to her apartment, slipping inside with practiced ease. The lock is laughably easy to pick, just as it had been every other time. The familiar scent of lavender and vanilla wraps around me like a second skin as I close the door softly behind me. Everything about this place is uniquely Rayne—warm yet meticulous, with little bursts of chaos that reflect her personality in ways I doubt she realizes. It's fascinating to me how someone can leave so much of themselves in their space without even trying.

My shoes make no sound against the hardwood as I move further into the apartment. I've done this enough times now that I know every creak and groan of the floorboards, every shadow cast by the dim light filtering through the curtains. And, like clockwork, her cat makes her appearance.

The small dark gray feline pads into view, her amber eyes narrowing as she spots me. She sits regally in the center of the living room, tail curling around her paws as though she's judging me for my tardiness. I smirk, pulling the package from my pocket.

"Demanding little thing," I murmur under my breath as I crouch down. I set the pouch of catnip on the ground along with a new toy—a feathery contraption I'd picked up earlier today. The cat tilts her head, giving me a look that speaks volumes. If looks could talk, I imagine hers to be saying, *"You're late again. But at least you brought a tribute."*

"Blame your human," I mutter, brushing my fingers lightly over the tips of her ears before straightening. The cat sniffs at the offerings, seemingly satisfied, before trotting off with the toy clutched in her mouth.

I take a moment to let the silence settle around me, listening for any sign of movement from the bedroom. Nothing yet. Perfect.

It's only been an hour since we'd followed her home from the bar, but the memory of watching her from the shadows still thrums through me. River and I had stayed tucked in the farthest corner, nursing drinks we never intended to finish. Her friend hadn't noticed us, too absorbed in whatever they'd been discussing, but Rayne? Oh, she'd felt us.

Even if she couldn't see us outright, I saw it in the tense line of her shoulders, the occasional glance over her shoulder as though expecting us to emerge from the dark again. She knew. Somewhere deep down, she knew.

"She's magnetic, isn't she?" River had murmured beside me, his voice low and edged with the same hunger I felt. "You can't help but watch her."

"Quite," I'd muttered, keeping my gaze locked on her. I couldn't look away. Every shift of her body, every flicker of emotion across her face—it was all consuming. She had no idea the power she wielded, or maybe she did, and that made it worse. Or better. I wasn't sure anymore.

We stayed until she left, her footsteps not completely steady after drinking, following her silently through the streets until she disappeared into the safety of her building. Only then had I turned to River, dragging him back to our own apartment to remind him just how patient I could really be when I wanted.

My pulse is steady as I move toward the bedroom, my footfalls nothing more than whispers against the floor. Control. Always control. Even when my blood burns and my mind screams to act, I wait. Because when the moment comes, it will be perfect.

And perfection is worth waiting for.

I don't need the dim light spilling through the window to know every detail of this place. I've committed it all to memory—the way the floor creaks faintly near the bedroom door, the uneven edge of the rug at the end of the hall, the slight dip in the mattress where she sleeps every night. It's all hers, all pieces of her life, and yet none of it feels enough. Not anymore.

As much as I want to deny it, River was right.

The thought grates against my mind. He had teased me, his words laced with that maddening mix of cheerfulness and malice only he could pull off, but there was truth buried there. The kind of truth I didn't want to acknowledge.

I am growing impatient.

Weeks ago, I would have stayed invisible—watching from the shadows, maintaining control even when the sight of her unraveled something deep inside me. But not now. Not after last night. I'd deliberately stepped into her line of sight, letting her see me. Letting her feel me.

I shouldn't have done it. I could have gone the entire night without her noticing me, slipping back into the dark like I always did. But something twisted and raw had clawed its way to the surface, demanding more. Demanding her.

The look on her face had been a mixture of surprise and something else—something curious, maybe even intrigued.

If River hadn't come into the hall when he did, I'm not sure what would've happened next. His timing was perfect, as always, dragging me back from the edge with that easy grin of his and a quip designed to diffuse the tension building between us. He's good at that, knowing how far to push before pulling back, but even then, the damage had already been done.

"I must be rubbing off on you" he'd said when we had moved to a table, his voice light but edged with something darker. "You're getting reckless. You know that, right?"

"Shut up," I'd muttered, though the words had no bite.

"Don't worry," he'd added with a grin, leaning close enough that I could feel the heat of him at my side. "I like it."

He wasn't wrong. I am being reckless. And probably worse. Because whatever patience I had left is wearing thin, unraveling with every breath I take in her presence.

I step inside her room, the air thick with her scent. I breathe in deeply, unable to stop the soft groan that escapes my lips. I'm thankful that I know she drank enough tonight to sleep deeply, unaware of my presence.

Because layered over her usual scent of lavender and vanilla is another aroma that's recently become a favorite of mine. My nostrils flare as I breathe it in. She must have touched herself after getting home, chasing the pleasure we'd denied her at the bar. The thought of her fingers sliding between her thighs, desperately seeking release, has my blood burning hot in my veins. A part of me is angry that she has stolen that release from me, that I wasn't there to watch her, to taste her as she succumbed to that pleasure.

The moonlight spilling through the gap in the curtains casts a silvery glow across her sleeping form. She's sprawled out on her back, one arm flung above her head, the other resting on her stomach.

The thin sheet has slipped down, revealing the swell of her breasts barely contained by a flimsy camisole. Her hair is a dark halo against the pillow, wild and untamed.

I move closer, silent as a shadow, drinking in every detail. The gentle rise and fall of her chest. The slight part of her full lips. The flutter of her eyelashes against her cheeks. She looks so peaceful, so vulnerable. It stirs a possessive hunger that threatens to consume everything in its path.

I lean in, close enough that I can feel the warmth radiating from her skin. My fingers itch to touch, to trace the curves and planes of her body that I've memorized over countless nights of watching.

A soft whimper escapes her lips and she shifts slightly, her legs parting unconsciously. The movement sends another wave of her scent washing over me and I have to bite back a growl. I imagine she's still wet, her arousal coating her inner thighs. I want to bury my face between them, lapping up every drop until she's writhing and begging beneath me.

Forcing my eyes away from her sleeping form, I scan the room, searching for any changes since my last visit. My gaze lands on a book resting on her nightstand–a new addition I haven't seen before. The cover is dark and sensual, clearly some kind of romance novel. Curiosity piques as I wonder if this is what fueled her self-pleasure earlier.

I pick up the book carefully, tilting it toward the faint moonlight filtering through the curtains. The spine is creased, suggesting she's already delved deep into its pages. A thin ribbon bookmark peeks out near the middle. Unable to resist, I gently open to the marked page, my eyes adjusting quickly to make out the words in the dim light.

As I begin to read, the heat in my blood ignites into an inferno. The scene describes a primal chase through moonlit woods, the heroine's heart pounding as she flees her pursuer. But there's an undercurrent of desire, a craving to be caught, to be claimed. The writing is visceral, dripping with tension and raw sexuality.

I can almost hear how Rayne's breath quickened as she read these words, can imagine her squirming with need. My cock hardens painfully as I continue reading, absorbing every sensual detail.

The chase culminates in a clearing, where the heroine is finally caught. What follows is a savage coupling, all teeth and claws and desperate need. It's animalistic, borderline violent, yet undeniably erotic. The hero takes her roughly from behind, one hand fisted in her hair as he drives into her relentlessly.

My breathing grows ragged as I picture Rayne writhing on this very bed, one hand between her thighs as the other clutches this book. Did she imagine herself as the heroine? Did she fantasize about being hunted, caught, ravaged so thoroughly?

The thought of her arousal building as she read, of her fingers working frantically to chase her release, has me achingly hard. I want to wake her, to recreate this scene and show her how much more intense reality can be compared to fiction. To hunt her through the shadows of her own home before claiming her against the wall, the floor, every surface until she's marked as mine, ours, inside and out.

With tremendous effort, I tear my eyes from the page and look back at Rayne, who is still passed out. Is she dreaming of us? Or the scene she read earlier? Of being pursued and possessed so completely?

Chapter 15
Knox

My control hangs by a thread as I set the book down and move closer to the bed, drawn to her like a moth to a flame. Carefully, reverently, I grasp the edge of the sheet pooled around her waist. With excruciating slowness, I begin to drag it down her body, exposing inch by delectable inch of her skin to my hungry gaze.

She doesn't stir, her breaths remaining deep and even as the sheet slides lower, revealing the gentle swell of her stomach before reaching the tempting shape of her hips. I hold my own breath, pulse thundering in my ears as I guide the fabric lower, anticipation coiling tighter within me.

When the sheet at last falls away completely, I can't bite back the rumble of approval that escapes my chest. Of course she would sleep in nothing more than a thin camisole and basic cotton panties–her body no doubt so hot that even that scant covering would have felt stifling against her flushed skin after her earlier ministrations.

My eyes rake over every inch of her, committing the sight to memory. The gentle curves capped by the peaks of her breasts, straining against the flimsy fabric. The juncture of her thighs, concealed yet hinting at the treasures hidden by the damp cotton clinging there. She's a living, breathing goddess lying before me, and the fact that she belongs to me, to us–that she simply doesn't know it yet–is almost too much to bear.

Moving with the silent grace of a predator, I reach out with one hand, allowing my fingers to brush over the scrap of material shielding her from my view. She doesn't even twitch at the featherlight caress, chest rising and falling in the steady rhythm of sleep. Emboldened, I hook my fingers into the waistband of her underwear, tugging it just enough to reveal a glimpse of those wet folds nestled in a thatch of dark curls.

A tremor races through me at the sight, my cock straining painfully against the confines of my jeans. But I refuse to rush, to miss a single moment of baring her to my hungry eyes. With a slow, steadying breath, I ease the cotton down over the lush swell of her hips, down the lengths of her thighs, until it joins the sheet in a crumpled heap at the foot of the bed.

"Such a good girl," I murmur, my voice a rumbling purr of approval as my hand returns to between her parted thighs. "You were thinking of us, weren't you?" One calloused finger traces along her slick heat, a featherlight caress that has her back arching infinitesimally off the bed.

I dip lower, circling her entrance with maddeningly light strokes, just barely dipping inside to gather her arousal on my fingertips. Her breath hitches, her thighs tensing as though seeking more friction, more pressure, but I deny her. Bringing my glistening digits to my lips, I taste her—that rich, tangy flavor I've already become addicted to.

A ragged groan tears from my chest as I savor her on my tongue. I need more.

Moving with exquisite care, I shift onto the bed, my weight causing the mattress to dip. Rayne doesn't stir, lost in the depths of her dreams as I position myself between her parted thighs. Up close, her scent is utterly intoxicating—a heady blend of arousal and feminine musk that has my mouth watering in anticipation.

Slowly, reverently, I trail my hands up the silken expanse of her thighs, pushing them wider to grant me unfettered access. Another soft sound escapes her lips as I expose her delicate folds, but she doesn't stir. I can't resist leaning closer, breathing her in as I commit every detail to memory. I allow the pads of my fingers to brush along her slick entrance, smearing the evidence of her desire. She shifts again, arching a little as her lips part on a breathy sigh that sends a tremor of need lancing through me. But still, she doesn't wake.

Inch by torturous inch, I sink two fingers into her velvet heat. She's scorching, her inner walls fluttering and clenching around the intrusion in her sleep. Carefully, I begin to thrust, savoring the lewd sounds of her arousal that fill the thick silence. Her hips roll subtly to meet each languid stroke, chasing the friction even in unconsciousness.

"That's it, baby girl," I rasp, the endearment falling from my lips in a rumbling purr. "Let me take care of you."

Using my thumb, I seek out the swollen bud of her clit, brushing it with the barest whisper of a touch. Instantly, Rayne's breath hitches, her back arching as her hips twitch, seeking more of the feeling I'm giving her. I keep the contact light and teasing, circling around the sensitive nub without ever applying direct pressure. She writhes beneath me, soft sighs and breathy mewls spilling from her parted lips as I steadily work her higher.

"Do you dream of me, Rayne?" I murmur, leaning so close that my lips ghost along her tender flesh with each word. "Of the things I could do to this perfect body?"

With each thrust of my fingers, I curl them slightly, searching... seeking...until I find that place inside her that makes her whimper, her thighs tensing around me. There. Her release will be exquisite.

I settle into a steady rhythm, fucking her with my fingers, my mouth so very close to tasting nirvana as it hovers over where my fingers are buried inside her. Her head shifts against the pillow as her release builds. She's exquisite like this—lost to the pleasure I'm giving her, unaware of how intently I'm watching. Drinking in every flutter of her lashes, every hitch of her breath, every subtle shift of her body as she chases her release. This moment is mine to savor. This pleasure is mine to give.

With one last deliberate curl of my fingers, I find that place inside her that shatters her control. Rayne's back bows as she crests. But no cries, no moans escape her parted lips. She shatters in utter silence, her inner walls pulsing and fluttering around my thrusting digits as wave after wave of release washes over her.

I can't tear my eyes away, enraptured by the play of rapture across her features, by the way her body writhes and shudders through the force of her orgasm. She's ethereal in this moment, transcendent. Lost to everything but the blinding ecstasy I've brought her.

Only when the last tremors fade and her body stills do I slowly withdraw my fingers, slick with her arousal. Gently, reverently, I spread her thighs wider, baring her to my hungry gaze. Rayne's body sinks deeper into the bed once more, her chest rising and falling with deep, even breaths. She's utterly unaware as I lower my mouth to her, my tongue lapping at her swollen folds in long, indulgent strokes.

She tastes of pure, carnal bliss. Musky and rich and so very her. I can't get enough, devouring every last trace of her release from her tender flesh. Her thighs tense briefly at the first swipe of my tongue, but she doesn't wake, just a soft whimper escaping her as I lave at her entrance with broad, unhurried strokes.

It's only when I'm certain I've licked her clean that I finally force myself to pull away, my own harsh breaths loud in the stillness of the room. I retrieve her panties from where they'd fallen, slipping them into my pocket to keep as a prize. A wicked smile pulls at my lips at the thought of her waking, blissfully unaware, confusion flooding her when she can't find them.

Rising from the bed, I drink in the sight of her once more. Rayne lies utterly spent, the sheet tangled around her feet, leaving her body shamelessly exposed. Satisfaction thrums through me at the sight.

Mine. Ours.

A low rumble of possession vibrates in my chest as I tear my eyes away and slip silently from the room. I will never get enough of her, of this. The hunger only grows, sharp claws sinking deeper into my being with each encounter. I want to drown in her, become utterly consumed until there is no line between us.

The realization should terrify me. But it doesn't.

If anything, the thought only fuels the ember of obsession smoldering in my veins into an inferno.

I move through the quiet apartment, steps light and unhurried. The gray cat watches me pass from her perch on the back of the couch, amber eyes unblinking. I swear she can see right through me, can sense the darkness lurking beneath my skin. But she doesn't appear to have any objections to me being near her human now.

Not like when I first visited.

"Keep her safe for me," I murmur under my breath as I retrieve the catnip pouch and let myself out.

Whether the small feline understands or not, I can't be sure. But one thing is certain–Rayne Bennett belongs to us now, even if she doesn't realize it yet. I will make sure of that.

The night air is cool against my heated skin, but it does little to douse the possessive fire burning in my veins.

Back at my own apartment, River is waiting in the shadows of the living room, his eyes glinting with wicked promise when I step inside. Before I can even speak, he's on me, claiming my mouth in a searing kiss as his fingers tangle in my hair. He tastes the lingering remnants of Rayne on my tongue and growls his approval against my lips.

"I can smell her all over you," he rasps when we finally break apart, both of us panting harshly. "Tell me you made her scream, Knox."

With a dark chuckle, I shake my head. "Not a sound. She slept right through it while I fucked her with my fingers and licked up every drop of her sweet release."

River's eyes blaze at my words, his tongue darting out to wet his lips.

"You're a cruel bastard, you know that?" He drags me back against him, his mouth hot and demanding on mine once more. "Denying me the privilege of watching her come apart."

"You'll get your chance," I promise against his lips, my hands sliding beneath his shirt to map the hard planes of his torso.

He shudders at the certainty in my tone, his hips rolling against mine in a tantalizing grind. "Soon?" he demands, desperation edging his voice.

Pulling back, I grin and tug Rayne's panties from my pocket, dangling them in front of his ravenous gaze. "Sooner than you think, my love."

With a feral sound, River snatches the scrap of cotton from my grasp and presses it to his face, inhaling deeply. His cock strains against the front of his pants as he breathes her in, and I can't resist palming the thick length, squeezing just enough to make him whine.

"I think maybe we have enough time before we have to get some work done for me to reward your patience," I growl, already guiding him toward the bedroom with the promise of taking him apart. His taste for depravity is insatiable, but then again, so is mine. And soon, so very soon, Rayne will understand just how deep that hunger goes.

She's already the most delicious addiction.

Chapter 16
Rayne

MORNING LIGHT FILTERS THROUGH the curtains, casting a warm glow over my bedroom. I blink slowly, emerging from a heavy, dreamless sleep. It's later than I normally wake, but I knew not to plan to run any errands the day after catching up with Kahlee. My body feels deliciously sated, a pleasant ache lingering in my muscles. Stretching, I relish the feeling for a few blissful moments before reality starts creeping back in.

I frown, realization slowly dawning as I take in my surroundings. The sheets are a tangled mess at the foot of the bed, and a quick glance confirms I'm completely naked from the waist down. Panic spikes through me as my mind races.

I don't remember undressing last night. Hell, I barely even remember coming home.

Standing abruptly from the bed, my heart starts pounding. What the hell happened? Flashes of the bar flicker through my mind—Kahlee's eager curiosity, the wine, the feeling of being watched, those intense hazel eyes finding me in the dim hallway...

Knox's piercing gaze sears through my memory, his presence utterly overwhelming. And River, his touch like a brand against my skin, his filthy words stirring heat low in my belly even now.

I shudder, as arousal wars with unease. I must have touched myself after coming home, getting caught up in imagining them. Or

I had an incredibly vivid dream? Or both, maybe. That has to be the only explanation for waking up almost naked and feeling so blissfully spent, right?

Except...something doesn't feel right. A sense of displacement hangs heavy in the air, leaving an ominous prickle racing over my skin. My gaze sweeps the room, searching for any sign of disturbance. Everything appears undisturbed...but that only makes the feeling of wrongness intensify.

Swallowing hard, I force myself to take a calming breath. I need to get a grip before I start spiraling into paranoia. It was just a sex dream, albeit an insanely hot one. Nothing more.

Shaking my head to dispel the lingering wisps of unease, I start straightening up the bed.

My discarded underwear must have been kicked off during...well, whatever happened last night. I glance around, frowning when I don't immediately see them.

With a sigh, I crouch down to check under the bed, sweeping my arm along the floor. Nothing but dust bunnies. Odd. I straighten and scan the room again, my brow furrowing. Surely they had to land somewhere.

A tiny flutter of worry tugs at me as I begin searching in earnest. I check the corners, pull back the curtains to let more light in, even shake out the pillows despite knowing they couldn't possibly have ended up there. But my underwear remains stubbornly absent, as if they've simply vanished into thin air.

Now I'm really starting to feel unsettled. I've lived alone for years, and not once have I just...misplaced an entire article of clothing like this before. Hell, even on my clumsiest mornings, I can always pinpoint where I've stripped off the day's garments. I distinctly remember wearing them to bed last night.

I press my lips together, trying to tamp down the rising sense of unease as I turn in a slow circle, scrutinizing every inch of the bedroom. Luna is suspiciously absent too, which is unusual for her. My fluffy gray shadow always comes slinking out from wherever she's curled up, meowing imperiously for attention and food the moment I stir each morning.

I grab my robe from where it's slung over the back of the chair, pulling it tightly around myself before heading for the living room, each step echoing hollowly in the oppressive silence. It's ridiculous how loud the thump of my racing pulse sounds in my ears. I half expect to turn a corner and—

Luna is sprawled on the back of the couch, her fluffy gray body rising and falling with each even breath. Her amber eyes open lazily at my approach, and she blinks at me with that trademark cat disdain she so expertly conveys.

I let out a shaky laugh, equal parts relief and embarrassment at my overreaction. "There you are," I murmur, reaching out to run my fingers along her spine. She arches into the touch with a rumbling purr, already forgetting my moment of panic.

"Good girl," I say as she rolls onto her back, all four paws splayed toward the ceiling. I take the invitation to rub her soft belly, the tension slowly ebbing from my shoulders.

With Luna's familiar rumbling purr and soft fur under my fingers, the lingering unease from the bedroom slowly dissipates. I take a deep, calming breath, feeling a bit silly for getting so worked up over a missing pair of underwear. Surely they'll turn up eventually, probably just kicked into some dark corner to be found later.

Giving Luna's belly one final rub, I straighten and head for the bathroom, dropping my robe as I go and pulling my camisole off. The hot spray of the shower works wonders in washing away the last lingering tendrils of tenseness due to my unease. I tilt my face into the pounding stream, letting the water sluice over my skin and soak into my hair. As steam fills the small space, my mind clears, focusing instead on the simple sensations—the heat loosening my muscles, the floral scent of my body wash, the rivulets trailing over my contours.

By the time I step out and begin toweling off, I've successfully shaken off the strange mood from earlier. A glance in the steamy mirror reveals my reflection looking much more like my usual self—dark hair tumbling in damp waves, cheeks flushed from the heat, blue eyes clear and calm once more. Whatever weirdness I felt upon waking up has dissipated, relegated to the back of my mind.

After dressing in a loose black sundress I make my way into the kitchen, unsurprised to find Luna already weaving between my feet and meowing insistently.

"Yes, yes, Your Majesty," I tell her with a fond eye roll. "I'm getting your food."

As soon as I scoop a portion of kibble into her bowl, she's purring and diving in like I haven't fed her in days. I watch her for a moment, smiling at her single-minded focus, before moving to retrieve the ingredients to make a breakfast smoothie from the fridge—Greek yogurt, fresh berries, spinach, and a banana.

After combining everything into a thick, creamy blend, my mind shifts to the tasks awaiting me today.

Sipping my smoothie, I lean back against the counter, my thoughts drifting to the boudoir shoot scheduled for later today. There's a familiar flutter of anticipation in my stomach—the kind that only comes before stepping behind the camera.

I picture the scene I'll be creating in the studio: sheer fabrics draped artfully, atmospheric lighting to bathe everything in a soft, inviting glow, music filling the air. It's my role to orchestrate an environment that allows my client to feel completely at ease, beautiful, and empowered. To create a space where they can let their most sensual self shine through.

A small smile tugs at my lips as I take another sip of the cool, fruity blend. This is what I live for—those moments of shamelessly celebrating the beauty of the human form through my art.

Once I finish today's photoshoot, I will save the images to my drives... Then there's...

My hand stills with the glass halfway toward my lips. The images from Knox and River's shoot. Just the thought has heat prickling along the back of my neck, a mixture of arousal and trepidation twisting low in my belly.

Do I really want to look through those photos, and the video, to relive that experience in vivid detail? Part of me craves it, yearns to see the evidence of what transpired in that studio captured in vivid color and clarity. But another part shies away, instinctively protecting the memory and the fiercer emotions it stirs within me.

Just the memory of their hands on me, their filthy words murmured against my skin, has arousal stirring low in my belly. I squeeze my thighs together, trying to regain my focus. Those photos are sure to be...intense, to say the least.

Part of me yearns to revisit that sensual haze, to pour over every detail captured forever in those frames. To study the expressions of rapture on my own face, immortalized by those photos and footage. It's tempting in a way that has little to do with vanity and everything to do with the deliciously wicked memories now tied to the images. I shiver, imagining my eyes raking over every bit of exposed skin, every bead of sweat, every explicit moment—all while reliving the taste of them, the scent, the exquisite way they utterly unraveled me.

But another part of me knows that indulging in that particular fantasy is...unwise. Even if the urge to pour over those photographs borders on obsessive. No, it would be far too easy to get lost in that spiral of need and longing. To have those images branded onto the backs of my eyelids in vivid, indelible detail.

I shake my head, as if to physically dislodge the heated thoughts. Prioritizing is key. I can't allow myself to get distracted, especially not today when there's real work to be done. Important work that allows me to create the kind of safe, sensual space I pride myself on.

Setting down my glass, I quickly rinse it out and place it in the drying rack before scurrying toward the studio door, Luna meowing indignantly at being abandoned so soon after her breakfast. I frown slightly for a moment at the toy mouse at her feet, one I don't recall buying. But knowing her, she probably had it hidden away for years in some sneaky hiding place. With a shrug, I turn away again. I'll have to remember to make it up to her later with some extra treats.

The door is silent as I push it open and lock it behind me before descending the stairs. The familiar sights and scents of the studio envelop me.

I move automatically through the space, adjusting lights, selecting lenses, positioning the backdrops just so. My fingers trail reverently over the delicate lace and satin of the lingerie outfits hanging on the rolling rack near the small dressing room, taking a moment to appreciate the exquisite details—the intricate embroidery, the sheer mesh panels, the tiny satin bows and ribbons.

This is my happy place, where I feel most centered and in control. Transforming this blank canvas of a space into an intimate boudoir setting is an art, one I've spent years perfecting. I have an eye for framing the human form in a way that transcends mere objectification. My goal is always to capture an essence, a glimpse into the soul behind the physical beauty.

A small, satisfied smile tugs at my lips as I take a step back, surveying my work. Everything is in place, ready to create an empowering experience for my client. As I give the studio one final sweep, my gaze drifts absently toward the entryway. That's when I notice it—a small, dark envelope just inside the door, its edges blending seamlessly with the shadowed hardwood. My brow furrows as I approach, wondering how I missed it before. No name adorns its surface, no postmark or stamp. Just a plain black envelope, unremarkable.

It's probably just junk mail, some glossy advertisement slipped under the door by an overzealous marketer. But as I bend to retrieve it, a chill races down my spine. The paper is thick, expensive—nothing like the flimsy stock used for run-of-the-mill flyers.

I turn it over in my hands, searching for any identifying marks. Finding none, I slide my nail under the flap, tearing it open with a soft rip that seems to echo in the stillness of the studio.

Inside is a single photograph. My breath catches in my throat as I pull it out, eyes widening in shock. It's me. Walking into the bar last night, my black dress swaying around my thighs, head turned slightly as if sensing someone's gaze. The image is crisp, professional—clearly taken with a high-end camera by someone who knows what they're doing.

But it's not the quality of the photo that has my heart hammering against my ribs. It's the single word scrawled across the bottom in bold, red ink:

MINE

For a moment, I'm frozen, my mind racing. Could River have taken this? The quality suggests a skilled photographer, and I remember the easy way he handled my camera during their session. But then, Knox's piercing gaze flashes through my memory—that predatory intensity that made me feel like prey caught in his sights. Either of them could have snapped this shot.

A small voice in the back of my mind whispers that maybe, just maybe, our encounter meant more to them than I assumed. The word scrawled across the image is full of possessive energy. Did they feel the same magnetic pull I did? Was our meeting in the bar hallway more than mere coincidence?

I shake my head, trying to dispel the swirling thoughts. I can't afford to get lost in speculation right now, not with a client due in only half an hour. Whatever this means, whatever is happening, I'll have to deal with it later.

I slide the photo back into the envelope, the thick paper feels heavy in my hands, weighted with unspoken implications. I hurry to my desk, tucking the envelope into the top drawer where it will be out of sight. But even as I close the drawer, I can feel its presence like a physical thing, impossible to ignore completely.

Taking a deep breath, I force myself to focus on the tasks at hand. I have a job to do, a client to empower and make feel beautiful. I can't let myself get distracted by... whatever this is.

Chapter 17

Rayne

As I'm adjusting one of the studio lights, I hear a familiar knock sequence at the studio door. A smile tugs at my lips as I call out, "Come in, Ainsley!"

The door swings open, revealing my friend and go-to hair and makeup artist. Her vibrant purple hair is twisted into an intricate updo, showcasing the shimmering silver hoops dangling from her ears. She's dressed in her usual all-black ensemble, which makes her colorful tattoos stand out even more against her pale skin.

"Rayne!" she exclaims, her green eyes sparkling as she sets down her massive makeup case, a tray of coffee cups balanced precariously on top. "I come bearing gifts," she continues with a grin, holding up the tray. "One caramel latte for you, and a cinnamon dolce double shot for me."

I laugh, crossing the room to relieve her of the coffees. "You're a lifesaver, Ains. How did you know I was in desperate need of caffeine?"

She quirks an eyebrow at me. "When are you not in need of caffeine, darling?"

"Fair point," I concede, taking a grateful sip of the latte. The rich, creamy flavor blooms across my tongue, and I let out a contented sigh.

"You will not believe the book I just finished. It was absolutely mind-blowing," she announces as she begins unpacking her supplies, arranging an impressive array of brushes, palettes, and products on a bench I have for that very purpose.

I can't help but grin, already feeling my earlier unease melting away in the face of Ainsley's infectious enthusiasm. "Oh yeah? Don't tell me—another dark romance that had you staying up until 3 a.m?"

"You know me too well," she laughs, retrieving her makeup chair that she stores in my office. "But seriously, this one was next level. The tension, the angst, the spice—I couldn't put it down."

As Ainsley continues setting up her station, we fall into our usual rhythm of excited chatter about our latest reads. It's a welcome distraction. I settle into the chair she just set up. There's still some time before our client arrives, and I can feel the tension from earlier slowly melting away in Ainsley's familiar presence.

"Okay, spill," I say, leaning back in the chair as Ainsley begins running her fingers through my hair, playing with it as she always does while we wait. "What was this mind-blowing book about?"

Her green eyes light up, a mischievous grin spreading across her face. "Picture this: a small-town librarian with a secret dark side. By day, she's all cardigans and sensible shoes. But by night? She's hunting down criminals that the justice system failed to punish."

"Ooh, vigilante justice. I love it already," I murmur, closing my eyes as she starts working some product through my locks.

"It gets better," Ainsley continues, her voice dropping to a conspiratorial whisper. "There's this brooding, mysterious newcomer in town. Tall, dark, and deliciously dangerous. Turns out, he's an undercover detective investigating a string of disappearances."

I crack open one eye, quirking an eyebrow. "Let me guess, the disappearances are actually our librarian's victims?"

"Bingo!" Ainsley laughs, starting to twirl sections of my hair and pin them up to create a twisted crown that I know will have my curls coming out when I let it all down again. "But here's the kicker—he figures it out pretty quickly. And instead of arresting her, he's... intrigued."

"Of course he is," I chuckle, shaking my head slightly.

"No, but listen," she insists, pausing to meet my gaze in the mirror. "It's not just about the thrill of the hunt or some twisted attraction. He genuinely sees the good in what she's doing, even if her methods are... extreme. And she challenges his black-and-white view of justice."

I hum thoughtfully, considering the premise. "Sounds like it could get pretty intense."

"Oh, it does," Ainsley nods emphatically. "The sexual tension is off the charts. But it's more than that. The way the author explores morality and justice, the blurred lines between right and wrong... it's surprisingly deep for a romance novel."

As she continues describing particularly gripping scenes, I find myself drawn into the story. The way she describes the characters' internal struggles, the push and pull between duty and desire, it makes my heart speed up in my chest.

"So, what happens in the end?" I ask, already invested. "Does the detective turn her in? Do they run off into the sunset together?"

Ainsley's grin turns wicked. "That would be spoiling the best part, wouldn't it? You'll just have to read it yourself to find out."

I roll my eyes good-naturedly. "Tease."

"You know it," she winks, just as she pins the last twist to my crown and a knock sounds at the studio door.

Our client is here.

As I move to answer the door, Ainsley gives my hair one final spritz of hairspray. The familiar scent mingles with the floral notes already perfuming the air, creating an intoxicating blend that speaks of femininity and sensuality.

I open the door to reveal Breanna, our client for today's boudoir shoot. She's a petite brunette with warm brown eyes that are currently wide with a mix of excitement and nerves.

"Hi Breanna, come on in," I greet her warmly, ushering her inside. "You look lovely."

She smiles shyly, tucking a strand of hair behind her ear. "Thank you. I'm a bit nervous, to be honest."

"That's completely normal," I assure her, guiding her towards where Ainsley is waiting. "But don't worry, we're going to take great care of you today."

Over the next hour and a half, I flit between final preparations and joining in on the lively chatter between Ainsley and Breanna. Ainsley works her magic, transforming Breanna's everyday look into something sultry and glamorous. I watch as Breanna's confidence grows with each brush stroke and curl set.

While they chat, I double-check all my equipment, ensuring every lens is clean and every battery fully charged. I adjust the lighting one last time, tweaking it until it casts the perfect soft glow across the boudoir set.

Ainsley regales us with tales of her latest dating adventures, her animated storytelling punctuated by the soft click of makeup brushes and the gentle hiss of hairspray. The conversation flows easily between the three of us, Ainsley's infectious enthusiasm drawing Breanna out of her shell bit by bit.

"So, Breanna," Ainsley chirps as she applies a shimmering eyeshadow, "tell us what inspired you to do this shoot. Anniversary gift? Just for fun?"

Breanna's cheeks flush slightly. "Actually, it's sort of a gift to myself. I recently got out of a long-term relationship that... well, let's just say it wasn't great for my self-esteem. This is my way of reclaiming my confidence, I guess."

"Good for you," I say genuinely, pausing in my work to meet her eyes in the mirror. "There's something incredibly empowering about celebrating your own beauty, just for yourself."

As Ainsley continues her work, transforming Breanna's already lovely features into something truly stunning, I find myself occasionally chiming in on their conversation. We discuss everything from favorite movies to dream vacation spots, the easy banter helping Breanna relax more and more.

I take the opportunity to go over some final details, explaining the process and reminding Breanna that she's in control at all times. "If there's anything you're uncomfortable with, just let me know," I assure her. "This is all about making you feel amazing."

Before we know it, Ainsley is finished and steps back, surveying her work with a critical eye before breaking into a wide grin. "Darling, you look absolutely stunning," she declares, spinning Breanna's chair to face the mirror.

Breanna's gasp of delight is audible. "Oh my god," she breathes, leaning in to examine her reflection. "Is that really me?"

I step closer, smiling at her reaction. "It absolutely is. You look beautiful, Breanna."

Ainsley beams at Breanna's reaction, her purple hair bouncing as she nods enthusiastically. "Told you I'd work my magic," she winks, already starting to pack up her extensive collection of brushes and palettes with practiced efficiency.

"Thank you so much," Breanna gushes, still admiring her reflection. "I can't believe that's me looking back."

I squeeze Breanna's shoulder gently. "That's all you, honey. Ainsley just helped bring out what was already there."

Ainsley finishes packing up her supplies in record time, slinging her massive makeup case over one shoulder with ease. She turns to me, green eyes sparkling. "Alright, darling, I'm off to my next gig. Try not to miss me too much!"

I laugh, pulling her in for a quick hug. "As if that's possible. Thanks for everything, Ains."

She releases me with a flourish, spinning towards the door in a whirl of color and energy. "Breanna, sweetie, you're going to absolutely slay this shoot. Own that gorgeous body of yours!"

With a final air kiss blown in our direction, Ainsley disappears out the door, leaving behind only the faintest trace of her floral perfume.

As the door clicks shut behind her, I turn back to Breanna with a warm smile. "How are you feeling?" I ask, genuinely interested in her state of mind. "I know all of this can be a bit overwhelming."

Breanna takes a deep breath, her shoulders relaxing slightly as she exhales. "I'm... nervous," she admits with a small laugh. "But excited too. I can't believe how amazing Ainsley made me look."

I nod understandingly. "It's perfectly normal to feel a mix of emotions. Remember, this whole experience is about celebrating you. There's no pressure to be anyone but yourself."

Moving towards the clothing rack, I gesture to the array of lingerie pieces hanging there. "Now, let's go over a few things before we get started. First, here's our selection of lingerie. Feel free to choose whatever you're most comfortable in. We have various sizes, styles, and colors to suit your preferences."

Breanna's eyes widen as she takes in the options, her fingers reaching out to stroke a delicate lace teddy. "These are gorgeous," she murmurs.

"Take your time selecting what you'd like to wear," I encourage her. "And remember, you can change outfits as many times as you'd like during the shoot."

I pause, my tone becoming a bit more serious. "Before we begin, I want to check if you have any injuries or sensitive areas I should be aware of. This helps me guide you into poses that are comfortable and flattering."

Breanna shakes her head. "No injuries or anything like that. I'm pretty flexible from yoga, actually."

"That's great," I nod approvingly. "Flexibility can definitely open up some fun pose options. Now, let's talk about the flow of the shoot. We'll start with some simpler poses to get you comfortable in front of the camera. As we go, we can gradually move into more sensual or daring poses if you're comfortable with that. At any point, if you feel uncomfortable or want to take a break, just let me know. This is all about you feeling empowered and beautiful."

Breanna nods, her eyes bright. "Okay, I think I'm ready."

Chapter 18
Rayne

I MOVE TOWARDS MY camera setup, picking up one of the bodies and attaching a lens. "I'll be shooting with this camera, but I also have a couple of others set up around the room to capture different angles. Don't worry about them—just focus on me and my main camera."

Breanna nods, her eyes following my movements with a mix of curiosity and nervousness.

"Alright then," I grin, gesturing towards the changing area. "Why don't you pick out your first outfit and we'll get started?"

As Breanna disappears behind the privacy screen with an armful of lacy garments, I walk over to the sound system and put on one of my standard playlists, Show Me by Alina Baraz starting to play through the room.

Breanna emerges from behind the screen a little hesitantly. She's chosen a deep burgundy lace bodysuit that hugs her body beautifully. Her cheeks are flushed, but there's a spark of excitement in her eyes.

"You look stunning," I tell her sincerely. "That color is perfect on you. How do you feel?"

Breanna takes a deep breath, smoothing her hands over the lace. "A little exposed," she admits with a nervous laugh. "But... good. Sexy, even."

"That's exactly how you should feel," I encourage. "Now, let's start with something simple. Why don't you come over to the couch here? I'm going to walk you through some poses but also once you feel more comfortable, if you want to move and try different angles between each of the images I take that's fine too. I'll point out any adjustments you need to make to your pose."

I guide her through a series of poses, starting with seated positions that allow her to feel more covered and secure. As we progress, I can see Breanna's confidence growing. Her movements become more fluid, her smiles more genuine.

"Beautiful, Breanna," I encourage as I capture a series of shots. "Now, let's try something a little more playful. Can you lie back on the chaise and stretch your arms above your head?"

She complies, arching her back slightly as she settles into the pose. I adjust my angle, framing the shot to accentuate the elegant line of her body.

"Perfect," I murmur, the camera clicking rapidly. "Now, bring one knee up slowly. That's it. Tilt your chin down just a touch. Gorgeous."

The music shifts to a sultry beat, and I notice her body subtly swaying to the rhythm. The shutter clicks rapidly as I move around her, seeking out the most flattering angles. Breanna's eyes meet mine through the lens, a mixture of vulnerability and empowerment shining in their depths.

"Rayne?" she asks softly, adjusting her position slightly. "Can I ask you something?"

I lower the camera, giving her my full attention. "Of course. What's on your mind?"

She hesitates for a moment, biting her lower lip. "What made you want to become a boudoir photographer? I mean, it's such a unique profession. I'm just curious about what drew you to it."

I pause, considering her question. It's not the first time I've been asked, and it certainly won't be the last. But something in Breanna's genuine curiosity makes me want to give her an honest answer.

I take a deep breath, my mind drifting back to memories I don't often revisit. "Well, I grew up in the foster system," I begin, my voice soft but steady. "And I was never what you'd call a small girl. I was always taller than the others there, curvier too. Kids can be cruel, and I was an easy target."

Breanna's eyes soften with sympathy, but I press on before she can interrupt. "For a long time, I hated my body. I felt awkward, out of place. But then, there was this boy, William, who came to the foster home for a brief time."

A small smile plays at my lips as I remember. "He was different from the others. He didn't tease me or make me feel like I was too much. Instead, he made me feel... beautiful. For the first time, I started to see my body as something other than a source of shame."

I pause, collecting my thoughts. "William didn't stay long, but the impact he had... it changed something in me. Before he left he told me he wished he could show me how he saw me, that I would never doubt my beauty if I could only see through his eyes. Because of him I started to realize that beauty comes in all shapes and sizes. That every body tells a story, and every story is worth celebrating. As I got older I realized I could give others that same feeling he gave me. Then I discovered photography. It became a way for me to capture beauty in all its forms. But it was more than just taking pretty pictures. I realized I had the power to show people a side of themselves they might never have seen before."

Breanna nods, her eyes wide with interest. "That's amazing, Rayne. It must be so rewarding to help people see their own beauty."

"It really is," I agree, a warmth spreading through my chest. "Every time I see that moment of realization in a client's eyes–that moment when they truly see how beautiful they are–it's like magic. It reminds me why I do this."

I lift my camera again, adjusting the angle slightly. "That's what today is all about, Breanna. Helping you see yourself the way others see you–as a strong, beautiful woman worthy of celebration."

Breanna's eyes shimmer with unshed tears, but she's smiling. "Thank you," she whispers. "I think I needed to hear that."

"You're welcome," I say softly. "Now, let's show the world just how gorgeous you are, shall we?"

With renewed enthusiasm, we dive back into the shoot. Breanna's movements become more confident. She experiments with different poses, her laughter ringing out as she tries something particularly daring.

"Alright, let's switch things up," I suggest, lowering my camera. "How about we try a different outfit? Something that makes you feel powerful and sexy."

Breanna disappears behind the screen again, and I take a moment to review the shots we've captured so far. Her growing confidence is evident in each frame, and I can't help but smile at the transformation.

When she emerges, my breath catches. She's chosen a strappy black number that leaves little to the imagination. Intricate lace panels hug her curves, while delicate straps crisscross her skin, creating tantalizing geometric patterns.

"Wow," I breathe, unable to hide my admiration. "You look incredible, Breanna. How do you feel in this one?"

She runs her hands over the fabric, a slow smile spreading across her face. "Powerful," she says, her voice low and sultry. "Like I could conquer the world."

"That's exactly the energy I want to capture," I grin, gesturing towards the bed set. "Let's move over there and try something a little more daring."

I guide her to the ottoman I've positioned at the foot of the ornate four-poster bed. The rich, burgundy velvet of the ottoman contrasts beautifully with the crisp white linens draped artfully over the bed.

"Okay, Breanna," I instruct, "I want you to lean back against the bed, letting your body form a gentle arch. That's it, perfect."

I climb up the ladder I've set up, giving me a bird's eye view of the scene. From this angle, the strappy lingerie creates an intricate web across Breanna's skin, the geometric patterns drawing the eye along the contours of her body.

"Beautiful," I murmur, snapping a few shots. "Now, I want you to look directly into the lens. Can you see your reflection in the glass?"

Breanna nods, her gaze locking onto the camera.

"Good. I want you to really look at yourself. See how beautiful you are, how powerful. Now, I want you to think about that person in the reflection being someone who desires you completely. Someone who's utterly captivated by you."

Her eyes darken, a flush creeping up her neck as she follows my instructions.

"That's it," I encourage, the camera clicking rapidly. "Now, imagine that person is completely obsessed with you. They can't get enough. Every little thing you do drives them wild. Show me how that makes you feel."

Breanna's expression transforms, becoming sultry and confident. Her lips part slightly, her eyes hooded with desire. She arches her back a little more, tilting her chin to elongate her neck. Every movement is deliberate, sensual.

"Perfect," I breathe, capturing shot after shot. "Now, run your hands slowly up your sides. That's it. Tilt your head back, expose that beautiful neck."

The music swells, a pulsing beat that seems to sync with Breanna's movements. She's lost in the moment now, fully embodying the seductress I knew was hiding beneath her initial shyness. Her hands trail sensually along her body as she moves through various poses, each one more daring than the last.

"Incredible, Breanna," I praise, descending the ladder to capture some close-up shots. "You're a natural at this."

She beams at me, her earlier nervousness completely gone. "This feels amazing," she admits, her voice husky. "I've never felt so... desirable."

"That's because you are desirable," I tell her sincerely. "You're absolutely stunning, inside and out. This shoot is just helping you see what's always been there."

We continue for another hour, cycling through various outfits and poses. With each new look, Breanna's confidence grows. By the end, she's suggesting her own poses, moving with a fluid grace that's captivating to watch.

As we wrap up the shoot, Breanna's eyes are full of happiness. "I can't believe how much fun that was," she gushes, wrapping herself in a silky robe. "Thank you so much, Rayne. This whole experience has been incredible."

I smile warmly at her as I begin packing up my equipment. "I'm so glad you enjoyed it. You did amazingly well, Breanna. I can't wait for you to see the final results."

After Breanna leaves, promising to book another session soon, I find myself alone in the studio once more. The silence feels heavy after the energy of the shoot, broken only by the soft whir of my computer as I begin uploading the images to my drives.

Curiosity gets the better of me and I open a few of the images as they transfer, I can't help but feel a surge of pride. Breanna's transformation is evident in every frame—from hesitant and shy to confident and sensual. This is why I love what I do. Helping people see their own beauty, their own power, is incredibly rewarding.

As the images continue transferring, I lean back in my chair, stretching my arms above my head. The soft glow of the computer screen illuminates the dimming studio, casting long shadows across the floor. Outside, the sky has turned a deep indigo, streaked with ribbons of pink and orange as the sun dips below the horizon.

My cursor hovers over the folder labeled "Knox & River," its innocuous text belying the intensity of what lies within. My heart rate picks up, a mix of anticipation and trepidation coursing through me. Those images... they're more than just photos. They're a vivid reminder of the most intense, passionate encounter I've ever experienced.

I can almost feel their hands on me again, hear their voices whispering filthy promises in my ear. The memory alone is enough to send a shiver down my spine, heat pooling low in my belly. My finger twitches on the mouse, so close to clicking, to diving back into that intoxicating world we created together.

But I hesitate.

Opening that folder feels dangerous somehow, like stepping off a cliff into unknown waters. Once I look, I know I won't be able to stop. I'll get lost in the images, reliving every touch, every kiss, every moan. And then what? I'll need to remind myself they're not mine to keep, not really. It was just one night, one incredible, mind-blowing night.

The rational part of my brain knows I should leave it alone, preserve the memory without obsessing over the details. But another part of me, a darker, needier part, wants to devour every pixel, commit each frame to memory until I can see them perfectly with my eyes closed.

My finger hovers, trembling slightly as I wage an internal battle. Just as I'm about to give in to temptation, a notification pops up on my screen. The file transfer is complete. I blink, snapping out of my trance-like state.

Glancing at the time display in the corner of the monitor, I'm shocked to realize it's already early evening. The grocery store will be closing soon, and my fridge is woefully bare. With a resigned sigh, I move the cursor away from the tempting folder and begin the shutdown process.

As the computer powers down, I can't help but cast one last longing look at the screen. Those images will have to wait for tomorrow. But even as I gather my things and head for the door, I know they'll be haunting my dreams tonight.

Chapter 19
Rayne

The soft glow of streetlights illuminates the sidewalk as I make my way home, plastic grocery bags swinging gently from my hands. The night air is cool against my skin, a welcome relief after the stuffy warmth of the crowded store. I'd managed to grab the essentials–milk, eggs, bread, and a few frozen dinners for those nights when cooking feels like too much effort.

My footsteps echo softly in the quiet evening, most of the shops already closed for the night. A few cars pass by, their headlights briefly illuminating the storefronts before fading away. The scent of jasmine drifts on the breeze from someone's garden, sweet and intoxicating.

I'm only a few blocks from my apartment now, my thoughts already drifting to a hot shower and comfortable pajamas. The day's work has left me pleasantly tired, muscles aching in that satisfying way that comes from doing something you love. Images from Breanna's shoot flicker through my mind and small smile tugs at my lips.

Lost in my musings, I barely register the dark alleyway I'm passing until hands suddenly grab me, yanking me roughly off the sidewalk. My heart leaps into my throat as I'm dragged deeper into the shadows, my mind struggling to catch up with what's happening. A man's voice, low and threatening, growls in my ear.

"Don't scream or I'll shoot you."

Fear floods my system, icy tendrils wrapping around my chest and making it hard to breathe. My body goes rigid, muscles locking up as panic takes hold. For several long moments, I can't even process what's happening. My fingers remain stubbornly curled around the handles of my grocery bags, as if clinging to that last shred of normalcy.

It takes what feels like an eternity, but is likely only seconds, for my brain to catch up. The plastic handles finally slip from my grasp, bags hitting the ground with a soft thud. Eggs crack, milk spills, but none of that matters now. All I can focus on is the iron grip on my arms and the paralyzing terror coursing through my veins.

My heart hammers as he shoves me roughly against the brick wall, waving a gun unsteadily toward my face. The cold metal of the barrel glints in the dim light filtering into the alley. His eyes are wild, pupils dilated, darting around erratically.

"Give me all your money." he snarls, his words slurring together. The stench of alcohol on his breath makes my stomach churn.

My breath catches as the gun tilts closer to my face before swaying slightly away. His hand trembles, the weapon weaving an unsteady path through the air. He doesn't seem steady, or sane. The manic gleam in his bloodshot eyes sends chills down my spine. This isn't just a desperate man looking for quick cash–there's something unhinged in his demeanor.

Time seems to slow to a crawl as I watch his finger tighten on the trigger. In the moments it takes my brain to catch up, I brace for the deafening bang of the gunshot.

But it never comes.

Instead, I watch in slow motion as a knife is suddenly thrust into the side of my attackers neck. The hand holding it twists the blade, using it to pull the attacker backward away from me. The metallic scent of copper fills my nostrils as I gasp in shock and blood starts pouring from the wound in the man's neck.

I stop breathing, paralyzed as I watch the crimson gush rapidly down his body. The man's eyes go wide with surprise and pain. When the hand pulls the knife back out, the gun clatters to the ground as my attackers hands fly to his neck, trying in vain to stem the tide of red.

He is still too close to me and I feel a few warm flecks of blood hit me.

A gurgling sound escapes his lips as he is jerked back further by the person behind him. The attacker is then pushed toward the opposite wall of the alleyway where he almost hits the dumpster there, before his legs give out and he crumples to the ground in a heap beside it. Twitching, gasping, drowning in his own blood.

I can't move. Can't breathe. Can't process what I'm seeing. My mind reels, unable to make sense of how quickly everything changed. One moment I was staring down the barrel of a gun, the next...

I'm staring at a completely different man, holding a blood stained knife up to the light. The black gloves on his hands almost blend seamlessly with the perfectly tailored black shirt and pants.

River.

But how is he here? How did he know I needed saving? How is it those black gloves on this man look so fucking hot?

"Were you... following me?" The question is barely a breath as I try to steady myself, my heart still racing in my chest.

He grins, that dark, dangerous grin as he steps over the body at our feet. His blue eyes glint with something wicked, and he brings the tip of the bloody knife to my throat, resting it there as if it's the most natural thing in the world. "Aww, so you really didn't notice?" His voice is taunting, mocking. "I was being *very* mindful... very demure."

A shocked, breathless laugh slips out before I can stop it, and he raises a brow, his grin widening as his gaze flickers over me, devouring every reaction. His empty hand presses just below where the knife sits, his fingers a firm, possessive weight on my skin, stealing the breath from my lungs.

River's eyes gleam with a dark satisfaction as he watches me, his hand pressed firmly against my chest, feeling the rapid, unsteady beat of my heart beneath his palm. "You feel that?" he murmurs, his voice low and rough. "That rush? The way the blood's pumping inside you? That's you feeling alive."

A shiver courses down my spine, and his hand trails slowly down my body, fingers grazing the curve of my breast before his palm cups and squeezes, coaxing a moan unbidden from deep within me. He chuckles darkly, noting my reaction. "Not crying... Not screaming," he observes, his eyes narrowing as he looks down at me.

"Should I be?" I manage to ask, my voice soft but steady, and he laughs softly, a sound that's both a little shocked and admiring.

"That would be the 'normal' response to what just happened," he murmurs, fingers curling into the material of my dress, tugging it higher, inch by inch. The air against my skin feels electric, each bit of fabric that rises sending a wave of heat curling low in my body. The edge of the knife still presses against my skin, and I can't help but wonder if the blood from my would-be attacker has smeared onto my throat. I shudder at the thought, a thrill running through me.

River's fingers reach my underwear, pushing them aside, sliding his fingers along my folds. His touch is rough and deliberate, the feel of the leather glove on his hand harsh against my skin and I can't suppress the groan that escapes me, mingling with his own as his fingers move. His leg nudges mine apart, keeping my dress raised, leaving me bare to him. He pulls his fingers back and brings them to his mouth, eyes locked onto mine as he licks them clean, his gaze smoldering. The sight of it makes my blood feel like it's on fire, heat pooling low and sharp in my body. I vaguely wonder if I taste good mixed with the leather of his glove.

"All that... just for me?" His voice is almost mocking, and his eyes glitter with dark satisfaction. "Watching me kill that man... did that turn you on?"

I can't respond. My throat is too dry, my words lost, all I can do is moan for him. I watch him, pulse pounding in anticipation. His carribean eyes look deep into mine, and whatever he sees there...

"Fuck it," he growls, his movements growing more frantic, his gaze primal. He drops the knife with a metallic clink before spinning me around. He presses me against the wall, his gloved hands rough as he positions me exactly where he wants, dragging my hips back until I almost stumble over the legs of the dead man on the ground. I brace my hands against the brick wall, the rough surface scratching against my skin. His fingers dig into my hips as he pulls my dress up again, higher this time, until the fabric pools around my waist. A low, growl fills the air as he kicks my feet apart.

I hear the clink of a belt and then the sound of his zipper, the anticipation making my body ache. The blunt head of his cock presses at my entrance, stretching me as he pushes in. His hand moves up to wrap around my throat, and the moan that escapes me this time is as raw as it is shameless.

River's thrusts are rough, his pace unforgiving, and it only makes my pulse race harder, my body pushing back against him despite the madness of it all. His hand tightens around my throat, not enough to cut off my air, just enough to feel the steady thrum of my pulse under his fingers.

He leans close, his mouth at my ear, his voice a low, dark growl. "I would kill anyone who threatens you," he murmurs, every word dripping with a terrifying sincerity. "If you want to watch next time... if you want to help... all you have to do is ask." His voice trails off into a sinister chuckle as his grip on me tightens, his other hand sliding up, pushing my dress further up my body. "Hell, I'd fuck you in their still-warm blood if you wanted."

The words should chill me, but instead, they burn, stoking a dark, hidden part of my soul that craves that reckless, almost sick level of possession. It's as if his brutal promises speak to something twisted and raw deep inside me, something I can't ignore, even if I want to. I gasp, and he must sense it, his fingers curling harder around my throat.

I'm barely able to breathe, but somehow I manage, "And... what about Knox?" The name slips from my lips, almost a whisper, as I wonder if the other man shares this same intensity, this same violent hunger.

River chuckles, his fingers pressing down harder. "Don't let that alpha act fool you," he murmurs. "Knox would slit the throat of anyone who so much as breathes too close to you." He thrusts harder, his hips slamming against mine, his voice a dangerous promise in my ear. "You're ours now. Do you understand?"

Another groan tears from my throat, as my mind stumbles over his words, over the implications. "I'm no one... and you only just met me," I manage, a desperate attempt to cling to reason, but he scoffs, his grip on me unwavering.

"Do you really think the photoshoot was the first time we saw you?" His laughter is almost mocking. "You have no idea how much we know about you, how long we've watched you... from a distance, waiting for the right moment."

River's words send shockwaves through me, but before I can even process their meaning, his thrusts become more frantic, more animalistic. His grip on my throat tightens, cutting off my air supply completely. Stars dance at the edges of my vision as he pounds into me relentlessly, the wet slap of skin on skin echoing obscenely in the alley.

His free hand snakes around to my front, gloved fingers finding my clit with unerring accuracy. He rubs furious circles against the sensitive bundle of nerves, the dual stimulation overwhelming my senses. My lungs burn for air, my body trembling on the precipice of something earth-shattering.

River's breath is hot against my ear, his words a feral growl. "Come for me, Rayne. Show me how much you love this. How much you need it."

The world narrows to a pinpoint of sensation–the rough brick scraping my palms, the fullness of him inside me, the pressure of his fingers on my throat and clit. My body obeys his command, convulsing violently as waves of pleasure crash over me. My vision goes white, mouth open in a silent scream as an intense orgasm rips through me.

Just as the edges of my consciousness start to blur, River releases his grip on my throat. Air rushes into my lungs in a desperate gasp, the sudden influx of oxygen intensifying every sensation tenfold. My inner walls clench and flutter around him as aftershocks roll through me.

River doesn't slow his pace, fucking me through my orgasm with savage ferocity. His fingers dig bruisingly into my hips as he chases his own release. I feel boneless, utterly at his mercy as he uses my body for his pleasure.

With a guttural groan, he slams into me one final time, burying himself to the hilt. I feel the hot rush of his release, filling me completely. He collapses against my back, his weight pinning me to the wall as we both struggle to catch our breath.

For several long moments, the only sounds are our ragged breathing and the distant hum of cars and people. The reality of our surroundings slowly filters back in—the coppery scent of blood, the cooling body at our feet, the eerie quiet of the deserted alley.

River pulls out slowly, and I have to bite back a whimper at the loss as I hear the sound of his zipper. He spins me around to face him, his eyes blazing with a possessive fire as he takes in my disheveled state. Without warning, he crashes his lips to mine in a bruising kiss that leaves me breathless all over again.

When he finally pulls back, that wicked grin is back in place. "We can't leave this mess for just anyone to find," he muses, his tone casual as if discussing the weather rather than a corpse. "I'll get Knox to come deal with the body. He's got a knack for making problems... disappear."

He pulls out his phone, fingers flying over the keys as he sends a rapid-fire text. The soft glow illuminates his face, casting eerie shadows that accentuate the sharp planes of his cheekbones and the predatory glint in his eyes.

"There," he says, slipping the phone back into his pocket. He leans down and picks up the discarded knife, casually pulling a cloth from his pocket to wipe it down before he lifts the back of his shirt. His hands are empty again when they reappear, moving to do up the belt that still hangs open at his waist.

He must have some sort of knife holster there.

"Knox will handle this. Now, let's get you presentable, shall we? Then I'll take you home."

With surprising gentleness, River smooths my dress back down, his fingers lingering on the fabric as if memorizing every curve beneath. He tucks a stray strand of hair behind my ear, his touch feather-light against my skin. The tenderness of the gesture is a stark contrast to the violence of moments before, leaving me dizzy with the whiplash of emotions.

"There," he murmurs, stepping back to admire his handiwork. "Almost as good as new. Though I do like you a bit... rumpled."

His wicked grin returns full force as he bends to retrieve my scattered groceries. The plastic bags rustle as he gathers them up. It's such a jarringly normal action amidst the surreal horror of the alley that I almost want to laugh. Miraculously there are still some unbroken eggs and half the milk remaining in the carton, but the broken shells crunch sadly and the bag and handle are slick with the spilled milk.

River straightens, grocery bags dangling from one hand as he reaches for me with the other. His arm snakes around my waist, pulling me firmly against his side. Not for the first time, I'm reminded of how much bigger he is; I feel small tucked in against him. The heat of his body seeps into mine, grounding me even as my mind still reels from everything that's transpired.

"Come on, gorgeous," he says, guiding me toward the mouth of the alley. "Let's get you home."

As we step back onto the sidewalk, the warm glow of streetlights feels almost painfully normal. A few cars roll past, their occupants oblivious to the violence we're leaving behind. River's arm remains a steady presence around me, his stride confident and unhurried.

I steal glances at him as we walk, marveling at how utterly calm he seems. There's no trace of the feral energy from moments ago, just an easy smile and relaxed posture. If not for the faint smears of blood still visible on both of our skin, one might think we were just an ordinary couple out for an evening stroll.

The weight of the grocery bags swinging gently in his free hand, the warmth of his body pressed against mine, the quiet hum of the city around us—it all feels surreal. Like a dream I can't quite wake up from. Or maybe I don't want to wake up from it.

Chapter 20
River

I GUIDE RAYNE ALONG the quiet streets, my arm secure around her waist. Her steps are uneven, whether from the lingering effects of adrenaline or the intensity of our encounter, I'm not sure. Probably both. I adjust my stride to match hers, keeping us moving at a casual pace that shouldn't draw attention.

The night air is cool against my skin, carrying the scents of the city—exhaust fumes, the greasy aroma of late-night takeout, a hint of rain on the horizon. Rayne's warmth seeps into my side, her body soft and pliant against mine. I can smell the faint traces of her floral shampoo mingling with sweat and sex and the coppery tang of blood. It's intoxicating.

We pass under pools of amber streetlights, emerging into shadows only to be illuminated again moments later. The rhythm of it is almost hypnotic. A few people pass us on the sidewalk, but their gazes slide right over us. Just another couple out and about. Nothing to see here.

I keep my senses alert for any sign of trouble, but the streets remain quiet. Good. Knox will handle the mess we left behind, and I'll make sure Rayne gets home safely. Then I can savor every delicious moment of what just transpired.

As we near her building, I feel Rayne tense slightly beside me. I give her waist a gentle squeeze, a silent reassurance. "Almost there,"

I murmur, my lips brushing the shell of her ear. She shivers, pressing closer to my side.

We enter through the door that leads directly to her photography studio. The space is dark and quiet, filled with the ghostly shapes of equipment and props. I navigate us through with ease, intimately familiar with the layout from the countless times I've been in here without her knowing.

At the door to her apartment, Rayne fumbles in her purse for her keys. Her hands are shaking slightly—the comedown from the adrenaline high finally hitting her, I suspect. After a moment of watching her struggle, I gently take the purse from her.

"Allow me," I say, reaching inside and retrieving her keys in one smooth motion. She blinks up at me, surprise evident in her wide blue eyes. I flash her a reassuring smile as I unlock the door and usher her inside.

The apartment is bathed in the soft glow of a lamp left on in the living room. As soon as we cross the threshold, a streak of gray fur comes bounding toward us. Rayne's cat—Luna, if I remember correctly—meows insistently, winding around our legs.

I crouch down, extending my hand toward the feline. "Hey there, pretty girl," I coo, my voice pitched low and soothing. Luna sniffs my fingers cautiously before butting her head against my palm, a deep purr rumbling from her chest.

"That's... odd," Rayne mumbles, her brow furrowing slightly as she watches Luna nuzzle against my hand. "She usually hates strangers."

I just grin, a secret dancing behind my eyes as I give Luna one final scratch behind the ears before standing. Of course the cat knows me –I've been in this apartment more times than I can count, though Rayne has no idea. Luna and I have come to an understanding over the months.

"Guess I just have a way with pussy," I quip with a wink, delighting in the way Rayne's lips twitch at my crude joke.

I scoop up the grocery bags and head for the kitchen, my steps sure and confident as I navigate her space. The layout is etched into my memory. I set the bags on the counter, making a mental note to replace the broken eggs and spilled milk tomorrow. Can't have our girl going hungry, after all.

When I turn back, Rayne is still in the entryway, her gaze unfocused as she absently strokes Luna's fur. My protective instincts surge, a primal need to care for her overriding everything else.

I cross the room in a few long strides, gently taking her elbow to guide her through the apartment. "Come on, sweetheart," I murmur, my voice low and soothing. "Let's get you cleaned up."

She doesn't resist as I lead her down the hallway to the bathroom, her steps slow and slightly unsteady. The cat follows at our heels, meowing softly as if concerned for her human. I flip on the light, wincing slightly at the harsh fluorescent glare before reaching for the shower knob. Water begins to pour from the showerhead, steam quickly filling the small space.

Turning back to Rayne, I find her staring blankly at her reflection in the mirror. There are smears of dried blood on her neck and cheek, stark against her pale skin. Her hair is a wild tangle, and her dress is rumpled and stained. She looks utterly wrecked, and a surge of possessive pride rushes through me at the sight.

"Arms up," I instruct gently, reaching for the hem of her dress. She complies without a word, allowing me to peel the garment off and toss it aside. Her bra and panties follow, leaving her gloriously naked before me. My eyes roam over her contour hungrily, drinking in every inch of exposed skin.

Rayne's eyes widen as I begin to strip off my own clothes, her gaze fixed on my hands as I unbutton my shirt. "What are you doing?" she asks, her voice barely above a whisper.

I grin, pulling off my gloves and placing them on her counter before shrugging off the shirt to reveal the toned planes of my chest and abdomen. "Can't very well help you get clean if I'm still dressed, can I?"

A pretty blush spreads across her cheeks as I undo my belt and step out of my pants and boxer briefs. Her eyes roam over my body, lingering on the ridges of muscle and the tattoos adorning my skin. I let her look her fill, reveling in the way her pupils dilate and her breath quickens. When her gaze finally meets mine again, I see a mix of desire and uncertainty swirling in those sapphire depths.

"River, I..." she starts, but I silence her with a gentle finger against her lips.

"Shh," I murmur, cupping her face in my hands. "No overthinking. Just let me take care of you."

Before she can protest, I guide her into the shower. The hot water cascades over us, washing away the blood and grime. Rayne lets out a soft sigh as the warmth seeps into her muscles, some of the tension visibly leaving her body and her eyes fluttering closed. I take a moment to simply admire her—water cascading over her curves, droplets clinging to her lashes, her lips parted slightly. She's breathtaking.

With reverent hands, I begin to wash her, starting with her shoulders. I work the soap into a rich lather, my fingers kneading gently at the tense muscles beneath her skin. I take my time, savoring every inch of her. My hands glide over the soft swell of her breasts, down the plane of her stomach, along the flare of her hips. I'm thorough in my ministrations, cleaning away the remnants of our encounter in the alley.

When I reach her hair, I gently tug at the pins holding her intricate updo in place. One by one, I remove them, letting her dark tresses tumble free. The wet strands cling to her skin, framing her face in inky tendrils. I work shampoo through her hair, my fingers massaging her scalp in slow, soothing circles.

Rayne remains silent throughout, her eyes closed and her breathing steady. But I can feel the way she leans into my touch, seeking more contact. It sends a thrill through me to see her so pliant, so trusting. Even after the violence she witnessed, she allows me this intimacy.

Once I've rinsed the last of the soap from her skin and hair, I turn off the water. The sudden silence feels heavy, broken only by the soft plink of water droplets hitting the tile. I step out first, grabbing a fluffy towel from the rack.

With the same care I used to wash her, I now dry Rayne off. I start with her hair, gently squeezing out the excess moisture before moving to her body. The soft terrycloth glides over her skin, leaving goosebumps in its wake. When I'm satisfied that she's thoroughly dry, I wrap the towel around her like a cocoon.

I dry myself off quickly with a second towel, more focused on Rayne than my own state. Her eyes are open now, watching me with a mixture of wariness and curiosity as I pull my briefs and pants back on. The shocked glaze from earlier has faded, replaced by a sharper awareness that makes my pulse quicken.

Guiding her to sit on the closed toilet lid, I retrieve her hairdryer from under the sink, plugging it in and flicking it on. The warm air ruffles her damp tresses as I run my fingers through them, separating the strands to ensure even drying.

As her hair begins to dry, soft waves forming around her face, I can see Rayne visibly relaxing. Her eyes drift closed again, head tilting slightly into my touch as I work. It's a strangely intimate moment, this quiet domesticity. One I look forward to repeating.

When her hair is finally dry, falling in silky waves around her shoulders, I set aside the dryer and pick up her brush. With long, smooth strokes, I begin to work out any remaining tangles. Rayne lets out another soft sigh of contentment, her body swaying slightly with each pass of the brush.

I set the brush aside and retrieve a hairband from her bathroom cabinet where I know she keeps them. Rayne's eyes have opened again, watching me intently as I move about her space with easy familiarity. I grin at her as I return, my fingers already beginning to separate her silky strands into sections.

"You're still not crying or screaming about what happened," I murmur, my voice low and intimate in the quiet bathroom. "You don't seem bothered at all really."

My fingers work deftly, weaving her dark locks into an intricate braid. The repetitive motion is soothing, almost meditative. I can feel the warmth of her scalp beneath my fingertips, the silky texture of her hair sliding between my fingers. The scent of her shampoo fills my nostrils as I breathe in deeply. I can't get enough of her scent.

Rayne's eyes meet mine in the mirror, a complex swirl of emotions dancing in their depths. There's curiosity there, and a hint of wariness, but also something darker. A spark of recognition, perhaps, of the beast that lurks beneath both our skins.

Though I doubt it. I'm not sure she understands or acknowledges that part of herself yet.

"Should I be?" she repeats softly, her voice barely above a whisper. "Bothered, I mean."

I chuckle, tugging gently at the braid to tighten it. "Most people would be," I point out. "I did just kill a man in front of you. Rather messily, I might add."

A small shiver runs through her, but it's not fear I see in her eyes. No, there's a heat there, a hunger that mirrors my own. My grin widens, becoming almost feral as I watch her reaction.

"But you're not most people, are you, Rayne?" I continue, my voice dropping to a husky murmur. "You didn't cry out for help. Didn't try to run. Instead, you let me bend you over and fuck you senseless while the blood was still warm on the ground."

Her breath hitches, a pretty flush spreading across her cheeks and down her neck. I can see the rapid rise and fall of her chest beneath the towel, her pulse fluttering visibly at the base of her throat. She's aroused, turned on by the memory and my words.

"I..." she starts, then falters, seemingly at a loss for words.

I finish the braid, securing it with the hairband before letting my hands come to rest on her shoulders. Our eyes lock in the mirror, my gaze holding her captive as I lean down to press a kiss to her temple.

"You don't have to explain yourself to me, little Rayne," I murmur, my thumbs tracing gentle circles on her skin. "I see you. The real you, not the mask you wear for the rest of the world."

I gently pull Rayne up and tug the towel away from her body, hanging it over the towel rack. My eyes roam over her exposed skin hungrily, drinking in every detail. The urge to touch her, to claim her again, is almost overwhelming. But I restrain myself, knowing she needs rest.

Taking her hand, I lead her out of the bathroom and down the short hallway to her bedroom. I turn on the bedside lamp and it casts a warm, intimate light across the space. I've spent countless hours in this room both with Knox and by myself, watching her sleep, memorizing every detail of her existence. But she doesn't know that. She has no clue how deeply our obsession with her runs.

The little grey cat is waiting on her bed for her, watching her human as she watches me.

I pull back the sheet, gesturing for Rayne to slide in. She hesitates for just a moment before complying, her movements slow and languid as she settles onto the mattress. Her eyes widen slightly as I pull the sheet back up, covering her naked form. She keeps watching me intently as I stretch out beside her on top of the sheet, propping myself up on one elbow.

"What are you doing?" she asks, her voice soft and slightly uncertain.

I smile, reaching out to brush a stray lock of hair from her face. "Staying until you fall asleep," I murmur.

Gently, I pull her against me, tucking her head under my chin. My fingers trail up and down her spine through the thin barrier of the sheet, tracing patterns only I can see. I can feel the heat of her skin, the softness of her body, even through the fabric. It takes every ounce of self-control not to rip away that flimsy barrier and lose myself in her again.

The cat stretches out on the other side of the bed, amber eyes tracking my movements as though guarding Rayne. Perhaps she still doesn't trust me completely with her human. I haven't succumbed to using bribery like Knox.

Rayne's body gradually relaxes against mine, her breathing evening out as exhaustion begins to take hold. I continue my gentle caresses, soothing her towards slumber. Rayne's breathing slows and deepens, her body completely relaxing against mine as she drifts into sleep. I remain perfectly still, savoring the weight of her in my arms, the soft puffs of her breath against my chest.

As I continue holding her, my mind wanders to all the nights Knox and I have spent watching her from the shadows. The countless hours we've devoted to learning every detail of her life, her habits, her desires. It's an obsession that's consumed us both.

We followed her, learned her routines, her favorite places. We watched her work, marveling at the passion and artistry she poured into every photograph. We saw the way she interacted with her clients, always professional yet warm, making them feel at ease even in their most vulnerable moments.

We memorized the cadence of her voice, the rhythm of her steps, the scent of her perfume. She's consumed our every waking thought. We've planned meticulously, biding our time until the perfect moment to make our move. And now that we have her, now that she's in our grasp, the obsession has only intensified.

Our obsession runs bone-deep, an all-consuming need. We'll create a fortress around her, eliminating any threat before it can even touch her. She'll be safe, cherished, worshipped.

But more than that, we'll nurture the darkness I've seen lurking beneath the surface.

Because she is ours.

And we are hers.

Chapter 21
Rayne

THE SHRILL BEEPING OF my alarm jolts me awake, tearing me from a dream filled with flashes of blood and heated skin. I groan, fumbling blindly for my phone to silence the incessant noise. As the quiet descends once more, I flop back against the pillows with a sigh.

Memories of last night flood back in vivid detail–the attempted mugging, the violence of River's intervention, the raw, primal encounter that followed. My body aches in the most delicious way, a pleasant soreness radiating from between my thighs and along my inner muscles.

I stretch languidly, savoring the dull throb that accompanies the movement. I can't remember the last time I felt so thoroughly used in the best possible way. Certainly not in the last few years, when intimacy has been more of an occasional indulgence than a regular occurrence.

As I swing my legs over the side of the bed, I notice my hair is still braided. River's handiwork. There's something both thrilling and unsettling about the mix of tenderness and violence he embodies and like a sentimental fool I leave my hair in the braid.

I pad to the bathroom, not bothering with the robe and ignoring Luna's cry for attention. The harsh fluorescent light makes me wince as I flip the switch, illuminating my reflection in the mirror. My eyes are drawn to the marks littering my body and neck that I've managed to collect in only a few days. My fingers trace the marks almost reverently, remembering the intensity of both encounters.

Stepping into the shower, I let the hot water cascade over me. It soothes my muscles but does little to wash away the memories or the lingering arousal they stir. I find myself wondering how long this delicious soreness will last, how long I'll get to enjoy this feeling, how many more encounters I'll have with River and Knox before they lose interest.

I quickly finish my shower, reluctant to linger too long under the warm spray. As I step out, wrapping a fluffy towel around myself, the humidity in the bathroom is already oppressive. Summer has arrived with a vengeance, promising another sweltering day.

Padding back to the bedroom, droplets of water trailing behind me, I survey my closet options. The thought of anything clinging to my skin in this heat makes me cringe. I settle on a lightweight sundress in a dark blue that brings out my eyes. The fabric is whisper-thin, floating around my body as I slip it on. The neckline dips low enough to be enticing without being scandalous, and the hem swishes around my knees.

Damp strands of my hair curl around my face as I make my way to the kitchen. Luna appears as if summoned, weaving between my ankles and meowing plaintively. Her cries grow more insistent with each step, a furry little drama queen demanding her breakfast.

"Yes, yes, I hear you," I mutter, careful not to trip over her as we enter the kitchen. "You act like I never feed you, you silly—"

The words die on my lips as I notice something out of place. There, on the counter where I'm certain nothing sat last night, is a pristine white bakery box. Beside it stands a travel coffee cup, tendrils of steam still curling from the small opening in the lid. The familiar logo of my favorite bakery is emblazoned on both items.

A bakery that is on the other side of town.

Frowning, I approach cautiously. Luna, momentarily forgotten, hops up onto a nearby stool to observe. I lift the lid of the box, and the heavenly scent of cinnamon and apples wafts out. Inside sits a single, perfectly frosted cupcake—my absolute favorite apple pie cupcake from the bakery.

Beside the cupcake and coffee, I notice a small folded note, I pick it up and unfold it. The handwriting is unfamiliar, a bold scrawl that seems to dance across the paper:

"Have a wonderful day, little Rayne. Since I couldn't also feed the pussy I wanted to this morning, I fed the other one. Don't let her tell you differently. I miss you already. - R"

I raise an eyebrow at Luna, who gives a half-hearted meow as though realizing her game is up. Her amber eyes blink slowly at me, betraying nothing of her morning visitor. He must have left after putting me to bed and returned this morning.

Lifting the cup to my lips, I take a cautious sip. The familiar flavor of caramel latte explodes across my tongue, and I can't suppress the moan of pleasure that escapes me. It's perfect—the exact blend I always order, with just the right amount of sweetness and a hint of salt to balance it out.

The fact that he knows my favorite cupcake, my preferred coffee order, and apparently how to get in and out of my apartment without waking me should be terrifying. And yet... I can't deny the warmth that blooms in my chest at the thoughtfulness of the gesture.

As much as the cupcake beckons me, I know I need to get my errands done first. Picking up the bakery box, I move to the fridge to store it out of the heat. As I open the refrigerator door, my breath catches in my throat.

The milk carton that had been half-spilled in the alley has been replaced with a pristine new one, condensation beading on its surface. Next to it sits a clean, unmarred carton of eggs–no sign of the cracked shells and sticky mess from last night. But it's not just these items that have my heart racing.

My eyes roam over the shelves, taking in the array of items that definitely weren't there last night. A pint of my favorite yogurt from the artisanal shop across town nestled in the corner. Beside it, a container of fresh strawberries. I spot a wedge of imported brie cheese that I only indulge in on special occasions, along with a small jar of fruit preserve—the perfect accompaniment.

In the produce drawer, I see a bunch of perfectly ripe bananas—not too green, not too spotty, just the way I like them. There's also a bag of organic baby spinach and a carton of blueberries, key ingredients for my morning smoothies.

In the door, a bottle of prosecco catches my eye. It's the same brand I'd mentioned offhandedly to Kahlee the other night, lamenting that I could never find it in stock at my local wine shop.

There's even a small container of chocolate-covered espresso beans, a guilty pleasure I usually hide in the back of my pantry for late-night editing sessions.

Each item is something I enjoy, little luxuries I don't often allow myself. Some are everyday staples, others rare indulgences, but all are unmistakably tailored to my tastes. The level of attention to detail is staggering. River—or perhaps Knox, or both of them together—must have spent considerable time and effort putting this together.

I place the cupcake box carefully in the fridge, letting out a small sigh as I close the door. As tempting as it is to indulge in the thoughtful treats River left, I know I need to stay focused. Sexy, dangerous men with a penchant for stalking and violence are not conducive to maintaining a proper work schedule.

Luna's insistent meow draws my attention back to her. I narrow my eyes at her, torn between amusement and exasperation. "Really? You're going to play this game after I just saw evidence that you've already been fed?"

She blinks up at me innocently, tail swishing back and forth. I can't help but chuckle at her audacity.

"Nice try, you little con artist," I tease, crouching down to scratch behind her ears. "But I'm onto you now. River may have charmed his way into feeding you, but don't think that means you get double breakfast every day."

Luna purrs, rubbing against my hand as if to say she has no idea what I'm talking about. With a resigned sigh, I stand and retrieve her food bowl. "Fine, you win this round. But only because I don't know exactly how much he gave you."

I pour a small amount of kibble into her bowl, about half her usual portion. Luna dives in eagerly, her earlier dramatic meowing forgotten in the face of more food. I watch her for a moment, torn between amusement and exasperation.

"Greedy little thing," I mutter fondly, giving her one last pat. "You're lucky you're so cute, you manipulative little furball."

I grab the coffee, savoring another sip of the perfectly crafted latte as I head out the door. The rich caramel notes dance on my tongue, a decadent start to the day. Locking up behind me, I make my way quickly down the stairs, the hem of my sundress swishing around my legs.

Without hesitation, I head straight for the basement stairs.

By the time I'm returning back up them, a good two hours have passed and sweat is trickling down my spine and plastering wisps of hair to my temples. I let out a relieved sigh as the blessed air conditioning envelops me.

As I move further into the studio, something catches my eye near the entry door.

There, on the floor, just inside the door... is another black envelope.

I freeze, my heart pounding as I stare at the innocuous black envelope on the floor. I bend to pick it up, feeling the thick, smooth paper. I take a deep breath, steeling myself before sliding my nail under the flap to open it.

Inside is another photograph, just as I feared. My breath catches as I pull it out, eyes widening as I take in the shadowy image. The details are hard to make out in the dimness, but I don't need clarity to recognize what I'm seeing. My own hands pressed against the rough brick of the alley wall. Behind me, River's powerful form is unmistakable as he takes me from behind, his body curved over mine, his face turned away from the camera.

And I know behind the dumpster on the opposite side of the alleyway, blocked from view is a dead body.

A shiver runs through me, equal parts arousal and unease. The photo captures a moment of raw, primal passion—my head thrown back in ecstasy, River's fingers digging into my hips. It's undeniably erotic, and yet...the fact that someone was there, watching us, photographing such an intimate moment without our knowledge, sends a chill down my spine.

Was it Knox? The thought flashes through my mind, remembering how River had texted him to clean up the scene. But as I turn the photo over, that theory is quickly dispelled.

Scrawled across the back in bold red ink are the words: "Touch him again and I'll kill him."

My blood runs cold as I stare at the threatening message. This wasn't Knox. This wasn't River. This was someone else entirely—someone who had been watching us, who had captured that intensely private moment on film.

Someone who felt they had a claim on me.

Chapter 22
Rayne

M\y hands shake as I carefully place the photograph back in the envelope. I take several deep breaths, trying to calm my racing heart. This is no longer a game or a twisted courtship. This is a serious threat from an unknown stalker.

I move to my desk, sinking into the familiar comfort of my chair. The leather creaks softly as I lean back, closing my eyes for a moment to gather my thoughts. When I open them again, I reach for my phone. The screen illuminates, displaying the time—8:43 a.m. I take another deep breath before dialing 911. The call connects almost immediately, a calm female voice answering:

"911, what's your emergency?"

I swallow hard, forcing my voice to remain steady. "I need to report a stalker. I've received threatening photographs."

The dispatcher's tone shifts, becoming more focused. "Are you in a safe location now, ma'am?"

"Yes," I confirm, glancing around my studio. "I'm at my place of work, below my apartment. It's secure."

"Alright, I'm going to dispatch officers to your location. Can you give me the address?"

I provide my studio's address, along with my name and phone number. The dispatcher assures me that help is on the way, advising me to stay put and not touch anything else that might be evidence.

After ending the call, I lean back in my chair once more, exhaling slowly. The wait begins. We are stuck somewhere between a small town and something that would mean the police wouldn't care, which means I won't be a priority.

The wait for the police feels interminable. To calm my frayed nerves, I busy myself with mundane tasks around the studio. I meticulously clean my camera lenses, wiping each one with gentle circular motions until they gleam. The familiar motions are soothing, allowing my mind to settle into a meditative state.

I move on to organizing my lingerie rack, arranging delicate lace veils and ornate jewelry on their hangers with careful precision. I lose myself in the details.

Time seems to stretch and warp as I work. The soft whir of the air conditioning becomes a comforting white noise, punctuated only by the occasional rustle of fabric or clink of metal as I sort through my collection. The scent of lavender from the sachet I keep hung on the rack wafts gently through the air, further calming my nerves.

As I work, my mind wanders to the stark difference between this threatening message and the oddly sweet gestures from River. It was one thing to think Knox or River was leaving reminders of their claim on me. Their intensity was thrilling in its own way, a dark seduction that spoke to something primal within me. But this... this is something else entirely.

A chill runs down my spine as I recall the menacing words scrawled across the back of the photo. This unknown person had witnessed one of the most intimate, raw moments of my life—and rather than being aroused or intrigued, they had responded with pure malice. The threat to River and no doubt Knox's life hangs heavy in the air, a stark reminder that this situation has escalated far beyond my control.

I find myself longing for River's steady presence, or even Knox's commanding aura. Their brand of danger feels almost comforting in comparison to this unknown threat. At least with them, I had some idea of where I stood. This new player is a complete wild card.

The sudden blare of a car horn outside startles me from my reverie. I glance at the clock, shocked to realize that nearly two hours have passed since I made the call. Just as I'm beginning to wonder if I should call again, I hear a sharp knock at my door.

My heart races as I approach the door, each step echoing loudly in the quiet studio. I take a deep breath, steeling myself before turning the handle. The door swings open, revealing two uniformed officers standing on my doorstep. Beyond them, I can see their squad car parked at the curb, its presence both reassuring and unsettling.

"Ms. Bennett?" the taller of the two officers asks, his voice gruff and businesslike. At my nod, he continues, "I'm Officer Daniels, and this is Officer Martinez. We're here in response to your call about threatening photographs."

I step back, gesturing for them to enter. "Yes, thank you for coming. Please, come in."

The officers move into the studio, their eyes sweeping over the space with practiced efficiency. I can see the moment they register the boudoir setup, the racks of lingerie, the artfully draped fabrics. Officer Martinez's eyebrows raise slightly, a look of poorly concealed judgment flashing across his face.

"Can you show us the photographs in question, Ms. Bennett?" Officer Daniels asks, pulling out a small notepad.

I nod, moving to retrieve the envelopes from my desk. As I hand them over, I can feel my cheeks heating with embarrassment. The intimate nature of the second photograph suddenly feels much more exposing under the scrutiny of these strangers.

Officer Daniels examines the photos carefully, his expression neutral. Officer Martinez, however, makes no effort to hide his disdain as he peers over his partner's shoulder.

"So, you're some kind of porn star?" Martinez asks, his tone dripping with judgment as he gestures to the boudoir set. "That why you've got all this... setup here?"

I bristle at his implication, anger flaring hot in my chest. "I'm a professional photographer," I say, my voice tight with suppressed fury. "I specialize in boudoir photography. It's a legitimate and respected art form."

Martinez snorts derisively, clearly unconvinced. "Right. 'Art.' And I suppose these 'artistic' photos of you getting railed in an alley are just part of your portfolio? Are you sure it's even a stalker? You know falsely reporting a crime is a federal offense, right?"

Before I can respond, a deep, authoritative voice cuts through the tension like a knife.

"That's enough, Officer Martinez."

My head whips around so fast I nearly give myself whiplash. There, striding into my studio with an air of absolute authority, are Knox and River. They're both dressed in suits... and they have badges gleaming on their belts. My eyes widen in shock, my mind reeling as I try to process their sudden appearance.

Knox's expression is thunderous as he fixes Martinez with a steely glare. "Your personal opinions have no place in this investigation. If you can't maintain a professional demeanor, you can wait in the car."

Martinez pales visibly, shrinking back under Knox's withering gaze. "Y-yes, sir. Sorry."

River steps forward, his eyes flashing with barely contained anger. "Victim-blaming isn't part of standard police procedure, Martinez," he says, his voice low and dangerous. "Ms. Bennett's profession has no bearing on this case. She's reporting a serious threat, and it's our job to investigate thoroughly and professionally."

The tension in the room is palpable, the air thick with unspoken hostility. Officer Daniels, clearly sensing the volatile situation, clears his throat and attempts to diffuse the tension.

"Now, now, let's all calm down," he says, his tone placating. "I'm sure there's no need for you gentlemen to trouble yourselves with a simple matter like this. We can handle it."

Knox's eyes narrow, his jaw clenching visibly as he turns his attention to Daniels. "A simple matter?" he repeats, his voice dripping with sarcasm. "I was coming from a scene and saw your squad car, so I decided to stop in and see if you needed any assistance. Imagine my surprise when I realized you were responding to a stalking case."

He takes a step closer to Daniels, his presence looming and intimidating despite the other officer's similar height. "Need I remind you, Officer Daniels, that there's a serial killer on the loose at the moment? One who's been targeting both men and women in this very area, with no identifiable type?"

The color drains from Daniels' face as the implications of Knox's words sink in. Martinez shifts uncomfortably, his earlier bravado completely evaporated in the face of the two detectives' ferocity.

River moves to stand beside Knox, his posture relaxed but his eyes sharp and alert. "Every threat should be taken seriously," he adds, his voice deceptively calm. "Especially given the current climate of fear in this town. Ms. Bennett's report deserves our full attention and resources."

I watch this exchange with a mixture of awe and confusion. The way Knox and River command the room is impressive, their authority unquestionable. But seeing them in this light—as detectives, as figures of law enforcement—is jarring. It's a stark contrast to the dangerous, primal men I've come to know in such an intimate way.

Knox turns to me, his eyes softening almost imperceptibly as they meet mine. "Ms. Bennett," he says, his voice professional but with an undercurrent of warmth that sends a shiver down my spine. "If you're comfortable with it, I'd like to take over this investigation personally. Detective Maddox and I have extensive experience with stalking cases and can ensure this threat is given the attention it deserves."

I nod, still somewhat dazed by the sudden turn of events. "Yes, of course," I manage to say, my voice steadier than I feel. "I'd appreciate that... Detective."

Daniels hesitates, clearly torn between following proper procedure and defying the intimidating presence of the two detectives. After a moment I take the envelopes containing the photographs from him and turn to Knox with them.

As Knox takes the evidence, his fingers brush against mine for the briefest moment. Despite the gravity of the situation, I feel a jolt of electricity at the contact. His eyes meet mine, a silent promise passing between us.

"Thank you for your initial response, officers," River says, his tone making it clear that they're being dismissed. "We'll take it from here. Ms. Bennett's safety is now our top priority."

Officers Daniels and Martinez exchange a look, clearly torn between relief at being off the hook and embarrassment at being dressed down by their superiors.

"Yes, sir," Daniels mumbles, not quite meeting either detective's eyes. "We'll, uh, we'll be on our way then."

Then the two uniformed officers shuffle towards the door, tails firmly between their legs.

When the door closes behind Daniels and Martinez, the atmosphere in the studio shifts palpably. The air feels charged, crackling with unspoken tension. Knox's eyes, which had been cold and professional moments ago, now burn with an intensity that makes my breath catch in my throat. He turns to me, his jaw clenched tight, a muscle ticking beneath the stubble that shadows his cheek.

"Why didn't you call me directly?" he demands, his voice a low rumble that sends shivers down my spine.

I blink, momentarily taken aback by the abrupt shift in his demeanor. The commanding detective is gone, replaced by the dangerous, possessive man I've come to know in such an intimate way. My mind races, trying to process the rapid changes of the last few minutes.

"When exactly did you tell me you were detectives?" I counter, finding my voice. "Because I'm pretty sure that particular detail never came up during our... encounters."

A frown pulls at Knox's lips, his brow furrowing as if he's genuinely surprised by this revelation. For a moment, he looks almost sheepish, an expression so at odds with his usual severity that I almost want to laugh. But the gravity of the situation quickly reasserts itself as Knox turns his attention to the photographs in his hands.

The first image—the one of me entering the bar—doesn't seem to bother him much. His eyes scan it clinically, taking in the details with professional detachment. But when he flips to the second photograph, the one capturing the raw, primal moment between River and me in the alley, his entire demeanor changes.

A growl, low and dangerous, rumbles from deep in his chest. His fingers tighten on the edges of the photo, crinkling the glossy paper. With a sharp movement, he thrusts the image at River, who has been watching the exchange with an uncharacteristically somber expression.

"Someone saw you," Knox snaps, his voice tight with barely contained fury.

River takes the photo, his eyes widening as he takes in the intimate scene captured on film. His usual easy-going demeanor vanishes, replaced by a cold, calculating look that sends a chill down my spine.

"Fuck," River breathes, running a hand through his hair. "This is... not good."

Knox begins to pace, his movements tightly controlled but radiating tension. Each step is measured, deliberate, like a caged predator assessing its confines. The soft thud of his expensive shoes on the hardwood floor echoes in the tense silence of the studio.

Knox stops his pacing abruptly, whirling to face River. His eyes blaze with barely contained fury as he fixes his partner with a withering glare.

"You were careless," Knox growls, his voice low and dangerous. "I told you to be more discreet, but you couldn't control yourself, could you? Had to have her right there in the alley, consequences be damned."

River has the grace to look somewhat chastened, but there's a defiant glint in his eye as he meets Knox's gaze. "You weren't there, Knox," he argues, his tone heated. He steps right into Knox's space, his free hand coming up to brush against Knox's stubble. "You didn't see how beautiful she looked, how responsive she was. I couldn't have stopped myself if I tried."

As I watch this exchange, a hysterical laugh bubbles up in my throat. "How is it that I have two detectives stalking me?" I ask, shaking my head in disbelief. "Isn't that, I don't know, against some kind of code of ethics or something?"

River's head snaps towards me, his earlier tension melting away as a wicked grin spreads across his face. "Oh, sweetheart," he purrs as he steps away from Knox again, his voice dropping to that sinful register that never fails to make my knees weak. "We're not stalking you. We're detecting."

I roll my eyes so hard I'm surprised they don't get stuck in the back of my head. "Right," I drawl, my voice dripping with sarcasm. "Because breaking into my apartment to leave baked goods and stock my fridge is standard police procedure."

Knox resumes his pacing, each step measured and deliberate, like the ticking of an ominous clock. His movements are tightly controlled, but I can see the tension coiled in his muscles, ready to spring at a moment's notice.

After what feels like an eternity, Knox stops directly in front of me. His eyes bore into mine, flecks of gold seeming to dance in their depths as he studies me intently. I feel pinned in place by the power of his gaze, unable to look away even if I wanted to.

"Tell us everything," he commands, his voice brooking no argument. "Every detail, no matter how small or insignificant you think it might be. Don't leave anything out."

I take a deep breath, steeling myself and I begin to recount the events leading up to this moment.

Chapter 23
Knox

THE PRECINCT HUMS WITH its usual controlled chaos as I settle into my desk chair, the familiar creak of leather doing little to soothe my frayed nerves. The fluorescent lights cast a harsh glare over the scattered case files and half-empty coffee cups littering the surface. I lean back, scrubbing a hand over my face, feeling the rough scratch of stubble against my palm.

Fuck. How did we miss this?

The question burns in my mind, a constant, mocking refrain. River and I have been watching Rayne for months, learning every detail of her life, memorizing her routines, her habits, her very essence. We thought we knew everything there was to know about her. And yet, somehow, we completely overlooked another predator circling our prey.

The realization sits like lead in my gut, a cold, heavy weight of failure. I've always prided myself on my observational skills, on my ability to see the things others miss. It's what makes me such a damn good detective. But in this case, I was blind. Blinded by my own obsession, by the all-consuming need to possess Rayne completely.

I pull out the photographs from the evidence bag, placing them both on my desk. The image of Rayne entering the bar is unremarkable, save for the fact that it exists at all. But the second photo... my fingers clench involuntarily as I stare at the captured moment of raw passion between River and Rayne.

The rage that had simmered beneath the surface since we left Rayne's studio threatens to boil over. The only person with any right to watch them is me. I want to tear the photo to shreds, to hunt down the bastard who dared to intrude on that private moment and make them suffer. Make them bleed. But I can't. I return the photos to the evidence bags and set them aside. The images are evidence now, a tangible reminder of my failure to protect what's mine.

Our carelessness could have cost us everything. If this unknown stalker had chosen to go to the police instead of threatening Rayne directly, our entire carefully constructed world could have come crashing down. Our careers, our freedom, our chance at a future with Rayne–all of it hanging by a thread because we let our guard down.

As much as we had wanted to stay with Rayne after she had told us the very limited information about her other stalker, she had work to do and so did we. There had been another body this morning, and then seeing the squad car outside of Rayne's place had me on edge and my control already almost slipped once.

I force myself to focus on the task at hand, pushing thoughts of Rayne to the back of my mind. As much as every fiber of my being screams to go back to her, to wrap her in my arms and never let go, I know we can't.

My eyes drift to the empty desk across from mine. River left the precinct within minutes of arriving, citing personal time. I know exactly where he's gone—to set up surveillance outside Rayne's studio. It's a necessary precaution, but part of me bristles at the thought of him being closer to her right now while I'm stuck here.

I turn my attention to the case file spread out before me, photos of the latest victim staring up accusingly. Another body found this morning, dumped unceremoniously in a back alley like garbage. The victim's blank eyes seem to bore into me, demanding justice, demanding that I do my job.

I almost want to laugh. The irony isn't lost on me–a killer hunting another killer.

But this one, he's different. He doesn't discriminate, doesn't choose his victims based on any discernible pattern or moral code. He's a true predator, striking at random, leaving a trail of brutalized bodies in his wake.

Or at least that's what we have led everyone else to believe.

As far as everyone thinks, the only thing that links each of the bodies are the very specific pattern of stab wounds, almost exactly the same on each body, and the very distinct two prong burn marks that are always found somewhere on the body. But what everyone else doesn't know is they are all on a list, a list known only to me and River, one we compiled of local criminals and abusers we deemed unfit to walk the streets.

My eyes linger on the most recent victim's photo, taking in the brutalized features, the glassy, lifeless stare. Gerald Kincaid, a drug dealer with a rap sheet longer than my arm and a penchant for violence against women and children. His name had been at the top of our list for over a year, but getting to him proved... challenging. He was well-insulated, always surrounded by a couple of lackeys or muscle.

I unlock my desk drawer and pull a worn leather journal from it, the cover soft and supple from years of handling. Flipping through the pages, I trace the names and details with my fingertip. Kincaid's entry isn't hard to find among the pages and a smile pulls at my lips as I take a pen and put a line through his page.

We keep a meticulous ledger, documenting every name that graces our list. Pedophiles, rapists, abusers of every variety—all those who have escaped the long arm of the law, we take it upon ourselves to punish them. Each entry is carefully researched, every shred of evidence scrutinized until we are certain beyond a shadow of a doubt that our target is guilty.

Once a name is on the list, it's only a matter of time.

We plan everything to the last detail – the location, the method, the cleanup. No traces left behind, no evidence to tie the kills back to us.

I feel River's presence before he takes a seat at his desk, the familiar scent of his cologne mingling with the acrid tang of station coffee and sweat. He moves with his usual fluid grace, settling into his chair with a soft sigh.

"It's done," he murmurs, his voice low enough that only I can hear.

I nod, not needing to ask for clarification. The thought of even that little extra security at her place eases some of the tension coiled in my chest, knowing that even if we can't be there personally, we still have eyes on her.

Without a word, I stand, motioning for River to follow. He falls into step beside me as we make our way out of the precinct, our footsteps echoing in perfect sync down the linoleum-tiled hallway.

We step out into the late afternoon sun, the humid air immediately clinging to our skin. The street isn't overly busy but there are still a few people rushing to and fro, oblivious to the predators walking among them. We make our way down the block to the bakery we frequent, the same one Rayne loves.

The bell above the door chimes softly as we enter, the rich aroma of freshly ground coffee beans enveloping us. The barista, a petite redhead named Mia, gives us a familiar nod as we enter. She already has our usual orders started before we even open our mouths to speak.

We take our usual table in the back corner, positioned perfectly to keep an eye on both the entrance and the rear exit. Old habits die hard, even in a place as familiar as this. I pull out the worn leather journal, sliding it across the table to River.

"I crossed out the entry," I say, my voice barely above a whisper.

River hums in response, his fingers tracing the embossed cover before flipping it open. His eyes scan the pages quickly, lingering on the freshly struck-through name. A small, satisfied smile plays at the corners of his mouth.

"Good riddance," he mutters, closing the journal with a soft thud. "One less scumbag on the streets."

I nod in agreement as River hops up again to retrieve our coffee from the counter, placing mine in front of me. Lifting the cup to my lips, I take a sip of my coffee and the rich and slightly bitter liquid burns a path down my throat, grounding me. River leans back in his chair, his posture relaxed but his eyes alert as they scan our surroundings.

"We need to stop it soon," he says after a moment, his voice low and serious. "It's drawing too much attention."

I nod again, knowing he's right.

My thoughts inevitably drift back to Rayne, as they always do. The image of her pressed against that alley wall, head thrown back in ecstasy, is seared into my mind now. I can almost hear her breathy moans.

"You're lucky that photo didn't show your face," I murmur, my voice low and rough. "Or the body on the ground."

River tries to hide his grin behind his coffee cup, but fails miserably. His eyes dance with wicked amusement as he sets the mug down. "Come on, Knox," he teases. "You can't tell me you didn't find it at least a little hot."

I glare at him, but there's no real heat behind it. Because if I'm being honest with myself, that image was fucking hot. Rayne's curves on full display, River's powerful form looming behind her, the raw passion evident in every line of their bodies. The only thing that would have made it hotter was if I had been there too. The thought of it sends a jolt of arousal through me—River's body caught between mine and Rayne's, all of us moving together in perfect sync.

I shift in my seat, trying to adjust myself discreetly. River's knowing smirk tells me I'm not entirely successful.

"Imagining yourself in that alley with us?" he purrs, leaning in close. His breath ghosts over my ear, making me suppress a shiver. "I bet you wish you'd been there, pressed up against my back, fucking me while I fucked her."

My hand shoots out, gripping his thigh hard enough to bruise. "Careful," I warn, my voice a low growl. "You're playing with fire, Riv."

He just grins wider, completely unrepentant. "Maybe I want to get burned," he murmurs, his eyes glittering with challenge.

The tension between us crackles like electricity, thick enough to cut with a knife. For a moment, I'm tempted to drag him into the bakery's tiny bathroom and remind him exactly what happens when he pushes me too far. But we're on duty, and more importantly, we have other priorities.

With supreme effort, I release my grip on his thigh and lean back in my chair. River pouts slightly at the loss of contact, but doesn't push further. He knows when to back off, at least for now.

"Once we deal with this stalker situation, we'll make it happen," I say, forcing my mind back to the task at hand. "This new player changes everything. We need to find out who they are and neutralize the threat before they can hurt Rayne or expose us."

River nods, his expression growing serious once more. "Agreed. Where do we start?"

I scroll through the notes on my phone, frustration mounting with each swipe. There isn't much to go on at all, just the two photos and nothing else. We should get the envelopes and images to forensics to see if there are any fingerprints or other DNA evidence to be gleaned from them, but I doubt it. Whoever this stalker is, they're careful. Meticulous.

I sigh heavily, running a hand through my hair. "We need to keep a closer eye on her without this other stalker knowing," I mutter, more to myself than to River. "Which means I need to be more careful when I go to her apartment tonight."

River raises an eyebrow, a hint of challenge in his blue eyes. "You mean we need to be more careful," he corrects, emphasizing the 'we.'

I fix him with a hard stare. "No, I mean I. You had your fun last night, River. You get to keep watch outside, like a good boy."

A slow, wicked grin spreads across his face. "Aww, is someone feeling left out?" he teases, his voice dropping to that low, seductive purr that never fails to send a shiver down my spine. "Don't worry, Knox. Our little Rayne has plenty of love to go around."

I growl low in my throat, my hand shooting out to grip the side of his neck, my thumb pressed firmly into the hollow of his throat. I pull him close, our faces mere inches apart. "Watch yourself," I warn, my voice a dangerous rumble.

River's eyes darken with lust as I grip his throat, his pulse quickening beneath my thumb. For a moment, we're suspended in that delicious tension, the air between us thick with unspoken desire.

Then River does what River does best—he pushes.

"Or what?" he breathes, voice husky. "You'll punish me? Maybe that's exactly what I want."

I squeeze River's throat tighter, feeling his pulse quicken beneath my fingers. "We need to focus," I growl, my voice low and dangerous.

River's eyes darken further, pupils blown wide. He tilts his head back in my grip, exposing the long line of his throat. "Yes, sir," he murmurs, the words coming out breathy and strained.

The sight of him like this—submissive, pliant, utterly mine—sends a jolt of desire straight to my cock. I want nothing more than to drag him out of this bakery and remind him exactly who he belongs to.

But we can't. Not here, not now. We have a job to do, a woman to protect.

I release my grip on River's throat. He lets out a small whimper, his eyes fluttering open to meet mine. The Caribbean blue of his irises is nearly swallowed by his dilated pupils, a ring of stormy desire.

"Later," I promise, my voice rough with restrained desire. "Right now, we have work to do."

River nods, straightening in his chair. I watch as he visibly pulls himself together, the playful, seductive energy giving way to professional focus. It's a transformation I've seen countless times, but it never fails to impress me—the way he can switch from carefree flirt to deadly serious detective in the blink of an eye.

"So, what's our next move?" he asks, all business now.

I lean back in my chair, considering our options. "We need to gather more information," I say slowly. "The photos are our only real lead at this point. We should get them to the lab, see if they can pull any prints or trace evidence."

River nods, his brow furrowing in thought. "What about the envelopes? Any postmarks or distinctive features?"

"Nothing obvious," I reply, frustration evident in my tone. "But maybe the lab can find something we missed. We should also look into any recent releases from prison or mental health facilities in the area. Someone with a history of stalking or violent behavior."

"Good idea," River agrees. "I'll start making calls when we get back to the precinct."

As we finish our coffee and prepare to leave, my mind is already racing with plans. Whoever this stalker is, they've made a grave mistake in targeting what's ours. We'll find them, get rid of the threat, and then...

Then Rayne will truly be ours, in every way possible.

The thought sends a thrill of anticipation through me. Soon, very soon, we'll have everything we've ever wanted. Everything *I've* ever wanted. And God help anyone who tries to stand in our way.

Chapter 24
Rayne

Flowers are delivered that same afternoon. For a few moments I think that perhaps they are from Knox and River, but I dismiss the thought before I even look at the card. They have been very obvious about knowing every tiny detail about me including my likes and dislikes.

Dislike isn't a strong enough word for the roses that are left on my doorstep.

I stare at the bouquet, a cloying sweetness filling the air. The roses are a garish shade of red, their petals already starting to wilt at the edges. The cellophane crinkles loudly as I pick up the arrangement, my nose wrinkling at the overpowering scent.

Roses. Of all the flowers they could have chosen, it had to be roses. I've never understood the appeal of these gaudy blooms, their thorny stems always seeming more a threat than a romantic gesture. Give me peonies or lavender any day.

I carry the unwanted gift into my studio, holding it at arm's length as if it might bite. The wrapping is a metallic gold tissue paper underneath the cellophane. A red satin ribbon, tied in an overly elaborate bow, completes the clichéd presentation.

With a sigh, I set the flowers on my desk and reach for my phone. My fingers hover over Knox's name in my contacts for a moment before I hit the call button. It rings twice before his deep voice answers.

"Sweetheart? Is everything alright?"

The concern in his tone sends an unexpected warmth through me. "I'm fine," I assure him quickly. "But I thought you should know... I received flowers today."

There's a sharp intake of breath on the other end of the line. "Describe them," Knox demands, his voice tight and I can hear the edge of anger.

I detail the garish arrangement, from the wilting petals to the tacky wrapping. As I speak, I notice a card nestled among the blooms. With trepidation, I pluck it from its plastic holder.

"There's a card," I tell Knox, my voice wavering slightly as I unfold the small piece of paper.

The message inside is a jumble of apologies and possessive ramblings, the handwriting alternating between careful precision and frenzied scrawl. My stomach churns as I read aloud:

"My dearest Rayne,

I'm sorry if I frightened you. That was never my intention. I only want to protect you, to keep you safe from those who would harm you. You are mine, my beautiful flower, and I will do anything to keep you. We belong together, can't you see that? Soon, very soon, we'll be together forever. No one will ever come between us again."

Knox's growl is audible even through the phone. "Don't touch anything else," he instructs. "I'll be there as soon as I can. In the meantime, get rid of those flowers. Throw them in the dumpster outside, not your trash can."

I nod, then remember he can't see me. "Okay," I agree. "I'll keep the card for you, though. It's... unsettling."

I stare at the card for a long moment as I hang up the phone, my skin crawling as I reread the possessive words. The paper feels tainted somehow, as if the stalker's obsession has seeped into the very fibers. Part of me wants to crumple it up, to set it aflame and watch the ashes scatter in the wind. To destroy this tangible evidence of the unwanted stalker hanging over me.

But I resist the urge, carefully placing the card on the corner of my desk instead. The crisp white rectangle stands out starkly against the dark wood. I'll leave it there for Knox to collect, another piece in the puzzle he's trying to solve.

With a shudder, I gather up the offending bouquet then head down the stairs and out into the alley behind the building.

The metal lid of the dumpster clangs open with a resounding bang that echoes off the brick walls. I toss the flowers in without ceremony, watching with grim satisfaction as they land among the other refuse. Good riddance.

Back in the studio, I try to shake off the unease that clings to me like a second skin. Already the scent of the roses stubbornly sticks to me, so I reach for the oil roller on my desk, freshening the lavender and vanilla scent on my skin. I need a distraction, something to occupy my mind so I turn to my computer, determined to lose myself in work.

I pull up the folder containing Breanna's initial gallery shots. The images from our boudoir session fill my screen—soft curves draped in delicate lace, coy smiles, and empowered poses. I begin the painstaking process of sorting through them, selecting the best shots for editing.

As I work, I'm acutely aware of another folder lurking in my digital files. The gallery I should be focusing on—the erotic session with Knox and River. The deadline is looming, but I can't bring myself to open it. Not yet. The thought of looking at that footage and all those images makes my heart race.

I tell myself I'll get to it tomorrow, knowing full well I probably won't.

Hours slip by as I lose myself in the familiar rhythm of editing. I adjust lighting, smooth skin tones, and enhance the natural beauty of each shot. The work is engrossing, allowing me to forget–if only for a little while–about stalkers and threats and the chaos that has become my life.

By the time I finally look up from my computer, the sky outside has darkened to a deep indigo. My eyes burn from staring at the screen for so long, and my back aches from hunching over my desk. With a groan, I stretch my arms above my head, feeling my spine pop in protest.

I'm about to shut down my computer when a small notification icon in the corner of my screen catches my eye. That's odd–I don't recall seeing it earlier, and I always keep my volume up to avoid missing alerts. Frowning, I click on the icon, watching as a news article pops up on my screen.

"Another Victim Found: Serial Killer Strikes Again"

My heart races as I scan the article, but it's still lacking in even the most basic details. The victim isn't named, just described as a "local man in his 40s." The body was discovered this morning in an alley downtown, not far from where River and I had our encounter the night before. A shiver runs down my spine at the memory.

The article mentions that the details of how the victim died can't be disclosed but it has been confirmed it's the same killer who's been terrorizing the town for over a week now, striking seemingly at random. The police are urging citizens to remain vigilant, to report any suspicious activity.

I lean back in my chair, mind whirling. Knox had mentioned something about a scene when he showed up at my studio earlier. This must have been what he was referring to. Another body, another victim of this ruthless killer.

My thoughts drift to Knox and River. These men who have shown me such passion and intensity, who stalk me with a predatory focus, are the same ones tasked with bringing this killer to justice. The weight of responsibility must be immense, knowing that with each passing day, another life hangs in the balance. I find myself longing to offer them comfort, to ease the burden they carry.

I close down the article with a heavy sigh before turning off the computer. For a moment, I sit in the stillness, listening to the soft hum of the air conditioning and the distant sounds of traffic filtering in from outside. The shadows in the corners of the room seem to deepen, and I can't shake the feeling of being watched. Shaking my head to dispel the paranoia, I gather my things and make my way to the door.

The lock clicks into place with a reassuring finality as I secure the studio. I double-check it, tugging on the handle just to be sure. Satisfied, I climb the stairs to my apartment, my footsteps echoing in the empty stairwell.

As I unlock and push open my apartment door, I'm greeted by an indignant meow. Luna sits in the middle of the entryway, her tail swishing back and forth in clear annoyance. Her amber eyes seem to glare accusingly at me as I step inside.

"I know, I know," I murmur, bending down to scratch behind her ears. "I've been neglecting you lately, haven't I? I've been a bad cat mom."

Luna allows the affection for a moment before sauntering away, her posture radiating disdain. I can't help but chuckle at her attitude. She's certainly not shy about expressing her displeasure at being left alone more often this past week.

With a sigh, I make my way to the kitchen, flicking on lights as I go. The warm glow chases away the lingering shadows, making the space feel more welcoming. I open the fridge, surveying its contents with a critical eye. After the day I've had, I deserve something nice for dinner.

I pull out an assortment of ingredients—fresh spinach, cherry tomatoes, a wedge of feta cheese, and a package of chicken breasts. A salad with grilled chicken sounds perfect, light yet satisfying. As I reach for a bottle of balsamic glaze on the top shelf, my eyes fall on a stack of unfamiliar cans.

Frowning, I pull one down to examine it. It's cat food, but not the usual brand I buy for Luna. This is the expensive stuff, the kind I've seen in specialty pet stores but always considered too pricey for everyday use. There are at least a dozen cans, neatly stacked and waiting.

I scoff, shaking my head in disbelief. "Really, River?" I mutter to myself. "Are you sneakily bribing my cat?"

Despite my exasperation, I can't help but feel a warmth blooming in my chest at the thoughtfulness of the gesture. It's such a small thing, but it speaks volumes.

I set the can of gourmet cat food on the counter, a wry smile tugging at my lips. "Well, Luna," I call out, "looks like you're in for a treat tonight."

I pop open the can, the strong aroma of salmon and tuna filling the air. Luna materializes as if summoned, her tail held high in anticipation. I scoop the food into her bowl, the pâté-like consistency a far cry from her usual kibble.

"Don't get used to this," I warn her as I set the bowl down. "And you can thank River for your fancy dinner, miss priss. Apparently, he's determined to win over both females in this household."

Luna dives in with gusto, purring loudly as she devours her meal. I watch her for a moment, amused by her enthusiasm. "At least one of us is easy to please," I mutter, turning back to my own dinner preparations.

I set about grilling the chicken, the sizzle and pop of meat hitting the hot pan filling the kitchen. The scent of herbs and garlic mingles with the lingering aroma of Luna's dinner, creating an odd but not unpleasant combination. As the chicken cooks, I assemble the salad, tearing crisp spinach leaves and halving plump cherry tomatoes.

Once the chicken is done, I let it rest for a few minutes before slicing it into perfect, juicy strips. I arrange them atop the salad, then crumble feta cheese over the whole affair. A drizzle of balsamic glaze completes the dish, the dark syrup creating abstract patterns across the colorful ingredients.

With dinner plated, I turn my attention to the wine River left in the fridge. The bottle or Prosecco is already chilled to perfection. I pour myself a generous glass, the pale golden liquid catching the light as it swirls in the glass.

Luna gives me a reproachful look as I take a sip. "Oh, don't judge me," I murmur to her. "You got gourmet cat food tonight."

I carry my meal to the living room, settling onto the plush cushions of my couch. Luna, having finished her own dinner, hops up to join me, curling into a contented ball at my side. I take a bite of the salad, savoring the interplay of flavors.

As I eat, my eyes keep drifting to the kitchen, where I know the bakery box sits in the fridge. The apple pie cupcake River left for me calls out like a siren song, tempting me with promises of sugary indulgence. I shake my head, forcing myself to focus on my healthy dinner. "Later," I promise myself, though I'm not entirely convinced.

With my plate cleared and my first glass of wine finished, I pour myself another. I flip through streaming services, searching for something to watch. After several minutes of indecision, I finally settle on an old favorite–a romantic comedy I've seen a dozen times before. The familiar plot is comforting, requiring little mental effort to follow. I sink deeper into the plush cushions, letting the tension of the day slowly seep from my muscles.

Luna stretches and repositions herself, draping her warm body across my lap. Her purr rumbles through me, a soothing vibration that seems to resonate in my very bones. I stroke her soft fur absently, marveling at the silky texture beneath my fingertips.

The movie plays on, its predictable twists and turns unfolding on the screen. The leading lady's quirky best friend delivers a witty one-liner, and I find myself chuckling despite having heard the joke before. The wine has left a pleasant warmth in my chest, softening the edges of the world and making everything feel just a little bit hazy.

As the movie progresses, I sink deeper into the comforting warmth of the couch. The soft glow of the TV bathes the room in a gentle, flickering light, casting dancing shadows on the walls. The familiar dialogue becomes a soothing murmur in the background, blending with the steady hum of the air conditioning and Luna's contented purrs.

On screen, the movie's climax unfolds–the typical misunderstanding that threatens to tear the main couple apart. But I know how it ends. They'll work it out, declare their love in some grand romantic gesture, and live happily ever after.

If only real life were so simple.

My fingers trace lazy patterns through Luna's fur, her warmth seeping into my lap like a living, breathing heating pad. Her whiskers twitch occasionally in her sleep, and I wonder what cats dream about. Chasing mice? Exploring sun-dappled gardens? Or perhaps she's dreaming of the gourmet meal she just devoured, courtesy of River.

Luna stirs beside me, stretching out to knead at my thigh with her paws. Her claws catch slightly in the fabric of my dress, and I gently disentangle her. She gives me an indignant look before hopping down from the couch, padding off towards the bedroom.

"Abandoning me already?" I call after her, taking the opportunity to stretch out along the couch. "And here I thought we were having a girls' night."

As the film enters its final act, my eyelids grow heavy. The wine has left me pleasantly warm and drowsy, my limbs feeling loose and relaxed. I struggle to keep my eyes open, not wanting to miss the climactic confrontation I know is coming.

But it's a losing battle.

The credits begin to roll, names scrolling by in a blur as the swell of orchestral music fills the room. I blink slowly, realizing I've missed the last few scenes of the movie. My wine glass sits empty on the coffee table, a faint lipstick stain marking where my lips touched the rim.

With great reluctance, I peel myself off the couch. My muscles protest the movement, having grown accustomed to the plush embrace of the cushions. I gather my empty wine glass and plate, padding softly to the kitchen, I rinse them and leave them in the drying rack to deal with in the morning.

As I turn to leave the kitchen, my eyes fall on the fridge. The bakery box inside calls to me, promising sweet indulgence. For a moment,

I'm tempted to give in, to savor the rich flavors of the apple pie cupcake as a late night snack. But the thought of the sugar high keeping me awake even longer makes me reconsider.

With another sigh, I flick off the kitchen light and make my way down the hallway. A quick shower and my bed beckons, the promise of sleep too enticing to resist.

And perhaps a sexy dream about a detective or two.

Chapter 25
Knox

I KNOW EXACTLY WHAT I'm about to do.

My movements are calculated, each step measured and deliberate as I cross the threshold into her bedroom, leaving her feline behind me in the living room with my offerings. Shadows stretch across the room, the faint glow of moonlight spilling through the crack in her curtains just enough to paint the edges of her belongings in silver.

I glance at the dresser first. The same delicate trinkets line its surface—small glass animals, a faded polaroid tucked carefully into the corner of her mirror, the faint smear of fingerprints on the glossy wood that only someone like me would notice. My lips curl slightly when my eyes drift to the bookcase beside it. The books have shifted again, their order rearranged since the last time I was here. She must've been reading before she went to sleep again.

My gaze slides back to the bed. Rayne. Her name echoes in my mind like a prayer I can't stop repeating, a mantra carved into my very bones. She's sprawled out on her back, the pale sheets clinging loosely to her body, one arm thrown back and the other resting limply against her stomach. I can see she is naked beneath the sheet and I wonder if she knew one of us might come tonight. Was she hoping we would? Her dark hair fans out around her head, a halo of ink against the ivory fabric, and even from here, I can see the subtle rise and fall of her chest as she sleeps.

She's still untouched by the world in this state, stripped bare not just of clothing but of the careful mask she wears during the day. No makeup, no practiced smiles or professional detachment. Just her. Pure and unguarded.

I move closer, silent, until I'm standing at the edge of the bed. For a moment, I do nothing, letting my eyes trace every curve, every dip and swell obscured by the sheet. My fingers twitch at my sides. This close, I can see how soft her skin looks, how warm she must be beneath the thin barrier separating us. It's maddening.

Leaning forward, I grip the edge of the sheet between my fingers. Slowly, deliberately, I peel it back, the fabric whispering against her body as it slides away. Inch by inch, the expanse of her naked form comes into view, her smooth skin catching the faint light in a way that makes something primal stir deep within me.

My breath hitches when I take her in fully, laid out before me like some forbidden offering. Heat coils through me, sharp and insistent, and for a fleeting moment, I consider burying my face between her thighs, tasting her while she's still lost in sleep again, seeing just how much I could do to her before she wakes. But no. That particular indulgence can wait for another night.

My shoes hit the floor with a soft thud, one after the other, and the cool air brushes against my skin as I strip away each layer of clothing. My pulse drums in my ears, a quiet rhythm that mirrors the ache building low in my core.

I move deliberately, lowering one knee onto the edge of the bed, the mattress dips under my weight. Slowly, I swing my other leg over her body, straddling her hips. She shifts beneath me, her movements instinctive, unconscious—just enough to send a flicker of heat through my veins.

As I lower myself closer, I press my hand firmly over her mouth. Her eyes snap open, wide and startled, glinting like shards of sapphire in the dim light. She reacts instantly, her hands flying up to grip my wrist. I feel the slight dig of her nails against my skin, the sharp sting cutting through the haze clouding my mind. God, I love it when she claws at me.

"Easy," I murmur, my voice low, roughened by restraint. Her panic is raw, electric, but it lasts only a heartbeat before recognition dawns in her gaze. That tension bleeds away, replaced by something softer, warmer—and far more dangerous.

"Knox," she breathes against my palm, her voice muffled but unmistakable. The sound of my name on her lips sends a jolt straight through me.

"That's better," I say, sliding my hand from her mouth to her throat. My fingers curl lightly around the vulnerable column of her neck, feeling the rapid flutter of her pulse beneath my thumb. She doesn't flinch. Doesn't fight. Instead, she looks up at me with an unreadable expression, her lips parting slightly.

"How did you get in here?" she asks, her tone calm—too calm for someone pinned beneath a man who shouldn't be in her bedroom. The question hangs between us, but I don't answer. Instead, I smirk, tilting my head as I take her in, savoring the way her chest rises and falls against me.

"You're awfully composed," I say, letting the words drip with amusement. "I could have done anything to you while you slept."

Her lips twitch, just barely, and there's a flicker of something dark behind her eyes—a shadow, a whisper of fascination that stirs something buried deep inside me.

Her shrug is almost imperceptible, a subtle roll of her bare shoulders against the sheets beneath her. The movement draws my attention momentarily to the smooth expanse of her collarbone before her voice pulls me back.

"Should I be scared, detective?" she asks, her tone deceptively light, almost curious. Her eyes hold mine steadily, it's certainly not fear swirling within them. "Are you planning to hurt me?"

I pause, tilting my head as I let her question hang in the charged air between us. My hand remains at her throat, my thumb idly brushing against the delicate skin just below her jaw. Her pulse beats steady now, no longer frantic but full of quiet anticipation. She doesn't flinch under my grip; instead, her gaze challenges me. My eyes flick to the new book resting on the nightstand next to the bed.

"So are you saying I could have fucked you while you were sleeping and you would have been okay with that? Perhaps I should put on a mask..." I counter, my voice low, gravelly, deliberate. My lips curl into a smirk as I lean in closer, watching every flicker of emotion that crosses her face. "Not let you know who I am while I fuck you... Maybe I should've held a knife to your throat..." My fingers tighten ever so slightly on her neck, not enough to harm, but enough to remind her who is in control. "...Cut into all that glorious skin just to paint you in blood and cum."

Her reaction is instantaneous, her pupils dilating until only the faintest ring of blue surrounds the black. Her breathing quickens, though it's not fear I see in her—it's something else entirely. Something far darker. Far more dangerous.

"I mean..." she starts, her lips curling into a wicked little smile that sends a jolt straight through me. It reminds me of River. "I wouldn't be opposed to the idea of any of that." Her voice is sweet, saccharine, but there's a razor-sharp edge beneath it. "I do read a lot of dark romance books, after all."

The sound that escapes me is involuntary—a chuckle, deep and throaty, vibrating from my chest. It fills the small space between us, and I see the way it affects her. Her thighs shift beneath me, the friction sending a delicious ripple of awareness through my body. God, I love how easily she reacts to me, how much control I have over her without even trying.

"Reading it and experiencing it are two very different things. Maybe I should read some to you out loud. Hmmm?" I murmur, amusement lacing my words. My free hand moves to the night-stand, and I pick up the book resting there. Its worn edges and well-thumbed pages tell me it's been read more than once. Perfect.

"Let's see what kind of twisted bedtime story you're reading now." I open the book one-handed, using my thumb to flip to the page marked by her bookmark. The words leap off the page, vivid and raw, and heat rushes through me as I skim the contents. My cock, already stirring from the proximity of her naked body, hardens fully, pressing insistently against her.

"Well, well," I say, my voice thick with arousal as I lower the book slightly to meet her gaze. My eyes burn into hers, taking in the way her lips part, her breath catching as she watches me. She would have to know exactly what I just read. "Is this what you like, baby girl?" My smirk widens, my control slipping now. "Should I threaten to breed this pretty little cunt?"

Chapter 26
Rayne

I DON'T KNOW WHAT'S come over me. I can't blame it on the alcohol—that had burned out of my system before I crawled into bed and long before I put the book aside and fell asleep again. But something deep and electric has taken hold of me this past week. Maybe it's knowing how closely they are following me like a predator stalking prey. Or maybe it's the book I couldn't resist reading before falling asleep, the one now open in his hands that whispers promises of dark, forbidden urges.

But the moment Knox's tattooed body loomed over me, that burn—the one I'd tried to ignore—flared back to life. A molten heat that started in my chest and spiraled down between my thighs. His voice, low and gravelly, ignited every nerve ending, making me feel like I was standing too close to an open flame. I'm thirsty, desperate... and somehow, I know he can quench this ache.

The room feels too small, the space between us suffocating. I try to answer, but the words stick in my throat.

I've never wanted children—I've always been sure of that. I love my friend's daughter, dote on her endlessly, but I've never felt the pull myself. And yet... the way Knox looks at me now, savage and unrelenting, makes my stomach twist with longing I don't fully understand. Not for the reality of it, no. But for this fantasy, this raw, carnal desire. For him.

My skin flushes hot, mortified and aroused all at once. I jerk my head in protest. "I—I have an implant," I stammer, the words tumbling out before I can stop them. "I'm not looking to get pregnant."

"Good," he growls, closing the book with a snap and setting it back on the nightstand. The sound makes me jump slightly, but his attention never wavers. "Because I don't give a damn about the reality of it. What I care about is the way you look at me when I say it. Like you want it anyway, like you want me to ruin you."

It's true. God, it's so painfully true.

"Well?" he murmurs. His voice is low, rough-edged, as though dragged over gravel, and it vibrates through the small space between us. His face is so close now, I can feel the heat radiating from him. His breath fans across my lips, intoxicating and maddening all at once. But he doesn't close the distance. He hovers, waiting, teasing.

I lift my head instinctively, desperate for contact, but he matches my movement perfectly, keeping that unbearable sliver of air between us. The corner of his mouth twitches, and I realize this is exactly what he wants—to watch me squirm, to make me chase something he's not ready to give.

"Well?" he repeats, his tone sharper now, more commanding. The question lingers in the haze clouding my brain. What was he asking? My thoughts stumble over themselves, tripping as I try to gather them. I want him to kiss me. I want him to do everything I've only ever imagined before. Every instinct in me screams to just throw myself into the fire he's ignited, but...

"River," I blurt out, my frown deepening as the name tumbles unbidden from my lips. "Does he even know you're here?"

Knox chuckles—a dark, rasping sound that scrapes against my nerves and sets me alight all over again. His grip tightens ever so slightly, a warning, though his thumb skims my jaw in a way that feels almost tender.

"Ohh little Rayne," he drawls, leaning closer until his lips hover near my ear. "He knows exactly where I am, and he wishes he were here too. Not being here is his punishment... for teasing me with the thought of fucking him while his cock is buried deep inside your delicious pussy." The confession hits me like a lightning strike, and I swear I feel it all the way down to my core. My thighs clench involuntarily, need coiling tighter and tighter inside me.

I shudder at his words, my breath hitching. There's something wickedly intimate about the way he says it—as though there's no room for shame or hesitation. Before I can stop myself, a vivid image of Knox and River together flashes through my mind, their bodies entwined, all raw power and unrelenting heat. A broken sound escapes me—a whimper—and Knox hears it, of course. His smirk sharpens, predatory.

"Now," he says, pulling back just enough to lock eyes with me again. His gaze burns, fierce and unyielding, pinning me in place. "Answer me. Tell me you love the idea of me taking you, owning you, ruining you..."

Yes. God, yes. That's what I want. All of it. Every dark, depraved thing I've only ever read about in secret and never dared to dream of experiencing. My heart races as I force myself to meet his gaze, drowning in the molten promise behind it.

"Yes," I whisper, the word slipping out before I can second-guess it. My voice is barely audible, but it feels deafening in the charged silence between us.

A slow smirk curls at the corner of his mouth, wicked and knowing. He tilts his head slightly, his lips still hovering achingly close to mine, but making no move to bridge the gap. "Beg me," he says, his tone calm, controlled, yet laced with a challenge that sends a fresh wave of heat pooling low in my belly.

My breath catches. He doesn't move, doesn't push further. He simply waits, his gaze locked onto mine, daring me to take the next step.

I blink up at him, my breath caught somewhere between my lungs and throat. The word reverberates in the charged air between us, a challenge that has been thrown at my feet.

"Wh-what?" My voice cracks slightly, and I hate how small it sounds.

Knox doesn't answer immediately. His piercing eyes—predatory and unwavering—remain locked on mine, his fingers tightening ever so slightly around my throat. My pulse hammers against his palm, betraying the storm inside me.

"Beg me," he repeats, his tone deliberate, gravel rough, each syllable dragged out as if savoring them. "Beg me to ruin you."

The heat of his body is suffocating, every part of him pressing into me without apology. His hard length digs into my stomach, nothing separating us. It sets my nerves alight, makes coherent thought impossible.

"Please," I blurt before I can stop myself, my voice trembling, but there's no hiding the need behind it. The sharp edge of amusement glints in his eyes, daring me to continue.

"Use your words, Rayne," he challenges, lowering his face until his lips are so close I can feel the ghost of his breath brushing mine. "Tell me exactly what you want."

The command sends a shiver down my spine, leaving a trail of goosebumps in its wake. My mind spins, torn between defiance and surrender, but my body has already made its choice. Everything in me aches for him—for the kind of destruction only he can offer.

"Ruin me," I whisper finally, the words tumbling from my lips unbidden, raw and desperate. "Please."

Knox's eyes darken at my words, molten gold flecks dancing in their hazel depths. A low growl rumbles in his chest, vibrating against me. But he doesn't move, doesn't give me what I crave. Instead, his grip on my throat tightens just a fraction more, his thumb pressing against my thundering pulse.

"Oh, sweetheart," he murmurs. "You can do better than that."

His free hand trails down my side, fingertips barely grazing my skin. The feather-light touch leaves goosebumps in its wake, my body arching instinctively into his caress. He chuckles darkly, clearly pleased by my responsiveness.

"Beg harder," Knox commands, his tone brooking no argument. "Make me believe you want this as badly as I do."

The weight of his body pins me to the mattress, every inch of his skin searing against mine. I can feel the coarse hair on his chest brushing my nipples, already painfully tight and sensitive. His cock, hard and insistent, presses into my stomach, a reminder of what awaits me if I can just find the right words.

I squirm beneath him, desperate for friction, for relief from the aching need building inside me. But Knox doesn't budge. His muscular thighs bracket my hips, holding me in place with effortless strength. The moonlight filtering through the curtains casts shadows across his face, highlighting the sharp planes of his cheekbones and the hungry glint in his eyes.

"Use that pretty mouth," he coaxes, his lips curling into a wicked smirk. "Tell me exactly how badly you want me to destroy you."

When he reaches my hip, his grip suddenly tightens, fingers digging into my flesh hard enough to bruise.

The pain mingles with pleasure, drawing a gasp from my lips. It's like a dam breaking, unleashing a torrent of words I didn't know I had in me.

"Please, Knox," I whimper, my inhibitions crumbling under the weight of his gaze. "I need you. I need you to ruin me, to break me apart and put me back together. I want your marks all over my body, inside and out. I want to feel you for days, to ache in places I didn't know could ache."

My cheeks burn with each confession, but I can't stop now. The words pour out of me, raw and unfiltered.

"I want both of you to use me, to take everything I have to give and demand more. I want to be yours and River's, completely and utterly. Please, Knox. Please ruin me. Make me yours."

His smirk deepens, and the hand around my throat flexes again, possessive and unrelenting. The control fraying at the edges now, tightening like a coiled spring, moments from snapping.

"Good girl," he growls, and the sound alone nearly undoes me.

Without warning, his lips crash into mine in a ferocious, devouring kiss. There's no gentleness, no restraint—only the raw, primal need to possess, to dominate. His tongue thrusts deep, tangling with mine as he swallows my moans.

I'm drowning in the scent of him, the taste, the overwhelming physicality that pins me in place. His hand tightens on my throat. The lack of air is dizzying, disorienting, but his lips are even more intoxicating.

I'm lost to everything but the feeling of him consuming me.

His free hand finds my breast, squeezing firmly, fingers kneading the soft flesh with delicious pressure. My back arches instinctively into his touch as he palms the generous curve, thumbing over the taut peak. A white-hot jolt of arousal lances through me at the rough caress.

His fingers twist at my aching nipple, the sharp pinch going straight to my throbbing core. A desperate whimper escapes me, my hips rocking uselessly against empty air in search of any friction. He chuckles darkly, the vibration sending tremors through my very bones.

I've never felt smaller or more deliciously overwhelmed by his sheer size and intensity. Every nerve is alight and hyper-aware of the hard planes of his body blanketing mine.

He lavishes the same rough attention on my other breast, squeezing and plucking until I'm writhing beneath him. I'm not a small woman by any means, but he makes me feel delicate and desired, as though I'm made to be devoured

When his mouth leaves mine again, he sits back, releasing my throat. Both of his large hands engulf the swell of my breasts, fingers sinking into the supple flesh as he watches me arch helplessly into his touch.

With a growl that vibrates in my very core, he pinches both hard nipples simultaneously, pulling hard. A strangled cry tears from my throat at the exquisite sting, the pain only amplifying the dizzying arousal swirling through me and I feel like he is pulling directly on my clit.

The rough sound seems to snap the taut leash on his control. In one fluid motion, he rises up on his knees and maneuvers me onto my stomach with an arm banded around my waist. I have no chance to even think before his big hands grasp my hips, wrenching me up onto my knees.

My trembling thighs are forced wide, and I start to push up on my hands, craving what I know is coming. But his palms are there in an instant, shoving my upper body back down to the mattress, bowing my spine into a delicious arch.

I'm utterly at his mercy, splayed out and aching for him.

A sharp tug at my hair wrenches a gasp from me. His fist knots in the long strands, the stinging bites across my scalp sending jolts of lighting straight to my molten center when he forces my head back. My back arches further as he bends my pliant form to his will.

Through the haze of need, I feel him then—the thick, hard head of his cock rubbing against my wet entrance. I clench around nothing, my walls fluttering hungrily. I'm so worked up and drenched for him, wanting desperately to feel him stretching me open again.

His harsh groan is like a caress against my flushed skin as he pushes just the tip into me...only to pull it back in slow, maddening torment.

"You sure, baby girl?" His gravelly words fan the flames burning through me. "Because I will fucking ruin you. I will give you every-thing you want, every dark and twisted fantasy."

A desperate, keening moan is torn from me. "Please..."

There's a beat of heated stillness, and then he slams home with brutal force.

The punishing thrust knocks the air from my lungs, choking me on the shocked, guttural "Fuck!" that bursts out. I don't get a chance to recover—he doesn't let up, doesn't show an ounce of mercy. He's primal, savage, pounding into me again and again with claiming strokes that rattle the bed and shake my very soul.

I'm mindless, overwhelmed by the loud, obscene noises of skin smacking wetly, the animalistic grunts being torn from him, and the high-pitched, desperate whimpers spilling shamelessly from my lips. I can hear how soaked I am for this rough treatment, the lewd sounds of his thick cock plunging relentlessly into me.

"I'm going to paint your womb with my cum," he growls, the filthy promise sending molten lava coursing through my body. "Fill you up until you can't take anymore and it drips from your pussy."

My fingers clutch painfully at the sheets beneath me as I keen again, higher and louder, the sounds coming from me seeming inhuman to my own ears. I'm undone, well on my way to shattering into a million pieces under his ruthless onslaught.

"I'll bury my cock so fucking deep inside you and just keep fucking you." He accentuates his crude vow with a series of short, sharp snaps of his hips that drive me closer to the edge. "And when I can't, River can...we can take turns until you know nothing but us. Our bodies, our scents, our cum. No one else."

His filthy words and ravenous pace ignite an inferno inside me. I'm keening, begging him in incoherent, barely audible rambling as he fucks me hard, violently. His fingers grip my hair tightly, pulling sharp and painfully as his other hand grips my hip, dragging my body back to meet his with each brutal thrust.

The dull ache lingering from the last two encounters only fuels the whirlwind of pleasure and pain that threatens to drown me in its chaotic storm. I can feel myself tightening around him, fluttering as my orgasm builds inside me like a coiled spring winding tighter with each punishing slam of his cock.

He releases his grip on my hip abruptly, and seconds later I feel the sharp sting of his palm landing hard across one ass cheek. Then the other. Fire rips through me, the burning ache of tender flesh only heightening the overwhelming sensations spiraling through my body. My walls clench impossibly tight and through the haze of lust and desperation, I hear his guttural command, "Come for me."

It's as if my body has been silently begging for permission. My orgasm slams into me with staggering force, the crest of ecstasy dragging me under its crashing wave. I cry out his name, uninhibited and shamelessly loud, as the pulses wrack through me. His pace stutters as I drag him over the edge with me, and I can feel the scorching heat of his cum flooding me. The sensation reminds me of his crude words, my hypersensitive pussy pulsing and fluttering around his twitching cock as he groans, "That's it, baby girl."

I can't move, utterly spent and limp against the mattress as I lose track of time, I'm only vaguely aware that he hasn't pulled out of me as he wraps himself around my body, rolling us onto our sides, but sleep is already dragging me under. The world feels hazy and distant, my body boneless and heavy in the aftermath of such intense pleasure. Knox's solid warmth envelops me completely, his chest pressed flush against my back, one muscular arm draped possessively over my waist.

His breath fans across the nape of my neck in slow, steady exhales, stirring the fine hairs there and sending little shivers down my spine. I can feel the steady thrum of his heartbeat against my shoulder blade, gradually slowing as we both come down from our shared high. The weight of his body anchors me, grounding me in this moment of utter contentment.

My eyelids grow heavier with each passing second, the soft cotton sheets beneath us feeling impossibly luxurious against my oversensitized skin. Knox's fingers trace lazy, abstract patterns along my hip and stomach, the calluses on his fingertips catching slightly on my sweat-dampened skin. It's soothing, hypnotic, lulling me further towards the edge of consciousness.

My last coherent thought before succumbing to slumber is how right this feels. How perfectly I fit against Knox's body, as if we were two pieces of a puzzle finally slotting into place. But there is still one piece missing. As darkness creeps in at the edges of my vision, I let out a contented sigh, sinking deeper into his embrace, wishing River was there too.

Chapter 27
Knox

I LIE AWAKE, SAVORING the warm weight of Rayne's body pressed against mine. Her soft curves mold perfectly to my harder planes, fitting together like we were made for this. My cock is still buried deep inside her, the tight, wet heat of her pussy a constant, maddening pleasure.

An hour has passed since our frenzied fuck, but sleep eludes me. I'm too consumed by the intoxicating scent of her skin, the silky texture of her hair splayed across the pillow, the gentle rise and fall of her chest as she slumbers. My fingers trace idle patterns along the skin of her hip, memorizing every dip and swell.

The room is bathed in the soft glow of moonlight filtering through the curtains. Shadows play across Rayne's face, accentuating the delicate arch of her brow, the fullness of her lips. Even in sleep, she's breathtaking. Just like I am with River, I'm obsessed with every tiny detail of the beautiful woman in my arms..

I can feel her pussy occasionally fluttering around me, little involuntary squeezes that send jolts of pleasure through my body. It takes every ounce of self-control not to start moving, to wake her with slow, deep thrusts. But I resist, content for now to simply be joined with her in this intimate way.

My mind drifts to thoughts of River, imagining him here with us. I picture him spooned behind her, his cock nestled between her ass cheeks, his arm draped over both Rayne and me. The three of us intertwined, a tangle of limbs and shared breaths. Soon, I promise myself. Soon we'll have that.

Rayne stirs slightly in her sleep, a soft moan escaping her lips. Her hips shift, grinding back against me, and I have to bite back a groan. My cock twitches inside her, hardening further. She settles again, but the damage is done. The embers of desire that had banked low now flare to life once more.

I nuzzle into the crook of her neck, inhaling deeply. My lips brush against her pulse point, feeling the steady thrum of her heartbeat. Slowly, carefully, I begin to move. Just the slightest roll of my hips, barely perceptible.

Rayne's breathing changes, becoming slightly quicker, though she doesn't wake. I continue my gentle movements, relishing the gradual build of pleasure. Her body responds even in sleep, growing wetter around me.

I trail open-mouthed kisses along the column of her throat, tasting the salt of dried sweat on her skin. My teeth graze the spot where her neck meets her shoulder, and I have to fight the urge to bite down, to mark her as mine. Instead, I soothe the skin with my tongue, drawing another sleepy sound of pleasure from her parted lips.

I lose track of time as I lazily fuck into her, my strokes long and unhurried. There's no urgency now, just the languid exploration of her body. My hands roam freely, gently cupping her breasts, thumbs brushing her nipples to stiff peaks. My hand drifts lower, splaying possessively across her lower abdomen. I imagine I can feel myself inside her, the hard length of my cock moving slowly within her depths.

The room is silent save for our mingled breaths and the wet sounds of our joined bodies. Rayne's skin is flushed and dewy with a fine sheen of sweat. I drink in every detail, I'm mesmerized by the flutter of her eyelashes, the occasional twitch of her brow.

I wonder if she's dreaming. If somewhere in her subconscious, she can feel me inside her, moving with exquisite slowness. Perhaps in her mind, River is here too. The three of us tangled together, a perfect union of flesh and desire. My cock throbs at the thought, imagining River's strong hands gripping Rayne's hips as I thrust into her mouth. Or maybe she dreams of being suspended between us, River's cock in her pussy while I take her ass. The possibilities are endless and intoxicating.

A soft whimper escapes Rayne's parted lips. Her hips push back against me instinctively, taking me deeper. I have to bite back a groan, not wanting to wake her just yet. I want to prolong this moment, to exist in this space between sleeping and waking where pleasure blurs the lines of reality.

My thrusts remain achingly slow, savoring every clench and flutter of her silken walls around me. I'm in no rush to find release. This isn't about chasing an orgasm, but about connection. About claiming her in the most primal way possible.

The sky outside begins to lighten imperceptibly, the inky black shifting to deep indigo. Dawn is still hours away, but already the world feels different. Charged with possibility. In this moment, anything seems achievable. River and I could keep Rayne forever, protected and cherished between us. We could build a life together, the three of us against the world.

I imagine a future where this is our norm—waking up with Rayne nestled between River and me, our bodies intertwined so completely it's hard to tell where one ends and another begins. No more sneaking into her apartment in the dead of night. No more pretending we don't want her with every fiber of our beings.

Just the three of us, together. Always.

The thought makes my chest tighten with an emotion I'm not quite ready to name. I bury my face in Rayne's hair, inhaling deeply.

Rayne shifts again in her sleep, pressing back against me more insistently. Her breathing quickens, little gasps and moans spilling from her lips. I wonder what she sees behind her closed eyelids. Does she picture River and me worshipping every inch of her body? Or perhaps she imagines us restraining her, teasing her to the brink of madness before allowing her release.

My own breathing grows ragged as I picture it. Rayne spread out before us, wrists and ankles secured to the bedposts. River's talented mouth between her thighs while I swallow her cries. My cock aches, throbbing deep inside her still-sleeping body. I could easily come right now, but I don't want this moment to end. Her tight pussy clenching around me is like a drug, and I'm a willing addict.

Rayne stirs slightly, her body tensing as she begins to wake. I slow my movements even further, barely rocking into her now. Her eyelashes flutter against her cheeks as consciousness slowly returns.

"Knox?" she murmurs sleepily, her voice thick and husky.

"Shh," I soothe, pressing a kiss to her shoulder. "I'm here, baby girl."

She hums contentedly, pushing back against me. A soft gasp escapes her as she realizes I'm still buried deep inside her.

"Oh," she breathes, clenching around me.

I groan low in my throat, my hips jerking involuntarily. "Fuck, Rayne."

She turns her head, seeking my lips. I oblige, capturing her mouth in a deep, languid kiss. My tongue sweeps inside, tasting her, claiming her. She moans into the kiss, her body undulating against mine.

When we finally break apart, both panting slightly, her eyes are hooded and dark with renewed desire. But I can see she is still hovering somewhere between sleep and awake, not quite ready to wake completely.

"How long have you been...?" she trails off, gasping softly as I give a particularly deep thrust.

"A while," I admit, nipping at her earlobe. "Couldn't help myself. You feel too good."

She shivers slightly, pressing back more insistently. "Don't stop," she rasps.

I have no intention of stopping. Now that she's partially awake, I increase my pace slightly. Still unhurried, but with more purpose now. I slide one hand down her body to where we're joined, my fingers finding her clit. She moans deeply at the touch, her pussy clenching around me.

"That's it, sweetheart," I encourage, rubbing slow circles. "Let me hear you."

Rayne grows louder, more desperate as I work her body. Her hand comes up to tangle in my hair, holding me close as I suck marks along her neck and shoulder.

"Knox," she whimpers. "Oh god, Knox..."

I can feel her getting close, her walls fluttering around me. My own release is building, a tight coil of pleasure low in my gut.

"Come for me, Rayne," I growl against her skin. "I want to feel you fall apart."

She obeys beautifully, saying my name like a prayer as her orgasm washes over her. Like I'm her god, and her worship and devotion belongs to me. The pulsing of her pussy around my cock drags me over the edge with her. I groan, burying myself deep as I spill inside her once more.

We lay tangled together in the aftermath, our bodies still joined as the last tremors of pleasure fade. Rayne's breathing gradually slows, her body relaxing against mine as she drifts back towards sleep. I remain buried deep inside her, still savoring the exquisite sensation of her warm, wet heat surrounding me.

As Rayne's breathing deepens, I'm struck by the perfection of this moment. The soft weight of her in my arms, the silky tangle of her hair, the gentle rise and fall of her chest–it's intoxicating.

I know with bone-deep certainty that this–right here, right now–is exactly where I'm meant to be. Where *we're* meant to be. Rayne belongs to us now, to River and me. And we belong to her just as completely.

As the first hints of dawn begin to color the sky, I find myself still wide awake, my body once again gently rocking into hers. The drag of her silken walls around me is exquisite torture, pleasure building with agonizing deliberation. I'm careful to keep my movements subtle, not wanting to wake her this time.

I continue my gentle, languid thrusts into Rayne's sleeping form, savoring every exquisite sensation. The soft light of dawn gradually illuminating her body, casting a warm glow on her skin.

Time seems to stretch and warp as I lose myself in the slow build of pleasure. Rayne's breathing remains deep and even, punctuated only by the occasional soft moan or sigh. Her body responds instinctively to mine once again, her hips rocking back to meet my shallow thrusts.

The coil of tension in my core winds tighter with each passing moment. Rayne's walls flutter and clench around me, drawing me deeper. I can feel her getting close, even in sleep. My fingers find her clit, circling with feather-light touches.

Her breath hitches, a whimper escaping her parted lips. I increase the pressure slightly, timing my strokes to match the quickening pace of my hips. Rayne's body goes taut, trembling in my arms as a soft cry of pleasure signals her release. Her pussy pulses around my cock and I let go, burying my face in her hair again to muffle my groan as I once more cum deep inside her.

As the last aftershocks fade, I carefully disentangle myself from Rayne's warm embrace. I take a moment to watch as our combined releases spill from her pussy and the sight has a possessive warmth blooming in my chest. My fingers twitch, wanting to push it back inside her.

Instead I restrain myself, settling for simply not cleaning her or wiping away the evidence of the night from her skin. Let her wake and remember, let her feel me there. Like I'm imprinted on her soul, a part of her as I was always meant to be. I dress quickly and silently, leaning down to brush a tender kiss across her temple before slipping out the way I came.

Chapter 28
Rayne

I'M STILL IN THE middle of admin work that I've been using as a way of procrastination when a knock at the door startles me. Frowning, I glance at the clock on my computer screen. It's just past 2 p.m, and I don't have any photoshoots scheduled for a few days. Knox and River wouldn't knock—they seem to have an uncanny ability to materialize in my space whenever they please. A flutter of unease ripples through my stomach as I push back from my desk and make my way to the door.

The studio is quiet save for the soft hum of the air conditioning and the muted sounds of traffic filtering in from outside. Afternoon sunlight streams through the high windows, casting long shadows across the polished hardwood floors. I pause for a moment, my hand hovering over the doorknob, before taking a deep breath and pulling it open.

To my surprise, Tash from the "Farewell to her Tah-Tahs" shoot stands on the other side, a sweet smile gracing her features. Her long blonde hair is pulled back in a messy bun, and she's wearing a flowy sundress that accentuates her curves beautifully. For a split second, I'm transported back to our photoshoot—the vulnerability in her eyes as she bared herself to my camera, the strength and courage radiating from her every pose.

"Tash!" I exclaim, genuine pleasure coloring my voice despite my initial wariness. "What a lovely surprise. Is everything okay?"

She nods, her smile widening. "Everything's great, Rayne. I hope I'm not interrupting anything important?"

I shake my head, stepping back to invite her in. "Not at all. Please, come in."

As Tash crosses the threshold, I notice she's carrying a small, nondescript box in her hands. It's about the size of a coffee mug, wrapped in plain brown paper with no visible markings or labels.

"Oh," Tash says, following my gaze. "This was on your doorstep when I arrived. I thought I'd bring it in for you."

She holds out the box, and I take it with a murmured thanks. The package is surprisingly heavy for its size, and a chill runs down my spine as I set it on the nearby side table. My mind races with possibilities—could this be another "gift" from my mysterious stalker? Could Tash be lying, could she be my stalker? Or am I wrong to mistrust everyone now? Or perhaps something more innocuous, like supplies I'd forgotten I'd ordered?

Pushing aside my concerns for the moment, I turn my attention back to Tash. "Can I get you something to drink? Water, tea, coffee?"

"Water would be lovely, thank you," she replies.

As I move to the small kitchenette tucked in the corner of the studio, I watch Tash out of the corner of my eye. She wanders over to the backdrop where we did her shoot, her fingers trailing lightly over the soft fabric. There's a wistful look on her face.

I return with two glasses of water, handing one to Tash. As she takes it, I notice a slight tremor in her hand. The vibrant, laughing woman from our photoshoot seems subdued now, a shadow of melancholy dimming her bright eyes.

"How are you doing, Tash?" I ask gently, gesturing for her to take a seat on the plush velvet Chesterfield.

She settles onto the cushions, smoothing her sundress over her knees. The afternoon light catches the delicate gold charm on her necklace—a tiny pair of angel wings that glint as she moves. Tash takes a sip of water before answering, her gaze fixed on some point beyond the studio walls.

"I'm..." she begins, then pauses, seeming to search for the right words. "I'm nervous, to be honest. The surgery is next week, and it's all starting to feel very real."

My heart clenches at the vulnerability in her voice. I sit beside her, close enough to offer comfort but not so near as to invade her space. "The double mastectomy?" I ask softly.

Tash nods, a sad smile tugging at the corners of her lips. It's so different from the joyous, infectious laughter that filled the studio during her session. Back then, even in the face of such a life-altering procedure, she had radiated strength and hope. Now, I can see the weight of her impending surgery pressing down on her shoulders. "Yes. I know it's necessary, I know it's the right choice, but..." She trails off, her hand unconsciously moving to rest over her chest. "It's hard not to feel like I'm losing a part of myself."

"I thought I was prepared," she continues, her fingers absently tracing the rim of her glass. "I've done all the research, talked to my doctors, even joined a support group and talked to survivors, even picked out some cute scarves for after. But now that it's so close... I'm terrified, Rayne." She trails off, blinking rapidly against the tears gathering in her eyes.

I squeeze her hand gently, offering what comfort I can. "It's okay to be scared, Tash. What you're facing is huge."

She nods, drawing in a shaky breath. "I know. I keep thinking about all the things I'll lose," she admits. "Not just my breasts, but... my hair, maybe. The feeling in my chest. The ability to breastfeed if I ever have kids." She takes a shuddering breath. "Part of my identity, in a way. It's just... I came here today because I wanted to thank you, Rayne. The proofing gallery you sent me... it was so beautiful."

Tash's eyes meet mine, brimming with unshed tears and heartfelt gratitude. "You have no idea how much it meant to me. To see myself through your lens, to feel beautiful and strong and... whole. Before everything changes."

Her words wash over me, and I feel my own eyes stinging with emotion. This is why I do what I do—to help women see their own beauty, their own strength. To capture moments of joy and empowerment that can sustain them through darker times. It's not the first time I've had a client like Tash who needed the photoshoot for a deeper reason, and it won't be the last.

Domestic violence survivors were also frequent clients, those who were so beaten down in the past that they no longer felt any self worth, or self confidence. And they affected me every single time.

Because they spoke to a part of my childhood that I could never forget. Of a mother I could never save.

"Oh, Tash," I murmur, shifting closer to her on the couch. I wrap an arm around her shoulders, and she leans into me, a few tears finally spilling over. "I'm so glad the photos meant so much to you. You were absolutely radiant during that shoot."

We sit in comfortable silence for a few moments.

"I've been looking at them every day since you sent them," she confesses, her voice thick with emotion. "They remind me of who I am, of the beauty and power I possess, regardless of what changes my body goes through."

I feel a lump forming in my throat, touched beyond words by her revelation. "Tash, I-"

She shakes her head, cutting me off gently. "No, please. Let me say this." She takes a deep breath, squaring her shoulders. "What you did for me, the way you captured not just my body but my spirit... it's given me strength I didn't know I had. When I look at those photos, I see a woman who is brave, who is beautiful, who is whole—no matter what."

As Tash speaks, I watch in awe as she seems to rebuild herself before my eyes. The slump in her shoulders gradually disappears, replaced by a straightening of her spine. The tremor in her voice fades, giving way to a quiet but unmistakable strength. Her eyes, which had been clouded with fear and uncertainty, now shine with renewed determination.

"When I first got the diagnosis," Tash continues, her voice steady now, "I felt like my world was falling apart. But looking at those photos... it's like I can see the woman I want to be after all this is over. Strong. Resilient. Beautiful, scars and all."

She reaches into her purse, pulling out a small, folded piece of paper. As she unfolds it, I recognize it as a print out of one of the images from her session—a stunning black and white image of her and her husband laughing, head thrown back, arms outstretched as if embracing the world as her husband embraces her.

"I'm going to keep this with me in the hospital," she says, tracing the outline of her image with a gentle finger. "To remind me of who I am, of the strength I have inside me. And that's thanks to you, Rayne."

My chest swells with pride and emotion. To know that my work has had such a profound impact on someone's life, to have played even a small role in helping Tash find her inner power—it's moments like these that remind me why I love what I do.

"Tash," I say, my voice thick with emotion, "you already had all that strength inside you. I just helped you see it."

She smiles at me, a full, radiant smile that lights up her entire face. "Maybe," she concedes. "But sometimes we need someone else to hold up a mirror, to show us what we can't see in ourselves. And that's what you did for me, Rayne. You held up a mirror and showed me my own power."

Tash stands then, smoothing down her sundress. There's a new energy about her, a quiet confidence that wasn't there when she first walked in. "I should go," she says. "I have a pre-op appointment to get to. But I wanted to come here first, to thank you in person."

I stand as well, and before I can react, Tash pulls me into a tight hug. She holds on perhaps a little too long, her arms wrapped firmly around me, her face buried in my shoulder. I can feel the slight tremor in her body, the way she clings to me as if drawing strength from the contact.

"Thank you," she whispers again, her voice muffled against my shirt. "For everything."

When she finally pulls away, there are tears in her eyes again, but they're accompanied by a smile—small, but genuine. I walk her to the door, feeling a mix of emotions swirling in my chest–pride, joy, a touch of sadness, but mostly a profound sense of purpose. This is the power of photography, of art, of truly seeing people.

"Good luck with your surgery, Tash," I say as we reach the threshold. "You've got this."

She nods, a determined glint in her eye. "Yes, I do. And I can't wait until I can come back and have another photoshoot with you once I recover. To capture the new me, scars and all."

Her words fill me with warmth. "I'd be honored, Tash. Truly. You just let me know when you're ready."

I squeeze her hand one last time before she steps out into the afternoon sun. As I close the door behind her, I lean against it for a moment, letting out a long breath. These encounters always leave me feeling drained yet oddly energized, as if I've absorbed some of my client's emotions.

Intending to dive back into work, I turn back toward my desk, when my eyes land on the package again. It sits there innocuously, a plain brown cube that could contain anything. A chill runs down my spine as I approach it cautiously, my earlier paranoia creeping back in.

There's nothing on the wrapping, no return address or name to indicate its origin. Could it have been from Tash? Could she have lied? I shake my head, trying to dispel the creeping tendrils of suspicion. Not everyone is out to get me, I remind myself firmly.

I carefully unwrap the package, peeling back the plain brown paper to reveal a nondescript cardboard box beneath. My heart pounds in my chest as I lift the lid, bracing myself for whatever might be inside.

Chapter 29
Rayne

THE FIRST THING I see is a flash of deep burgundy silk. As I gingerly lift the fabric from the box, it unfurls in my hands, revealing itself to be a delicate nightgown. The material is impossibly soft, slipping through my fingers like water. Intricate lace adorns the plunging neckline and hem, a pattern of intertwining roses and thorns that seems both beautiful and menacing.

The nightgown is exquisite, exactly the kind of thing I might have chosen for myself. But perhaps in a different color and pattern. That realization sends a chill down my spine. Whoever sent this knows my tastes.

As I examine the garment, something small and white flutters to the floor. My stomach drops as I bend to retrieve it, instantly recognizing the now-familiar handwriting. The note is written on thick, creamy paper, the ink a deep blood red that stands out starkly against the pale background.

"My dearest Rayne,

This reminded me so much of you, delicate yet strong. I couldn't resist getting it for you. Perhaps you could wear it to bed tonight? I'll be dreaming of you in it, just as I hope you'll dream of me. Soon, my love. Soon we'll be together, and these gifts will pale in comparison to what I have planned for us.

Until then, sweet dreams.

Yours always"

My blood runs cold as I read the words, bile rising in my throat. The intimacy of the gift, the possessive tone of the note–it's all too much. I drop the nightgown as if it's burned me, watching it pool on the floor in a puddle of silk and lace. Like blood.

Without hesitation, I grab the nightgown and shove it back in the box, throwing the note on the side table for Knox to collect. My skin crawls at the mere thought of touching it again, of imagining the stalker's hands on it, picturing me wearing it.

I march purposefully down the stairs, my footsteps echoing loudly in the empty stairwell, through the basement and out through the door next to the entrance to my basement parking. If this person is watching my front door I don't want them to see this. The afternoon sun is blinding as I push open the door, heading straight for the dumpster where I'd discarded the roses just days ago.

The metal lid creaks loudly as I lift it, the stench of rotting garbage assaulting my nostrils. Without ceremony, I hurl the box into the depths of the dumpster, hearing it land with a satisfying thud among the other refuse.

Anger washes over me. How dare they? How dare this person invade my life, my space, with these unwanted "gifts" and messages? "Fuck you," I spit out, my voice shaking with anger. "Fuck you and your sick games."

I slam the lid shut with enough force to make the entire dumpster rattle, as if I could somehow contain the threat, lock away the fear and disgust roiling inside me. But even as I turn to head back inside, I know it's not that simple. The stalker is still out there, watching, waiting. And no amount of discarded "gifts" will change that chilling reality.

As I calmly move back inside, I take several deep breaths, feeling the tension slowly drain from my body. The cool air of the studio washes over me, a stark contrast to the oppressive heat outside. I won't let this person have the satisfaction of rattling me. I am stronger than them.

At my desk, I sink into the familiar embrace of my chair. The leather is soft and worn in all the right places, molding to my body like a second skin. I take a moment to roll my oil roller on my wrist, taking another deep breath to inhale the calming scent.

My phone sits where I left it, screen dark and innocuous. With steady hands, I pick it up, unlocking it with a swipe of my thumb. The background image—a picture of Luna—fills the screen momentarily before I open my messaging app.

Selecting Knox's name, my fingers hover over the keyboard for a moment as I consider my words carefully. I don't want to worry him unnecessarily, but I know he needs to be informed.

Hey Knox, I received another package today. I've left the note for you on the side table. If you want the 'gift' itself, you'll have to fish it out of the dumpster behind the studio. I couldn't stand to keep it in the building.

I hit send and wait, watching as the message status changes from "Delivered" to "Read" almost immediately. The three dots indicating Knox is typing appear, then disappear, then reappear. Finally, his response comes through:

Are you okay? We aren't far if you need us to come by now.

The concern in his message is palpable, even through the impersonal medium of text. A warmth blooms in my chest at his concern, a flicker of something I'm not quite ready to name. I stare at Knox's message, my thumbs hovering over the keyboard. A part of me longs to accept his offer, to have him and River rush to my side, to feel safe in their protective embrace. But I can't. I can't let myself become dependent on them, can't risk opening myself up only to have them inevitably grow tired of me.

I'm fine, I type back, keeping my tone light and casual. *No need to worry. We can talk about it later. I've got a lot of work to catch up on right now.*

I hit send before I can second-guess myself, then set my phone face-down on the desk. Out of sight, out of mind.

Taking a deep breath, I turn my attention to my computer screen. The familiar interface of my social media management tool greets me, a blank canvas waiting to be filled with carefully curated content. I throw myself into the task, losing myself in the minutiae of scheduling posts, crafting captions, and selecting the perfect images to showcase my work.

Time slips by unnoticed as I work, and when I run out of things to distract myself with, I sigh. It's late enough that I could easily shut down and go upstairs, spend time with Luna and ignore it for yet another day, but something has me clicking my way into the folder on my storage drive.

Images and video files fill my screen and I instantly flush. It's not as though I haven't since been fucked repeatedly by them, but there's something different about seeing it all laid out before me like this. The raw, unedited footage of our encounter feels almost voyeuristic, even though I was an active participant.

I hesitantly click through some of the images and my heart stops when I open one I distinctly remember him capturing. It's a close up of my face right at the point of climax, I remember seeing my reflection in the lens but it had nothing on what he saw through that glass. I quickly close out of the image as my core throbs with arousal.

I swallow down my nerves and click on one of the video files.

The video starts from the beginning, it's high quality because I pride myself on my equipment. So I can clearly see the two of them standing in the center of my studio, their eyes hot and hungry as they watch me move around and finish turning all the cameras on. I never noticed it at the time, but I see it now. When I turn back to them in the video, they have focused on each other again.

I give them the go ahead and I watch as Knox reaches for River. I watch and my body feels just as hot at the replay as it did when I watched it in person. The way they move together, how perfectly they fit against each other, each touch, kiss and look clearly showing the level of intimacy and connection between the pair.

I watch, transfixed, as Knox and River move to the bed. Their bodies undulate together, all tattooed hard planes and taut muscle. Knox's hand tangles in River's hair, yanking his head back to expose the long column of his throat. River lets out a guttural moan as Knox's teeth scrape over his pulse point.

My heart races, pounding against my ribcage as if trying to escape. I strain to hear their muffled words and breathy gasps. Without thinking, I reach for the volume, turning it up until their sounds of pleasure fill the room.

"Fuck," River groans, his voice rough with desire. I didn't hear it the first time, either too distracted or it was just too low, but I hear it through the speakers. "Need her between us."

Knox growls in response, grinding his hips up against River. The friction draws a whimper from River that sends heat pooling low in my belly. I shift in my seat, thighs pressing together as arousal builds.

On screen, I see the moment I lost control of the session. River's eyes locking onto me, a wicked gleam in their depths. I hear us talking, not realizing exactly where he was leading me. In a fluid motion, he plucks the camera from my hands. I remember the jolt of surprise, the thrill of excitement as the tables turned.

Knox wastes no time, his large hands gripping my waist. I watch as I throw my professionalism out the window, but this time I watch the looks pass between them leading up to it, I can see how I had no hope of escaping what they obviously had planned. I listen as the moans and sounds from the speakers grow louder, I watch as Knox devours me. I feel my cheeks flush hot as I watch River set the camera down, angling it to capture the bed. He stalks towards us, predatory grace in every movement.

Unbidden, my own hand drifts lower, skimming over my stomach. I know I should stop, should close the video and shut down the computer.

Instead I skip ahead, unable to bear the building tension. The video jumps to the three of us on the bed, a tangle of limbs and heated skin. Louder moans and desperate whimpers echo through my speakers.

Suddenly my phone rings and I scramble to stop the video, my heart pounding as I fumble with the mouse. The sudden silence is deafening as the moans and gasps cut off abruptly, broken only by the cheerful ringtone. I look down at the screen to see who is calling, my breath catching in my throat as I read the words flashing across the display: 'Your Cute Psycho'.

For a moment, I stare at it, my mind racing. When did River add his contact name in my phone? How did he even get access to it?

With a deep breath, I steel myself and swipe to answer the call. "Hello?" My voice comes out breathier than I intended, a hint of the arousal I'd been feeling moments ago still evident in my tone.

The silence stretches for a long moment. I can almost picture River on the other end of the line, a knowing smirk playing on his lips. My heart pounds in my chest, so loudly I wonder if he can hear it through the phone.

Finally, a low, wicked chuckle breaks the quiet. "Oh sweetheart," River purrs, his voice honey-smooth and dripping with amusement, "what are you up to?"

I have to clear my throat, trying desperately to erase the huskiness from my voice. "I'm working," I insist, wincing at how unconvincing I sound even to my own ears.

River hums, the sound rich with disbelief. I can practically see him shaking his head, those Caribbean blue eyes sparkling with mirth.

I sigh, leaning forward to rest my elbows on the desk. My free hand moves to swipe over my heated face, hoping to cool my flushed cheeks. But fate, it seems, has other plans.

As I shift, my elbow catches the mouse. Before I can react, the video springs back to life on my screen. The room is suddenly filled with the unmistakable sounds of passion–breathy moans, the slap of skin on skin, and then as though to prove it could get worse Knox's voice growls loudly through the speakers, "Fuck, you feel so goddamn tight wrapped around our cocks."

For a heartbeat, I'm frozen in horror. Then I lunge for the mouse, frantically clicking to stop the playback. But in my haste, I only succeed in turning the volume up higher.

"Fuck, fuck, fuck," I mutter, my cheeks burning as I finally manage to silence the video.

The silence that follows is deafening. I hold my breath, praying that somehow, miraculously, River didn't hear any of that.

But of course, I'm not that lucky.

"Well, well, well," River's voice comes through the phone, low and dangerous. I can hear the smirk in his tone, the predatory edge that makes my stomach flip. "It seems our little Rayne has been enjoying a private show."

I open my mouth to deny it, to make up some excuse, but nothing comes out. My mind is blank, consumed by mortification and a traitorous surge of arousal.

"I..." I start, then trail off, unsure what I can possibly say to salvage this situation.

River's chuckle is dark and wicked, sending shivers down my spine. The sound reverberates through the phone, rich and velvety, wrapping around me like a physical caress. I can almost see the dangerous glint in his eyes, the way his lips would curl into that devastating smirk that never fails to make my heart race.

"Oh sweetheart," he purrs, his voice dripping with sinful promise. "You have no idea how much trouble you're in now."

Before I can formulate a response, there's a rustling on the other end of the line. I hear muffled voices, as if River is talking to someone else. My stomach flips as I realize who it must be.

Suddenly, Knox's voice fills my ear, low and commanding. The change is jarring, like being doused in ice water only to be immediately thrust into a raging inferno. Where River's tone was playful and teasing, Knox's brooks no argument. It's the voice of a man used to being obeyed without question.

"Switch to video. Now."

Chapter 30
River

I WATCH AS RAYNE's flushed face fills the screen of the phone in Knox's hand. Even through the small display, her arousal is clear–pupils dilated, cheeks stained a delicious pink, plush lips parted slightly. There's a hint of embarrassment underneath it all, but it only adds to her allure. She looks utterly delectable, and I have to clench my fists to resist reaching out to touch the screen.

We had spent the day questioning locals about any suspicious activity, investigating Rayne's stalker while we pretended to follow up on leads for our official case. It had been frustrating, hours of dead ends and unhelpful witnesses. But now, seeing Rayne like this, all of that fades away.

Knox takes control immediately, his voice dropping into that commanding tone that never fails to make both Rayne and me shiver with anticipation. "Show us what you were watching," he orders, and I can see the effect his words have on her. Her breath catches, chest rising and falling rapidly.

For a moment, she hesitates, her teeth worrying her bottom lip. I can almost see the gears turning in her head, weighing her options. But then, beautifully, she obeys. The camera angle shifts as she turns her phone, giving us a view of her computer screen.

The video is paused, but the image on display sends heat coursing through my veins. It's a frame from our photoshoot—Rayne sandwiched between Knox and me, her head thrown back in ecstasy, lips parted in a silent scream of pleasure. I remember that moment vividly—the velvet heat of her wrapped around us, the way Knox's fingers dug into her hips, the intoxicating sounds she made as we pushed her to the edge.

"Good girl," Knox purrs.

The camera swings back to Rayne's face, and the sight nearly undoes me. Her eyes are heavy-lidded, lips parted as she pants softly. There's a vulnerability in her expression that makes me want to reach through the screen and pull her into my arms.

"Tell us, baby girl," Knox growls. "Have you touched yourself while watching this?"

Rayne's blush deepens, spreading down her neck to disappear beneath the neckline of her dress. "N-no," she stammers. "I... I wanted to, but..."

"What were you thinking about while you watched it?" I chime in, unable to resist joining the game. "Were you imagining us there with you, touching you, tasting you?"

She whimpers, a soft, needy sound that goes straight to my cock. "Yes," she breathes, her voice barely above a whisper. "I was thinking about your hands on me, your mouths..."

"Show us," Knox demands, his voice rough with desire. "Put the phone somewhere so we can see all of you. And show us that pretty pussy of yours."

Rayne hesitates, there's a flicker of uncertainty in her eyes, a question she seems afraid to ask. Knox's gaze sharpens, reading something in her expression.

"We're at our apartment, sweetheart," he says, his tone softening slightly. "We had planned on showering and changing before handling some business. We were going to bide our time until we could come to you under the cover of darkness."

The tension visibly drains from Rayne's shoulders at his words. She nods, a mixture of relief and renewed arousal flooding her features. With trembling hands, she props the phone up on her desk, angling it to capture her entire body where she sits in her leather desk chair. She's wearing a simple black dress, the fabric clinging to her curves in all the right places. My mouth goes dry at the sight.

Slowly, teasingly, she reaches for the hem of her dress. Her fingers play with the fabric for a moment before she begins to inch it upwards. Inch by tantalizing inch, she reveals more of her creamy thighs. The dress rises higher, exposing the lacy edge of her panties.

"That's it, little Rayne," I encourage, my voice husky with want. "Show us what's ours."

Rayne's breath hitches at my words. In one fluid motion, she shifts and pulls the dress over her head, letting it fall to the floor beside her.

I feel my breath catch in my throat. She's left in a black lace bra and matching panties, the delicate fabric a stark contrast against her pale skin. The lingerie hugs her body perfectly, accentuating the generous swell of her breasts and the dip of her waist. Her long, dark hair cascades over her shoulders, a few errant strands falling across her collarbone in a way that makes me ache to brush them aside.

I press myself against Knox's back, feeling the solid warmth of his body against mine. My hands snake around his waist, fingertips tracing the hard planes of his abs through his shirt before drifting lower. I can feel the rigid length of him straining against his pants, and I can't resist palming him through the fabric. Knox grunts, a low, guttural sound that sends shivers down my spine.

"Take off your panties," Knox orders, his voice rough with desire. "Slowly. Show us how wet you are for us, baby girl."

Rayne's lips part, her breathing growing heavier as she hooks her thumbs under the waistband of her panties. With agonizing slowness, she begins to slide them down her thighs. The black lace catches slightly on her skin, clinging as if reluctant to let go. As she lifts her hips to work the fabric past her ass, I hear Knox's sharp intake of breath.

Finally, the panties fall to the floor, joining her discarded dress. Rayne leans back in her chair, spreading her legs to give us a full view. Even through the phone screen, I can see the glistening evidence of her arousal coating her inner thighs.

"Fuck," I breathe, my hand tightening around Knox's cock. He pushes back against me, grinding his ass against my own straining erection.

Rayne whimpers, her hips shifting restlessly in the chair. Her hand drifts down her body, fingertips grazing her stomach, inching closer to where we know she's aching to be touched.

Knox catches the movement, a wicked smirk curling his lips. "Do you like to watch, sweetheart?" he asks, his voice low and dangerous. "Do you want to see River come on my cock while we watch you play with that pretty pussy?"

Rayne's eyes widen. Her tongue darts out to wet her lips, a gesture so unconsciously sensual it makes my cock throb. She nods frantically, a breathy "Yes, please" escaping her lips.

Without taking his eyes off the screen, Knox turns his head slightly towards me. "You heard her, River," Knox growls, a glint in his eyes. "Show our girl what she wants to see."

I don't need to be told twice. My hands make quick work of Knox's belt, the clink of metal loud in the charged atmosphere. I push his pants and boxers down in one swift motion, freeing his cock. It springs free, hard and flushed.

Knox steps out of his clothes with practiced ease, his movements fluid and purposeful. He stalks towards our couch, every step radiating raw power and barely contained desire. The late afternoon sunlight streaming through the windows catches on the intricate tattoos adorning his muscular form, making the ink seem to dance across his skin.

He positions the phone carefully on the coffee table, angling it to capture the full expanse of the couch while still allowing us a clear view of the screen where Rayne watches, her eyes wide and hungry. The leather of the couch creaks softly as Knox lowers himself onto it, his powerful thighs spread wide in invitation.

Slowly he unbuttons his cuffs, then each button of his shirt before pulling it off in a smooth, effortless motion that never fails to set my blood on fire. The fabric slides over his sculpted abs, revealing more inked skin and the dusting of dark hair trailing down to his groin. He tosses the shirt aside, then raises an eyebrow at me, a silent challenge in his eyes.

I grin wickedly, feeling the familiar surge of heat and anticipation coursing through my veins. My hands move to the buttons of my own shirt, slowly undoing them one by one. I can feel his eyes on me, his gaze almost tangible as it roams over my body.

The shirt falls open, revealing the planes of my chest and stomach. I let it slide off my shoulders, pooling on the floor behind me. My pants follow suit, and I step out of them, kicking them aside. Now fully naked, I stretch languidly, putting on a show for my captive audience.

I move to the side table, retrieving the bottle of lube we keep there. The cool plastic is a stark contrast to my heated skin as I wrap my fingers around it. Knox's eyes follow my every movement, dark with lust and impatience.

As I approach the couch, I can hear Rayne's breathing growing heavier through the phone's speakers. A quick glance at the screen shows her squirming in her chair, one hand ghosting over her breast, the other inching ever closer to the apex of her thighs.

"Don't you dare touch yourself yet, baby girl," Knox growls, his voice rough with desire. "Not until I say so."

Rayne whimpers but obeys, her hands gripping the arms of her chair tightly. The sight of her restraint, the way she trembles with need, sends a fresh wave of arousal surging through me.

I come to stand between Knox's spread legs, drinking in the sight of him. His cock stands proud, flushed and hard against his stomach. I can't resist reaching out to trail my fingers along its length, reveling in the way it twitches at my touch.

Knox's hand shoots out, gripping my wrist tightly, painfully. The way I like it. "Enough teasing," he growls, turning me to face away from him and pulling me down onto his lap. I straddle Knox's muscular thighs, facing the phone propped on the coffee table. The leather of the couch is cool against my skin and his breath fans across the nape of my neck, sending shivers down my spine.

"Open yourself up for me," Knox commands, his voice a low rumble that I feel more than hear.

I uncap the bottle of lube, the sharp click echoing in the charged atmosphere. The cool gel coats my fingers as I reach down between my legs. My fingertips brush against Knox's hard length, and I feel it twitch against my skin. A smirk tugs at my lips, but before I can tease him further, Knox's large hand wraps around my wrist, guiding my fingers to my entrance.

Slowly, teasingly, I circle my entrance with slick fingers. The muscles there flutter under my touch, anticipation building low in my gut. Knox's hands grip my hips tightly, his fingers digging into the flesh hard enough to bruise. The slight pain only heightens my arousal.

"That's it," Knox murmurs, his lips brushing the shell of my ear. "Get that tight little hole nice and wet for me. Show Rayne how you get ready for my cock."

At the mention of her name, my eyes flick to the phone screen. Rayne is watching us intently, her chest heaving with each ragged breath. Her hands are clenched tightly on the arms of her chair, knuckles white with the effort of restraining herself.

I press one finger inside myself, a low moan slipping past my lips at the sensation. Knox's hips buck slightly, his cock sliding against the cleft of my ass. I work the finger in and out, gradually adding a second. The stretch burns deliciously.

Suddenly, Knox's fingers join mine. He pushes two thick digits in alongside my own, and I whimper at the sudden fullness. His other arm wraps around my waist, holding me steady as he begins to pump his fingers in and out.

"Fuck," I gasp, my head falling back against his shoulder. "Knox..."

He scissors his fingers, stretching me further. The burn intensifies, riding the knife's edge between pleasure and pain. My thighs quiver with the effort of holding myself up.

On the screen, Rayne whimpers. She's shifting restlessly in her chair, her thighs pressing together as if seeking friction. Her eyes are dark with lust, fixed on where Knox's fingers disappear inside me.

"Please," she breathes, her voice barely audible through the phone's speakers. "Can I... can I touch myself?"

Knox chuckles darkly, the sound vibrating through his chest and into my back. "Not yet, baby girl," he says. "But you can play with those pretty tits of yours. Show us how sensitive they are."

Rayne doesn't hesitate. Her hands fly to her breasts, still encased in black lace. She kneads the soft flesh, her head falling back as she pinches and rolls her nipples through the delicate fabric. A soft moan escapes her parted lips, the sound sending a jolt of arousal straight through me.

I feel Knox shift behind me. His fingers withdraw, leaving me feeling achingly empty. "Enough," he growls, his voice rough with desire. "I need to be inside you. Now."

I whimper at the loss, but eagerly lift my hips, positioning myself over his straining cock. Knox's hands grip my waist, guiding me down onto him with agonizing slowness. The blunt head of his cock presses against my entrance, and I take a deep breath, willing my body to relax.

Inch by delicious inch, I sink down onto him. The stretch is intense, bordering on painful, but in the most exquisite way. I can feel every ridge, every vein of his thick length as it fills me completely.

When I'm fully seated, I pause, panting heavily. Knox is breathing hard too, his chest heaving against my back. I can feel the tension in his body, the way he's restraining himself from thrusting up into me.

"Fuck," I groan, my head falling back against his shoulder. "So fucking good."

His only response is a guttural growl as his hips snap up, driving himself even deeper inside me. I cry out, my back arching at the sudden movement.

On the screen, Rayne whimpers. Her hands are still on her breasts, fingers toying with her nipples through the lace of her bra. Her hips rock subtly, unconsciously seeking friction.

"Look at her, River," Knox murmurs in my ear, his voice low and dangerous. "Look at how badly she wants to touch herself. How desperate she is to feel what you're feeling right now."

I meet Rayne's gaze through the screen, seeing the raw need in her eyes. "Please," she whispers, her voice breathy and strained. "Please, I need..."

"Not yet," Knox says firmly. "You'll wait until we say so. Until you've earned it."

With that, he begins to move in earnest. His hips snap up, driving into me with brutal force. He knows just how I like it, hard and unrestrained. Each thrust sends shockwaves of pleasure coursing through my body. I brace my hands on his thighs, using the leverage to meet him thrust for thrust.

The room fills with the sounds of our pleasure–skin slapping against skin, our mingled moans and grunts, and Rayne's soft whimpers from the phone.

Knox's hand snakes around my body, wrapping around my neglected cock. His grip is tight, almost painfully so, as he strokes me in time with his thrusts. The dual sensations are overwhelming, pushing me rapidly towards the edge.

"That's it," Knox growls, his breath hot against my ear. "Fuck yourself on my cock."

I ride Knox with abandon, my body moving in perfect sync with his powerful thrusts. Every nerve ending feels electrified, sparks of pleasure shooting through me with each roll of our hips. The coil of tension in my core winds tighter and tighter, threatening to snap at any moment.

Knox's grip on my cock is relentless, his calloused palm dragging exquisitely along my length. His thumb swipes over the sensitive head on each upstroke, spreading the beads of precum gathering there. The slick sound of his hand working me mingles with the obscene slap of skin on skin.

"Fuck, fuck, fuck," I chant, the words falling from my lips in a breathless litany. My thighs burn with the effort of lifting and lowering myself onto Knox's thick length, but the ache only adds to the overwhelming sensations.

I can feel my climax approaching rapidly, a tingling heat spreading from the base of my spine outward. My balls draw up tight against my body, ready to release. Just as I'm about to tumble over the edge, Knox's voice cuts through the haze of pleasure.

"Don't you dare come yet," he growls. "Remember, not until I say so."

I whimper, fighting against my body's desperate need for release. It takes every ounce of willpower to hold back, to force down the impending orgasm. My muscles tremble with the effort, sweat beading on my skin.

"Good boy," Knox purrs, rewarding me with a particularly deep thrust that has me seeing stars. "Now, Rayne. Fuck that pretty pussy with your fingers. Show us how wet you are for us. And keep your eyes on us, your pleasure belongs to us now."

My eyes snap to the phone screen just in time to see Rayne's hand dip between her spread thighs. She gasps as her fingers make contact with her slick folds, her head falling back against the chair. The sight of her pleasuring herself, knowing it's because of us, nearly undoes me.

"Oh god," Rayne moans, her fingers working furiously at her clit. "Oh fuck, you two look so hot together. I wish I was there, I wish I could feel you both inside me again."

Her words send a fresh wave of arousal shooting through me. I clench around Knox's cock, drawing a guttural groan from him. His hips snap up harder, faster, driving into me with bruising force.

Rayne's moans and whimpers join mine, filling the air with a symphony of pleasure. Her eyes are locked on us, drinking in every detail of our joined, sweat slicked bodies. I can see the flush spreading across her chest, the way her breasts heave with each panting breath. She's already close, her movements growing frantic as she chases her release.

"That's it, baby girl," Knox encourages, his voice rough with exertion. "Come for us. Let us see how pretty you look."

Rayne's eyes roll back as her orgasm crashes over her. Her body arches beautifully, a strangled cry escaping her parted lips. I watch, mesmerized, as waves of pleasure wash over her features. She's breathtaking in her ecstasy, utterly abandoned to the sensations wracking her body.

The sight of her coming undone is too much. "Knox," I gasp, my voice breaking. "Please, I need to come. Please let me come."

Knox's hips stutter, his rhythm faltering as he nears his own climax. "Come now," he growls, his hand tightening around my cock.

His permission is all I need. With a hoarse shout, I let go, surrendering to the overwhelming pleasure. My release paints my chest and Knox's hand in thick ropes as my body convulses. Knox fucks me through it, his thrusts growing erratic as he chases his own orgasm.

With a guttural groan, Knox buries himself deep inside me one last time. I feel the hot pulse of his release filling me. We stay like that for a long moment, both panting heavily, our bodies trembling with aftershocks.

Slowly, carefully, I lift myself off Knox's softening cock. A trickle of his cum leaks down my thigh as I collapse onto the couch beside him. Knox immediately pulls me against his side, his arm wrapping around my shoulders. He presses a soft sweet kiss to my lips, it's his way of checking in and reassuring me without words.

Our attention turns back to the phone screen. Rayne is slumped in her chair, looking thoroughly debauched. Her chest heaves as she catches her breath, a satisfied smile playing on her lips.

"Fuck," she breathes, her voice husky. "That was..."

"Incredible," I finish for her, a lazy grin spreading across my face.

Knox hums in agreement, his fingers tracing idle patterns on my shoulder. "You did so well, baby girl," he praises, his voice warm with affection. "Both of you did."

Rayne blushes at the compliment, ducking her head slightly. It's endearing how she can still be shy after what we have shared.

"Now," Knox continues, his tone shifting to something more serious. "Tell us about this package you received."

Chapter 31

Knox

THE CITY IS QUIET as we pull up in the alleyway behind Rayne's building in the early hours of the morning. Streetlights cast long shadows across the empty sidewalks, the usual bustle of daytime traffic replaced by an eerie stillness. I kill the engine, sitting for a moment in the darkness of the car as I breathe through the chaos of thoughts in my mind.

River's hand finds mine across the center console, his touch grounding me. "You good?" he asks softly, his blue eyes searching my face in the dim light.

I nod, squeezing his hand before releasing it to exit the vehicle. We'd spent the evening poring over security cameras and chasing down leads that all led to dead ends. No matter which direction we look or what time of day it is, they manage to know exactly where the cameras are to hide their identity. The frustration of another fruitless day weighs heavily on my shoulders.

River walks beside me, his usual cheerful demeanor subdued. His eyes scan our surroundings constantly, alert for any sign of the stalker who's been tormenting Rayne. I can see the tension in the set of his shoulders, the predatory grace in his movements. He's like a coiled spring, ready to unleash violence at a moment's notice.

I love when he is like this, on the edge and ready to draw blood, I just wish it wasn't because Rayne was in danger.

As we approach the building, I fish out the key we copied long ago, using it to slip silently into her studio. The studio is dark and silent as we enter, the familiar scent of Rayne lingering in the air. My eyes adjust quickly to the dimness, scanning for any signs of disturbance.

I move to the side table where Rayne said she left the note. The creamy card stands out starkly against the dark wood, the blood-red ink a sinister contrast. With gloved hands, I carefully lift the note, my jaw clenching as I read the possessive words even though she prepared us for what it said. I want to tear it to shreds and use it for kindling but instead I slide it into an evidence bag, sealing it with practiced efficiency. We will check it for prints but there won't be any, just like there wasn't with the others.

River touches my arm lightly, a silent signal that he's finished his own inspection of the studio. I nod, and we make our way to the staircase leading up to Rayne's apartment. Each step is carefully placed, our movements fluid and silent. Years of training and shared experience allow us to move as one, perfectly in sync.

We slip inside her apartment, closing the door behind us with barely a whisper of sound. The space is bathed in shadows, moonlight filtering through the partially drawn curtains to cast strange, elongated shapes across the floor.

A soft meow breaks the silence, and I turn to see Rayne's cat padding towards us, her grey fur almost silver in the dim light. Her amber eyes fix on me accusingly, as if I've personally offended her by arriving empty-handed. It makes me feel like she is an addict and I'm some sort of dealer that's arrived without her latest fix. River crouches down, extending his hand to the feline. Her tail swishes once, imperiously, considering him for a moment before deigning to accept his attention, rubbing her head against his palm. "Hey there, beautiful," he murmurs, his voice barely audible.

I watch the interaction with a mixture of amusement and exasperation. The damn cat has never warmed to me, despite my best efforts. But with River, she's putty in his hands. He scratches behind her ears, eliciting a louder purr.

I leave River to placate the cat, moving deeper into the apartment. My eyes roam over every surface, every shadow, searching for anything out of place. The living room is as we left it, with the exception of a throw blanket draped haphazardly over the arm of the couch, as if Rayne had just risen from a nap.

Having now moved to the kitchen, River is already opening the fridge, his movements swift and purposeful. He examines the contents critically, checking expiration dates and assessing the freshness of the produce. It's a habit of his. Too many years of going hungry, of barely surviving on scraps.

He grabs a bag and removes a few items and I know he will be sneaking back in later to replace them without her knowing. Unless he makes it a lot more obvious like last time.

As River methodically works through his demons, my gaze drifts absently around the apartment again and something near the apartment door catches my eye. At first, it's just a vague dark spot on the floor, barely noticeable in the dim light. Frowning, I move closer, pulling out my phone to illuminate the area.

The beam of light reveals a small, crumpled object. My breath catches as I realize what I'm looking at. A rose petal, its deep crimson hue unmistakable even in the harsh glare of my phone's flashlight. But it's not just the petal that sends a chill down my spine. Next to it, almost invisible against the dark hardwood, are a few tiny droplets. Blood.

My mind races, piecing together the scene. The stalker must have tried to gain entry, likely attempting to leave another "gift" for Rayne in the form of more roses. But something—or someone—stopped them.

I crouch down, examining the area more closely. There are faint scratch marks on the door frame, barely perceptible unless you know what to look for. They're low to the ground, about the height a cat might reach if it were rearing up on its hind legs.

Suddenly, Luna's earlier behavior makes perfect sense. Her accusatory stare, the way she seemed to be demanding something from us. She wasn't just being a typically aloof feline—she was expecting praise. Recognition for a job well done.

"River," I call softly, my voice tight with a mixture of anger and grudging respect. "Come take a look at this."

He's at my side in an instant, his eyes widening as he takes in the scene. "Is that...?"

I nod grimly. "Looks like our little gatekeeper here did more than just keep watch." I gesture towards the cat, who has followed River and is now sitting regally a few feet away, her tail curled neatly around her paws. In the dim light, her amber eyes seem to glow with an almost supernatural intelligence.

River crouches down, extending his hand towards the cat once more. This time, she approaches more eagerly, butting her head against his palm with a soft chirp. "You're quite the fierce protector, aren't you?" he murmurs, scratching under her chin. She preens under the attention, her purr growing louder.

I shake my head, a reluctant smile tugging at my lips. "I'll be damned," I mutter. "Never thought I'd be grateful for that furball."

River shoots me a reproachful look, but there's a glimmer of amusement in his eyes. "Don't let her hear you call her that. She might decide you're not worthy anymore even with your bribes."

I snort, but I can't deny the swell of affection I feel for the cat. She protected Rayne when we couldn't be here. That alone earns her a lifetime supply of the fanciest cat food money can buy.

River murmurs that he will go get the kit from the car and he slips out the door silently. He is only gone a few moments before he's back, kneeling down while I continue to shine my camera light on the area for him to take a sample of the blood so we can run it for DNA. There isn't much there and I doubt there is even enough but we will still try. River extracts a sterile cotton bud from the case and delicately swabs at the tiny crimson drops, rotating the tip to collect as much of the scant evidence as possible. His brow furrows in concentration, his movements meticulous.

When he has captured what little he can, River seals the swab in a clear plastic tube, securing the cap with a click. Even such a minuscule sample could potentially yield priceless information if properly processed and analyzed. He stows the tube carefully in the interior pocket of his jacket.

Satisfied that we've collected everything possible from the area, River rises gracefully to his feet. His eyes meet mine, a silent exchange passing between us. A muscle ticks in his jaw, the only outward sign of the fury simmering beneath his calm exterior.

I can read the promise in his gaze—whoever this bastard is, they won't get away with threatening what's ours. Rayne's safety is paramount, and we'll stop at nothing to eliminate this threat. Permanently.

"You know what this means, right?" he says, his voice low and dangerous.

I meet his gaze, seeing the feral viciousness flash in his eyes. His bloodlust is hovering just below the surface, barely contained. I feel an answering surge of violent anticipation course through my veins.

"The stalker hasn't tried to enter before. They're escalating. We can't keep splitting our attention between the serial killer case and the stalker," I growl, my fists clenching at my sides. "The deaths have to stop."

River nods, his expression hardening. "Agreed."

We move as one, silently making our way down the hallway to Rayne's bedroom. The door is slightly ajar, and we slip inside without a sound.

Moonlight spills through the gap in the curtains, casting a silver glow across the room. Rayne lies curled on her side, her dark hair fanned out across the pillow. The sheet has slipped down, revealing the curve of her shoulder and the soft swell of her breast. She looks peaceful, untroubled by the dangers circling ever closer.

River's hand finds mine, squeezing gently. I know he is having to force himself not to go to her, not to brush her hair from her face or lie there and play with it. We stand there for a long moment, watching the steady rise and fall of her chest. In sleep, she looks impossibly innocent and vulnerable. Even though we know she isn't. The urge to protect her, to shield her from all harm, rises up in me with overwhelming force. That need, that urge is a part of me now.

But we don't wake her, can't burden her with the knowledge of how close the danger truly came this time. So we let her continue sleeping, blissfully unaware.

Letting go of River's hand, I move silently to the bed. I want badly to slide into bed beside her, to feel the warmth of her body against mine, to bury myself inside her and stay there until the world fades away. The urge is almost overwhelming, a physical ache that resonates through my entire being. I can almost taste her on my tongue, can almost feel the silken heat of her wrapped around me.

But I resist, forcing myself to focus on the task at hand. I reach for her phone on the bedside table, the device unlocking as soon as I lift it, recognizing my face from me programming it in long ago. The soft blue glow of the screen illuminates my features, casting eerie shadows across the room.

I navigate to her alarm settings and the alarm for 6 a.m stares back. With a quick tap, I disable it, ensuring she'll sleep in. She needs to rest.

As I set the phone back down, my eyes are drawn once again to Rayne. A small frown creases her brow for a moment, and I have to resist the urge to smooth it away with my thumb. Instead, I allow my gaze to roam over her, committing every detail to memory for the millionth time. The way her lashes fan out against her cheeks, impossibly long and delicate. The soft fullness of her lips, slightly parted as she breathes. The elegant line of her collarbone, begging to be traced with fingers and tongues.

A soft rustle behind me reminds me of River's presence. I turn to find him watching me, his eyes dark with a mixture of desire and understanding. He knows exactly what I'm feeling because he feels it too. The need to touch, to claim, to protect.

With a silent nod, we both move towards the door. But before we leave, I pause, turning back for one last look. Rayne has shifted in her sleep, one arm now flung out across the empty space beside her. As if even in sleep, she's reaching for us.

The sight makes my chest tighten with an emotion. I swallow hard, forcing down the lump in my throat.

We slip out of the room as silently as we entered, leaving Rayne to her peaceful slumber. As we make our way back through the apartment, Luna appears from the shadows. She meows softly, as if bidding us farewell.

I crouch down, extending my hand towards her. To my surprise, she deigns to approach, butting her head against my palm. "Good girl," I murmur, scratching behind her ears. "Keep watching over her for us."

Luna purrs contentedly, arching into my touch. For a moment, I'm struck by how surreal this all is—praising a cat for fending off a stalker, sneaking around the apartment of the woman we're both obsessed with. But then, nothing about our lives has ever been normal.

River collects the bag from the kitchen bench, carefully checking its contents one last time. His movements are swift and silent, his blue eyes, usually sparkling with mischief, are now focused and intense as he mentally catalogs each item.

I watch him from the doorway, marveling at the care he takes in this simple task as he finishes and heads toward me. It's more than just restocking her fridge; it's an act of devotion, a tangible expression of his need to provide and protect. This side of him—the nurturer, the provider—never fails to warm my heart. It's a stark contrast to the cheerful psychopath the world sees, the man who can slit a throat with a smile. But this, this is the River only I get to see.

And soon so will Rayne.

The thought of him cooking for her makes my chest tighten with anticipation and longing. I can almost see her face lighting up as she takes that first bite, her eyes widening in delight. The pride and joy that would radiate from River at her reaction, his eyes sparkling with happiness.

Then I'm sure he would fuck her over the table between the potatoes and peas.

Chapter 32

Rayne

I STARTLE AWAKE, MY eyes flying open as something cold and wet presses against my cheek. A loud, insistent meow pierces the fog of sleep,
and I find myself staring into Luna's amber eyes, mere inches from
my face. Her whiskers twitch as she lets out another plaintive cry,
clearly displeased.

"Alright, alright," I mumble, my voice thick with sleep. "I'm up."

Sunlight streams through the gap in my curtains, painting golden
stripes across my rumpled bed sheets and the air conditioning is
already struggling against the heat again. The light seems unusually
bright, and I squint against its intensity as I fumble for my phone on
the nightstand. Luna takes this opportunity to headbutt my hand,
demanding attention. With a sigh, I oblige, scratching behind her
ears as I finally manage to grab my phone.

I blink blearily at the screen, waiting for my eyes to focus on the
numbers displayed there. When they do, a jolt of adrenaline surges
through me, instantly banishing any lingering drowsiness.

"Shit!" I bolt upright in bed, nearly dislodging Luna from her
perch beside me. The cat lets out an indignant meow, jumping
gracefully to the floor. "No, no, no. This can't be right."

But the glowing numbers on my phone screen don't lie. It's well
past 10 a.m, hours later than I'd planned to wake up. My mind races,

trying to make sense of the situation. I could have sworn I set my alarm for 6 a.m last night when I came to bed.

"Fuck," I mutter, running a hand through my tangled hair. "Luna, why didn't you wake me earlier?"

The cat, now sitting primly on the floor, merely blinks at me, as if to say, *"Not my job, human."*

I throw off the sheet, swinging my legs over the side of the bed. The cool hardwood floor beneath my feet sends a shiver up my spine, but I barely notice as I tap frantically through my phone. There it is—my usual 6 AM alarm, clearly switched off. But I don't remember doing that. Did I disable it in my sleep? It wouldn't be the first time my subconscious decided I needed more rest.

A frustrated groan escapes me as I realize how this throws off my entire day. I had a whole list of errands I wanted to run before diving into work—a package to drop off, dry cleaning to pick up, getting groceries in the daylight instead of night for once. Now, with client inquiries to respond to and a mountain of editing waiting for me, there's no time for any of it.

"Don't look at me like that," I grumble at her, shooting Luna a glare. "This is your fault. You're supposed to be my backup alarm."

Luna blinks slowly at me, utterly unimpressed by my accusation. She yawns widely, showing off her tiny pink tongue and sharp teeth, before sauntering out of the room. Clearly, she considers her duties fulfilled.

With a resigned sigh, I head for the bathroom. I remind myself of one of the perks of being my own boss—I don't have to rush. Sure, I've overslept, but there's no angry supervisor waiting to reprimand me, no time clock to punch. I can still take a moment to breathe, to center myself before diving into the day.

The bathroom mirror reflects a slightly disheveled version of myself—hair mussed from sleep, eyes still heavy-lidded. I turn on the shower, letting the water heat up and steam begins to fill the small space, fogging the mirror and wrapping around me like a warm embrace.

I step under the spray, letting out a contented sigh as the hot water cascades over my body. The steady drumming of droplets against my skin helps to wash away the last remnants of sleep, invigorating me for the day ahead. I quickly work shampoo through my long dark hair, but nothing can compare now to how it felt when River did it.

I grab my favorite lavender-scented body wash, lathering it between my hands before smoothing it over my skin. The familiar scent fills the steamy air, soothing my frazzled nerves. As I work the suds across my body, my mind drifts to the events of yesterday and a shiver runs through me that has nothing to do with the water temperature.

Shaking off those distracting thoughts, I quickly finish washing up, regretfully cutting my shower shorter than I'd like. While I may not have a traditional boss, I do have responsibilities, and a growing list of tasks won't complete themselves.

I dress quickly, pulling on simple black lace lingerie before slipping into one of the loose, flowing dresses I prefer. As a boudoir photographer I know the power of lingerie, including on the person wearing it simply for themselves. The soft fabric of my dress caresses my skin as I move, the hem swishing around my calves. The deep blue color brings out the sapphire tones in my eyes, and the loose fit skims over my curves without clinging. I relish the feel of the cool fabric against my skin. It's perfect for the sweltering heat outside, allowing air to circulate while still looking put-together enough for any impromptu client meetings.

As I make my way to the kitchen, the hardwood floor cool beneath my bare feet, Luna appears as if summoned. She weaves between my legs, nearly tripping me, her meows growing more insistent with each step. "Yes, yes, I know," I mutter, reaching down to scratch behind her ears. "Breakfast time for the queen, right?"

I open the fridge, the cool air washing over me as I reach for one of the cans of gourmet cat food River had left. My hand pauses as I grab it, a small frown creasing my brow. I could have sworn there were only three cans left yesterday after I'd used one, but now there are four sitting neatly in a row.

For a moment, I stand there, staring at the cans as if they might offer an explanation. Had I miscounted yesterday? Or perhaps I'm more sleep-deprived than I thought. Luna's impatient meow breaks me from my reverie, and I shake off the odd feeling. Whatever the explanation, it's hardly the strangest thing to happen lately.

I quickly blend up a smoothie while Luna eagerly devours her breakfast. The whir of the blender fills the kitchen as I toss in a mix of frozen berries, banana, spinach, and almond milk. The vibrant purple concoction swirls hypnotically, tiny flecks of green from the spinach dancing through the vortex.

As Luna licks her bowl clean, I transfer the smoothie to a glass and rinse the blender, the cool water sluicing over my hands. Droplets cling to my fingers, catching the morning light streaming through the window and scattering tiny rainbows across the sink.

With a final scratch behind Luna's ears, I grab my smoothie and head for the door. The lock clicks softly behind me as I step into the stairwell.

At the bottom, I pause, my free hand resting on the banister. My eyes scan the studio, drinking in every detail. Sunlight streams through the high windows, dust specks dancing lazily in the golden beams. The polished hardwood gleams, reflecting the light. My gaze is drawn to the floor near the entrance. I hold my breath, scrutinizing every inch. But there's nothing there—no envelopes, no roses, no ominous packages, no signs of disturbance. Just a clean, empty floor.

I release the breath I'd been holding, my shoulders relaxing slightly. Maybe I am being paranoid. Maybe it's a good thing I slept in, I hadn't thought about my unwanted stalker when I planned my errands.

Shaking off the lingering unease, I make my way to my desk. The familiar space welcomes me, my computer humming softly as it wakes from sleep mode. I settle into my chair, the leather creaking slightly as it molds to my body.

As I take a sip of my smoothie, the sweet-tart flavor bursting across my tongue, I try to focus on the day ahead. There's work to be done, clients to contact, images to edit. No time for paranoid thoughts or mysterious stalkers.

But even as I immerse myself in my tasks, a small part of my mind remains alert, watchful. Just in case.

As my computer screen flickers to life, I'm instantly reminded of exactly what I was doing the night before. The folder of Knox and River's session is still open, dominating my display. My breath catches as I'm confronted with a sea of thumbnails, each one a snapshot of raw passion and desire.

I shift in my chair, uncomfortably aware of the warmth pooling low in my belly. This is precisely why I shouldn't be looking at these images right now. How can I possibly maintain any semblance of professional objectivity when just looking at the thumbnails has me ready to combust?

For a wild moment, I consider giving Knox a refund and moving all the files to another drive–a personal one, for my own private use. The thought of having these images, this record of our passion, all to myself is tempting. I could revisit that night whenever I wanted, could lose myself in the memories without the pressure of delivering a final product.

But no. That wouldn't be right. As much as I might want to keep these images for myself, they don't belong to me alone. They belong to Knox and River too, and they trusted me to capture this intimate moment for them. I can't betray that trust, no matter how much I might want to.

With a deep breath, I force myself to navigate out of the folder. The thumbnails disappear, taking with them the temptation to lose myself in those heated memories. Instead, I open my administration console, determined to focus on more mundane tasks.

As I scan through my emails and messages, a small smile tugs at my lips. Breanna has already made her final image selections from her recent session. I open Breanna's selections, my smile widening as I see which images she's chosen. They're all stunning shots, capturing her journey from hesitant to empowered. I make a mental note to reach out to her later, to check in and see how she's feeling now that she's had time to really look at the photos.

I dive into editing Breanna's photos, grateful for the distraction from my more complicated thoughts and feelings. As I work, I lose myself in the familiar rhythm of adjusting colors, smoothing skin, enhancing the natural beauty of my client. It's meditative, allowing my mind to quiet and focus solely on the task at hand.

Hours slip by unnoticed as I work my way through Breanna's selections. The world outside my studio fades away as I focus intently on bringing out the best in each image.

A sudden knock at the door startles me from my focused state. I blink, realizing how stiff my body has become after hunching over my computer. Stretching languidly, I feel my muscles protest, joints popping as I extend my arms overhead. The early afternoon sun slants through the windows at a different angle now.

I stand, wincing slightly as blood flow returns to my legs. My bare feet pad silently across the cool floor as I make my way to the entrance. As I approach the door, a flicker of unease ripples through me. My hand hovers over the doorknob, fingers trembling slightly. For a wild moment, I wish I had a weapon. But of course, I don't. I'm in my own studio, a place that's always felt safe. Until recently.

Taking a deep breath, I steel myself and open the door. The first thing I see is a large travel coffee cup from my favorite local bakery. The familiar logo brings an involuntary smile to my face. The rich aroma of freshly brewed coffee wafts towards me, making my mouth water. As my eyes travel up from the large travel cup, they meet a pair of striking Caribbean blue eyes, twinkling with mischief. River stands before me, his trademark wicked grin spreading across his face.

The sight of him sends a jolt through my system more potent than any caffeine could provide.

He's leaning casually against the doorframe, one hand holding out the coffee while the other is tucked into the pocket of his tailored slacks. His crisp white shirt is rolled up to the elbows, revealing the corded muscles of his forearms and swirls and lines of the tattoos that wind their way up his skin. A loosened tie hangs around his neck, the deep blue silk complementing his eyes perfectly.

As my gaze drifts past River, I notice Knox standing just behind him. My breath catches in my throat. Knox is dressed similarly to River, in a crisp white shirt and tailored slacks that hug his powerful thighs in all the right ways. His sleeves are also rolled up, revealing the intricate tattoos that wind their way up his forearms. The top few buttons of his shirt are undone, offering a tantalizing glimpse of tanned skin and the edges of his intricate tattoos.

Knox's dark hair is slightly tousled, as if he's been running his hands through it all day. The hint of stubble along his strong jawline makes me ache to reach out and touch him, to feel the rough texture against my palm. His hazel eyes, flecked with gold and green, meet mine with an intensity that makes my knees weak.

I find myself lost in the sight of them, drinking in every detail. The way River's golden hair catches the afternoon sunlight, creating a halo effect around his head. The subtle shift of muscles beneath Knox's shirt as he adjusts his stance. The contrast between River's easy, wicked grin and Knox's smoldering gaze. They're a study in opposites that somehow fit together perfectly–light and dark, mischief and intensity, playfulness and control.

A low chuckle breaks me from my reverie. I blink, realizing I've been staring openly at them for far too long.

River waves the coffee at me again, the rich aroma wafting towards me. "We come bearing sustenance," he says, his voice a sexy purr that sends shivers down my spine.

I blink, trying to gather my scattered thoughts. "Since when do either of you knock?" I manage to ask, my voice coming out huskier than I intended.

Knox's eyes darken at my tone, but it's River who answers. "Since someone else is stalking you and could be watching," he says, his cheerful tone at odds with the serious nature of his words.

The reminder of my stalker is like a bucket of ice water, dousing the warmth that had been building in my core. I feel my shoulders tense, my eyes darting past them to scan the street behind them.

"Step back and let us in," Knox orders, his voice low and commanding. There's an edge to his tone.

I comply without hesitation, retreating into the safety of my studio. River follows close behind, his presence warm at my back. As Knox enters, he turns to lock the door. The soft click of it sliding into place echoes in the sudden silence.

Chapter 33
Rayne

RIVER SETS THE COFFEE and a small box I hadn't noticed before on the side table. The box is pristine white, a stark contrast to the dark wood beneath it. My brow furrows as I stare at it, a chill running down my spine. Was another "gift" left? But no, this box is different–white instead of the plain brown of yesterday's package.

I'm so distracted by the sight of the box that I don't notice Knox approaching until his hand is on the back of my neck, large and warm against my skin. His touch is firm, fingers tangling in the soft hairs at my nape. He draws me into a soft, slow kiss that makes my toes curl. His lips move against mine, coaxing a small sigh from me. I melt into him, my body molding to his as if we were made to fit together.

When we finally part, I'm breathless. "I thought you were being careful," I whisper, my voice barely audible. "In case I was being watched."

Knox's eyes, a swirling mix of green and gold, bore into mine. "No," he murmurs, his breath ghosting over my lips. "We need whoever it is to be curious instead of angry. We didn't want them storming off at us coming in unannounced, we want them to see this is an official visit and get closer to find out why."

My eyes widen, my heart stuttering in my chest. "Why?" I breathe, searching Knox's face for answers.

River steps closer, his presence warm at my back. "They always avoid the known cameras," he explains, his voice low and intense. "So we installed some more in the middle of the night, but facing out all the windows. If the stalker comes to investigate, we should hopefully get a face shot."

I blink rapidly, my attention ping-ponging between the two men. The realization hits me like a physical blow—they weren't really here to see me. They want to solve a case. Am I too much of a burden to them?

The thought sends a cold tendril of doubt coiling through my gut. I take an unconscious step back, bumping into River's solid chest. His arms come around me instinctively, steadying me.

"Rayne?" Knox's voice is tinged with concern. His brow furrows as he studies my face, clearly sensing the shift in my mood.

I shake my head, trying to dispel the negative thoughts. "It's nothing," I mutter, averting my gaze. But even as I say it, I can feel myself withdrawing, building walls around my heart.

River's arms tighten around me, his chest rumbling as he speaks. "Oh no, little Rayne. Don't you dare start thinking what I think you're thinking."

I stiffen in his embrace, feeling exposed and vulnerable. How can he read me so easily? Am I that transparent? The doubts swirl in my mind, growing louder with each passing second.

Knox narrows his eyes at me, his gaze sharp and assessing as he rubs a thumb across his lower lip. For a moment, I imagine he's rubbing away the taste of me, erasing the evidence of our kiss. The thought sends a pang through my chest, intensifying the swirl of insecurity already churning in my gut.

I'm acutely aware of how I must look to them—tall and awkward, too curvy, too large. Nothing like the svelte, graceful women I'm sure they're used to. My loose dress suddenly feels like a shapeless sack, hiding my flaws but also obscuring any hint of femininity. I resist the urge to cross my arms over my chest, to make myself smaller under their scrutiny.

River's teeth graze the back of my neck, a sharp nip that sends shivers cascading down my spine. His breath is warm against my skin as he speaks, voice low and husky. "You're thinking too loud, little Rayne. And I bet every thought in that pretty head of yours is wrong."

I open my mouth to protest, but before I can form the words, Knox moves. He takes two swift steps away from us, his broad shoulders taut with tension. My heart sinks, convinced he's about to leave, to walk away from the complicated mess I've become. But then he stops, turning back to face us with a predatory grace that steals my breath.

"Come here," Knox commands, his voice a low growl that reverberates through my body. River's arms loosen around me, his hands sliding to my hips. With gentle pressure, he propels me forward toward Knox. My bare feet glide across the cool hardwood, each step bringing me closer to Knox's imposing form.

As I reach him, Knox's strong hands wrap around my upper arms, his touch firm yet tender. He turns me with deliberate slowness until I'm facing the ornate full-length mirror propped in the corner of the studio. The antique gold frame gleams in the afternoon light.

In the reflection, I see myself–tall and curvy, the loose fabric of my dress rippling softly with each breath. Knox stands close behind me, his broad chest nearly touching my back. The contrast between us is striking–his crisp white shirt against the deep blue of my dress, his tanned skin a warm backdrop to my paler complexion.

I turn my head, intending to locate River, but Knox's arm snakes around my body. His fingers grip my chin firmly, forcing me to face forward again. The pads of his fingers are slightly calloused, a delicious friction against my skin.

"Eyes on the mirror, baby girl," Knox growls, his lips brushing the shell of my ear. "I want you to see what we see when we look at you."

Knox's hand splays across my stomach, the heat of his palm seeping through the thin fabric of my dress. His fingers flex, pressing me back against his solid chest. I can feel the steady thrum of his heartbeat against my spine, a soothing counterpoint to my own racing pulse.

"Look at yourself, Rayne," Knox commands, his voice a low rumble that I feel more than hear. "Really look."

I force myself to meet my own gaze in the mirror. My eyes are wide, pupils dilated with a mixture of arousal and uncertainty. A flush has spread across my cheeks, staining them a delicate pink. My long, dark hair falls in soft waves over my shoulders, framing my face.

Knox's eyes lock with mine in the reflection. The intensity of his gaze makes me want to look away, but his grip on my chin prevents it. "You encourage others to love themselves almost every day," he says, his voice soft but firm. "You show them their beauty, their strength, their worth. But you neglect to take any of your own words to heart."

His words hit me like a physical blow. I want to protest, to deny it, but I know he's right. How many times have I told my clients to embrace their bodies, to love themselves unconditionally, while secretly criticizing every perceived flaw in my own reflection?

"We see you, Rayne," Knox continues, his lips brushing against my ear. "We see all of you. Your strength, your compassion, your fierce protectiveness of those you care about. We see the way you light up when you're behind the camera, how you come alive as you work your magic. The way you coax beauty and confidence out of even the most hesitant subjects."

His hand slides up from my stomach, skimming over my ribs to cup my breast through the thin fabric of my dress. I gasp at the contact, my nipple hardening against his palm.

"We see this body that you try so hard to hide," Knox murmurs, his voice low and intense. "These lush curves that you drape in loose fabric, as if you're ashamed of them. But there's nothing to be ashamed of, Rayne. Your body is a work of art."

His other hand releases my chin, trailing down my neck to trace my collarbone. "Your skin is like porcelain, flawless and soft. I want to map every inch of it with my tongue, to learn every freckle and beauty mark."

Knox's hands move to my hips, gripping them firmly. He pulls me back against him, and I can feel the hard length of him pressing against my ass. "These hips were made for our hands," he growls. "Perfect for gripping as we thrust into you, for steadying you as you ride us."

"Your breasts," he murmurs, cupping them gently through my dress, "are perfect. Full and soft, they fit my hands like they were made for me. I love the way they bounce when you move, the way your nipples harden at the slightest touch."

He trails his fingers down my stomach, splaying his hand across my abdomen again. "This softness here, it's not a flaw. It's a testament to your strength, to the life your body has lived. It's beautiful, just like every other part of you."

Knox's hands move to my thighs, squeezing gently. "These legs... They're long and shapely, strong enough to wrap around my waist and hold me close as I fuck you."

His voice drops lower, becoming almost a purr. "And your ass, Rayne... God, your ass... so round and firm, perfect for gripping, for spanking, for worshipping with our hands and mouths."

His touch is electric, sending shivers of pleasure coursing through my body. But it's not just the physical sensations that overwhelm me–it's the raw emotion in his voice, the way he speaks about me with such reverence and desire.

"But it's not just your body that captivates us, Rayne," Knox continues, his voice softening. "Your mind, Rayne, is a marvel. The way you see the world, the beauty you find in the smallest details—it's breathtaking. We've watched you work though you didn't know it, we've seen the way you can put even the most nervous client at ease with just a few words and a gentle smile. Your empathy, your ability to connect with people on such a deep level, it's a rare and precious gift."

His fingers trace the dip of my waist, skimming over my hip and down my thigh. "The way you throw yourself into your passions, whether it's photography or helping others—it's inspiring. You have this fire inside you, this drive to make the world a better place, one person at a time. It's intoxicating to watch."

Knox's lips brush against my ear as he continues, his voice low and intense. "Your laugh, Rayne—it's like music. The way your eyes crinkle at the corners when you're truly happy, how your whole face lights up—it's mesmerizing. And your smile, god, your smile could outshine the sun."

His eyes meet mine in the mirror, his gaze intense and unwavering. "I told you a long time ago that I wished you could see yourself the way I see you," Knox murmurs, his voice thick with emotion. "You would never doubt your beauty if you saw yourself through my eyes."

My breath catches in my throat, memories flooding back in a dizzying rush. A warm summer day, the scent of freshly cut grass in the air. Two children, a boy and a girl, sitting side by side on a rickety porch swing. His hand, small but already calloused, wrapped around mine. The weight of secrets shared, of promises made.

"William," I whisper, the name falling from my lips unbidden.

Chapter 34

Rayne

KNOX GENTLY KISSES MY temple, his lips lingering against my skin. "You know I hated that name," he says softly. "It was my father's name, and I was never going to keep it after what he did."

The weight of unspoken history hangs heavy between us. I remember him as a young boy with haunted eyes, bruises hidden beneath too-large clothes. How we bonded over lost mothers to violent fathers. I remember whispered promises in the dark, dreams of a better life. And I remember the day he disappeared, leaving nothing but a hollow ache in my chest.

Knox's arms tighten around me, as if he can sense the direction of my thoughts. "I'm sorry," he murmurs against my hair. "I'm sorry I left you behind. I didn't want to, but they wouldn't let me stay. I tried."

I turn in his arms, facing him directly instead of through the mirror's reflection. His eyes are dark with regret and something deeper, more intense. "Knox," I breathe, reaching up to cup his stubbled jaw.

He catches my hand and presses a fervent kiss to my palm. "I did what I had to, to protect you," he rumbles, lips brushing my skin before he moves his hands to my hips. "I overheard that boy saying things, vile things he planned to do to you. I couldn't let that happen, no matter what."

A frown creases my brow as my mind rushes to make sense of his words. What boy? What is he talking about? Sensing my confusion, Knox's expression tightens, a muscle ticking in his chiseled jaw.

"You don't remember him," he states flatly. It's not a question. "He was one of the older kids at the home. Always lurking in corners, watching you with eyes that made my skin crawl." Knox's hands flex against my hips, fingers digging in almost painfully. "I overheard him telling his buddies exactly what he wanted to do to you once you turned thirteen. The things he described..." He shakes his head, jaw clenched so tightly I fear he might crack a tooth.

Bile rises in my throat as the implication of his words sinks in. A nameless, faceless threat from my past, one I have no recollection of. But Knox remembers.

"I couldn't let that happen to you," Knox rumbles, his voice vibrating with barely contained fury. "Even back then, I knew that you were mine, something inside me just...snapped."

He draws in a ragged breath, the tendons in his neck standing out in stark relief. "I waited until after lights out, when the halls were deserted. When he came sneaking out of his room, I was ready. I attacked him from behind, slamming his head into the wall until he crumpled to the floor."

Knox's eyes burn with an intensity that I can feel deep in my soul. "I just kept hitting him, over and over, until my knuckles were raw and bloody. All I could think about was protecting you, keeping that monster away from you at all costs."

His hands flex, fingers curling as if remembering the feel of flesh yielding beneath his knuckles. "By the time the night staff pulled me off him, that piece of shit was barely conscious. He could barely move, let alone touch you. You thankfully slept through the whole thing, even back then you were a heavy sleeper."

"Of course, when the staff found out why I did it, they just shuffled us off to new foster homes," Knox continues bitterly. "They put that sick fuck with a whole new crop of little girls to terrorize. I couldn't let him hurt you or anyone else ever again. So I waited until he recovered from that first beating before taking him by surprise when he was alone. He was the first person I killed, to protect you and other girls like you."

My heart is pounding in my chest. A part of me should be horrified by his admission, but a darker part is captivated and aroused by this glimpse into Knox's uncompromising nature when it comes to defending what's his.

River steps up behind me, his solid chest pressing against my back as his arms snake around my waist. "You aren't even shocked, gorgeous," he purrs in my ear, his breath hot on my skin. "You know there's an edge to us, a darkness that draws you in like a moth to a flame."

His tongue traces the delicate shell of my ear, and I whimper softly at the erotic sensation. "Knox didn't do it alone, you know," River continues in that low, wicked tone. "I was in that home they transferred him to and I could sense it in him—that willingness to go to any lengths to protect what's precious to him. It sang to the darkest parts of my soul."

One of River's hands slides up to caress the curve of my breast, his thumb brushing over my hardened nipple through the thin fabric of my dress. His other hand threads through my hair, twirling the strands around his fingers, tugging gently. He leans in, his lips brushing the shell of my ear as he speaks in a low, seductive rasp. "Your soul sings the same dark song as ours, little Rayne. I see it in your eyes—that flash of desire whenever we speak about getting a little...messy."

His tongue darts out, tracing the whorled ridges of my ear in a maddeningly slow circle. I shudder against him, my core clenching with need. "You're not horrified, are you?" he murmurs, his breath hot on my sensitized skin. "That we were willing to kill, even back then. That darkness within us, that capacity for violence—it doesn't repulse you. It excites you."

Another whimper escapes my parted lips as River's teeth graze my earlobe with delicious pressure and he tugs on my hair again. "I know it wouldn't matter who we killed," he whispers darkly. "Like that man in the alleyway that thought he could touch what didn't belong to him. I could see it in your eyes—watching me kill him, watching the life drain from his body...it didn't horrify you. It turned you on."

His words send a molten wave of arousal crashing through me. He's right—none of this repulses me. Quite the opposite. My soul resonates with that same primal darkness, that willingness to do whatever it takes.

River's hand tightens in my hair, tugging my head back to expose the long column of my throat. Knox shifts closer, the heat of his body searing me even through the thin fabric of my dress. His lips brush against my bared neck, teeth grazing my thundering pulse.

"You're ours, Rayne," Knox growls against my skin. "Your soul, your body, your very existence—it all belongs to us and always has. We'll worship every inch of you, cherish you in a way no one else ever could."

Knox's hand slides possessively down my body as he steps away, leaving a trail of heat in its wake. I lean back into River's solid embrace, seeking solace from the whirlwind of emotions swirling within me. His arms tighten around my waist, anchoring me.

An alert chimes loudly from my computer, the unexpected sound making me jump. I nearly groan at the interruption, desperate to remain lost in this heated moment with Knox and River. Their touches, their words—they've unraveled me in the most delicious way.

I try to step out from between them, to deal with whatever message or notification has intruded on our moment. But River merely tightens his grip, refusing to let me go. His lips trail scorching kisses down the side of my neck as he murmurs, "Ignore it. Nothing is more important than this. Than us."

Knox, however, moves towards my computer with a predatory grace. He leans over the desk, fingers flying across the keyboard and mouse. There's a slight furrow in his brow as he navigates to the source of the alert.

It doesn't concern me much at first—I assume it's simply an automated news alert about the ongoing serial killer case. Those pop up frequently in the corner of my screen, whenever it's mentioned in any news.

The sound of Knox's sharp inhale cuts through the sensual haze clouding my mind. Instantly, I'm on high alert, adrenaline spiking through my veins.

"What is it?" I ask, trying to move around River to get a better view of the computer screen. But he holds me firmly in place, his arms like steel bands around my waist.

Knox doesn't answer right away. His jaw is clenched so tightly I fear he might crack a tooth. The tendons in his neck stand out in harsh relief as his eyes rapidly scan whatever he's seeing on the display.

Then, with a harsh exhale, he spins the monitor around so I can see.

My breath catches in my throat as I take in the image filling the screen. It's one of the photos from the session with Knox and River—the three of us tangled together in the throes of passion. Sweat-slicked limbs, expressions of rapturous pleasure, the evidence of our joining glistening between our bodies. It's an incredibly private, deeply intimate moment, captured forever in vivid digital detail.

Except it's not just the image itself that has dread coiling in the pit of my stomach. Scrawled across it in jagged, angry red text are the words: YOU'RE MINE. THEY ARE ALREADY DEAD, THEY JUST DON'T KNOW IT YET.

A choked sound escapes my lips as the weight of the threat sinks in. This psychopath, this deranged stalker, has somehow gained access to files that were stored on my secure drive.

Knox's jaw tightens as he stares at the vile message scrawled across one of our most intimate moments. A muscle ticks in his chiseled jaw, betraying the barely leashed fury simmering beneath his controlled exterior.

With a harsh exhale, he pulls his phone from his pocket, thumbs flying across the screen. A look of grim determination settles over his features as he raises the device to his ear.

"It's me," he growls into the phone, the deep timbre of his voice reverberating through the tense air of the studio. "We have a situation. I need you to trace an email address for me, now."

A pause, during which I can almost picture the person on the other end scrambling to comply with Knox's terse demand. His free hand clenches into a white-knuckled fist at his side, tendons standing out in stark relief.

Knox's voice drops lower, a hint of exasperation creeping in. "No, I can't give you direct access to the computer or the email itself. We just need you to trace who the account belongs to." He pauses, listening to the response on the other end.

"Yes, I know it's not as simple as it sounds," Knox growls, pinching the bridge of his nose. His eyes flick to me for a moment before returning to the screen. "Look, I don't care what methods you have to use. Legal, illegal, borderline–I don't give a fuck. Just get me a name or an address."

There's another pause as Knox listens, his jaw clenching tighter with each passing second. "No, I'm not going to tell you why it's so urgent. But I promise this one's worth your while. It's... personal."

Suddenly, his expression shifts, a hint of amusement breaking through the tension. "Oh, don't give me that bullshit. You love a challenge." He chuckles, the sound low and rich. "Yeah, yeah, I know. You're a delicate flower who needs constant praise and validation."

Despite the gravity of the situation, I feel a sharp pang of jealousy. Who is this person on the other end of the line that can make Knox laugh so easily in the midst of such a tense moment?

"Don't get your panties in a twist, gorgeous," River purrs, his lips brushing my sensitized skin. "That's just Zeke, our off-the-books IT contact. Useful for situations like this where we need to keep things...discreet."

His tongue darts out, tracing the delicate shell of my ear in a slow, maddening circle. "You know Knox would never look at another woman, right? Not when he's got you—a delicious little morsel to devour whenever he pleases."

Knox hums for a moment, his brow furrowed in concentration as he listens intently to the person on the other end of the line. "Thank you," he says finally, his voice low and gravelly. "I owe you one." With that, he ends the call, slipping the phone back into his pocket with a smooth, practiced motion.

Both River and I watch intently as Knox stalks towards us, his movements fluid and predatory. Each step is measured, purposeful, like a lion approaching its prey. The air around him seems to crackle with tension and barely leashed energy.

When he reaches us, Knox cradles my face in his large, warm hands. His calloused palms are rough against my skin, a delicious contrast to the softness of his touch. He leans in, capturing my lips in a slow, deep kiss that makes my toes curl and my heart race. His tongue traces the seam of my lips, demanding entry, and I yield to him willingly, melting into his embrace.

The kiss is thorough, almost possessive, as if Knox is trying to imprint himself on every part of me. When he finally pulls away, I'm breathless, my lips tingling and my head spinning.

"Stay here," Knox murmurs, his voice a low rumble that sends shivers down my spine. His eyes bore into mine. "Stay safe. We don't know what this psychopath is capable of."

I feel River's arms loosen around me, his warmth retreating as he prepares to step away. But Knox's hand shoots out, gripping River's wrist with a force that makes the tendons in his arm stand out in stark relief.

"No," Knox growls, his gaze flicking to River. "You stay here too. Keep her safe."

River nods, a silent understanding passing between them. His arms encircle me once more, pulling me back against the solid warmth of his chest.

"When I get back, we are going to discuss the consequences of breaching the NDA you signed." My jaw drops as Knox turns, his movements fluid and purposeful as he strides towards the door. The late afternoon sunlight streaming through the windows catches on his crisp white shirt, highlighting the play of muscles beneath the fabric as he moves.

A part of me wants to call out, to beg him to stay. The thought of him out there, potentially in harm's way, makes my heart clench painfully. But before I can voice my concerns, River gently turns me in his arms, drawing my attention back to him.

His blue eyes capture mine, a mix of mischief and concern swirling in their depths. "Now, little Rayne, back to you doubting our love of your smoking hot body," he says, his voice a low, seductive purr. "Is that why you didn't eat the cupcake I gave you?"

Chapter 35

Rayne

I BITE MY LIP and look away from River, not wanting to answer. A flush of shame creeps up my neck as I realize he's right–a part of me did hesitate to eat the cupcake he gave me because of my insecurities about my body. The memory of wanting so badly to indulge but holding back out of misplaced guilt, makes me cringe inwardly.

River chuckles, the sound low and wicked. His fingers brush my chin, gently urging me to meet his gaze again. His eyes dance with mischief as he asks, "You know what's good about being here on official business?"

Before I can respond, he lets go of me but gently takes one of my hands. His other hand reaches behind him, and when it comes back into view, my breath catches. Dangling from his fingers is a set of handcuffs, the metal gleaming in the late afternoon light.

"These," River purrs, his voice dripping with sin. With a swift, practiced motion, he snaps one cuff around my wrist. The metal is cool against my skin, a stark contrast to the heat building inside me. The weight of it is unfamiliar, yet strangely thrilling. I can feel my pulse quickening, a mix of anticipation and nervousness coursing through my veins.

River's eyes darken as he watches my reaction, his pupils dilating with desire. "Oh, little Rayne," he purrs, tugging gently on the cuffs. "Do you like being bound?"

I open my mouth to respond, but no words come out. My throat feels dry, my tongue heavy in my mouth. River's gaze is intense, his blue eyes seeming to see right through me, reading every unspoken desire written on my skin.

Without breaking eye contact, River leads me across the studio. When we reach the foot of the bed, River's voice drops to a low, commanding tone. "Raise your arms for me, little Rayne."

Without hesitation, I comply. My arms lift above my head, the loose fabric of my dress shifting with the movement. I can feel my breasts straining against the thin material, my nipples hardening into tight peaks. River's eyes rake over my body, drinking in every detail.

His eyes gleam with wicked intent as he steps closer, his body radiating heat. His fingers trail up my arms, leaving goosebumps in their wake. The touch is feather-light, almost reverent, as if he's mapping every inch of my skin. I shiver involuntarily, my body arching towards him, seeking more contact.

He leans in, his breath hot against my ear as he whispers, "You're so beautiful like this, Rayne. All flushed and trembling for me." His lips brush the sensitive spot just below my ear, and I have to bite back a moan.

His touch is maddening, simultaneously too much and not enough. I'm so lost in the sensations that I barely register the soft clink of metal.

Suddenly, there's a cool pressure around my other wrist. My eyes fly open—when had I closed them?—just in time to see River securing the second cuff to my other wrist, having hooked it over one of the bars of the canopy bed. The realization hits me a moment too late as I instinctively tug against the restraints.

The metal is unyielding, cold and hard against my skin. The cuffs are snug but not tight, allowing just enough movement to tease but not enough to escape. I test them again, feeling the solid weight of the metal, the way it restricts my movements.

River grins at me, his expression a mix of wickedness and unbridled glee. It's the kind of smile that would make most people take a step back, a primal part of their brain recognizing the predator before them. But I'm not most people. I feel an answering thrill of excitement race through me, my body responding to the dangerous edge in his eyes.

I give him a droll look, trying to maintain some semblance of composure despite the heat pooling low in my belly. "You know," I say, my voice huskier than I intended, "I have leather cuffs over there." I motion with my head towards the far wall, where the St. Andrew's cross stands proudly alongside an array of other BDSM equipment. The leather cuffs in question hang from a hook nearby, their soft black surface a stark contrast to the cold metal currently encircling my wrists.

River's eyes follow my gesture, his grin widening impossibly further. His gaze lingers on the cross, and I can almost see the wheels turning in his mind, no doubt imagining all the delicious scenarios we could explore with that particular piece of equipment. When he turns back to me, his eyes are dark with desire, pupils blown wide.

He chuckles, the sound low and wicked. "Oh, of course I know about those lovely leather cuffs, sweetheart," he purrs, his voice a seductive rumble that sends shivers down my spine. "But these," he taps the metal cuffs with one long finger, "were convenient. And every time I look at them from now on I will be able to picture you just like this. Besides, you might struggle a bit less against them.

Though we will definitely be playing with those leather ones another time. I have so many delicious ideas for them."

He steps back, his gaze raking over my restrained form with obvious appreciation. Then he turns and walks away. I watch, transfixed, as he retrieves the white box and coffee cup from where he left them earlier.

River returns, his eyes never leaving mine as he approaches. The air between us feels charged, crackling with tension. He stops just inches from me, close enough that I can feel the heat radiating from his body. My breath catches in my throat as he lifts the coffee cup to my lips. The rich aroma of caramel latte fills my senses, mingling with River's own intoxicating scent.

"Drink," he growls, his voice low and commanding. Before I can fully process what's happening, the first drops of liquid touch my tongue. The latte has cooled to a comfortable temperature, no longer scalding but still holding a pleasant warmth.

The sweetness of caramel mingles with the bitter notes of espresso, creating a perfect balance. I close my eyes, savoring the flavors as River carefully tips the cup, allowing me to drink.

As I swallow, I feel a drop escape the corner of my mouth, trailing slowly down my chin. Before I can react, River's thumb is there, catching the errant liquid. His touch lingers, the pad of his thumb tracing the curve of my lower lip with agonizing slowness as he pulls the cup away. When I open my eyes, his gaze is fixed on my mouth.

He slowly lowers the coffee cup, setting it gently on the hardwood floor beside us. The soft thud as it meets the ground seems amplified in the charged silence of the room.

With a flourish, he lifts the lid on the white box, revealing the treasure within. My breath catches at the sight of the apple crumble cupcake nestled in its paper wrapper. The cake itself is a rich, golden brown, studded with chunks of tender apple and crowned with a generous swirl of cream cheese frosting. A dusting of cinnamon-sugar crumble adorns the top, glittering like edible jewels in the late afternoon light.

The aroma wafts up, an intoxicating blend of warm spices, tart apple, and sweet vanilla. It's a scent that speaks of comfort, of indulgence, of moments stolen from the rush of everyday life. My mouth waters involuntarily, and I feel a pang of regret for not enjoying the one he'd given me the other day.

River's voice breaks through my reverie, tinged with a mix of amusement and something darker. "Since you didn't eat the other one," he purrs, his blue eyes locked on mine, "I got you a fresh one. This time, you're going to eat it."

There's no room for argument in his tone. It's not a suggestion, but a command.

His finger dips into the luscious cream cheese frosting, coming away with a generous dollop. Slowly, teasingly, he brings it to my lips. Without breaking eye contact, I dart my tongue out, licking the frosting from his skin. The sweet, tangy flavor explodes on my tongue, a perfect balance of cream cheese and vanilla. River hums appreciatively, his eyes darkening as he watches my tongue swirl around his finger.

"Good girl," he murmurs, his voice husky. He breaks off a small piece of the cupcake, holding it to my lips. Without being told, I part them, allowing him to press the morsel between them.

As he feeds me another bite, River's voice drops lower, taking on a more serious tone. "I ended up in foster care when I was eleven," he begins, his eyes distant for a moment before refocusing on me. "My parents... well, let's just say they weren't fit to raise a goldfish, let alone a child."

He breaks off more cupcake, this time smearing it with frosting before bringing it to my lips. As I take the bite, a dollop of frosting escapes, clinging to the corner of my mouth. River leans in, his tongue darting out to lick it away. The heat of his mouth against my skin sends a shiver down my spine.

His fingers trail down my neck, leaving a trail of goosebumps in their wake. His eyes, usually sparkling with mischief, are now dark and serious as he continues his story.

"My parents," he says, his voice low and controlled, "were addicts. Heroin, mostly, but they'd take anything they could get their hands on." He breaks off another piece of cupcake, once again dragging it through the frosting before bringing it to my lips. As I take the bite, he leans in, his tongue darting out to catch a stray crumb at the corner of my mouth.

"They owed money to their dealer," River continues, his fingers tracing abstract patterns on my collarbone. "A lot of money. And one day, when they couldn't pay..." He pauses, his jaw clenching. "They decided I was worth enough to cover their debt."

My heart clenches at his words, a wave of sympathy and anger washing over me. I want to reach out, to comfort him, but the hand-cuffs prevent me from moving. River seems to sense my distress, because he leans in, pressing a soft kiss to my forehead.

"Don't worry, little Rayne," he murmurs against my skin. "It has a happy ending. Well, for me at least." His trademark wicked grin returns, though there's still a hint of darkness in his eyes. "The dealer came to collect. My parents were too high to put up much of a fight. I remember my mother's vacant stare as the man dragged me out of our dingy apartment. I kicked and screamed, but no one came to help."

He breaks off another piece of cupcake, holding it to my lips. As I take the bite, his thumb brushes my lower lip, lingering there. "The dealer took me to this abandoned warehouse. It was cold and damp. It smelled like mold and despair. There were other kids there, all looking as terrified as I felt."

River's hand trails down my neck again, his touch feather-light. "I quickly realized what was going to happen to us. The other kids, they were resigned to their fate. But not me. I refused to be a victim."

His eyes meet mine, and I see a flash of that dangerous edge that lurks beneath his cheerful exterior. "When one of the men came for me, I was ready. I'd found a rusty nail in a pile of debris. As he reached for me, I struck. Right in the eye."

River's grin is feral now, all sharp edges and dark satisfaction. "The screams were music to my ears. In the chaos that followed, I managed to escape. Ran until my lungs burned and my legs gave out."

"I ended up in the system after that. Never staying anywhere long. I was... difficult. Angry. Lashing out at everyone and everything."

He breaks off another piece of cupcake, gathering more frosting before bringing it to my lips. "Then I met Knox," River says, a soft smile playing on his lips. "Or William as he still went by back then. He was different from the other kids. Quiet, watchful. But I could see the darkness in his eyes, the same darkness I saw in the mirror every day."

His fingers go back to trailing down my neck, tracing abstract patterns on my collarbone. "We recognized something in each other. A kindred spirit. Someone who understood the ugliness of the world, who wasn't afraid to do what needed to be done."

River's hand moves lower, skimming over the swell of my breast. His touch is feather-light, teasing. "We became inseparable. Partners in crime, literally and figuratively. We protected each other, watched each other's backs. And when the time came, we killed together."

Chapter 36
Rayne

As River's words sink in, a maelstrom of emotions swirls within me. My heart aches for the scared little boy he once was, thrust into a world of cruelty and darkness far too soon. I can almost see him–small, scrawny, eyes wide with terror as he was dragged from the only home he had ever known. The image makes my chest tight, a lump forming in my throat.

River watches my face intently, his eyes studying every minute shift in my expression. I know he can read the thoughts racing through my mind as clearly as if I'd spoken them aloud. His lips curl into a knowing smirk, a glimmer of appreciation flickering in his gaze.

"Oh, little Rayne," he purrs, his voice low and rich with dark promise. "I can see those beautiful wheels turning in that pretty head of yours. Tell me, what are you thinking?"

I swallow hard, my mouth suddenly dry despite the lingering sweetness of the cupcake. "I... I wish I could go back," I whisper, my voice trembling with emotion. "I wish I could hold that little boy, protect him from all that pain and fear."

River's eyes soften for a moment, a flicker of vulnerability passing across his features before it's swallowed by his usual wicked grin. "You're too good for this world, aren't you?" he murmurs, tracing the contour of my cheek with his thumb.

But that's not all. The words tumble out of me, raw and unfiltered. "I wish I could hunt down your drug-addicted parents," I continue, my voice growing harder, colder. "I want to cut them to pieces for how they treated you. For betraying you, for selling you like you were nothing more than a commodity."

His hand slides to my throat, not squeezing, just resting there. I can feel my pulse thundering against his palm.

"And what else?" he prompts, his voice thick with anticipation. "What other deliciously violent thoughts are dancing through that sexy mind?"

"That dealer," I hiss, baring my teeth in a feral snarl. "I wish I could slaughter him for daring to think he could touch you, or any of those other boys. I'd make him suffer, River. I'd take my time, peeling back his skin inch by agonizing inch. I'd carve my rage into his flesh, make him feel every ounce of pain and terror he inflicted on those innocent children."

My voice grows darker, a vicious edge creeping in as I continue. "I'd gouge out his eyes, slowly, so the last thing he'd see is my face, twisted with hatred and disgust. I'd cut out his tongue so he couldn't beg for mercy. And then, when he's nothing but a broken, bleeding mess, I'd leave him for the rats. Let them feast on him while he's still alive, still able to feel every gnawing bite."

River's eyes darken with lust, his pupils blown wide. A low, guttural groan escapes his throat, the sound vibrating through his chest. "Fuck, Rayne," he growls, his voice thick with desire. "Do you have any idea how hot that makes me? How much I want to bend you over right now and fuck you senseless?"

His hand tightens slightly on my throat, not enough to restrict my breathing, but enough to make me acutely aware of his strength, his control. "The things I want to do to you," he purrs, his voice a low, seductive rumble. "You are absolutely fucking perfect for us. Do you know that? Do you have any idea how rare it is to find someone who not only accepts our darkness but embraces it? Who matches it with her own?"

He leans in close, his lips brushing the shell of my ear as he speaks. "You're like a dark goddess come to life, all soft curves and razor-sharp edges. Your beauty is intoxicating, but it's your mind—that deliciously twisted, brilliantly creative mind—that truly captivates us."

River's free hand traces the skin of my waist, his touch feather-light yet electrifying. "The way your eyes light up when we talk about violence, about retribution... it's breathtaking. You don't shy away from the ugliness of the world. You see it, understand it, and want to shape it to your will. Just like us. You can't hide it from us, Rayne. We see you. All of you. The light and the dark, the sweet and the savage. And we fucking love every inch of it."

He pulls back slightly, his eyes locking with mine. There's a vulnerability there that I've never seen before, a raw honesty that makes my heart clench.

"You know," he says softly, breaking off another piece of the cupcake, "as much as I hated those experiences at the time, they made me who I am today." He brings the morsel to my lips, and I accept it, savoring the sweet, spiced flavor as he continues, his voice tinged with a mix of nostalgia and hard-won wisdom. "The pain, the fear, the anger—they all shaped me, forged me into the man I am now."

His fingers trail along my jawline, a feather-light touch that sends shivers down my spine. "I used to dream about changing my past, about having a normal childhood with loving parents and a white picket fence. But now?" He shakes his head, a wry smile playing at his lips. "Now I wouldn't change a single moment."

River's hand moves to cup my cheek, his thumb brushing gently over my skin. "Because every hardship, every moment of darkness, led me here. To this exact point in time and space. To Knox. And to you, Rayne."

His eyes lock with mine, intense and unwavering. "This, us, it's not just chance or coincidence. It's destiny. Everything I've been through, everything I've done, it was all leading me to you two."

As River's words sink in, I feel something shift deep within me. It's as if a final piece of a complex puzzle has clicked into place, revealing a picture I've always known was there but couldn't quite see. The realization washes over me like a tidal wave, powerful and all-consuming.

Love.

It's not just obsession or lust or even a deep connection. It's love, pure and fierce and terrifying in its intensity. A part of me has loved Knox since that first day in the foster home, when his haunted eyes met mine and I saw a kindred spirit. But we're not those same lost children anymore. We've grown, changed, been shaped by the darkness and pain of our pasts.

And River... he completes us in a way I never knew was possible. He's the missing piece, the balance to Knox's intensity, the spark to my smoldering flame. Together, we form a perfect trinity, a three-sided puzzle that fits together flawlessly.

The emotion swells in my chest, threatening to overflow. I want to tell them, to shout it from the rooftops, but the words stick in my throat. How can I possibly articulate the depth of what I'm feeling?

As if sensing the frenzy of emotions coursing through me, River's expression softens. His thumb traces my cheekbone again, a tender gesture that belies the darkness we were just reveling in moments ago.

"I see it in your eyes, little Rayne," he murmurs, his voice uncharacteristically gentle. "But don't worry, I won't make you say it. Not yet."

His words send a wave of relief washing over me. I'm not ready to voice these feelings aloud, not when they're still so new and overwhelming. River seems to understand this, his eyes twinkling with a mix of mischief and tenderness. Instead he breaks off another piece of the cupcake, holding it to my lips.

"You know," he says softly as I take the bite, "Knox never told me much about how you ended up in foster care. He always said it was your story to tell, if you ever wanted to."

I swallow hard, the sweetness of the cupcake turning to ash in my mouth as River's words stir up my own painful memories. Taking a deep breath, I begin to share my own story.

"I'm sure Knox has told you his story, my story isn't so different from his," I say softly, my voice barely above a whisper. "I had a loving mother, but my father..." I trail off, the words sticking in my throat. River's hand comes up to cup my cheek, his touch grounding me.

"My father was an abusive asshole," I continue, drawing strength from River's steady gaze. "He'd beat my mother regularly. She never fought back, never defended herself. I used to be so angry with her for that, for just taking it. But later, I learned why."

I close my eyes, remembering the fear in my mother's eyes, the bruises she'd try to hide with makeup and long sleeves. "He threatened to turn on me if she ever fought back. So she endured it, suffered in silence to protect me."

River's thumb strokes my cheek gently, encouraging me to continue. I lean into his touch, grateful for the comfort.

"For years, it went on like that. My mother shielding me from the worst of it, taking the brunt of his anger and violence. But then..." I pause, my breath catching in my throat. "Then he decided he wanted a piece of me too."

River's eyes darken, a storm of fury brewing in their depths. His hand tightens on my cheek, not painfully, but with a fierce protectiveness that makes my heart clench.

"When he made those comments to my mother," I continue, my voice barely above a whisper, "something in her just... snapped. It was like watching a switch flip. One moment, she was the same quiet, submissive woman I'd always known. The next, she was a raging inferno of maternal fury."

I close my eyes, the memories flooding back with vivid clarity. "She lunged at him, her hands clawing at his face, her screams of rage echoing through our tiny house. For a moment, I thought she might actually overpower him. She was so fast, so fierce in her determination to protect me."

"She managed to grab a kitchen knife," I say, my voice trembling. "I remember the way the blade glinted in the harsh light of our kitchen. She stabbed at him wildly, her eyes wide and feral. But he was bigger, stronger. He caught her wrist, simply ripping the knife from her hand."

I swallow hard, the taste of fear and desperation still bitter on my tongue after all these years. "There was so much blood. It seemed to be everywhere—splattered on the walls, pooling on the linoleum floor, soaking into my mother's floral dress. The metallic scent of it filled the air, so thick I could taste it on my tongue."

"I was only twelve," I whisper, my voice cracking with emotion. "But somehow, in that moment of chaos and terror, I found the strength to run. I bolted from that house, my lungs burning as I screamed for help."

I can still feel the rough asphalt beneath my feet, the way the cold night air stung my tear-streaked cheeks. The memory is so vivid, it's as if I'm reliving it all over again.

"I ended up collapsing on a neighbor's porch. I remember the porch light flickering on and the door opening, and then I looked up to see our elderly neighbor, Mrs. Jameson, looking shocked and concerned."

River's hand moves to my hair, gently stroking the long, dark strands. The soothing motion grounds me, helping me continue through the painful recollection.

"Everything after that is a blur of flashing lights and stern faces. Police cars and ambulances everywhere. Neighbors whispering... The trial was a nightmare," I continue, my voice barely above a whisper. "I had to testify, to recount every horrific detail in front of a room full of strangers. My father's eyes bore into me the entire time, cold and unfeeling. But I refused to let him break me. I spoke clearly, my voice steady even as tears streamed down my face."

River's hand continues its soothing motion through my hair.

"In the end, justice prevailed. My father was sent to prison. But the victory felt hollow. My mother was gone, and I was alone in the world."

I take a shaky breath, steeling myself to continue. "I was placed in foster care. I was angry too, but I was withdrawn. I pushed away anyone who tried to get close. But then, a few months after entering the system, I met Knox. We gravitated towards each other, two broken souls finding solace in each other's company."

I close my eyes, remembering those precious few months. "For the first time since losing my mother, I felt safe. Knox became my protector, my confidant. We'd spend hours talking, sharing our dreams and fears. He promised me that one day, we'd leave the system behind and make a life for ourselves."

A wistful smile tugs at my lips. "We even made a pact, swearing that we'd be together forever. It was childish, perhaps, but it felt so real, so important at the time."

My voice catches as I continue, "But then, a few months later, he was gone. I woke up one morning, and his bed was empty. No note, no goodbye. He'd just... vanished."

I blink back tears, the old pain still raw after all these years. "I was devastated. It felt like losing my mother all over again. I withdrew even further, building walls around my heart that I thought were impenetrable."

River's eyes soften as he takes in my vulnerable state. Without a word, he reaches up and gently undoes the handcuffs from around my wrists. The metal clinks softly as it releases, and I feel the blood rushing back into my arms. River's fingers trace delicately over the faint red marks left behind, his touch soothing and tender.

He brings each wrist to his lips, pressing soft kisses against the sensitive skin. His tongue darts out, tracing lazy circles that send shivers down my spine. I watch, mesmerized, as he lavishes attention on my wrists, erasing any lingering discomfort with his ministrations.

When he's satisfied, River tucks the handcuffs away in his pocket. Then, in one fluid motion, he scoops me up into his arms. I let out a small gasp of surprise, my arms instinctively wrapping around his neck for balance. He cradles me against his chest, my head tucked under his chin. I can feel the steady thrum of his heartbeat, strong and reassuring.

With careful movements, River crawls onto the bed, still holding me close. He settles us both down onto the plush mattress, arranging our bodies so that he's curled protectively around me. His chest presses against my back, one arm draped over my waist, our legs tangled together.

I shift slightly, aware of the work still waiting for me. "River, I should really get back to editing. I have deadlines to meet and-"

"Shhh," River murmurs, his breath warm against my ear. "Let's just take a moment."

His arm tightens around my waist, pulling me flush against his chest. I can feel the steady rise and fall of his breathing, the solid warmth of his body enveloping me. The tension slowly begins to seep out of my muscles as I sink into his embrace.

River's fingers trace lazy patterns on my hip, the touch soothing and grounding. The late afternoon sunlight filters through the curtains, casting a golden glow across the room.

I relax, letting the warmth of his body and the steady rhythm of his breathing soothe me. The tension from reliving those painful memories slowly ebbs away, replaced by a sense of comfort and safety I haven't felt in years.

Chapter 37
Rayne

I'M NOT SURE HOW long we lay there, River's body a warm cocoon around mine. Time seems to stretch and blur, measured only by the steady rise and fall of his chest against my back. River's hand moves to my hair, his fingers gently combing through the long, dark strands. The repetitive motion is soothing, almost hypnotic. I find myself drifting in a hazy state between wakefulness and sleep, lulled by the comforting sensations.

His fingers work through any small tangles they encounter with surprising gentleness, carefully teasing apart the strands without causing discomfort. It's clear he has some sort of fascination with hair, and I'm certainly not complaining. The attention is both relaxing and oddly intimate, making me feel cherished.

I'm hovering in that hazy space between wakefulness and sleep, lulled by River's warmth and the rhythmic motion of his fingers in my hair, when suddenly, everything changes.

In a move so swift I can barely follow it, River twists behind me. There's a soft metallic click, and suddenly his gun is out, aimed unerringly at the studio doorway. The weapon seems to have materialized out of thin air–one moment we were cuddling peacefully, the next River is coiled and ready to strike, all trace of softness gone from his body.

My heart leaps into my throat, adrenaline flooding my system. I hadn't heard a thing, but River's reaction tells me something is wrong. My eyes dart to the doorway, following the line of River's aim.

And there, standing silently in the threshold, is Knox.

His posture is relaxed, hands tucked casually in his pockets, but there's a dangerous glint in his eyes. "Good boy... Nice reflexes," Knox says, his eyes flick from River's gun to my face, then back again.

I scramble out of the bed, my heart racing. "Knox! What did you find out?" I ask urgently, my voice tinged with anxiety.

Knox's expression remains impassive as he meets my gaze. "Secure the studio," he says simply, his tone brooking no argument. Without another word, he strides over to the little cabinet where I keep my shoes.

I frown, confusion and frustration warring within me. Part of me wants to demand answers immediately, but I know better than to push Knox when he's in this mood. With a resigned sigh, I move to shut down my computer, fingers flying over the keyboard as I close programs and save files.

As I work, I can hear Knox rummaging through the cabinet, the soft rustle of fabric and the quiet thud of shoes being moved aside. The normalcy of the sound is at odds with the tension thrumming through the air.

I grab my keys from their usual spot on my desk, the metal cool against my palm. The familiar weight grounds me, a small anchor in the storm of uncertainty swirling around me.

When I turn back, Knox is approaching with a pair of my most comfortable flats in hand. Without a word, he kneels before me, his movements fluid and graceful despite his imposing size. I watch, transfixed, as he gently lifts my foot, sliding the shoe on with a tenderness that makes my heart clench.

He repeats the process with the other foot, his touch lingering perhaps a moment longer than strictly necessary. As he finishes, his hands begin a slow, sensuous journey up my legs. His palms are warm against my skin, leaving trails of heat in their wake.

Knox's fingers trace over my calves, skimming over my knees and continuing their ascent along my thighs. When his hands reach my hips, Knox pauses. His hazel eyes, flecked with gold and green, lock with mine. There's an intensity in his gaze that steals my breath, a mix of desire, protectiveness, and something deeper.

In one fluid motion, Knox rises to his feet, his hands never leaving my body. As he stands, he pulls me up with him, drawing me flush against his chest. I can feel the solid warmth of him through his shirt, the steady thrum of his heartbeat against my palm.

For a moment, we stand there, bodies pressed together, breathing in sync. The world around us seems to fade away, narrowing down to just this—the heat of Knox's body, the strength of his arms around me, the depth of emotion in his eyes.

Knox leans in, his lips brushing against my ear as he whispers, his voice low and husky. "When I walked in and saw you and River together, it felt like coming home." He presses a soft kiss to my temple, his breath warm against my skin. "Seeing you two together, it felt right in a way I can't even begin to explain."

Another kiss, this time to my cheek. "It was like all the pieces of my life finally falling into place." His lips ghost over my jaw, feather-light. "You have no idea how long I've dreamed of this, of having both of you."

Knox pulls back slightly, his eyes boring into mine with an intensity that steals my breath. "It meant everything to me, Rayne. Everything."

Before I can respond, Knox takes my hand in his, his grip firm and reassuring. He turns, leading me towards where River waits by the door. For a moment, my heart races, thinking of the stalker potentially watching us. But Knox's demeanor is calm, almost casual. There's no tension in his shoulders, no wariness in his movements. Whatever he discovered during his absence, it clearly alleviated some of his immediate concerns.

As we step out of the studio, the late afternoon sun bathes everything in a warm, golden glow. River turns back to the door, his movements fluid and practiced. I watch, bemused, as he produces a key from his pocket—a key I definitely didn't give him. The lock clicks into place with a soft, satisfying sound.

I raise an eyebrow at him, a mix of exasperation and amusement tugging at my lips. "Really?" I ask, jingling my own set of keys pointedly.

River's response is a grin that's equal parts mischievous and unrepentant. His eyes dance with barely contained glee as he pockets the key with a flourish. "What can I say?" he quips, his voice light and teasing. "We like to be prepared."

Before I can question him further, Knox's hand finds the small of my back, gently guiding me towards the curb. Parked there is a sleek, navy blue car. Its polished surface gleams, exuding an aura of quiet power and luxury.

Knox opens the passenger door and I slide into the seat, the supple leather cool against my skin. Knox gently closes the door behind me, the soft thud resonating with a sense of finality. Through the tinted windows, I watch him walk around the front of the car, his movements fluid and purposeful. The fading sunlight catches on his dark hair, highlighting the hints of auburn hidden in the rich brown strands.

River slides into the back seat, but instead of settling back, he drapes himself over my seat. His presence is warm and solid behind me, his breath tickling my ear as he leans forward. The scent of his cologne - a heady mix of sandalwood and something distinctly masculine - envelops me.

Knox slips into the driver's seat, his large frame fitting perfectly in the space. With a press of a button, the engine purrs to life, a low, powerful rumble that I can feel vibrating through the seat. He pulls away from the curb with smooth precision, merging effortlessly into the flow of evening traffic. He drives the car like it's a part of him, and he has full control over it like he does with everything else.

The silence in the car is thick, almost palpable. Questions swirl in my mind, a tornado of curiosity and anxiety that threatens to overwhelm me.

I watch as Knox moves, the muscles in his arm flexing as he changes gears. The sleek car responds instantly to his touch, accelerating smoothly as we make our way through town. The leather-wrapped steering wheel seems like a natural extension of his body, his large hands gripping it with casual confidence.

My eyes trace the line of his forearm, admiring the way his rolled-up sleeve only accentuates the intricate tattoos beneath. The inked swirls and lines disappear under the crisp white fabric, making me want to trace the artwork hidden from view.

"You dropped thousands on the shoot," I muse aloud, my gaze sweeping over the luxurious interior of the car. The dashboard gleams with high-end tech, while the seats cradle us in sumptuous leather. "And now this car... It looks like some sort of very expensive extension to your cock."

River's laughter erupts from the backseat, loud and unrestrained. His mirth is infectious, and I find myself fighting back a grin despite the tension still thrumming through my body.

Knox's lips twitch, a hint of amusement breaking through his stoic facade. "My father may have killed my mother," he says, his voice low and controlled, "but she had planned ahead. Left me a substantial amount of money in trust."

The casual way he mentions such a traumatic event makes me turn to face him, studying his profile as he focuses on the road. I open my mouth to ask more, but something in his expression makes me hesitate. Instead, I turn my attention to our surroundings.

"Where are we going?" I ask, unable to contain my curiosity any longer. The question hangs in the air, unanswered.

Knox's eyes remain fixed on the road, his jaw set in a hard line. The muscles in his forearm flex as he grips the steering wheel tighter, the only outward sign of any tension.

"Knox," I try again, my voice taking on a pleading edge. "Please, tell me what's going on. Who is the stalker? What did you find out?"

Still, he remains silent. The quiet hum of the engine and the soft whoosh of passing cars are the only sounds filling the luxurious interior.

Frustration bubbles up inside me, threatening to spill over. I turn to River, hoping he might help, but he merely shakes his head, a small, apologetic smile playing at his lips.

"Seriously?" I huff, crossing my arms over my chest. "You're both just going to sit there and say nothing?"

The silence stretches on, broken only by the soft click of the turn signal as Knox smoothly navigates a corner. I growl in frustration, my patience finally reaching its breaking point. But before I can unleash the torrent of questions and demands building inside me,

Knox smoothly pulls the car into a hidden parking garage. The sleek vehicle glides effortlessly into a shadowy corner, far from prying eyes.

As the engine purrs to a stop, Knox finally breaks his silence. "We don't want the car seen near the address," he explains, his voice low and measured. "We'll leave it here and walk the rest of the way. It's not far."

I huff, my irritation still simmering just beneath the surface. Without waiting for either of them, I turn to open the door myself, eager to escape the stifling silence of the car. But before I can even touch the handle, River is there, opening the door. Knox makes his way around the car and extends his hand to me, his eyes intense and unreadable. For a moment, I consider refusing, petulantly clinging to my frustration. But something in his gaze - a mix of determination and something softer, almost pleading - makes me relent. I place my hand in his, allowing him to help me out of the car.

Knox's hand remains firmly clasped around mine as we exit the parking garage, his grip both reassuring and possessive. River falls into step beside us, his usual carefree demeanor replaced by a focused alertness. The late afternoon sun casts long shadows across the sidewalk as we make our way down the street.

We walk in silence, the only sounds are the soft tapping of our shoes on the pavement and the distant hum of town life. I can feel Knox's thumb absently stroking the back of my hand, a soothing gesture that seems almost unconscious.

As we turn the corner, the landscape begins to shift. The sleek, modern buildings of the business district give way to a curious blend of old and new. Here, the city's attempts at gentrification are on full display.

Knox's grip on my hand tightens almost imperceptibly as he guides us towards a nondescript alleyway. The entrance is partially obscured by an overflowing dumpster, the acrid smell of garbage mingling with the damp, earthy scent of the narrow passage.

As we step into the alley, the world seems to close in around us. The walls on either side are a canvas of urban art–layers upon layers of graffiti tags and elaborate murals competing for space. Splashes of vibrant color peek through the grime and decay, like flowers blooming in the cracks of a forgotten garden.

We come to a stop in front of a nondescript metal door, its surface marred by rust and graffiti. It's so similar to the one behind my studio that for a moment, I feel a disorienting sense of déjà vu. Knox opens the door, revealing a dimly lit stairwell beyond. As we step inside, the heavy door swings shut behind us with a resounding thud. The sound reverberates through the narrow space, making me jump slightly. Knox's hand finds the small of my back, a steadying presence as my eyes adjust to the gloom.

The stairwell is illuminated by a single bare bulb, casting long shadows that dance and flicker with our movements. The concrete steps are worn smooth in the center, testament to years of use. A musty scent hangs in the air, mingling with the faint smell of damp stone.

Finally, we reach the bottom. Before us stands another metal door, this one even more weathered than the first. Rust creeps along its edges like a slow-moving infection, and the paint is peeling off in large flakes.

"Who's place is this?" I ask softly, looking between them.

"Your stalker's," Knox says simply, his voice a low rumble that echoes in the confined space.

River steps forward, opening the door for us and motioning us through. Knox stays close behind me, his presence solid and reassuring at my back. His hand rests on my lower back, gently guiding me forward into the gloom.

There isn't much light in the room, only two tiny windows that don't really provide much light. But then an overhead light flares to life, illuminating a figure bound and gagged to a chair in the center of the room.

My breath catches in my throat. "Lacy?"

Chapter 38
River

I WATCH THE SURPRISE and confusion cross Rayne's face, her eyes widening as she takes in the sight before us. Even I have to admit, seeing this woman tied up here surprises me. I shoot a look at Knox, raising an eyebrow in silent question. He gives me a subtle nod, confirming that this is no mistake.

Lacy sits bound to a metal chair in the center of the dimly lit room, her wrists and ankles secured with zip ties. A strip of duct tape covers her mouth, muffling what I assume are protests or pleas. Her usually perfectly styled blonde hair is disheveled, mascara streaks her cheeks, evidence of recent tears.

How we missed that one of Rayne's clients had become obsessed with her and started stalking her was beyond me. A week of her little "surprises" was a week too many. We should have seen this coming, should have caught on sooner. The thought leaves a bitter taste in my mouth.

I look back at the woman, really studying her now. Lacy's designer clothes are rumpled, her silk blouse partially untucked from her pencil skirt. There's a wild, desperate look in her eyes as they dart between the three of us.

My mind races, piecing together the puzzle. Lacy had been overly enthusiastic when I had watched her visit the studio both times I saw her. And both times she had lingered a little too long outside the studio.

She has focused her pleading eyes on Rayne. Knox strides over to her and peels off the tape from her mouth in one swift motion. Lacy wastes no time in trying to plead with Rayne, her voice hoarse and trembling.

"Rayne! Oh thank God you're here!" Lacy cries, her words tumbling out in a frantic rush. "I don't understand what's happening. Why are they doing this to me? Please, you have to help me!"

I have to hand it to her, she's good. Her performance is almost flawless, each word dripping with fear and desperation. Her blue eyes, wide and brimming with unshed tears, are fixed solely on Rayne. It's as if Knox and I don't even exist in her world right now.

I watch as Lacy's words wash over Rayne, her desperate pleas tugging at the compassionate heart I know beats within our girl's chest. Rayne's eyes cloud with doubt, her brow furrowing as she tries to reconcile the sobbing woman before her with the stalker who's been tormenting her.

"I-I don't understand," Lacy continues, her voice quavering. "I had only just gotten home and was making myself a tea when that man," she nods towards Knox, her eyes never leaving Rayne's face, "broke in and grabbed me. He tied me up and brought me down here to this... this basement. Rayne, please, you have to believe me!"

Her act is impressive, I'll give her that. The tremor in her voice, the way her body shakes with apparent fear, it's all very convincing. If I didn't know better, I might be swayed myself. But I do know better, and I can see the cracks in her facade.

There's a glint in her eyes that doesn't match her terrified words. A hint of calculation behind the tears. It's subtle, but it's there. I wonder if Rayne can see it too.

I glance at Knox, seeing the same thoughts reflected in his eyes. He catches my gaze, a silent communication passing between us. Then, with a small huff of laughter, he speaks.

"That's funny," Knox says, his voice low and dangerous, a predatory gleam in his eyes. "You seem to be forgetting the part where you laughed and said you hoped River and I would die slow, painful deaths."

Lacy's eyes widen, a picture of wounded innocence. "No! That's not true!" she cries, her voice pitched high with desperation. "Rayne, please, you can't believe them. They're lying!"

I watch the scene unfold, fascinated by the interplay of emotions flickering across both women's faces. Lacy's performance is Oscar-worthy, each trembling word and tearful glance carefully calculated to elicit sympathy.

My gaze shifts to Rayne, and I feel a surge of pride and affection. The doubt that had clouded her eyes mere moments ago is rapidly clearing, like storm clouds parting to reveal a brilliant sky. Her jaw sets, a steely determination replacing the uncertainty that had briefly flickered across her beautiful features.

It's reassuring to see how quickly Rayne's faith in us solidifies. All it took was a single word from Knox to tip the scales, to remind her of the unshakeable trust that binds us together. In that moment, I fall even deeper in love with her, if such a thing is possible.

Rayne takes a step closer to Lacy, her movements slow and deliberate. There's a new energy about her now, a predatory grace that sends a thrill down my spine. This is a side of Rayne we've only glimpsed before, and seeing it emerge fully is intoxicating.

"You know, Lacy," Rayne says, her voice calm and controlled, "I've always prided myself on my ability to read people. It's part of what makes me good at what I do."

As Rayne speaks, I watch the facade melt away from Lacy like wax under a flame. The trembling lip stills, the wide-eyed innocence fades, replaced by something altogether more sinister. It's as if a mask has been lifted, revealing the true face beneath, and it's not a pretty sight.

I reach down and lift my pants leg, my fingers wrapping around the familiar grip of the knife strapped there. The blade slides free with a soft whisper of steel against leather, the weight comforting in my palm. It's the same knife I used in the alley the other night, when I saved Rayne from that would-be attacker. The memory of how easily the blade sank into flesh, how warm blood coated my glove, sends a delicious shiver down my spine.

The knife is a vicious thing, designed for one purpose and one purpose only. Its serrated edge gleams dully in the dim light, promising pain and suffering to whoever feels its bite. I begin to circle them, my movements slow and deliberate, like a shark scenting blood in the water.

Lacy's eyes narrow, the fear and desperation replaced by a cold, calculating gleam. Her lips twist into a snarl, baring her teeth in a feral grin that sends a chill through me. Now revealing the true face of madness that had been lurking just beneath the surface.

"You're right, Rayne. You are good at reading people. But not good enough, it seems. Not good enough to see what was right in front of you all this time," Lacy hisses, her voice dripping with venom.

"You have no idea how long I've waited for this moment. To finally show you who I really am, Rayne." She leans forward in her chair, straining against her bonds. "I've watched you for months, you know. Followed your every move. Did you like my little gifts? The photos? The messages? I put so much thought into each one. I wanted them to be perfect."

A low growl builds in my chest as I listen to her deranged ranting. My grip tightens on the knife, knuckles white around the handle. I dart forward and press the tip of the blade against Lacy's sternum, just hard enough to dimple the skin beneath her silk blouse.

"Do we really need to know anything else?" I snarl, my voice rough with barely contained fury. "Or can I kill this bitch now?"

Knox tilts his head, considering. His eyes are cold and calculating as he regards Lacy. "We could always pass this off as another victim of the serial killer," he muses. "What do you think, Rayne?"

Rayne's eyes slide to Knox, and I see a twinkle of humor dancing in their sapphire depths. "I mean, sure, we could," she says with a nonchalant shrug, her tone light and casual as if we're discussing dinner plans rather than murder.

Knox steps closer to her, his imposing frame towering over her curvy figure. The contrast between them is striking–his dark, dangerous intensity against her soft femininity.

His large hand comes up, the backs of his fingers brushing tenderly against Rayne's cheek. The gentleness of the gesture is at odds with the predatory gleam in his eyes. "Are you done playing games yet, baby girl?" he asks softly, his gravelly voice barely above a whisper.

A wicked little grin spreads across Rayne's beautiful lips, transforming her face. It's a look I've never seen on her before–equal parts mischief and darkness, innocence and sin. Her eyes sparkle with a dangerous light, like the glint of a knife in the shadows. That grin speaks of hidden depths, of secrets and desires long kept buried. It's a promise and a challenge all at once.

I feel my breath catch in my throat at the sight. This–this right here–is my new favorite look on her. It's like watching the final piece of a complex puzzle slide into place, revealing the full, glorious picture we've only glimpsed hints of before.

The air in the room seems to shift, crackling with an electric tension. Rayne's transformation is palpable, her energy changing from uncertain victim to confident predator in the blink of an eye.

Rayne's eyes sparkle with mischief as she looks up at Knox through her lashes. "With you? Never..." she purrs, her voice low and sultry. The tension in the room shifts.

Knox huffs out a soft laugh, shaking his head slightly. His eyes dance with amusement and something darker, more primal. "Can we at least all stop pretending like we don't know you're the one killing off our targets in very public ways?"

The words hang in the air, heavy with implication. For a moment, the only sound is Lacy's ragged breathing and the soft hum of the overhead light.

Rayne raises an eyebrow, her grin widening impossibly further. The expression transforms her face further, revealing the predator that's always lurked beneath her sweet exterior. It's like watching a flower unfurl its petals, only to reveal razor-sharp thorns hidden within.

"Well," she drawls, each word dripping with dark humor, "you weren't making a move. You had been stalking me for months and still hadn't done anything. What was a girl to do?"

Her words send a thrill through me. The casual way she admits to her kills, the playful challenge in her tone—it's intoxicating. I feel a surge of pride and desire, marveling at how perfectly she fits with us. This beautiful, deadly creature who's been dancing on the edge of darkness all along, waiting for us to catch up.

Knox's eyes darken with desire, his pupils dilating as he drinks in the sight of Rayne's transformation. A slow, predatory smile spreads across his face, matching her wicked grin. The tension in the room ratchets up another notch, crackling like electricity in the air.

"You knew we were stalking you this whole time?" Knox asks, his voice a low rumble that sends shivers down my spine. "Did you know who I was the whole time?"

Rayne tilts her head, regarding Knox with an expression that suggests he should have realized the obvious by now. Her eyes dance with mischief and dark humor as she lets the silence stretch, savoring the moment.

"Oh, Knox," she purrs, her voice rich with amusement. "Do you think I moved to this town for the scenery?" She pauses, letting her words sink in before continuing. "Or that I just randomly chose to frequent a bakery a block from the police station on the opposite side of town?"

A bark of laughter escapes me before I can stop it. This is absolutely delicious. I move the knife away from our captive, bringing it up to my lips as I hum and send a wicked grin toward Knox and Rayne. As much as I want to carve Lacy up, I already know what Knox is thinking—we need a scapegoat, and Lacy is the perfect volunteer.

I turn toward Knox and Rayne, my eyes glinting with mischief. "You're going to take away my fun, aren't you?" I ask, my voice a playful whine that belies the darkness lurking beneath.

Knox's lips twitch, fighting back a smile. "Sorry, River," he says, not sounding sorry at all. "But you have to admit, this is too perfect an opportunity to pass up."

I sigh dramatically, twirling the knife between my fingers with practiced ease. The blade catches the dim light, sending little flashes across the room. "I suppose you're right," I concede, my tone mock-reluctant. "It would be a shame to waste such a golden opportunity."

Rayne's eyes follow the movement of the knife, her gaze hungry and appreciative. There's no fear in her expression, only a dark fascination that makes my blood sing. She steps closer to me, close enough that I can feel the heat radiating from her body.

"Don't worry, darling," she purrs, her voice low and sultry. "I have a feeling we're going to have plenty of fun together very soon."

Her words send a shiver of anticipation down my spine. The promise in her tone, the wicked glint in her eye–it's fucking hot.

Knox reaches behind his back, his movements fluid and practiced. When it reappears it's gripping a beautiful black gun, the metal gleaming dully in the dim light. He levels it at Lacy, his aim steady and unwavering.

"We can plant some evidence," Knox says, his voice low and controlled. "Zeke can help set up the tech side of things. Make it look like you resisted arrest, had a weapon of your own."

I nod, understanding the implication. "I may need to lose my knife, wipe it down and make sure hers are the only prints found on it," I say, a hint of regret in my tone. "But I'm sure you'll buy me a nice, sexy new one to replace it."

Knox's lips twitch in the barest hint of a smile. "Of course," he murmurs. "Only the best for you, baby."

Rayne tilts her head, a playful pout forming on her lush lips. She huffs softly, her eyes twinkling with mischief. "I mean, at least she gave me flowers," she says, her tone a perfect blend of mock indignation and dark humor.

I can't help but grin at her words, my heart swelling with adoration for this beautifully twisted woman. I turn to face her fully, my eyes locking with hers. "I will happily give you flowers every day if you want, gorgeous," I purr, my voice low and seductive. "Would you like them from my left hand or my right?"

With a flourish, I raise both hands, palms facing towards me, showcasing the intricate tattoos that adorn the backs of them. Delicate peonies and sprigs of lavender intertwine across my skin, their petals and stems flowing seamlessly. The flowers are rendered in exquisite detail, each petal lovingly shaded to create depth and texture. Soft dusky pinks and purples dominate the design, with greys and hints of dark green providing a natural contrast.

I remember the day I got these tattoos, not long after I discovered Rayne's favorite flowers. The artist had looked at me strangely when I requested flowers on my hands, but I didn't care. I wanted to carry a piece of Rayne with me always, even before she knew who I was.

Her gaze traces every delicate petal, every carefully shaded leaf. The wonder in her expression is breathtaking—it's like I've just offered her the moon and stars, or blood diamonds.

I shift to the side so Knox can take care of Lacy so we can go home. I'll let her look at them all she wants before I wrap them around her pretty throat while I fuck her.

But what happens next catches us all off guard.

Lacy throws her head back and laughs.

It's not the nervous giggle of someone facing death, nor the hysterical cackle of a mind unhinged by fear. No, this is a full-bodied, genuine laugh. The sound echoes off the bare walls, filling the small space.

Knox tilts his head, narrowing his eyes at our captive. His finger tightens imperceptibly on the trigger, but he doesn't fire. Not yet.

When Lacy finally calms, she shakes her head, a sardonic smile playing at her lips. "You seem to be missing a tiny detail," she says, her voice dripping with smug satisfaction. "I may have delivered all those little presents, but they weren't from me."

As though she timed it perfectly, in the silence that follows her words, we hear noises from upstairs. A muffled voice, calling out and getting louder as it approaches. Whoever it is, they're coming down toward the basement.

The atmosphere in the room shifts instantly. Knox's grip on his gun tightens, his knuckles turning white. My body tenses and I pull out my own gun, aiming it toward the basement door.

But it's Rayne's reaction that truly catches my attention. Something shifts on her gorgeous face, a flicker of... something? Her eyes widen slightly, a mix of emotions swirling in their depths–surprise, confusion, and something else I can't quite place.

The footsteps grow louder, echoing in the stairwell outside. A shadow passes across the small, grimy window in the door. The handle turns with an ominous creak.

As the door swings open, light from the stairwell spills into the room, momentarily blinding us. A silhouette fills the doorway, tall and imposing.

"Well, well, well," a deep voice drawls.

It's then I realize what the other emotion is as it fills her face and I want to set the world on fire; it's fear.

Her voice is barely audible but it makes me murderous. "Dad?"

Chapter 39

Rayne

THE EUPHORIA OF FINALLY revealing my secrets vanishes in a microsecond. Fear claws at my insides, threatening to overwhelm me as I stare at the man who had haunted my nightmares for so long. My father. The monster who murdered my mother when she tried to protect me from his vile intentions.

For a heartbeat, I feel like that terrified little girl again, cowering in the corner as violence erupted around me. The metallic scent of blood filled my nostrils, phantom echoes of my mother's screams ringing in my ears. My legs tremble, threatening to give out beneath me.

But then, as quickly as it came, the fear recedes. In its place, a tidal wave of pure, incandescent rage washes over me. My hands clench into fists at my sides, nails biting into my palms hard enough to draw blood. The pain grounds me, fueling the inferno building inside.

I am not that helpless child anymore. I am not a goddamn victim.

I am a fucking killer.

My eyes narrow as I take in every detail of the man before me. He looks older, of course—prison will do that to a person. His once-dark hair is now shot through with gray, and deep lines etch his face. But his eyes... those cold, cruel eyes are exactly as I remember them. They sweep over the room, taking in Knox and River with their weapons drawn, before finally landing on me.

A slow, predatory smile spreads across my father's face as his eyes lock with mine. It's a look I know all too well—the expression of a man who thinks he holds all the cards, who believes he is about to crush his opponents beneath his heel.

How wrong he is.

I can feel Knox and River tensing behind me, their weapons trained steadily on my father. The air crackles with tension, thick enough to cut with a knife. One wrong move, one twitch of a finger, and bullets will fly.

But this isn't their fight. Not yet.

Without taking my eyes off my father, I raise my hand. "Wait," I say, my voice low but firm.

"Rayne?" Knox questions, a note of concern in his gravelly tone. I can hear the unspoken questions in that single word. Are you okay? Do you want us to take him out? What's the play here?

I don't answer immediately. My mind is racing, piecing together the puzzle before me. How is he here? He should be rotting in a prison cell, not standing in this dingy basement with that smug grin on his face. And Lacy... how does she fit into all of this?

My father's grin widens, no doubt thinking he has caught us off guard. He probably expects me to cower, to shrink back in fear at the sight of him. But the fear that had initially gripped me has burned away, leaving nothing but cold fury.

I feel my lip curl in disgust as I stare at the him. "How the hell did you get out of prison?" I ask, venom dripping from every word. "I was hoping you'd been shanked by now. Save the taxpayers some money."

My father throws his head back and laughs, the sound grating against my nerves like nails on a chalkboard. His amusement only serves to stoke the fires of my rage.

"Oh, my dear," he drawls, his voice dripping with condescension. "Good behavior, a sympathetic parole board, and prison overcrowding can work wonders. It's amazing what a cocktail like that can do for a man's prospects."

The smug satisfaction in his tone makes my skin crawl. He stands there, so fucking pleased with himself, as if he's pulled off some great feat. As if conning his way out of a well-deserved prison sentence is something to be proud of.

"Besides," he continues, gesturing vaguely towards Lacy, "it helped that I had a good woman waiting for me on the outside." Oddly, he makes no move to free her, shows no concern for her predicament.

I scoff, unable to contain my disbelief and disgust. "How the hell did you two even meet? What, did you put an ad in the prison newsletter? 'Convicted murderer seeks deranged stalker for long walks on the beach and terrorizing my daughter'?"

My father's eyes narrow slightly at my sarcasm, but then his expression shifts, a look of mock hurt crossing his weathered features. "Now, now, Rayne. Is that any way to talk to your dear old dad? She was a pen pal, she gave me the only comfort I could get in that prison." He tsks, shaking his head. "And here I thought we could have a nice family reunion."

He takes a step closer, his movements slow and deliberate. I stand my ground, refusing to give an inch. From the corner of my eye, I can see Knox tensing further, ready to spring into action at a moment's notice. River steps up behind me, pressing against my back and I reach down to grasp his hand.

"You want to know how this all came about?" my father continues, spreading his arms wide as if he's about to tell a grand story. "It's quite simple, really. A beautiful twist of fate, you might say."

He pauses, clearly savoring the moment, relishing the attention. "When I got out, I had no intention of finding you. As far as I was concerned, that chapter of my life was closed. I was going to start fresh, make a new life for myself."

A sardonic smile plays at his lips. "But then, one night, as I was picking up a few essentials at the grocery store, who should I see but my darling daughter?" His eyes lock onto mine, a predatory gleam in their depths. "You were standing there in the produce section, deliberating between two different types of apples. So focused, so oblivious to the world around you."

My father's eyes glint with a sinister light as he continues his tale, each word dripping with a perverse satisfaction. "I couldn't believe my luck. There you were, all grown up and beautiful. The spitting image of your mother." His gaze rakes over me, leaving me feeling dirty and exposed. "I followed you that day, all the way back to that quaint little studio of yours."

He takes another step closer, and I have to fight the urge to back away.

"After that, it was easy," my father says with a casual shrug. "I did some digging, found out about your little photography business. It wasn't hard to... convince Lacy to help me."

Lacy shifts in her chair, a proud smile spreading across her face despite the circumstances. "He told me all about you, Rayne," she says, her voice sickeningly sweet. "How you two had been estranged for so long, how he just wanted to reconnect with his little girl. It was so touching, so romantic in a way. I couldn't resist helping. He even got me to book a session with you so we could connect and become friends."

She's a fucking nutcase.

I stare at Lacy, incredulous at her delusion. A bitter laugh escapes my lips, harsh and humorless.

"Oh, he told you all about me, did he?" I ask, my voice dripping with sarcasm. "I bet he painted quite the picture. Poor, misunderstood father, just wanting to reconnect with his ungrateful daughter." I take a step closer to Lacy, my eyes boring into hers. "Tell me, Lacy, did he also mention how he brutally murdered his first wife? My mother?"

The words hang in the air, heavy and charged. For a moment, the only sound in the room is our collective breathing and the soft hum of the overhead light.

I watch as my father's smile falters, just for a fraction of a second. It's barely noticeable, but I catch it. That tiny crack in his facade is all the confirmation I need.

Lacy's eyes narrow, darting between me and my father. "No," she says, shaking her head vehemently. "No, you're lying. You're just an ungrateful child who doesn't appreciate everything your father has done for you. He told me you might say things like this, try to turn me against him."

I can't help it. I look at her like the crazy bitch she is, my disgust and disbelief written plainly across my face. This woman who thought she was living out some twisted romantic fantasy, who the hell believed the lies of a murderer without question. The pity I might have felt for her earlier evaporates like mist in the morning sun.

"He was in prison for murdering her, you stupid bitch," I snarl, my words sharp enough to cut glass. "He killed her because she stopped him from trying to fuck me. That's the sort of man you crawled into bed with."

As the words leave my mouth, I watch the transformation unfold on my father's face. The mask of civility he had been wearing crumbles away, revealing the monster I remember from my childhood. His features contort with rage, twisting into an ugly snarl that sends a chill down my spine despite my determination to stand my ground.

His eyes, once coldly calculating, now burn with a manic fury. The lines on his face deepen, etching canyons of hatred across his weathered skin. His jaw clenches so tightly I can almost hear his teeth grinding together. The veins in his neck and forehead bulge, pulsing with each ragged breath he takes.

"You little cunt," he spits, his voice a guttural growl that barely sounds human. Flecks of spittle fly from his lips as he continues his tirade. "You were always an ungrateful little bitch, just like your whore of a mother!"

He takes a menacing step forward, his hands curling into fists at his sides. The knuckles stand out white against his skin, scarred and calloused from years of violence. I can see the tension in his arms, the way the muscles bunch and coil beneath the fabric of his shirt. He's like a serpent preparing to strike, all coiled rage and deadly intent.

"I should have had you killed years ago," he snarls, his words dripping with venom.

The sight of him, ranting and raving like the unhinged psychopath he truly is, solidifies something within me.

I've heard enough. Like fuck am I standing here having any more 'sparkling conversation with dear old dad'.

Time seems to slow as I bring up my right hand–the one that had been grasping River's, the one he had subtly slipped his gun into when he stepped behind me. The weight of the weapon is unfamiliar yet comforting in my palm. My finger curls around the trigger.

I don't hesitate. I don't second-guess. I simply act.

The loud crack of the gunshot echoes through the small room, reverberating off the concrete walls. The acrid scent of gunpowder fills the air, mingling with the musty odor of the basement. My father's scream of agony follows a split second later as he crumples to the ground, clutching his shattered kneecap. Blood seeps between his fingers, a vivid crimson against his pale skin.

The sight of him writhing on the dirty floor, his face contorted in pain, sends a rush of dark satisfaction through me. This man, this monster who had tormented me for so long, reduced to a pathetic, mewling wreck by my hand. It's intoxicating.

Lacy's shriek of outrage cuts through my father's pained groans. "You bitch!" she screams, her face twisted into a mask of fury and disbelief. "I'll fucking kill you!"

As her shrill threat pierces the air, I pivot smoothly, the gun an extension of my arm. Her eyes widen in shock, mouth still open mid-scream as I squeeze the trigger. I watch the bullet's impact. It strikes Lacy square in the chest, the force of it jerking her body back against the chair. A small, perfect circle appears in her silk blouse, rapidly blooming into a crimson flower. Her eyes, wide with disbelief and pain, lock onto mine for a brief moment before the light in them begins to fade.

As Lacy's final breath rattles from her lungs, I calmly switch on the gun's safety. Without looking, I hold it out to River, butt first. "Is she still a sufficient scapegoat?" I ask, my voice eerily calm in the aftermath of violence.

I can practically feel the grins spreading across Knox and River's faces. There's a beat of silence, then River's low chuckle breaks the tension. "Oh, little Rayne," he purrs, taking the gun from my hand, his fingers lingering on mine for a moment longer than necessary. "She'll work just nicely."

Knox nods, his eyes gleaming with a mix of pride and dark desire. "Agreed," he rumbles, holstering his own weapon. "This works out perfectly."

"Good," I say, a wicked smile curving my lips. I gesture to the chairs along the wall. "Then grab a seat and watch, boys. I have something truly beautiful in mind for dear old dad."

River passes me his knife as he and Knox exchange heated looks before moving to do as I've instructed. The scrape of chair legs against concrete echoes in the small space as they settle in, eyes locked on me with rapt attention.

I turn back to my father, still writhing on the floor in agony. Taking my time, I circle him slowly, savoring each pained gasp and whimper. When I speak, my voice is low and dangerous. "You know, I've thought about this moment for years. Dreamed of all the ways I could make you suffer."

My heel comes down hard on his shattered kneecap, grinding the shards of bone together. His scream is music to my ears. "And now that I have you here, I find myself feeling... creative."

I take my time, savoring every moment as I inflict pain upon the monster who tormented me for so long. My hands are steady as I work, methodically carving my rage into his flesh. Blood flows freely, staining the concrete floor crimson.

As I carve into my father's flesh, I pause momentarily and look up, catching sight of Knox and River watching me intently from their seats. Their expressions send a thrill through me unlike anything I've ever experienced.

Knox's eyes are dark with desire, pupils blown wide as he drinks in every detail of my bloody work. His jaw is clenched, the muscles twitching with barely restrained lust. One large hand grips the arm of his chair so tightly his knuckles have gone white, while the other is wrapped firmly around River's cock, stroking in time with my movements.

River looks utterly entranced, his eyes gleaming with a mix of awe and carnal hunger. His lips are parted slightly, chest heaving with each ragged breath. He leans into Knox's touch even as his own hand works Knox's length. The sight of them pleasuring each other while watching me is intoxicating.

But it's more than just physical desire I see reflected in their eyes. There's reverence there, a look of absolute worship that makes my heart soar. They're seeing me—truly seeing me—perhaps for the first time. Not as a victim to be protected or a delicate flower to be shielded from the darkness, but as their equal.

They look at me like I'm a goddess made flesh, terrible and beautiful. A being to be feared and adored in equal measure.

In this moment, covered in my father's blood with a knife in my hand, I've never felt more powerful or more alive. Every experience that led me to this point–the pain, the fear, the loneliness—it all crystallizes into perfect clarity. Every step of my journey, every dark impulse I've nurtured in secret, has led me to this exquisite moment. It was all worth it. River was right. I wouldn't trade my past for anything, because it forged me into who I am now.

A killer.

Their queen.

I return my attention to my father, relishing his agonized whimpers as I continue my bloody work. I lose myself in the rhythm of it–the slice of the blade, the screams of agony, the wet sounds of tearing flesh. Time seems to stretch and blur, measured only by my father's weakening cries and rasping breaths.

When I finally step back, my arms are coated in gore up to the elbows. My father lies motionless, barely recognizable as human. A sense of peace washes over me, years of fear and anger releasing their hold on my soul.

Epilogue
River

6 Months Later

TONIGHT, RAYNE IS HAVING drinks with her friend Kahlee, giving me the perfect opportunity to have Knox all to myself. Well, with the exception of Luna, who is currently sprawled in one of the beds of a brand new cat tree with a small pouch of catnip Knox snuck her.

It's been six months since we wrapped up the serial killer investigation, and while we couldn't use Lacy as a scapegoat like we planned, we managed to cover our tracks well enough. The case was closed as unsolved, but we all knew the truth.

As amazing and awe inspiring as it was watching Rayne torture and kill her father, it meant a good hour had passed since she had shot Lacy. It's a little hard to get away with waiting that long to call it in. So we simply disposed of them and since then have been on our best behavior.

We did manage to convince Rayne to move in with us with the promise of her own reading room and a new studio space on another floor of our building. She initially hesitated until Kahlee told her she needed to move again, stating someone she thinks works for her ex was sniffing around. So Rayne told Kahlee to move into her place and transfer her studio into a family photography space.

We got Zeke to set up some security and keep an eye out just in case. But there hasn't been anything suspicious since then so the girls decided to have a night out to let off some steam.

I sprawl lazily across the plush leather couch, a tumbler of whiskey dangling from my fingers as I watch Knox move about the kitchen cleaning up from the dinner I cooked. The late afternoon sun streams through the floor-to-ceiling windows, bathing him in a golden glow that highlights every muscular curve of his body. He's wearing nothing but a pair of low-slung sweatpants, and I can't help but admire the way the fabric clings to his ass as he bends to return something to a lower cabinet.

"You know," I drawl, a wicked grin playing at my lips, "It's been a while since I've had you all to myself like this."

Knox glances over his shoulder, a smirk tugging at the corner of his mouth. "Don't get too comfortable," he warns, his voice a low rumble that sends shivers down my spine. "Rayne will be home before you know it."

I hum in acknowledgment, taking a sip of my whiskey. The amber liquid burns pleasantly as it slides down my throat. "True," I concede, "but we've got at least another hour before she's done with her girls' night with Kahlee. Plenty of time for some fun."

Knox chuckles, the sound rich and deep. He turns fully towards me, leaning back against the kitchen counter. The movement causes his sweatpants to ride even lower on his hips, revealing that delicious V that makes me hot every time. He knows what they do to me, so I know he wears them on purpose.

I can't help but marvel at how far we've come. From two lost, broken boys in the foster system, to this—lovers, partners, and now, part of a twisted trio with the most extraordinary woman I've ever known.

Knox stalks towards me, his movements fluid and predatory, and I feel my breath catch in my throat. The intensity in his eyes sends a thrill of anticipation coursing through my body. Without breaking eye contact, he reaches down and plucks the tumbler from my hand. I open my mouth to protest, but the words die on my lips as I watch him tip his head back, draining the remaining whiskey in one smooth motion.

Before I can react, Knox's hand shoots out, fingers wrapping firmly around my jaw. His grip is tight, bordering on painful, as he forces my mouth open. My pulse quickens, a mix of excitement and arousal flooding my system. Knox leans in close, his breath hot against my skin. I can smell the whiskey on him, rich and intoxicating.

Slowly, deliberately, Knox parts his lips. The amber liquid begins to trickle from his mouth into mine, a warm, sensual cascade. The alcohol burns as it hits my tongue, mingling with the taste of Knox himself—a combination that makes my head spin.

As the last of the whiskey passes between us, Knox closes the distance, crushing his mouth against mine. The kiss is fierce, almost brutal in its intensity. His tongue invades my mouth, chasing the lingering taste of whiskey. I moan into the kiss, my hands coming up to tangle in his hair, pulling him closer.

Instead Knox pulls back slightly, pushing back against my grip, his teeth grazing my lower lip. "Swallow," he growls, his voice rough with desire.

I obey without hesitation, swallowing the whiskey. Knox watches intently, his eyes dark with lust as my throat bobs. The moment the last drop disappears, he surges forward again, reclaiming my mouth in a searing kiss.

He pulls me up off the couch and then his hands shift, one pressing firmly on my shoulders, guiding me down. His growl is both rough and irresistible as he commands, "On your knees."

I sink down until I'm on my knees before him. My heart races, anticipation and desire coursing through me.

Knox's hand threads through my hair again, gripping firmly. "Good boy," he murmurs, his deep voice sending shivers down my spine. I melt at his praise. His other hand moves to the waistband of his sweats, slowly pushing them down.

I watch, transfixed, as his impressive length springs free. He's large, thick and hard, the sight making my mouth water. Knox guides my head closer, the tip of his cock brushing against my lips.

"Open," he commands.

I hesitate for just a moment, a wicked grin pulling at my lips before he grips my hair tightly. The heat pooling low in my belly and the ache in my cock overrides everything else. I part my lips, allowing Knox to guide himself into my waiting mouth.

He groans low in his throat as I take him in, the sound sending another jolt of arousal through me. His fingers tightens in my hair harder as he begins to move, setting a slow but insistent rhythm.

I hollow my cheeks, swirling my tongue along his length as he slides in and out. The taste of him, the weight on my tongue, the stretch of my lips around him, the sounds he makes when I move my tongue just right–it's intoxicating, it's addictive. I moan softly, the vibrations making Knox's hips jerk. The head of his cock hits the back of my throat and I swallow around him before forcing myself to relax.

"That's it, fuck, you're mouth is perfect," he growls, pushing deeper. My eyes flick up to his and the look I see there tells me everything I need without words. Before Knox, I never knew it was possible to have a look of pure worship on your face when you aren't the one on your knees.

I'm consumed by the taste and feel of Knox in my mouth, my senses overwhelmed. His grip in my hair is tight as he guides my movements, controlling the pace. I focus on relaxing my throat more, taking him deeper with each thrust.

I'm lost in the sensation of Knox, the taste of him on my tongue, when suddenly he's pulling me to my feet. His hands are rough as he yanks down my own sweatpants, exposing my aching cock to the cool air. I shiver, partly from the chill and partly from anticipation.

Knox's eyes rake over my body, dark with lust. "You little tease," he growls, his voice husky. "Wearing these all day, knowing what they do to me."

I open my mouth to retort about him doing the exact same thing, but I'm cut off by the sound of the front door opening. We both freeze, turning towards the entrance.

Rayne steps in, a knowing smirk playing on her full lips as she takes in the scene before her. She's wearing a long winter coat over her dress, which isn't surprising given the frigid temperatures outside. What is surprising is the way her eyes gleam with a predatory light, a look we've come to know well over the past six months.

"Don't stop on my account, boys," she purrs, her voice low and sultry.

As she speaks, she lets the coat slip from her shoulders, allowing it to pool at her feet. The sight that greets us steals the breath from my lungs.

Rayne stands before us in a form-fitting black dress that clings to every luscious contour of her body. But it's not the dress that captures our attention. It's the blood. Rich, crimson blood coats her arms up to the elbows, splattered across her chest and face in a macabre pattern. It glistens wetly in the soft light of our apartment, still fresh and vibrant. The sight is both terrifying and breathtakingly beautiful.

Knox's grip on my hip tightens, his fingers digging into my flesh hard enough to bruise. I can feel the tremor that runs through his body, a mix of surprise and arousal. My own cock twitches in response, hardening further despite the shock of Rayne's unexpected appearance.

"Rayne, sweetheart," Knox breathes, his voice a mix of concern and dark curiosity. "What happened?"

She shrugs nonchalantly, as if coming home covered in blood is an everyday occurrence. "Oh, you know," she says casually, her eyes glinting with wicked amusement. "Some guy decided he wanted to follow Kahlee home, so I took care of him." Her blood-stained lips curl into a predatory smile. "You can never be too careful, detectives. There are so many stalkers out there, after all."

The way she says it, so matter-of-fact and unapologetic, sends a shiver of excitement down my spine. This woman, this beautiful, deadly creature, never ceases to amaze me.

Rayne begins to walk towards us, her hips swaying hypnotically with each step. Her hands move to the zipper of her dress, slowly pulling it down. The black fabric parts, revealing tantalizing glimpses of creamy skin and lacy lingerie beneath.

She shrugs the dress off her shoulders, letting it fall to the floor in a whisper of silk. My breath catches in my throat at the sight of her standing there in nothing but a black lace bra, matching thong, and sky-high stilettos. The blood splattered across her pale skin creates a stark, erotic contrast that makes my cock throb with need.

As Rayne reaches behind her back to unclasp her bra, I find my voice. "Leave it," I command, my tone rough with desire. "The lingerie and the heels stay on."

A wicked smile pulls at her blood-stained lips. "As you wish," she purrs. Her eyes gleam with mischief as she adds, "Why don't you go get the lube, my cute little psycho? It looks like ass fucking is on the menu for all of us tonight."

I shiver at her words, anticipation coiling low in my belly. I nod, reluctantly tearing myself away from the intoxicating sight before me. As I head to the bedroom to retrieve the lube, I detour to the corner of the living room and switch on the camera we have set up there. When I turn around the sight that greets me nearly takes my breath away. Rayne is kneeling in the center of the room, her back arched gracefully, presenting herself to us. The blood splattered across her pale skin glistens in the soft lighting, creating an erotic contrast with her black lace lingerie. Knox kneels behind her, his large hands caressing her body with reverent touches.

I stride over to them, unable to resist kneeling and pulling Rayne into a deep, passionate kiss. Her lips are soft against mine. When we part, both breathless, I grin wickedly at her.

"Pose for me, little Rayne," I purr, gesturing towards the camera. "Let's make sure we capture every delicious moment of this."

Rayne's eyes light up with mischief and desire. She shifts her position, lowering her front onto the pile of pillows Knox has arranged, facing the large mirror on the side wall. The position raises her ass while giving her a perfect view of everything that's about to unfold.

I move behind her, sliding between her and Knox, drinking in the sight of her perfect ass framed by the delicate lace of her thong. With deliberate slowness, I pour a generous amount of lube onto my fingers, making sure Rayne can see every movement in the mirror.

I tease my slick fingers along the cleft of Rayne's ass, watching her shiver in anticipation. Slowly, I pull the lacy thong to the side and circle her tight hole with my lubed fingers. Rayne's breath hitches as I press one finger inside, her inner muscles clenching around the intrusion.

"Relax, sweetheart," I murmur, working my finger in deeper. "Let me open you up."

As I prepare Rayne, I feel Knox's presence behind me, his body radiating heat. His hands grip my hips, thumbs digging into the dimples above my ass. I hear the snap of the lube cap and then cool wetness drizzling between my cheeks.

Knox's thick finger probes at my entrance and I groan, pressing back against him. The dual sensation of fingering Rayne while Knox opens me up is intoxicating. My cock throbs, heavy and aching to be touched.

When Rayne is ready, I line myself up with her slick hole. I push forward slowly, savoring the tight heat as I sink into her slowly. At the same time, Knox presses the head of his cock against my own entrance. The pressure builds until he buries himself inside me in one smooth thrust.

For a moment, we're all still, adjusting to the intense sensations. Then Knox begins to move, setting a slow, deep rhythm. Each thrust drives me deeper into Rayne, making her cry out in pleasure.

The sensations are incredible–Knox's thick length stretching me open as I bury myself in Rayne's perfect ass. I'm surrounded, filled, caught between them in the most delicious way.

Rayne's eyes meet mine in the mirror, heavy-lidded with pleasure. The sight of her—cheeks flushed, lips parted, eyes wild with lust—nearly undoes me. I reach forward, tangling my fingers in her long, dark hair. With a firm grip, I pull her head back, exposing the elegant line of her throat. Her gasp of pleasure echoes through the room, mingling with the obscene sounds of flesh against flesh.

Behind me, Knox is a solid wall of muscle, tattoos and heat. His large hands grip my hips with bruising force, guiding my movements as he thrusts into me. His rhythm picks up, his thrusts becoming harder, more insistent. Rayne pushes her hips back to meet me with each thrust, pulling guttural moans from both of us. The sound of skin slapping against skin echoes through the room, punctuated by our ragged breathing and desperate cries of pleasure.

I feel myself getting close, the dual sensations of Knox filling me and Rayne's tight heat around my cock pushing me towards the edge. But I want more. I need more.

"Knox," I growl, my voice rough with desire. "Harder. Fucking *wreck* me."

Knox's response is immediate and fierce. His grip on my hips tightens, fingers digging in hard enough to leave bruises. He pulls almost all the way out before slamming back in with brutal force. The power of his thrust drives me hard into Rayne, making her cry out in a mix of pleasure and pain.

"Like that, River?" Knox growls, his voice low and dangerous. "Is this what you want?"

He sets a punishing pace, each thrust harder than the last. The force of it rocks me forward, driving me relentlessly into Rayne's ass. I can feel every inch of him as he pounds into me, stretching me open, filling me completely. The burn and stretch is exquisite, riding the razor's edge between pleasure and pain.

"Fuck, baby," Knox growls, his voice a low rumble that sends shivers down my spine. "You feel so fucking good. So tight for me."

Rayne's cries grow louder, more desperate. Her inner muscles clench around me, milking my cock with each thrust. I tighten my grip in her hair, pulling her head back further. The arch of her spine is beautiful, a perfect curve of pale skin marred by splashes of drying blood.

Knox's thrusts turn brutal, each snap of his hips driving into me with punishing force. The power behind his movements is my undoing. I lose all semblance of control, my rhythm becoming harsh and erratic as I pound into Rayne.

The sensations overwhelm me. It's too much, too intense. I feel myself hurtling towards the edge, unable to hold back any longer.

I drive into her with wild abandon, all finesse lost to primal need. The sound of flesh slapping against flesh echoes through the room, punctuated by our collective grunts and moans. Rayne's cries grow louder, more desperate with each punishing thrust.

"Oh god, oh fuck," she gasps, her voice raw and broken. "River, Knox, I'm so close. Please, please, I need..."

Her words dissolve into incoherent whimpers as I angle my hips, hitting that perfect spot inside her. The pressure builds, a coiling tension low in my belly that threatens to snap at any moment.

Knox's hand snakes around, gripping my throat and pulling me back against his chest. The new angle drives him impossibly deeper, hitting that spot inside me with unerring accuracy. Stars explode behind my eyes, pleasure crackling along every nerve ending.

"Come for me," Knox commands, his voice a low, dangerous rumble in my ear. "Both of you. Fucking come now."

Like a dam breaking, it hits me all at once. My orgasm crashes over me in waves of white-hot ecstasy. I cry out, my voice raw and animalistic as I empty myself into Rayne's tight heat. My vision blurs as I feel Rayne shatter around me. Her body convulses, inner walls clamping down on my cock as she cries out. I feel the heat of Knox's release as his own pace stutters to a stop.

As the last tremors of our shared orgasm fade, we collapse onto the floor in a tangle of sweaty limbs and heaving chests. The room is thick with the scent of sex and the metallic tang of blood. For a moment, the only sounds are our ragged breaths and the faint hum of the air conditioning.

I lie there, sandwiched between Knox and Rayne, feeling utterly spent and blissfully content. Knox's solid warmth presses against my back, his arm draped possessively over my waist. Rayne is curled into my chest, her blood-spattered skin sticky against mine. The contrast of her soft contours and Knox's hard planes is exquisite, a perfect balance of feminine and masculine.

As we bask in the afterglow, a soft thump draws my attention. I crack open an eye to see Luna gracefully descending from her cat tree, her tail swishing behind her with regal disdain. She pads across the room, her paws making no sound on the hardwood floor, before settling a few feet away from our sprawled bodies.

Luna sits down, wrapping her tail neatly around her paws. Her amber eyes survey us with a mixture of disgust and accusation, as if we've committed some grave feline faux pas by engaging in such debauchery in her presence. Her whiskers twitch, nose wrinkling slightly as she catches the mingled scents of blood, sweat, and sex hanging in the air.

Rayne catches sight of Luna's judgmental stare and dissolves into a fit of giggles. The sound is light and musical, a stark contrast to the passionate cries that filled the room just moments ago. Her body shakes with mirth.

Luna's tail twitches in annoyance at us, her eyes narrowing to slits. She looks for all the world like a disapproving matron who's caught us in some scandalous act. Which, I suppose, she has.

"I'm sorry, Your Majesty," Rayne manages to gasp out between giggles. "We'll try to keep our depraved human activities to a minimum in your presence."

Luna's tail twitches again, her whiskers quivering with disdain. With one last withering look, she turns her back on us and begins to fastidiously groom herself, as if to cleanse away the very sight of our debauchery.

Knox chuckles, the sound rumbling through his chest. "I think we've offended Her Royal Highness," he says, his voice still husky from our exertions. His hand traces lazy patterns on my hip as he speaks.

I grin, pressing a kiss to Rayne's temple. "Well, we can't have that, can we? We'd better make it up to her."

Rayne hums in agreement, her giggles subsiding. "Extra treats for Luna tomorrow," she declares. "And maybe a new toy. We wouldn't want her plotting our demise. The treats might just buy us some time."

Bonus

Luna

Humans. Utterly ridiculous creatures.

I watch as my three pets sprawl on the floor, their naked bodies tangled together in a most undignified manner. The air is thick with strange scents—sweat, blood, and that musky odor they produce when engaging in their bizarre mating rituals. How completely un-civilized.

I settle myself a safe distance away, wrapping my tail neatly around my paws. Really, they should know better than to carry on like this in my presence. I am royalty, after all. Such debauchery has no place in the court of Queen Luna.

My smallest pet, Rayne, notices me first. She dissolves into a fit of giggles, her body shaking in a most unseemly fashion. Does she not realize how ridiculous she looks, covered in dried blood and writhing about on the floor?

"I'm sorry, Your Majesty," she manages to gasp out between bouts of laughter. "We'll try to keep our depraved human activities to a minimum in your presence."

At least she has the decency to apologize, though her tone lacks the proper reverence. I narrow my eyes, fixing her with my most withering stare. Let her feel the full weight of my disapproval.

Do they have no shame? No sense of decorum? I'm a royal creature, descended from the sacred cats of Egypt. I shouldn't have to witness such... debauchery.

They're talking now, their voices low and affectionate. I catch something about "treats" and "toys," which piques my interest despite my disgust. Perhaps there's hope for them yet.

I turn my back on them, focusing instead on grooming my beautiful fur. Let them see what real grace and elegance looks like.

My two larger pets have odd fur, all patchy and colorful. I've tried grooming them before, but it never comes off. Maybe they both needs a proper tongue bath.

These humans truly have no sense of proper etiquette. Here I am, forced to witness their unseemly behavior, and now they also have the audacity to ignore my dinner time which has long passed? Unacceptable.

I rise gracefully to my paws, stretching languidly to remind them of my feline perfection. My claws extend, tiny daggers of gleaming ivory, as I flex my toes against the hardwood floor. Perhaps a gentle reminder of my displeasure is in order.

With silent steps, I approach the tangled mass of limbs that is my trio of pets. They remain oblivious to my presence, lost in their own little world of soft touches and whispered words. How rude. Do they not realize that I, Queen Luna, require their full attention?

I pause at the edge of their little cuddle puddle, tail swishing in irritation. The smallest one, Rayne, has her back to me. Her pale skin is marred by drying streaks of red—honestly, these humans and their messy habits. It's almost as bad as when they insist on "bathing" in that strange waterfall room instead of properly grooming themselves with their tongues like civilized creatures.

Well, if they won't acknowledge me of their own accord, I'll simply have to take matters into my own paws.

With precise aim, I extend one paw and delicately press my claws against Rayne's exposed back. Not hard enough to break the skin—I'm not a savage, after all—but just enough to make my presence known. The effect is immediate and most satisfying.

Rayne yelps, her body jerking in surprise. The sudden movement causes a chain reaction among my other two pets. The one called Knox raises his head, those strange hazel eyes of his scanning the room for potential threats. River, ever the more excitable of the two, actually scrambles to his feet, nearly tripping over his own gangly limbs in the process.

I watch their antics with regal disdain, my tail swishing lazily behind me. Honestly, you'd think they'd never felt the gentle caress of claws before. Such drama queens, the lot of them.

"Luna!" Rayne exclaims, twisting around to face me. Her sapphire eyes are wide with surprise. "What was that for?"

I fix her with my most imperious stare. Really, do I need to explain myself? I am Queen Luna, ruler of this domain. My word—or in this case, my claw—is law.

I meet her gaze steadily, unimpressed by her indignation. With deliberate slowness, I retract my claws and begin to groom my paw, as if to say, "Oh, was that your back? How careless of me." Let her interpret that as she will.

The largest one, Knox, chuckles as he sits up. "I think Her Majesty is reminding us of our duties," he says, his voice still rough from their earlier activities. His large hand reaches out to scratch behind my ears. I allow it this time, magnanimous ruler that I am, and even deign to lean into his touch. His fingers are pleasantly warm and he now knows just the right spot to scratch. Perhaps I'll keep this one around after all. After all, he was the one who brought that delightful catnip pouch earlier.

River, the lanky one with the blue eyes lighter than my first pet, scrambles to his feet. His movements are jerky and uncoordinated compared to my feline grace. How these humans manage to function with such clumsy bodies is beyond me.

"Oh shit, we forgot to feed Luna!" River exclaims, his voice tinged with a mixture of guilt and alarm. At least one of them has some sense of priorities.

I watch with regal amusement as River hurries towards the kitchen, nearly tripping over his own feet in his haste. The sound of cabinet doors opening and closing, followed by the telltale rattle of my food container, fills the air. It seems my little reminder has had the desired effect. Discipline does work, it seems. I'll remember this tactic for future use.

Author's Note

Thank you so much for reading Pose For Me! I really hope you enjoyed it. I want to thank my amazing teams, all of you are wonderful and I appreciate you all so much. And I want to thank you, my readers, everyone who takes a chance on any of my books. THANK YOU.

On a more personal note... There was a little bit of me in this FMC, so I think she will always be a little closer to my heart. Having spent years doing boudoir photography with the aim of showing those who visited my studio just how beautiful they truly are it meant a lot to write this particular character. And even if they never see this note, I want to thank every single one of the people for stepping into my studio and trusting me with that honor. The farewell to her tah-tah session mentioned at the start, was an actual session I did with a couple who did giggle their whole way through the entire thing. And it is true that a large number of domestic violence survivors reached out to me for sessions. I strived to show everyone who came to me that beauty comes in all shapes and sizes, and no matter what you have been through in life, you are strong and you are powerful and you deserve to be celebrated for no reason but for being you. So I do hope everyone who reads this book also gets to take that same message away from this experience.

xx Maree Rose

About the Author

Maree is an indie author who, although she has been writing most of her life, never thought she would ever get something published, which is now why she published this herself. She has always been an avid reader since a young age after roaming through book exchanges with her mum when she was just starting to read serious big girl books.

Maree lives on the East Coast of Australia with her wonderful husband, her son, and her two gorgeous squishy british bulldogs.

When she is not writing, she is working in a financial career (for something completely different to the creative side) or she is working on her photography (which is just as hot as her books).

Stalk Me

Please feel free to stalk me.
Like metaphorically, not literally of course!
https://linktr.ee/mareeroseauthor

Also By

DARLING WORLD

hunt me darling
hide me darling
seek me darling

DEAD DEVIL'S WORLD

Dead Devil's Night
Dead Devil's Playground

WHISPERS OF WICKED FAE

The Wild Hunt

SHATTERED WORLD

Shattered Safety Duet:
Untouchable & Unbreakable
Shattered Memories Duet:

Unforgettable & Unstoppable

STANDALONES

Home Sweet Home
Pose For Me
Push My Buttons
The Darkest Gift